SPREE

A Jon Steadman Thriller

Nellie Neeman

ISBN: 978-1-7351505-1-2 (Paperback)
ISBN: 978-1-7351505-0-5 (E-book)

Author Photo by: Elan Sachs

Library of Congress Control Number: 2020909899
Printed in the United States of America

For Yechezkel
When you were born...

For Glenn
Here's to all the adventures yet to come

PART I

THREE YEARS AGO

CHAPTER 1

Boston Technological Institute

Early May

"Congrats Grads!"

Ashleigh Lewis eyed the flashy banner above the doorway with an unsettling mix of fear and exhilaration. Next week, she would be a graduate of BTI, one of the country's most prestigious universities. Forging blindly into the unknown.

The uproarious sounds of a party in full swing blared from the rec center. They only served to amplify her jitters. Taking a deep breath, she lifted her left hand to her face, studying her ring. It sparkled brilliantly, the diamond reflecting the fluorescent lights overhead.

Jon.

Her heart lurched, the fears quickly subsiding, allowing her to focus on the celebratory night ahead. She wore her favorite light blue dress, the one Jon said brought out her eyes and luminous complexion. She smoothed her long hair back behind her shoulders, the scent of her lavender shampoo still potent. Ashleigh stepped inside.

The DJ was working on all cylinders, spinning a mix of pop and hip-hop, the crowd responding in kind. The room pulsated as dancers bounced to the music, releasing tension built up over finals week, the unmistakable stench of sweat, weed, and hormones filling the air.

The utilitarian space, spruced up for the occasion, was crowded beyond capacity. Helium balloons lined the ceiling, their dangling ribbons shimmying with icy blasts from the ceiling vents. Colored strobes flashed to the beat, each burst of light revealing an altered scene of dancers in new positions. It reminded her of a game she'd played as a child, where everyone froze on the leader's command.

Ashleigh scanned the crowd for Jon, spotting him on the dance floor. By some mutual telepathy, he met her gaze, grinning broadly. He began playfully swinging his hips to the electronic beat, making come-hither gestures to her with his hands. Amused, Ashleigh stepped onto the parquet floor. Jon drew her close, the adoration in his eyes mirroring her own.

Ashleigh wrapped her arms around Jon's neck, her fingers skimming his thick to-the-nape brown hair. Broad-shouldered with intense hazel eyes, at 5'10" Jon Steadman enveloped her delicate frame. Swaying in unison, Ashleigh giggled as Jon's goatee gently grazed the top of her cheek.

Jon took a step back, spoke loudly, just above the music. "How's Gabe?"

Her older brother Gabe was under the weather. At the last minute, he'd backed out of joining them, missing the final party before her graduation. She'd just come from dropping off a container of chicken soup and a bottle of aspirin.

"He'll be alright. Once he's had a decent night's sleep."

They danced, building a sweat, Jon's face red from exertion.

"I'm going to grab us some beers," Ashleigh said. "You deserve it for helping me with my psych paper until 2:00 a.m."

Jon gestured a thumbs up. She felt him watch her as she squeezed through the crowd. She headed toward the bar at the far end of the room, nearly bumping into a dancer gyrating to the music.

The man was tall and lanky, dressed in worn-out khakis and an ill-fitting red plaid button-down. His long, drawn features and bony cheekbones lent him an emaciated appearance, oddly akin to a weather-beaten scarecrow. No partner in sight, his moves were conspicuously out of sync with the throng of fist-pumping students surrounding him on the dance floor.

At the bar, Ashleigh paid for two beers, tacking on a generous tip. Grabbing the chilled bottles, she began to turn away when she saw the strange dancer again.

Without warning, the man stopped cold, calmly pulled a revolver from the waistband under his shirt and started shooting.

Ashleigh gawked in disbelief. The bottles slipped from her hands, glass shattering at her feet, the liquid snaking in all directions.

For a few morbid seconds, the partiers continued dancing to Lady Gaga's *Paparazzi,* unable to hear the gunshots above the music.

But then, people on the dance floor were dropping, screaming in terror, and all at once everyone was running, stumbling. Stampeding.

The shooter was moving through the room, firing indiscriminately, no clear target. In the chaos, Ashleigh couldn't spot Jon.

Some primal instinct forced her to duck down beside the bar, her hands held protectively over her head, doing her best to stay out of the line of fire.

"Jon!" she shouted in desperation, but was drowned out by the mad cacophony.

Finally, she caught sight of him hunched down between her and the front door, fighting against a frenzied current of bodies determined to get out. He was coming for her!

More shots. More screaming and trampling.

Ashleigh noticed Jon's fraternity brother frantically trying to pry open a window when his body went slack and dropped to the floor, blood spurting from the back of his head.

Oh God.

Staying low to the ground, Ashleigh struggled to reach Jon, the crushing horde an impenetrable barrier between them.

She realized the muffled *pop-pops* had stopped. Maybe the shooter had run out of bullets. Or maybe he was reloading.

As Ashleigh neared the threshold, there was an earsplitting boom. The ground shook violently beneath her and then all was silent.

CHAPTER 2

Boston Technological Institute

"Jon! Open your eyes. Come on, buddy. Please!"

Jon could barely make out the familiar sound of Pauly Hendrix's voice, now hysterical, forcing its way through the ringing in his head.

Why is Pauly yelling? Jon's eyelids felt like lead, and he was suddenly aware of sharp pain all over his body.

With great effort, he opened his eyes. His vision was blurry, but he could make out the scene around him. It looked as though he had woken up on a battlefield. He was lying on the quad lawn, halfway between Mason Hall and what was left of the rec center. The building was engulfed, the cloudy sky ablaze with raging flames, sparks shooting fifty feet high.

Dazed survivors stumbled past, looking shell-shocked, moaning, coughing and bleeding. Others lay unmoving, with no one to attend to them.

And then it came rushing back like a tsunami. He didn't see Ashleigh.

"Jon?"

"I'm okay," is what he meant to say, but it came out as "m'kay."

Pauly let out a sigh of relief. "Oh, thank God."

Jon gingerly turned his head. Pauly was leaning over him,

his face covered in black soot and streaked with blood, his hair coated in ash and his designer jeans ripped at the knees. Though his mouth was moving, Jon could barely hear him. He gestured weakly to his ear. Pauly's face registered dismay. He spoke louder, exaggerating his lip movements. "I said, thank God you're okay."

Jon looked down at his splayed body. His favorite BTI t-shirt was drenched in sweat, blood, and something once human he didn't want to identify.

He tried sitting up and felt a stabbing pain in his right leg. "Ashleigh?" he croaked.

"I don't see her," Pauly cried, loud enough to be heard.

Hearing that, Jon stumbled to a stand. With one leg trailing behind, he broke into a hunchback-like lope, making a beeline to the fiery site.

Pauly nearly tackled him. "You can't go in there! You'll kill yourself. The place is falling down."

"Let me go!" Jon tried to pry Pauly off him. He was outweighed by thirty pounds. Falling to his knees, Jon let loose a heart-wrenching sob. "Please. We need to find her."

Intense heat radiated off the building, Helplessly, they watched as pieces of the roof plummeted to the ground, scorching nearby shrubbery.

Near collapse, Jon began coughing violently, every nerve ending firing, a blinding pain searing his chest. He took a few deep breaths, attempting to get vertical again, but his body wouldn't obey.

Reluctantly, Jon allowed Pauly to help him to safer ground. Exhausted, he leaned against an old oak, scanning the area for any sign of Ashleigh. His gaze settled on his friend. "You're bleeding."

"I'm fine," Pauly said. "It's you I'm worried about. Take a minute and catch your breath. Help will be here any second. I hear sirens."

Ears ringing, Jon couldn't hear them. The pain in his leg spiked and his body throbbed horribly. It felt as though a truck was parked on his chest, crushing his insides. Trying for a more comfortable position, Jon placed his hand beside him and felt a sharp object puncture his skin.

"Ow!" Nestled in the grass beneath his palm was a small warped metal box, hot to the touch, sticky with bloody residue and debris. Lifting it with the edge of his shirt, Jon examined what had poked him. "What is this thing?"

Pauly assessed the smoking device. "Some kind of electrical box. We'd better let the police have a look at it."

Jon shifted his position, laying the object down.

"Sit still," Pauly ordered. "I think your leg is broken."

Wails of approaching sirens grew louder as police cars, ambulances and fire trucks barreled down the main campus road, one after the other. The quad was soon swarming with emergency personnel.

Jon moaned, and Pauly eyed him with a mixture of fear and anxiety. "You don't look so good. I'll get someone over here to help you."

"Thanks. Keep a lookout for Ash."

Pauly spotted a young medic wearing a red slicker, the ubiquitous snake-and-staff caduceus emblazoned on the back. He held a black tote in hand.

"Hey, over here!" he called.

The medic ran over, eyes widening at the sight of Jon. "We're setting up triage. Since he's conscious, he'll be second tier. We need to get the worst ones onto the ambulances immediately. As soon as they're cleared, we'll get to him. In the meantime, stay with him. If he loses consciousness, let one of us know right away."

Within minutes, firefighters were scurrying about, donning their gear and setting up the ladders and hoses. A police car screeched to a halt twenty feet from where they sat. Two uniformed officers—one male, one female—bolted from their car. They dashed from one victim to the next, looking for the seriously wounded, calling to medics just arriving on the scene.

The female officer hurried over to Jon and Pauly. Her name-plate read "D. Kearns." Late thirties, fair-skinned with a sprinkle of persistent freckles, her cap snug atop a tightly wound, auburn-haired bun.

"You guys okay?" she asked, her attention focused on Jon.

Pauly answered. "No, my friend needs help, but I was told they can't take care of him yet."

Kearns sized up Jon, seated at an odd angle. "Okay, don't move. I'll see if I can get someone over here. I'll be right—"

Jon interrupted, trying to sit up. "My fiancée may still be in there. Someone needs to find her."

Horrified, the policewoman looked at the inferno, then back at him. "What's her name?"

"Ashleigh Lewis."

"I'll tell the fire chief." Her eyes met Jon's. "Don't do anything foolish. The pros are here. Let them do their job. All right?"

When Jon didn't respond, Kearns turned to Pauly, "All right?" tilting her head in Jon's direction.

"Yeah, okay. I'm on it," said Pauly. When she turned away, Pauly called after her. "One second. We found something." He pointed to the metal device. "Not sure what it is."

"Don't touch it. I'll be back to check it out."

A few minutes later, a somber Kearns returned with gloves and an evidence kit. Jon and Pauly watched as she carefully inspected and bagged the metal box.

"Looks like you located the detonator," she said. "I need your names and phone numbers, to follow up later." She took out her notepad.

"I'm Paul Hendrix and this is Jon Steadman." He recited both their numbers.

She wrote as she spoke. "Paul, let's get your friend over to triage now. They'll treat both of you as soon as they can." She handed him a card. "Here's my number. Call me if you think of anything that might help the investigation. Take care of yourselves." To Jon, she added, "I hope we find your fiancée soon."

Pauly read the card. *Lt. Donna Kearns Boston PD Detective, Homicide Division*

With Pauly holding Jon up by the waist, the two limped together to the nearest medic.

CHAPTER 3

Boston

Ashleigh's body was never found. The explosion had toppled the rec center, reducing it to rubble, fire incinerating any remains. Within minutes of their arrival on the scene, a thirty-person team of first responders redirected efforts from a rescue mission to a recovery operation. Three students had died, not counting the bomber—a freshman named Joseph Amos Abadi. He had no prior record. The police were looking for a motive.

On the day of Jon's discharge from Mass General, the nurse brought him forms to sign, painkillers, and his bag of bloodied clothes. He'd suffered four broken ribs, a fractured hip bone, and a shattered right leg. He was fit for a cast, and scheduled for intense rehab over the next three months.

Jon's Granny Eunice pleaded with him to come home with her to South Boston to recuperate. Her modest split-level was only a thirty-minute drive from the BTI campus, but he declined. All he wanted was to get back to his dorm. Back to normal.

Now, sitting on his dorm room bed, he readied the soiled clothes for either the laundry or garbage, horrified by the blood stains and grime on his jeans and t-shirt. He was about to toss the shirt into the trash bin when he noticed something small and black stuck to the hem. It looked like dark plastic. Upon closer inspection, he saw it was a fingernail, badly charred, large enough to be from a grown male.

Detective Kearns words came back to him. *You located the detonator.*

Jon had a vague memory of lifting the device with his shirttail to avoid being burned. Could the killer's fingernail have attached itself to the detonator?

As a forensics and criminology major, Jon was acutely aware of DNA's sensitive nature. He had long ago decided on a career in intelligence, with hopes of landing a job with a federal agency.

He found a pair of tweezers and wiped them down with rubbing alcohol from the first aid kit Granny Eunice had bought him. He rinsed them thoroughly and carefully picked the nail off his shirt, dropping it into a glass test tube, one of many kept in his room from years of science classes. He secured the tube with its rubber stopper, putting it in the shoebox in which he stored important papers. The clothes then got thrown into the garbage. He never wanted to see them again.

* * *

Austin, Texas

Two Weeks Later

Ashleigh's memorial service drew hundreds. The Lewises of Austin were an established, well-known family, and Gabe invited Jon to Austin to join them in the final goodbye.

Jon emerged from the taxi, looking up at the stately home.

The house evoked a sense of authentic Southern charm with two inviting rocking chairs, a brightly cushioned swing, hanging flower baskets and a golden retriever lazing on a grand wrap-around porch. Twin boys dressed in matching crisp white shorts and bow ties peeked through the porch's narrow spindles, making faces at the flow of guests. Jon watched as a tall blonde woman, who looked too much like Ashleigh, took each boy by the hand, guiding them to the backyard. *Jillian.*

Using his crutches for support, Jon approached the wide entryway and proceeded through the ornate beveled glass door.

The house was decorated with all of Ashleigh's favorite flowers—gardenias, lilacs and of course, lavender. The aroma was everywhere—in scented candles, sachets of potpourri, even the bathroom soaps. Friends and family milled about, moving from room to room, speaking in hushed voices. Others sat on deep sofas, awkwardly balancing plates of devilled eggs and buttered biscuits on their laps.

Jon made his way towards the back of the house, finding himself in a massive kitchen with an opulent yet tasteful cathedral ceiling. Modern appliances and fixtures offset the traditional wainscoting and painted glass window above the farm sink.

Gabe, dressed in a tailored navy blazer with gold buttons, was leaning against the island, drink in one hand, his other arm around his mother, Jillian. A fair-skinned, rail-thin woman, she was holding an old-fashioned lace handkerchief, sobbing. Jon had met her only once before, shortly after he and Ashleigh had announced their engagement.

"Oh, I'm sorry to interrupt." Jon turned away veering back towards the front of the house.

"Jon, you're here!" said Gabe. "Please stay."

Mrs. Lewis looked at him through puffy, watery eyes. Glancing down at Jon's cast, she froze a moment, then opened her arms wide. Jon went right to her and fell into a tight embrace, Mrs. Lewis weeping. It took every last ounce of restraint for

Jon not to break down. Neither wanted to let go but after a minute, they stepped back, regarding each other.

Placing a hand gently on his cheek, she said in a Texas drawl, "I'm sure you know that Ashleigh truly loved you. She sang your praises each time we spoke." She choked back another sob. "She couldn't wait to start making wedding plans."

Heartbroken, Jon told her the feelings were mutual, expressed his deepest condolences and asked if he could be of help.

"What would be a great help is if you would stay for dinner this evening. Charles and I invited some of Ashleigh's dearest friends to reminisce and offer personal memories of her." She dabbed her eyes. "We don't want just to mourn. We also want to celebrate her life."

Jon was touched. "It would be an honor."

"Thank you. In the meantime, please make yourself comfortable. Gabe can show you around and fix you a nice plate."

"Okay," Gabe said, hesitatingly.

"Go on, you two. I'll be fine. I could use a few minutes alone with my thoughts."

Gabe gave his mom a peck on the cheek, grabbed two beers from the fridge, then led Jon to a winding staircase just off the family room.

"Come on, buddy. Let's find somewhere to hang out. Think you can make it up these stairs in one piece?"

Accepting the challenge, Jon leaned his crutches against the wall, grabbed the railings, and hoisted himself up one stair at a time. Gabe followed with the crutches, handing them to Jon at the top landing. They walked down a long, wide corridor, into a light-drenched room filled with books arranged in floor-to-ceiling built-ins, an ornate oak desk and several wood-paneled file cabinets. The walls were covered with framed photos of Mr. Lewis with politicians, sports stars and celebrities.

"This is my Dad's study. It's the quietest room in the house, as it faces the back. Take a look at this."

Gabe opened a set of French doors that led to a vast terrace and a spectacular view of gentle green hills.

"Wow, this is beautiful."

"Yep, it's where I go when I need some thinking time. Here, have a seat."

Jon settled into a comfortable lounge chair and took the offered beer Gabe had cracked open.

Gabe raised his bottle. "To Ashleigh."

"To Ashleigh."

Each man took a long pull, then sat quietly side by side, looking out on the breathtaking vista.

After several minutes, Gabe broke the silence.

"Jon, there's something I need to say to you, and hope you're ready to hear it with an open mind."

"Everything okay? Besides the obvious, of course."

"These last few days have been devastating, more for my parents than anyone. But what I want to say is about you."

"What's on your mind?"

"It's about that night. Pauly told me that you barely made it out alive. He said when you came to, your first instinct was to run into the fire to find Ashleigh."

Jon looked down at his beer. "Look, Gabe, I really don't—"

"Just let me finish. I need you to know that nothing you could have done would have saved her. It...it was just awful bad luck."

"Bad luck?" Jon nearly shouted. Something dangerously close to anger roiled up within. "We were dancing, having a great time. She offered to buy me a drink." He paused, collecting himself. "If I'd gone to the bar instead, she'd still be here."

"You can't know that. There's no way to predict these things. It was her time, not yours."

"How can you be so cavalier about this? Ashleigh was your sister!"

"I'm well aware," Gabe said softly. "All I'm saying is what you tried to do was incredibly brave. I'm eternally grateful for that, and for the happiness you brought her while she was here

16

with us. You will always be a brother to me. I mean it. Anything you ever need, come to me."

Jon was doing all he could to keep feeling angry, a defense mechanism he learned long ago to protect the raw feelings from bursting out. But then Gabe stood up, put down his beer and gestured to Jon to stand for a hug.

When they embraced, Jon lost all control. "I loved her, Gabe," he wept. "I loved her so much."

"I know, buddy, so did I. So did I."

PART II

Present Day

CHAPTER 4

University of North Texas
Dallas Campus

On the third anniversary of the BTI bombing, Jon and Gabe went out for drinks at The Blue Fox, an upscale bar within walking distance of Dallas' University of North Texas. It was Gabe's last weekend before returning for the summer to Austin, where he would intern at his father's brokerage firm. Jon planned to use the break making money working on campus as a tutor and TA.

The two friends shot pool for a while before phoning Gabe's parents, a tradition begun the first year after Ashleigh's death. Even now, the loss was incomprehensible, not unlike the death of Jon's parents. Three people he had loved were ripped away from him in the blink of an eye. Without rhyme or reason. One day here, gone the next.

In the aftermath of the attack, Jon had descended into a downward spiral, allowing the fall semester to pass him by. And then the spring. He became solitary, spending most of his time alone in his room binge watching episodes of *CSI* and *Cops*. While his friends felt badly for him, they could no longer relate to the brooding, melancholy person he'd become.

Before long, he was notified that his BTI scholarship had been suspended. Only students taking a full course load could claim the funds. It was just as well. Granny Eunice had been telling him for months that he needed a fresh start.

Jon applied to University of North Texas' criminology program, and was accepted with a full ride, the school happy to steal him away from the elite New England academy. Gabe had already transferred to UNT's doctoral program in chemical engineering. Two years older than Jon, Gabe was now three years ahead of him in his studies.

Jon knew it would be good to be around his old buddy, one of the few people whose grief matched his own. But unlike Jon, Gabe found solace in speaking of Ashleigh often. Jon vividly recalled the first time he'd met Gabe—playing together on BTI's soccer team. He assumed the pretty blonde cheering Gabe on from the sidelines was his girlfriend. It was an honest mistake—they looked nothing alike. Gabe, with his brown curly locks and solid football-player build was a direct contrast to Ashleigh, petite and fair.

The few weeks leading up to this third anniversary had been Jon's best in a long time, with him showing more interest in life outside his dorm room. But the thought of her was still a punch to the gut.

Now, sitting at the bar in the Blue Fox, Gabe asked Jon if he felt justice had been served.

Jon picked at the label on the beer bottle. "Not sure how to answer that since there was no one to prosecute. When Abadi offed himself, he robbed everybody of the closure they needed. Seems to me, there can be no real justice."

Gabe nodded. "True."

Jon looked up. "What I can't get past is they never found a motive. Three years and nothing."

Gabe took a sip of beer and said, "I never mentioned it, but a few months ago, my parents flew up to D.C. along with the other victims' families, to meet with reps from the FBI. They demanded an update, but left with only spotty information. Seems the Bureau spent an incredible amount of manpower investigating the guy, speaking to everyone who knew him. They all said the same thing. Abadi was a normal dude, never demonstrated any hint of psychological problems. The Feds combed his laptop but found no terrorist ties or extremism in his past, and no possible accomplices. They never even figured out how he got his hands on a bomb. He had no known skills in that area, no paraphernalia, nothing. It's as if the explosives materialized out of nowhere."

Jon was disgusted. "Incompetents." As far as he was concerned, the FBI was an organization of bumbling idiots in need of a complete overhaul with fresh blood, new thinkers. He could feel himself getting worked up. *Stay focused.* "Tell me again what they know about Abadi's background."

Gabe's gaze drew him far away. "His parents immigrated to the U.S. from Egypt when he was a baby. They ran a restaurant in Stamford—or they did, until the bombing. After that, they closed it and moved away. Abadi was an honors student, had lots of friends and had just started dating someone. He didn't fit the classic profile of a loner or bullied teen. Even his handgun was licensed. His parents had bought it for protection when they opened their restaurant. Apparently no one saw what happened at BTI coming."

Jon shook his head. "That's what I'm saying. I don't get it either. Why would a guy with no known bone to pick decide one day to go on a shooting rampage? And why blow the whole place up? Wasn't it enough to wreak havoc by shooting into a crowded party?"

They sat quietly nursing their drinks, pondering the rhetorical. Jon drained his beer and signaled the bartender for another. He placed a ten-dollar bill on the bar in front of him. "Remember I told you about the fingernail I found that night?"

"Yeah."

"What do you think about analyzing it?" Jon asked. "We each have to do a research project for our final thesis and we can ask the dean to do it jointly. Me for my master's, and you for your doctorate."

Gabe appeared skeptical. "I don't see the point."

"The families deserve to know why Abadi did what he did."

"I'm with you on that, but what if there is no reasonable explanation?"

Jon was emphatic. "Something inside was gnawing at Abadi that this is what he should do. *Needed* to do."

"All right," said Gabe. "Your instincts are better than most, but one fingernail does not a project make."

Jon sat up straighter. "Agreed, but what if we cover several bombings, not just the one at BTI? There have been many since then, all over the world, with tons of accessible reports and news coverage. Maybe we can get our hands on more evidence to analyze. If our work is sound, we could submit the thesis as an article for publication, say, in the Journal of Applied Sciences."

"And in the process learn more about Abadi and why he did it."

Jon nodded at his friend. "Exactly."

"Let's say I go along with this. What would the dissertation be about?"

Jon mulled it over, rubbing his clean-shaven chin, still expecting to find his goatee. "How about the correlation between genetics and criminal behavior? We could try and prove homicidal behaviors can be traced back to chemical imbalance."

"Hmm, it *would* probably satisfy both our majors." He was starting to see the potential. "We have access to lab equipment. And anything else we need, we can ask one of the professors...I like it! The Feds have had long enough. It's time we figure this out for Ash and the others."

Jon was now fully animated. "First thing is to clear it with a professor. Then come up with how we're going to access evidence from other crime scenes." He downed the last of his beer. With newfound purpose, he smacked his empty glass down on the bar and stood up. "I'll nose around. There isn't anything you can't find on the Internet these days."

CHAPTER 5

University of North Texas

J on closed his laptop, massaging his temples in an attempt at easing a burgeoning headache. It was only the beginning of the new semester, but he'd spent most of the day conducting research for the project. It had been several weeks since the dean accepted the joint thesis proposal, and he had used the summer break to get a leg up on the work.

Every morning Jon scoured the Internet, reading blogs focusing on forensics—specifically, DNA analysis. He subscribed to chatrooms posting his interest in specimens found at killing sites over recent years, and even went old-school, putting up fliers in the cafeteria and library.

He webcammed Gabe regularly to review what they'd each been working on. So far, they'd identified three other shooting rampages perpetrated by college students. Each was followed by an explosion, incinerating the killer. Same as BTI. Yet despite all their efforts, the search for new hard evidence proved fruitless.

Famished, Jon stepped over a pile of dirty laundry, and checked his mini-fridge. Last week's leftovers were long gone. A quick glance around reminded Jon he needed to clean up his side of the dorm room. Weeks of intense research had resulted in a pile-up of used take-out cartons, stained chopsticks, and a mess of stuff under his bed, likely causing the moldy odor permeating the room. That his neatnik roommate Ken put up with this was a testament to how awesome he was. More than one friend had referred to them as the Odd Couple.

Jon left the room untouched, promising himself to get to it later. He dry-swallowed two aspirins, and headed out to the cafeteria. The setting sun cast a purplish hue across the sky. The clock atop McConnell Tower chimed, reminding him the bookstore would soon be closing. He decided to stop there first, and buy a Mean Green t-shirt for Granny Eunice, and a ticket to their upcoming game. He made a mental note to call her before booking his flight to Boston for Thanksgiving. He'd last seen her over Spring Break, and couldn't wait to chow down a plateful of her chocolate chip cookies.

Stomach grumbling, Jon left the bookstore and headed to the dining hall. As he rounded the fountain, he glimpsed someone kneeling beside a folding table, collapsing its legs. He noted the booth's excellent placement and admired the strategy. Now that classes were starting up, every student on campus had to pass this spot. A makeshift sign lay on the ground, reading, "Help an Orphan and Save Yourself."

Jon's first thought was *Missionary...keep walking and don't make eye contact.*

From over his shoulder, he heard, "Hi there. Can I have a few moments of your time?" *Ugh, caught.*

And then he turned around.

CHAPTER 6

University of North Texas

"**I**'m sort of in a rush." Jon said, searching for a quick exit strategy. He changed his mind when the solicitor stood up.

She was tall, maybe just an inch or two shorter than him in her Keds. Her wavy chestnut hair was left loose, cascading around her sweatshirt hood—same one he was wearing. And her eyes. The bluest eyes he'd ever seen were focused solely on him.

Her hopeful smile was dazzling. "It will only take a minute."

"Sure, why not?" he said, momentarily flustered. "Can I give you a hand?"

She stopped packing up her things. "I'm nearly done. Thanks anyway. We're collecting for orphans from Haiti. Any amount is welcome." She added, "By the way, I'm Melanie Ridgefield."

"I'm Jon. I can relate to your cause, being an orphan myself." *Did I just say that out loud?*

Melanie's expression turned soulful. "Oh, I'm so sorry to hear that. Must've been tough, growing up without parents."

"It was. But I'm lucky enough to have the best grandma ever." Knowing this was TMI, Jon changed course. "I transferred here from BTI. I'm doing a graduate program in criminology and forensic science. How about you?"

"I'm majoring in biochemistry. One year to go—undergrad,

that is." Smiling again, she said, "Funny, looks like we're twins today."

"What? Oh, the sweatshirts. Right. I guess you're also a Mean Green fan. Just came from buying my grandmother some team gear." *Seriously, did I just bring Granny into this conversation again?* "Are you going to the game tomorrow night?" Jon threw in, hoping to get back on track.

"Depends if I can get some studying in before kickoff. How about you?"

"Yep, have my ticket right here." He patted his jeans pocket. "I just finished preliminary work on a research project that's been taking over my life, so the pressure's off for a day or two."

"Great. If I go, I'll come by and say hello."

He was doing a good job looking chill while they exchanged numbers. "Yeah, maybe I'll see you there. Good luck with the fundraiser." He tossed a buck into the jar and silently cursed his never-ending stupidity as he moved on.

* * *

Jon's stomach reminded him where he'd been heading. Nearing the cafeteria, he caught sight of Sam running past him.

Sam Delgado was the first guy he met when transferring to UNT. Sam had made a point of introducing himself when he spotted Jon unpacking his car, offering to give him a hand. A top-notch dude.

Now, Sam caught his eye and changed course, catching up just as Jon was halfway through the door.

A big guy—six-four, with retro glasses, and always in need of a haircut—Sam was in perpetual motion. He rarely finished what he started, whether a school assignment or a conversation, but he was by far one of the most likeable people Jon have ever known. Sam always wore a smile on his face. When he walked into a room of people he had never met before, he rarely left without knowing something interesting about each person there.

Sam's personality fit his size—big all the way around. All that was missing from the picture was the axe and overalls. He had a lumbering gait that made him identifiable from across campus.

Despite a lifelong learning disability, Sam had been determined to go to college. On his second try, he was accepted to UNT receiving a need-based scholarship.

"Sam, where are you headed in such a rush?" Jon asked.

Sam was breathless. "I'm trying to find where they're holding those ADHD trials. I'm going for an interview to see if I qualify for an experimental treatment. If I get in, they'll pay twenty bucks an hour just to get inside my head."

"Good luck to them, man! There's more going on in that brain of yours than they could ever bargain for."

Sam chuckled. "You got that right. By the way, who's bringing the keg tonight?"

"I'm pretty sure Ken's got it covered," Jon answered. "You know how organized he can be when it comes to beer."

"I'll meet up with you guys later." With a smirk, Sam added, "By the way, buddy, you got a goofy look on your face. Stab in the dark ...a girl get to you?"

Before Jon could dish it back to him, Sam patted him good-naturedly on the shoulder and trudged off.

Jon entered the dining hall, thinking it odd that ADHD trial interviews were running so late into the evening. After getting in line, he ordered a burger, fries and diet cola. He spotted classmates sitting together and—with Granny Eunice's voice echoing in his head, encouraging Jon to socialize more—he took his tray and joined them.

After dinner, he returned to his room, showered, and changed into a blue flannel shirt, a fresh pair of Levi's, and broken-in leather Timberlands. He recalled how Ashleigh had dubbed him "ruggedly handsome," claiming his preferred wardrobe made him look more a homegrown Southerner than the New England bookworm he was. Ironically now, his limp from the BTI bombing might be misconstrued as a cowboy swagger.

In no rush to head to the party, he decided to clean his side of the room, convinced it was a respectable form of procrastination. Parties were no longer his thing, but tonight he would step out of his comfort zone. Before he could change his mind, he texted Ken that he was on his way to the frat house.

A local boy, Ken knew the whole town and had promised his buddies to invite pretty sorority girls he knew from high school, and whom he was sure would get into a party mood on short notice.

Jon threw a final dirty sock in the hamper, switched off the lights, and taking two deep breaths, headed out.

CHAPTER 7

University of North Texas

"**P**sych Dept. Interview Session" was written on a piece of paper taped to the door. When Sam entered, two other people were in the room. A bespectacled Asian student sat at a computer, pecking the keyboard one letter at a time. Behind him, an older man, dressed in a suit and tie, shuffled through some files.

"Can I help you?" asked the student.

"I'm here for the ADHD profile interview."

"You missed it by an hour or so."

Not easily discouraged, Sam said, "I guess if nothing else, that shows I would be a perfect candidate. Disorganized, poor time management..."

The kid at the computer laughed as the professor turned to face Sam. He lowered his glasses, peering over them at Sam. "You make an intriguing point, young man. I'm Professor Mo Siddiqui." His English was precise, his South Asian accent distinct.

"Thanks, sir. Any chance you can still fit me in?"

"Though I am known for my punctiliousness, I will make an exception, given your accurate self-assessment...and my need for additional participants."

"Great! What do I need to do?"

"Take a seat in my office. I'll get the paperwork and we'll get started in a minute."

* * *

Phi Beta Epsilon was housed in a ramshackle edifice with an interior that would scare away even the most determined renovation expert. Originally designed as a small social hall with billiards and ping pong tables, over the years, more rooms had been haphazardly added. The result was a building that should have been condemned long ago, but the frat brothers weren't complaining, and for now campus administration had bigger fish to fry.

By the time Jon arrived, a game of beer pong was in full swing. Ken and Sam were already there, with three girls Jon had never seen before, cheering on the players. Someone had connected an 80's playlist to the speakers, and Bon Jovi was singing about giving love a bad name.

Immediately, Sam pulled him in. "Hey, buddy. Let me introduce you to Karen, Sandy and Lauren." They giggled as Sam spoke, suggesting they'd had a head start on drinking. True to form, Sam already learned fun facts he couldn't wait to share. "Karen has an extra toe on her left foot. Sandy teaches a high-impact Zumba class at Sky's the Limit gym, and Lauren is fluent in five languages."

Dressed in hot pink spandex, Sandy was pouring a shooter down Ken's throat while tall, dark-haired Karen only had eyes for Sam. That left Lauren. Jon turned to her, saying, "Which five languages do you speak?"

She was a cheerful redhead with the straightest teeth Jon had ever seen, but after a few minutes the conversation fizzled. He found himself thinking of Melanie, the charity girl.

He excused himself and took a look around. *What am I doing here? I'm a grad student now, not an underclassman. I'm too old for this scene.*

Shouting from the ping pong table brought him out of his reverie. As the place got more crowded, Jon became increasingly uncomfortable, sweat accumulating on his forehead. He recognized the signs—claustrophobia, a racing pulse. The beers hadn't helped calm him. It was time to say his goodbyes, and quickly. He smiled weakly, and offered a wave to the crew, struggling to cover up his panic.

"It's not even midnight yet," Sam called to him. "You have somewhere or someone better to go to?"

"Yeah, my bed. She's been beckoning me all night, wondering where I am."

"Good one, man. Catch you *mañana*." Sam turned his attention back to Karen. Ken and Sandy were nowhere to be seen.

Jon grabbed his jacket and got the hell out of there.

* * *

Jon woke to a killer hangover. Gingerly, he turned over in bed to look at the clock. 12:20 in the afternoon! What had he been thinking? He knew he should analyze his anxious reaction to the growing crowd last night. But not right now.

He dragged himself out of bed, took a cold shower, and got dressed. Before he lost his mojo, he picked up his phone and texted Melanie, asking if she was going to the game later.

She replied moments later. *Yes. Hope to see you*, followed by a smiley face with sunglasses and a football icon.

* * *

The Mean Green lost the game that night 21-10, but he met up with Melanie at the concession stand, bought her a hot dog, and asked her out on a real date. Things went really well from there.

CHAPTER 8

Georgia Tech

Atlanta

A s the dorm room door closed behind him, Andrew Capaletto used the back of his hand to wipe pink lipstick off his mouth. He smiled to himself. He really liked Jessica. A Southern belle. And a hot tamale. He laughed at the cultural mashup. He could still taste her mochaccino on his breath, smell the intoxicating rosy perfume of her bed sheets.

He felt light-headed. Hopefully he wasn't coming down with a cold. More likely a reaction from the passionate workout with Jess. An overwhelming urge came over him.

Go to the cafeteria now.

Andrew looked at his shiny new watch. There was just enough time to stop at the cafeteria before meeting his buddies for a few hands of Texas hold 'em. He blinked repeatedly, trying to shake off the encroaching brain fog. Andrew placed his white and gold Georgia Tech ball cap atop his mop of unruly red hair. As if his legs had a mind of their own, he hastily set out for the campus cafeteria.

* * *

The spacious Georgia Tech dining hall was half-filled with

students eating an early dinner. An aproned worker donning a netted hair bonnet collected abandoned trays from the laminated tables, while plugged-in students stared at their laptop screens.

Andrew entered the cafeteria and made a beeline for the salad bar, ten feet from a coffee klatch laughing loudly. Shanice, a long-haired hippie from his Advanced Calculus class, was among them.

"Hey Andrew, want to join us?" Shanice asked.

Andrew didn't respond, his mind shrouded in a heavy fog. He registered Shanice's frown at the snub, aware her eyes remained on him. He bent down retrieving a hard-sided picnic cooler from the skirted space beneath the salad bar, he *somehow* knew would be there, and worked the latches open. Inside was a two-cylinder device with black and yellow wires attached to a red trigger button.

Aghast, Shanice screamed, "Bomb!" Those nearby stopped what they were doing, turned to Shanice in shock, tracking her accusatory finger pointed at Andrew. Awareness turned to pandemonium. Screaming students leapt off their seats and ran to the closest exit. The thundering crash of metal chairs hitting the ground ricocheted off the walls.

Ten excruciating seconds passed as Andrew felt his body shudder. He gritted his teeth fighting an internal battle against the violent seizure. His eyes twitched furiously, the detonator iron-clenched in his tremoring hand.

Everyone managed to escape moments before Andrew Capaletto exploded.

CHAPTER 9

University of North Texas

J on was waiting for his electric kettle to boil, when an alert popped up on his phone with news of an attack at Georgia Tech. Facebook, Instagram and Twitter were aflame with updates. The Atlanta school was on lockdown, but a few daring students were moving about, taking live-action video of the ongoing tragedy, allowing Jon to watch the gruesome drama as it was unfolding. Switching to his computer, Jon saw police in full riot gear, brandishing assault rifles. Smoke was billowing out the windows of one campus building. Scrolling newsfeed at the bottom of the screen identified it as the dining hall. Ambulances were parked askew, lights flashing with their backdoors open, ready to receive the dead and wounded.

It brought it all back. *BTI*. Jon took a deep breath, trying to get control of the anxiety, aware that lately there were more triggers to sidestep.

Why am I putting myself through this? He turned off his computer and made himself a chamomile tea, allowing it to steep. He'd begun to believe that any useful DNA evidence would be locked away at a police headquarters or the FBI evidentiary facility, places he'd never gain access to. He understood going into this that, unlike himself, most civilians would not hold on to seemingly inconsequential detritus. All his research seemed to do was stir up difficult memories.

This is for Ashleigh, he reminded himself. He wasn't giving up. When he set a goal, he stuck with it until the work was done, oblivious to anything else around him, including his anxieties. Melanie called it being in the "Jon Zone." Despite his heavy workload, he'd managed to keep up his good grades, maintaining his place on the Dean's List. *I can do this.*

His cellphone dinged with a text notification of a shared tweet. It was forwarded by a user on Criminal Minds—one of the chatrooms Jon had joined—dedicated to discussing psychological profiles of historical and present-day killers. *Thought this would interest you.*

It was a close-up of a red hair. The caption read, *This is all that remains of the jackass who stole our innocence. #Enraged.* It was posted by @JessJensen.

He quickly took a screenshot and enlarged it to get a better look, then texted it to Gabe with the message, *What do you think? Found this on a student's feed from Georgia Tech.*

Gabe wrote back. *Can u track it down?*

I'll try.

Gd job. Lmk what u find out. Ttyl.

Jon went to his Twitter account and followed JessJensen. *Hey Jess, this is Jon. I saw your post. Could we speak? I survived a similar attack.*

He got an immediate response. *Really, when?*

BTI.

OMG! I remember that. PM me your number and I'll call.

Thirty seconds later, his phone rang. The caller ID showed up with a 404 area code.

A lilting Southern accent came across the line. "Hi, this is Jessica." Her tone was subdued. Jon knew people reacted to tragedy in different ways. Some became hysterical, others depressed. He guessed Jessica was the latter. Like him.

"Hey. Thanks for calling."

"What did you want to talk about?" she asked tentatively.

"As I wrote, I went through something similar. It stays with you a long time."

Her voice was somber, weighted down as if she'd just been

crying. "Yeah, my aunt's a psychologist, and I'm sure she'll force me into therapy."

"That could be a good idea."

"Did *you* go?" Jessica asked.

"No," he admitted, "but I hear it can do wonders for most people." He then added, "I saw you posted a photo of a hair and your tweet was pretty mysterious."

"It's sort of embarrassing, but I was so angry I needed to do *something*. I went out with that guy...the guy who did it." She sounded miserable.

"The police already identified him?"

"They didn't need to. His name's Andrew Capaletto. Everyone's posting about it. A bunch of people saw him in the cafeteria opening a cooler and pulling out a detonator. It must've been hidden there beforehand. He didn't have it with him when he got there."

"Sounds premeditated."

"Yeah. But I heard Andy hesitated. It's so crazy, it makes no sense. If he was going to blow the place up, why wait for people to leave?"

"So no one was killed?"

"I don't know. My friend saw a few people taken to the hospital."

Jon looked at his computer screen. "From the livestream, it looks like the building's still standing."

"It is. I heard they built it to withstand earthquakes and other natural disasters."

The silver lining. "Forgive me for asking, but you never got the sense that Andrew was off somehow?"

"Not at all. We met a few weeks ago at the student union. He was playing darts and I bet I could beat him. He took my challenge. We went out twice since."

"Did you?"

"Did I what?"

"Beat him."

"By a mile. He took it well. That's what impressed me

enough to go out with him. He wasn't the look I normally go for. Redhead and on the short side. But not many guys out there can take a bruise to the ego and still ask you out, you know?"

"When was the last time you saw him?"

It sounded like she suppressed a sob. "Maybe an hour before he did it! I'm freaking out. We went out for Frappucinos. He liked salted caramel." She paused. "I still can't believe it. He seemed so chill. We had plans to meet up again Saturday night."

Jon found that odd. Maybe Andrew had set up the date as a cover. "So what's the story with the red hair you posted?"

She got quiet for a minute. She seemed to be deciding whether or not to continue but then plunged in. "At the risk of sounding like a totally pathetic judge of character, after the café, we went back to my room and made out for a while."

"Gotcha." Given what happened, Jon gave Jessica credit for admitting that.

"After the bomb went off, they put the school on lockdown. I got stuck in my classroom for over an hour. I got back to my room a few minutes ago and noticed his hair under my pillow."

"What makes you think it's his?"

"No one else I know has red hair. And I found it where he had been, if you know what I mean. If my parents find out I was with this guy, they'll think I'm demented, and push for me to come home. This is exactly what my mother's been worrying about since I got here. She told me college is breeding ground for psychos."

"Any reason to tell them?"

"I wish I didn't have to, but it's just a matter of time till the police come speak with me. They'll hear we went out."

He agreed. "You're probably right about that. But maybe something you know can help them figure the guy out."

"I didn't have a clue Andy had this in him. I mean, he could've killed me! The guy was nuts, and I was alone with him. I just don't get why he did this."

"I know how you feel. They never found out what motivated the guy who blew up the social hall at BTI. But Jessica, count your blessings and try not to think of the what-ifs. Take my word for it. They will make you nuts. Just be happy you got another chance at life."

"Is that how you feel?"

"Every minute of every day."

Jon heard her sob softly and gave her a moment.

"Do you think I could've done anything to stop him? I keep asking myself if I might have done something to set him off."

"Jessica, listen to me very carefully. Blame lies solely on his insane shoulders." The irony wasn't lost on Jon. He'd never taken this sage advice when it was offered to him.

"You're not just saying that to make me feel better, are you?"

"I'm saying it because it's the truth."

His words seemed to calm her.

Jon continued, "I have a favor to ask. I'm working on my thesis and looking for evidence from attacks such as this one. The red hair you found would really be helpful."

"Don't you think the police may want it?"

"You told me they already identified him from firsthand witness accounts."

"That's true." She sounded uncertain.

Jon gave her a small push. "DNA is used for identifying someone, and they already did that, right?"

"That makes sense."

"It would be really helpful," Jon repeated. "If you have a plastic baggie, please seal it in there. I'll take care of the postage." He gave her his address.

Her voice was now steadier. "Don't worry about it. It's been good to speak with you. Maybe you could, you know, help victims of these kinds of crimes, since you understand how they feel. That's what I think my aunt would say. And I'll bet it would be a kind of therapy for you as well."

"You know, Jessica, that's not a bad idea. I'll give it some thought."

An awkward pause ensued. "Um, good luck with your project."

"Thanks." *I'm gonna need it.*

CHAPTER 10

University of North Texas

J on escorted Melanie across campus and then to her apartment. The kiss good night was steamy, and it took all his self-control to leave. Though the attraction was off the charts, he wasn't ready to take it to the next level. Even after three years, it felt like cheating on Ashleigh. He knew it wasn't rational, but when were feelings rational? For now, Jon was satisfied with how things were progressing.

Dating Melanie was a welcome distraction from his workload. They went on hikes, played tennis, and occasionally met up with friends.

Jon knew he and Melanie had their differences, but that only made things more interesting. Though never obvious about it, Mel had been born into old money. The Ridgefields, long-time Southerners had made their fortune selling cotton to the Confederate Army, which was used to make the soldiers' uniforms, bedding and bandages. With the Union victory, the Tennessee family reinvented themselves when the family patriarch built a thriving whiskey business, still in operation today.

When Melanie heard about Jon's project with Gabe, she offered to show the specimens to her favorite professor. She described Professor Breitler as a genius, scatterbrained at times, but she expected he would help if he had time.

She was right. The professor agreed to analyze their samples, apparently eager to use his newly acquired lab equipment. He had even informed Melanie of the department's recent endowment, a generous donation given to the university to be used for research grants at his discretion, pending the dean's approval. With Melanie's help, Gabe submitted a detailed application and request for financial backing. Two weeks later, they got the go-ahead. Any reasonable expenses related to the project would be reimbursed. To celebrate, the three friends went out to Melanie's favorite sushi place.

Over rainbow rolls and edamame, they charted their course. Melanie put down her chopsticks, and took a sip of her sake. "I nearly forgot to tell you that Professor B. has a contact overseas who may be able to help decipher the killers' genetic components—something he won't be able to achieve himself without a fuller understanding of his new equipment's capabilities. We'd learn more about the bombers and their predispositions and, you never know, maybe it will lead to motive. Either way, it will help your project."

"That's great," said Gabe. "Who is it?"

"A geneticist, Dr. Terry Lavi from Israel."

"Israel? Aren't there any geneticists closer to home?"

"I'm told Dr. Lavi is the premier expert in advanced DNA mapping and has access to the latest technology, designed to work on even the most compromised specimens. I'll forward you the email address."

The rest of the evening had been all play and no work. Just three friends kicking back, enjoying a night out.

After another scintillating kiss, Jon took the long way home. A drizzle misted the air, the humidity painfully reminding him of his bum leg. Melanie hadn't yet asked him about the limp, probably out of politeness, and he was offering no explanation. Actually, he rarely spoke of his past at all with anyone but Gabe or Granny Eunice. He had learned there was no point rehashing what couldn't be undone. After the bombing, Pauly had encouraged him to see a therapist and talk it out, but Jon knew instinctively not to go. He had already been through the loss of his parents and counseling hadn't helped. He still struggled with it every day. He pulled up his sweatshirt hood, took out his cellphone and dialed Boston. Granny Eunice picked up on the first ring.

"Hi sweetheart, how are your classes going?" she asked cheerfully. She sounded thrilled every time he called.

"Going well."

"I'm not surprised. You're a star student."

"Still my biggest fan, huh?"

"Always.

"Just wanted you to know that I've met a girl."

He could hear the smile in her voice. "Really, now? Let's have it."

Jon took a seat on a wet bench. "Her name's Melanie. She's a senior at UNT. I'm texting you a picture of us at a Mean Green game." He pulled up his photos, found the one he loved, and sent it.

He heard the ping of her phone on the other end. "She's a beauty. I'm so proud of you for moving on with your life, honey. I know it hasn't been easy for you. I hope you'll bring Melanie to Boston to meet me."

"It's a little early for that but if things stay the course, you may have to set one more place at the Thanksgiving table."

CHAPTER 11

FBI Regional Office
Dallas

Special Agent in Charge Doug Matthews was sitting in his downtown Dallas office reading the morning status reports when his assistant walked in with a cup of black coffee. He marveled that no matter the time of day, Kelly Flanagan always looked put together, her fiery Irish hair in place, dress precisely pressed, sporting full makeup. By contrast, Agent Matthews had a hard time keeping his shirt tucked in, something that made his wife Erica crazy. It wasn't for a lack of trying but sitting on his butt for so many hours each day left him looking perpetually sloppy.

Tall, with a full head of close-cropped dark hair, Matthews was fit for a man closing in on fifty. Photos of his high school classmates on social media made him realize he was better preserved than most. No protruding gut or receding hairline. He attributed it to never having had kids and all the agita that came with parenting. He and Erica had married after her short-lived urge for babies had passed, but he had never really pictured himself the fatherly type anyway.

If it weren't for his assistant, his office would look like a hoarder's closet. Kelly kept him organized and on schedule.

He accepted the coffee. "What's on the docket for today?"

Tapping her tablet, Kelly pulled up the day's itinerary.

"Let's see," she began, in her Texas twang. "You have a ten a.m. phone meeting with Lieutenant James of the Atlanta Police about the Georgia Tech bombings."

"Terrific. I bet he wants to *share* information with us." Matthews gestured finger quotes on 'share.' As one of the leaders of the investigation, he had neither the time nor patience to review details of his work with every cop looking for a lead.

He blew in his cup, taking a careful sip of the steaming coffee. "What else?"

"Your weekly two p.m. review with the Colonel. He's in town so it's in-person this week."

Another winner. "Colonel" Victor Gomez had been in a foul mood for weeks. Each killing spree made him ornerier, particularly since it was his job to oversee the investigation's progress. By extension, that meant Matthew's team. The increased crankiness was too bad, as the two men had been getting along particularly well these recent months.

Gomez had earned the moniker by serving his country as a Marine colonel for many years. At the FBI, he was Matthews' boss. Soon after Matthews' promotion, the Colonel and his wife had invited him and Erica to their annual dinner party at their D.C. area home, introducing them to powerbrokers Matthews had only read about in the papers.

Erica had made darned sure to be in town that evening, despite a hectic travel schedule. She enjoyed herself tremendously. Coming face to face with the elite was exhilarating. With both of their jobs demanding every spare moment, they rarely had time together but he couldn't complain. They had clawed their way near the top of their respective fields, he as a SAC with the FBI, Erica as an Assistant District Attorney.

That evening at the Gomezes had been a magical one, giving them a chance to reconnect while surrounded by the well-heeled members of Washington high society. Thanks in large part to his oil-rich father-in-law, the Colonel and his wife lived on a beautiful estate nestled on a secluded riverfront property. A yacht was docked at their private pier. A leg up and some good investments made the Colonel financially independent. But a soldier's duty was never complete. Word was he would stay active until either forced into retirement or transferring to the great bunker in the sky.

Kelly broke Matthews' train of thought. "Sir, I don't know if you even want to hear about this, but a call came in to the main desk from a UNT student claiming to have evidence that could help us with our investigation into the recent killings."

Even kids are connecting the dots between the massacres. BTI, San Bernardino, Newtown, Colorado, Virginia Tech, Georgia Tech, and Orlando all appeared as isolated incidents to the average citizen, but the most recent ones were shaping up as potentially connected events, something his team was diligently studying. He had hoped the lone-wolf theory would hold up for a while longer in the public consciousness. Otherwise, he'd be inundated with conspiracy theorists incessantly calling his office, not to mention the widespread panic that would ensue.

"Why bring it to me?" Matthews asked, annoyed.

"He heard you were the local agent in charge of investigating attacks on college campuses."

"He must have seen my name in some article. How many times do I have to tell those stupid reporters to keep my name out of the papers? If he calls back, forward him to PR."

"Yes, sir."

"That will be all, Kelly."

His assistant left, closing the door behind her.

Agent Matthews looked at the pile of classified documents on his desk, sighed, and reached for the one at the top, preparing himself for a long and grueling day.

* * *

At 3:00 p.m., Matthews was returning from his meeting, his mood considerably improved. The meeting with the Colonel had gone better than expected. While Matthews didn't have any new intel to share since the previous week, he left feeling appreciated for his hard work.

As he walked past Kelly's desk, he overheard her on the phone. "I'm sorry, but Special Agent Matthews is in a meeting and cannot be disturbed."

She paused to listen to the other party. "Yes, I understand you have valuable information. Please call the number I gave you the last time you called. I'm sure they'll be of help." After another pause, "Mr. Steadman, that will not be necessary. Showing up here in person will not make any difference."

Matthews saw her exasperation and felt sorry for her. "I'll take the call in my office." He entered his office, grabbing an apple from the fruit basket delivered for his birthday the day before. Though no note had accompanied it, he had assumed it was from his team. He sat down and picked up the phone.

"Special Agent Matthews."

"Whoa! Finally. You're one tough guy to reach." The kid had the voice and attitude of a Northerner.

"I'm a busy man. How can I help you, Mr. Steadman?"

"It's Jon, and as I explained to your formidable assistant, I'm a student at UNT, majoring in criminology and forensic science. I'm working with another student on a research project focusing on DNA analysis from crime scenes. As it happens, we've obtained samples from two different attacks that we plan to analyze."

"And may I ask how you came by these samples?" He took a bite from the apple.

"Suffice it to say, we weren't involved in the incidents in any way, but for now, I'd like to keep our acquisition methods under wraps.."

Deciding to humor the kid, Matthews said, "You may not be in a position to make that choice."

"I thought you might say that. Obviously, our main object-ive is to help the investigation and we'll share what's required of us. But, if we could work alongside your analysts, it would be greatly appreciated. Without hard data, our paper has no basis."

The kid had no clue what he was trying to get involved in. As far as Matthews was concerned, Good Samaritans were just another name for more paperwork. "Mr. Steadman...Jon, I'm impressed you would jeopardize what I imagine took months of work in order to help your country. You sound like a bright young man, and the FBI appreciates you coming forward to protect your fellow citizens. However..."

"I'll be there in ten minutes."

"Excuse me?"

"Like I told your assistant, I'm in the area and will be happy to show you what I have."

Agent Matthews was about to stop him in his tracks but thought better of it. A kid like this would not take no for an answer, and with Matthews' luck would report the stonewalling. In a post-9/11 world, that could turn into a media nightmare for the FBI.

He resigned himself to another detour in an already demanding schedule "When you get to the front desk, ask to be sent to my office. I'll take a look at what you have."

"Awesome!"

Matthews returned the phone to its receiver, mumbling, "It's unbelievable what I put up with."

* * *

Precisely ten minutes after they hung up, Kelly ushered Jon into Matthews' office. The young man was tall and good looking, walking with a distinct limp. He made full-on eye contact, giving off an air of self-assuredness bordering on arrogance. He didn't appear quite as clueless as he had sounded over the telephone. Jon Steadman had also failed to mention he was bringing a friend along, an attractive young woman named Melanie Ridgefield.

"Have a seat," said Matthews.

Jon and Melanie sat in the faux leather chairs across from the agent's desk.

"Thanks," said Jon. "You know, your assistant Kelly is much nicer in person."

"I'm sure she'd be relieved to hear that."

Jon either didn't notice or chose to ignore the sarcasm. "Anyway, I recalled your name from a write up a while back in the *Post* on the FBI and the rising pressures to keep Americans safe. The journalist wrote she respected you and your position, and how difficult the burden must be in this day and age."

Matthews began seeing Steadman in a new light. Smart kid —complimenting him, though Doug understood an unorthodox request would soon follow.

"No truer words."

"Here are the samples I mentioned."

Matthews watched the kid pull a lab pouch from his pocket.

"I can't actually take them out to show you. This isn't a sterile environment and we don't want to contaminate the evidence. But, as you can see, these are specimens extracted from two of the crime scenes."

Matthews looked at the glass vials. He put on his reading glasses, and saw a black fragment that appeared to be a human nail, and a single strand of red hair about ¼ inch in length.

"These are miniscule specimens. They can't be analyzed reliably," said Matthews.

Melanie chimed in. "With all due respect, sir, we believe they actually can be coded using the latest cutting-edge technology. Major advances are being made in genetic testing." She spoke with a confidence Matthews had not expected.

"That may be true, young lady, but these emerging methods may not be used at the FBI. Can you guess why?"

"Probably because you don't want your cases ripped to shreds by skilled defense attorneys looking for acquittals based on a technicality."

Smart young woman, he thought. "Skilled and unscrupulous, may be a more accurate depiction. We can't allow investigations that take months, or sometimes years of round-the-clock work, to be undermined. If the technology isn't tried and true, we risk letting dangerous criminals walk free."

The three sat silently for a moment until Agent Matthews stood up.

"I'm sorry to have disappointed you," said Matthews, "but that's the reality of today's jurisprudence."

"Okay." Jon stood up, as did by Melanie. "Thanks for your time," he said. "At least we can say we tried."

"Your perseverance is quite admirable," said Matthews. "Good luck with your research." Smiling diplomatically, the agent extended his hand like a seasoned politician. Hands were shook.

Agent Matthews watched as the pair walked past Kelly's desk, smiling as he saw his assistant give them the evil eye.

* * *

Jon and Melanie hopped on the DART.

"That was one weird meeting," Melanie said.

"Yeah. What a condescending asshole. Why even let us into his office only to shut us down so fast?"

"Maybe he decided it would just be easier to meet us for a few minutes than argue about it for an hour on the phone."

"Maybe. I admit, though, the Bureau was pretty awesome. All those special agents in one building. What I wouldn't do to be a fly on the wall."

"What now?"

"We continue, as planned. I'll call Gabe and tell him to book a flight to Israel."

"You don't think that's a bit impulsive?" asked Melanie. "You never even asked if Dr. Lavi is willing to become more involved. Until now, it's just been professional courtesy by email."

"That's the idea. If Gabe shows up in person, there's little chance he'll be sent away without at least a meeting. People feel pressured in those circumstances."

"You're a regular steamroller, Jon. Let's hope you're right or Gabe will be making a very expensive trip for nothing."

"I would go myself but I promised Granny Eunice I'd go home for Thanksgiving. I'm all the family she has." Jon paused, looking into Melanie's extraordinary eyes. "You know, I've been thinking about it, and I'd love if you would come with me."

"To Boston?"

"Yeah. My grandmother would be thrilled to meet you, and she makes a killer sweet potato pie. Marshmallows and all."

Touched, Melanie replied, "My parents will be disappointed...but sure, I'd love to come!"

"Great!" he said hugging her. "I'll show you my old stomping grounds. You know, it's too bad Gabe will be spending the holiday all alone, bored and without pie."

"Yeah, poor guy."

CHAPTER 12

FBI Regional Office
Dallas

Eleven p.m. in Dallas meant it was midnight on the coast. The twelfth floor was empty with the exception of a few other workaholics and those pulling an all-nighter on active investigations. The mole locked the office door, walking across the room to stand by the floor-to-ceiling window. The city looked beautiful at this hour, the Dallas skyline glittering, the Trinity River, a dark blanket, still and peaceful.

Unlocking the bottom desk drawer, the mole took out the iPhone that remained off until needed, powered it up, and dialed a number memorized long ago. The call was answered on the first ring.

"Good evening. Do you have any updates for me?" asked the familiar, cultured voice.

All business all the time. "Nothing has changed so we're still set for Phoenix. Our operative is in place and will be in receipt of the necessary equipment by the deadline."

"Well done. Has there been any progress in the investigation?"

"Fortunately, things remain at a standstill. No leads so far. Unless you want to count a ridiculous impromptu visit the FBI had today." The mole chuckled.

"Visit?"

"Yes, two students trying to help the cause. I don't know why I even brought it up. Silly, really. They offered what they think is evidence from two killing sites. Of course, they have nothing at all."

"What sort of evidence?" A concerned tone seeped in.

"I wouldn't give it a second thought. They're working on a school project and were excited just to be in an actual FBI office building. They claimed to have a fingernail and strand of hair. Even if they're authentic—and I highly doubt that to be the case—they cannot be analyzed with the procedures available today."

"Are you certain of that?"

"Of course. Nothing out there could map a quarter inch hair strand without the follicle attached—or, for that matter, a burnt chip of nail. We are years away from that technology, and when it does arrive, its cost will likely be prohibitive."

"Very well. But to be on the safe side, it would be better to accept their offer."

The mole was surprised by this. "May I ask for what purpose?"

"For my piece of mind. And, in turn, for yours."

Unsettled, the mole said, "I have no way to secure the samples at this point. They took them and left."

"Then I would think it prudent to keep an eye on these young people and find another way to acquire their so-called evidence." A note of irritation was conveyed. "You have the number of our friend?"

"I do," said the mole, "but he could draw unwanted attention to our work."

"Not if he's careful. "

"I suppose I could have him shadow these kids until an opportunity arises to access the samples."

"I suppose you could."

The mole was about to hang up, but not before hearing the parting words. "I do hope you all enjoyed the fruit basket."

CHAPTER 13

Dallas/Fort Worth International Airport

René Leduc pulled a cellphone from his pocket and dialed the emergency number. An annoyed voice picked up. "Why are you calling? I'm at work. You know this number is only for emergencies."

"I'm at the airport."

"Hold on," whispered the mole. "I'm going to find somewhere to talk."

A few minutes later, the voice came back on the line, now louder and more insistent. "Steadman's leaving town?"

"He gave the samples to his friend. They met at the school cafeteria a few hours ago and made the exchange. I followed the guy and he came here."

"Where he's heading?"

"Tel Aviv."

"As in Israel?"

"Can you think of another one?" He was losing patience with this pompous dolt. He continued. "I'm calling to give you the update and ask what you want me to do now."

"This is going way further than expected. Follow him."

"Then what?"

"Find out who he's meeting and relieve him of the package."

"To what lengths should I go to accomplish that?"

"Any lengths necessary. You'll be compensated accordingly."

"Understood." Leduc hung up, checked the departure time on the overhead screens, and purchased a wheeled carry-on bag, pair of pants, two shirts, underwear and a toothbrush from the terminal shop. Anything else he needed he could buy in Israel. If the airline's security personnel noticed him attempting to fly internationally without any luggage it would raise a red flag, a risk he couldn't afford. Given the unpredictability of his occupation, he always kept his passport on him. This was not his first trip to Tel Aviv, and while he knew better than to use a fraudulent document with the Israelis who were quick to pick up even the best quality forgery, using his real passport would create more problems.

New bag in hand, Leduc went to the El Al ticketing desk, paid for his ticket and waited in line. As expected, the security questions were extensive. Israelis had no problem offending people by profiling when it came to the safety of their countrymen. After intense minutes of questioning, Leduc cleared security, found his gate and took a seat in the corner, with a good view of the waiting area.

Gabe Lewis sat twenty feet away, earbuds in place listening to his playlist, completely unaware that he was being watched.

CHAPTER 14

Ben Gurion International Airport
Tel Aviv, Israel

Gabe awoke just as the plane was approaching Ben Gurion Airport. He clicked in his seatbelt and tilted his seat forward. He had never seen the Mediterranean Sea, let alone flown over it. Outside his window, the coast glowed with the impending sunset, a spectacular display of gold and purple hues streaking across a dusky sky. Passengers leaned over each other, edging to get a glimpse of the glorious show.

Gabe's body felt like it was not yet noon, but here the sun was already setting, causing a sense of disorientation. Hopefully, he would quickly adjust to the new time zone. Jon had called only two days ago to tell him the trip was a go and instructed him to pack only absolute necessities for the three-day excursion. Following the failed FBI meeting, they could now go forward with clear conscience, holding onto their evidence for further study. Professor Breitler had worked his magic, and successfully granted funds to cover trip expenses.

Just hours before leaving for the airport, Gabe met Jon in the campus cafeteria to discuss Gabe's impending trip and for Jon to hand over the specimens retrieved from the professor. They were waiting for Dr. Breitler to share preliminary results.

"Do your best to persuade Dr. Lavi to accept the samples for analysis," advised Jon. "Tell him it's a matter of life and death, which of course it is. We're asking a lot of him, so you may have to lay it on thick."

"He's only expecting a short consult. It feels like we're blindsiding him with a huge undertaking."

"No question that's what we *are* doing. But in our defense, in our email dialogue Lavi seemed curious to learn more about our research. If you think it will help, you might offer to name him as a co-author... as an incentive."

"Always the salesman, my friend." Gabe laughed. "I know you need to visit your grandmother, or you'd be the better man for this job. I'll do my best to win him over with my good looks and charm."

Jon laughed. "Try harder than that. You can do it. Stay in touch and good luck."

The friends shared a bro-hug and parted ways.

* * *

Gabe felt the wheels touch ground. Many around him began to clap, including the two passengers seated beside him, an elderly, frail-looking woman and her grandson.

"Why are passengers clapping?" Gabe asked.

She whispered reverentially, "This country is a miracle. It is the homeland of my people. We will never take for granted that she is here to welcome us into her open arms."

Touched by the demonstration of unbridled patriotism, Gabe unbuckled his seatbelt, eager to begin his adventure. He waited for his seatmate and her companion to exit the row before making his way into the aisle. As he reached up to retrieve his carry-on bag, he caught the eye of an olive-skinned man with a thick well-trimmed mustache, several rows behind. The man quickly looked away, and Gabe had the unsettling feeling he'd seen him before. He couldn't place when or where.

After deplaning, he cleared customs and exited to the curb-side taxi line. It took only seconds to realize he had arrived in a whole new world.

CHAPTER 15

Boston Technological Institute

The BTI campus was alive with vibrant shades of amber, red and gold, pumpkins and fall wreaths decorating the grounds. Mounds of scattered leaves rejected by old maples carpeted the lawn. The library's dome loomed above, its majestic pillars testament to the great minds who had founded the prominent academy. Though the American flag stood at half-mast, yellow mums cheerfully surrounded the flagpole.

The women's track and field team was running laps around the quad. Dressed in shorts and long-sleeved t-shirts emblazoned with school logos, their ponytails danced in time with their strides, like hypnotizing metronomes. Tomorrow, classes would break for the Thanksgiving holiday.

Jon zipped up his jacket, rubbed his hands together, blowing warm breath over them. The air was brisk and invigorating. Autumn conjured up bittersweet childhood memories of his five-year-old self, leaping into heaps of packed leaves raked by his dad.

It was difficult to imagine that in this bucolic setting a mass killing took place only three years before. Jon wasn't sure what compelled him to return today, but knew any therapist worth their salt would say it was unresolved issues. On autopilot, Jon found himself a quiet corner off the quad.

There, a large sculpted rock marked the place where the

student union building once stood, where his friends had died. Erected on the last anniversary of the attack, the school had held a formal unveiling, inviting all alumni. Jon didn't attend but he had seen posts on Facebook.

He sat on the grass as a heaviness filled him. Dried up bouquets wrapped in colorful ribbons lay nearby, the petals falling off long ago. Extinguished votive candles rested below faded photos of the dead and injured taped haphazardly to the memorial. Each name was engraved in the gray granite.

Cameron Beales

Ashleigh Lewis

Shawna Pearson

Ashleigh.

Jon stared at her name. *Why am I still here and she's gone?* He was the poster child for survivor's guilt and knew it. He made a mental note to call her parents to wish them a Happy Thanksgiving.

The memorial rested just yards from a construction site. A diagram of the future Ashleigh Lewis Memorial Recreation Center showed Phase 1 plans were nearly complete. Charles and Jillian Lewis had established a fund in their daughter's memory, a large percentage earmarked for rebuilding the center. It would be a state-of-the-art facility with all the bells and whistles. At least one good thing had risen from the ashes.

Feeling lightheaded, Jon slowly stood up and made his way back to the paved path, trying to keep the sorrow at bay. He'd been given a second chance at life, and had no intention of squandering it by asking the unanswerable.

He turned to find Melanie running toward him. She looked beautiful in her blue turtleneck and faded jeans, her long tresses blowing in the breeze. He shook away the painful memories.

"Hey, space cadet, what are you mulling over?" Melanie asked, catching up with him.

"Just thinking about the old days, and that you and Granny Eunice are going to get along great."

Melanie took his hand in hers. "I can't wait to meet her. Anyone who's contributed to you being such an awesome guy has to be wonderful herself."

Jon pulled Melanie closer, taking her face in his hands, kissing her tenderly. He marveled at how much his life had changed since the last time he was here.

"Did you enjoy the campus tour?" asked Jon. "Sorry I didn't join you. I needed a few minutes alone."

"No problem. It must be hard for you being back here after what happened. They spoke about it on the tour. Three students besides the bomber died that day. The quad flag will remain at half-staff indefinitely. So sad."

Jon had never spoken of the event other than to Granny Eunice and Gabe. After the bombing, he and Pauly drifted apart, infrequently catching up on social media. No one from his new UNT circle knew of his past, and Jon wasn't ready to speak of it now. Maybe not ever.

Jon made a sweeping gesture with his free hand. "So, what do you think of my alma mater?"

"It's gorgeous. Feels like we're meandering inside a Norman Rockwell painting."

He laughed, "True, but the workload was anything but serene." He looked at his wristwatch. "It's almost time for the Skype call with Professor B. I think our best bet is to call from the forensics lab where it's quiet and they have Wi-Fi."

"Sounds good. Lead the way."

"It's great the professor looked over the samples before Gabe left. I just hope he's able to answer a few questions."

"His email said he had some interesting findings to discuss," said Melanie. "I'm impressed he's making himself available for the call today. Now that classes are on hiatus, he must have tons of exams to grade."

* * *

Scott Breitler was indeed grading papers when Melanie and Jon rang in. He accepted their Skype call, squinting at their faces on his laptop screen. His unruly white hair and lopsided bow tie made Jon think of the quintessential absent-minded professor. A miniature toy dinosaur stood guard on his desk.

"Hello, Melanie."

"Hi, Professor. How're you doing?"

"I'm well. It's been a hectic few days with exams but I'm muddling through. And who may I ask is your friend?"

Melanie made the introductions. "This is Jon. Jon, Professor Breitler. He's overseeing my project on autoimmune oral treatments. Professor, we're calling from New England. BTI, to be exact."

Jon said, "Hello, sir."

"Pleasure to meet you, son. Beautiful country, up there. I suppose you have family in the area?"

"My grandmother. She invited us for Thanksgiving."

"That should be lovely. Well then, Melanie, would you like to review your most recent study?"

"Actually, sir, we're calling about Jon's project."

The man donned a perplexed expression. "Oh, yes, yes, that's right, isn't it?"

Jon interjected, "I understand you had a chance to analyze the specimens."

"Of course, young man. Melanie dropped them off the other day. It was a good excuse for me to test-drive what I refer to as our new toy. The TR-X is the latest, most advanced machine—only three of which are available in academia. The other five went to major pharmaceutical laboratories around the world. We were one of the lucky few, thanks to generous benefactors. It doesn't hurt to have the sitting US Surgeon General among our prestigious alumni."

Trying to politely redirect him, Jon said, "Impressive. Were you able to find out any more information from the DNA than what we started with? We're anxious to know if there are any genetic abnormalities to explain criminal behaviors."

"You brought me a burnt nail sample and a short hair specimen."

"That's right, sir, and...?"

"I found no genetic mutation in either sample. The nail proved to be the more challenging of the two, given its condition and the length of time that has gone by."

Jon wondered if any new discovery was forthcoming or if this was just the professor's way of expounding on the greatness of his new equipment.

Breitler rummaged through papers on his desk. "I can't seem to find my glasses."

"They're on your neck string, sir," Melanie offered, good-naturedly.

"Yes, of course." He picked them off his chest, put them on and began perusing below the screen level. "Here we are. A tox screening on the hair sample showed a highly unusual result."

Jon perked up. "Oh?"

"Chrysanthemum Unclassified or Exotic is a species of the Asteraceae family. It's found only in the deep Amazon—specific to northeast Brazil. Ancient Awa Indians used it for rites of passage, possibly as a hallucinogen."

Melanie asked, "And you found traces of *that* in the hair?"

"Indeed."

"That seems weird. If it's a type of opiate, does it have a street name?"

"Well, that's the point. This botanical isn't accessible anywhere, as far as I could tell. Not as a pharmaceutical or a street drug. It's not out there. The only reason I was able to identify it is that the TR-X holds an exhaustive database of all plant species that can be used for drug use, regardless of their accessibility to the masses."

"If you had to guess, how would someone come across this drug?"

"I'm not in the business of guessing. My role is to acquire data and report it, not to make assumptions."

Melanie pushed. "But if you had to, for the sake of this conversation only?"

The professor pursed his lips, seeming uncomfortable with the notion. "If only for this chat, I'd say that the hair belonged to someone who was in the Amazon and came in contact with it, or there's an industry for this drug that I am unaware of."

"What are the effects of this plant?"

"After I learned of its rarity, I did some research. The plant was harvested at its peak in the early fall, then boiled down to essence within a span of no longer than an hour of its gleaning. It must be preserved in a dry cool environment remaining potent for up to six months before it loses its effects."

"And what are those?" Jon asked.

"The available information was severely limited and would require greater resources than I was able to locate in the short time I had."

"You've actually found out a great deal already. Thank you, professor," Melanie said.

"I wouldn't thank me yet. I'm very interested in finding out more about this esoteric plant and its effects. It's very exciting when a new drug potential is located." He paused. "But for now, you know what this means?"

Jon answered. "I think it means the Georgia Tech bomber was under the influence of a rare drug at the time of the killing."

"Quite right," said Dr. B. "But that's not all TR-X found." He peered intently into the camera. "You had better sit down for this one."

CHAPTER 16

Jerusalem, Israel

G abe had never experienced so many smells, sights and sounds at once like he did at the shuk, Machane Yehuda. Without realizing it, he had wandered into the open-air Jerusalem marketplace. A wild scene lay before him. Vendors perched at stands shaded by tattered awnings, indecipherably barking their wares. Throngs of shoppers pushed through the narrow outdoor space, bargaining for the best price on everything from chicken liver to pomegranates. He accepted a sample of halva, and decided he'd never tasted anything so good. From there it was a freefall. The dates tasted as sweet as sugar, the tea as if the leaves had been picked just hours before.

Gabe's map app showed a twenty-five-minute walk time to the Zion Hotel. Reluctantly, he pushed through the crowd, promising himself he'd be back. As he headed east on cobblestone Yaffo Street, Gabe was imbued with a sense of wonder. This city was a combination of old and new, and somehow the modern glass buildings made sense rising beside ancient stone edifices.

Was it only yesterday that Jon met me at the school cafeteria and handed over the samples he retrieved from the professor? Gabe pondered. Seemed hard to believe, given his current surroundings. He would do his best to convince Dr. Lavi to help. The need for answers had not faded, but instead became more pressing with time. Though he had never told anyone, it would always weigh on Gabe that he'd been sick that night at BTI. Logically, he knew he had no control over the events, but deep down he still felt he'd failed to protect his younger sister.

Gabe entered the hotel lobby, his shoes resonating loudly off the polished marble floor. The décor was Middle Eastern, with rich fabrics and decorative wrought-iron archways. He made his way past the reception desk to the café. Just a few tables were taken, and at one sat an elderly well-tailored gentleman donning a yarmulke.

"Dr. Lavi? I'm Gabriel Lewis. So glad to finally meet you."

The man smiled. "Ah, an American! The pleasure is all mine, but I am disappointed to inform you that I am not the doctor you seek," he declared in heavily accented English. My name is Gershon Pinsker, a retired jeweler from the Lower East Side of New York."

"Oh, I assumed you were the man I'm meeting. I guess he's not here yet." Turning to find a seat, he heard a soft chuckle.

Gabe found himself looking down at a woman, her age just either side of thirty, sitting near the corner window of the lobby. She had shoulder length hair the color of autumn wheat, intelligent green eyes, and on her face was a Cheshire cat grin. Petite, dressed in a fitted dark suit, she was a knockout.

"I never expected an alumnus of BTI to be so closed-minded in this day and age," the woman said teasingly. "I am Terry Lavi—*Doctor* Terry Lavi."

Gabe tried to recover. Dr. Lavi looked more like a co-ed than a celebrated researcher at Technion Institute. He settled in the seat across from her.

"Rookie mistake. Your name threw me off.," he said, flustered. "And given your impressive body of work, I also assumed you'd be older. As a budding scientist, I've been trained never to jump to conclusions but I suppose I haven't truly learned the lesson until now."

Dr.. Lavi extended her hand and they shook. "Forget it. As

luck would have it, I presented recent work findings at a symposium at Shaarei Tzedek Medical Center earlier today. When I received your call, I was already in Jerusalem. But to be blunt, I have very limited spare time. My bus to Haifa leaves at six thirty tomorrow morning. And surely you have other business to attend to while in our country."

Taking the hint, Gabe switched to all-on work mode, pushing his glasses further up the bridge of his nose. "Actually I flew here with the sole purpose of meeting you."

Terry raised a brow. "But I can't—"

"Since you're rushed, let's get right to it." He took out his iPad, entered his password and opened the classified file. "As you no doubt recall from our emails, there has been a spate of killing sprees in the United States. These attacks have occurred in every corner of the country, both in large cities and small college towns. We've spent a great deal of time looking for common denominators and have found various abnormalities that have proven challenging."

Gabe described the research he and Jon were conducting, elaborating on the basics they had already emailed her. He was outlining the results when Professor Lavi interrupted.

"You have succeeded in capturing my attention," she said. "But I'm famished. Perhaps we should, how do you say, 'kill two birds with one stone?' There is a small bistro a few blocks from here that has the best foie gras in the Middle East. Would you be up for continuing this discussion over dinner?"

Gabe didn't need to hear more. He quickly shut down his device, jammed it into his backpack and offered her his hand, helping her up.

Professor Lavi's eyes met Gabe's. "Has anyone ever said you look a lot like Clark Kent?"

"Superman, huh?" Gabe chuckled. "Those are big boots to fill but I'll try."

She smiled, smoothed her skirt, and grabbed her handbag. Together they walked into the Jerusalem night.

CHAPTER 17

Jerusalem

The evening air was pleasant, cooling. Gabe slowed to keep pace with Dr. Lavi, who was a full foot shorter than him, walking beside her along cobblestone alleyways lined with cafés and art galleries. Quaint shops housed in ancient buildings made of Jerusalem stone displayed handmade jewelry and Judaica in their windows. Turning a corner, the walls of the Old City came into view. The lingering iridescent glow of sunset lit billowy clouds above David's Citadel, evoking awe and feelings of wonder.

Sensing his emotional reaction, Terry walked on silently. After several blocks, she stopped in front of a small restaurant that Gabe thought might charitably be referred to as a "hole in the wall." Yet, when he opened the door, he was surprised. Soft Yemenite music played in the background. Stained glass sconces adorned pale limestone walls shedding jewel tones across the tabletops. A rough-hewn bar of dark acacia wood was manned by a hipster donning a fedora.

They were shown to a tiny table wedged between other diners. Gabe studied the professor as she perused her menu.

"If I may ask, Doctor, where did you acquire such a good command of English?" he asked.

"Please call me Terry. In Israel, it is highly unusual to address people by their titles. We are even on a first name basis with our prime minister." She laughed softly, a sound Gabe thought lovely. "But to answer your question, I have spent a lot of time in the United States. My father was a visiting professor of mechanical engineering at BTI. During my grade school years, we lived in the Boston area and moved back to Israel when my mother's job was transferred home. She is a genealogist at Haifa University. I returned to Yale for med school."

"A family of academics, then?"

"Yes, with the exception of my younger brother who lives in Tel Aviv with his wife and baby boy. He works in the hi-tech industry. Unfortunately, with our hectic schedules, I don't see them often." She paused. "Enough about me. Tell me how a doctoral student from Texas ended up in a Jerusalem bistro meeting with a geneticist."

Gabe wanted to ask her many questions, more personal than professional, but went along with the change in focus. "After I graduated from BTI, I moved back to Texas to start grad school. I wasn't cut out to live through another one of those crazy Northeast winters."

Terry nodded. "I can relate. A sabra like me can never fully adjust to cold climates. If I recall correctly, you're working on your project with a partner."

"My friend Jon. The idea for our study came about after he and my sister Ashleigh were at a school party when a bomb went off. Since then, we heard of similar bombings in different cities."

"Oh my. With my connections at BTI, of course I remember that attack. Were the two of them okay?"

Looking down at his plate, he replied, "Ashleigh was killed in the blast."

"How awful. I'm so sorry for your loss. I had no idea how personal this project was. We Israelis know all too well the effects of terror."

The waitress came for their orders. Foie gras for Terry, and for Gabe, a combination plate of babaganoush, hummus, and tahini sauce with fresh baked pita bread.

When the food arrived, Gabe took his first bite, and let out an audible moan. "Oh, that's good."

The couple at the next table gave him a once over. Terry laughed, causing Gabe to do the same.

"Gabe, as much as I am enjoying our dinner, I will have to leave shortly. I suppose you want my feedback on your research. I am intrigued with what you have already shared and wonder how I can help, especially given my tight schedule."

"Yes, of course. One consistent data point is that all the attacks resulted in the decimation of the attacker. Each bomber was burnt beyond recognition."

"Any DNA obtained?"

"Yes, in two cases trace evidence was acquired. We've grappled with the idea that perhaps the heat levels reached were intentional to erase as much information about the attackers as possible. It's almost as if the resulting devastation was secondary to that objective."

"The objective being to destroy all evidence of the attacker?"

"Exactly."

Terry contemplated. "When ambient temperatures approach significant levels, not only is identity in question, but extreme heat erases the genetic map we use to collect vital data such as the individual's eating and smoking habits, drug use, overall health and probability of developing certain diseases."

"That last point is quite interesting. Maybe these attackers were sick or likely to become sick."

"It's a possibility. Bear in mind, in some cultures dying for a cause is a noble venture. Western cultures may find this beyond comprehension, but much of the world adheres at least in principle to this tenet. Terrorist organizations seek out believers who show signs of impending illness to enlist as suicide bombers, selling it as a glorious way to depart this world."

Gabe was fascinated. "That doesn't explain any efforts to

cover up DNA."

"Perhaps they're covering up health habits, drug use and such."

"To what end?"

They sat in silence, thinking it over.

From his backpack, Gabe took out a small pouch, placing it on the table between them. "I wasn't sure if this would be helpful but now I'm certain it will be. I've brought samples extracted from two of the bombings. One was from an attacker's fingernail from the BTI attack. It was attached to the detonator. The other is from a hair left behind by the Georgia Tech attacker shortly before he struck. Professor Breitler says your developing technology is the most advanced to analyze compromised samples like these."

"True, but how did you acquire these?" Terry asked, dubiously eying the pouch.

"Jon found the fingernail at the BTI scene."

"Why didn't he call the police and give it to them?"

"He was an emotional mess and wanted to just put the whole thing behind him. Besides, the police already had the detonator. I'm just thankful Jon had the presence of mind to keep it."

"And the hair strand?"

"That one took a longer route to us. And to be honest, not in the most aboveboard way."

"Do you mean illegally?"

"Truthfully, I don't know. But what's done is done, and there's no going back."

Terry raised an eyebrow at his flippant response.

Gabe went on. "Just to be clear, once Jon got the hair, he went to the FBI, offering them both samples. They refused them, due to poor quality and the challenge of reliable analysis."

"I appreciate your candor. Am I to assume you want me to assess them?"

Gabe looked at her expectantly. He needed to tread gently.

"Professor Breitler, who referred us to you, looked at them and should have preliminary results any day. He has access to the TR-X but is still learning its full capabilities."

"Brilliant man, though some might say eccentric. Often comes with the territory."

"Not in your case," Gabe blurted. Embarrassed that he had overstepped his bounds, he looked at the menu, even though he couldn't read a word of it.

She let the comment pass. "Please clarify what you are asking of me."

"I was hoping after you heard more about this from me you'd consider making a more in-depth analysis. Our motives are more than academic. We're dedicated to bringing the perpetrators to justice."

Terry looked at her watch and motioned to the waitress to bring the check. "That's quite a request—ncredibly time-consuming. None of this was mentioned in your correspondence."

Gabe recalled Jon's words, *You may have to lay it on thick.* "Your reputation is stellar as is your facility's cutting-edge technology."

Terry's face remained neutral.

Gabe kept trying. "I know you're extremely busy, but I did come all this way to meet you, and we have no other avenues to explore." He paused and then added, "Of course we would name you as a co-author in any published work."

Disappointment shadowed her features. "Why do I feel like I'm being manipulated?"

"That's not my intention," he said with downcast eyes.

Her facial expression made it clear she didn't believe it. The next few minutes were spent in an uncomfortable silence. When the check arrived, Gabe insisted on paying the tab despite Terry's initial objections.

She stood, picked up the pouch, paused and set it back down on the table. "Thank you for an interesting evening. I must get some sleep."

"I'll walk you back to your hotel," Gabe offered, rising.

"No thanks. I would enjoy a solitary evening stroll."

"Is it safe?"

"Absolutely, and I am perfectly capable of defending myself." She tapped her purse.

"Well then, all right," Gabe conceded.

"I will have an answer for you tomorrow. In the meantime, please hold on to your samples." Terry shook his hand formally and left the restaurant.

Gabe didn't know what to think. *That took an unfortunate turn. I guess I pushed too hard.*

He never noticed the mustached, olive-skinned man slip out behind Terry and follow after her.

CHAPTER 18

Boston Technological Institute

"**O**kay, Professor B., we're sitting," Melanie said, leaning forward. The Boston Tech laboratory was pristine, microscopes, test tubes and petri dishes lined up neatly on sterile counters. Nearby a skeleton crew of student researchers were packing up their belongings. Jon sat beside her, his arm draped over the back of her chair.

"The nail was the more challenging of the two given its condition," said Professor Breitler. "Please understand the TR-X is new to us. New to the world, for that matter. I'm still learning how to engineer it for best practice, which is why I put you in touch with Dr. Lavi."

Jon fidgeted in his chair. Melanie put a calming hand on his.

"As I understood, your two samples were acquired years apart and are from different people. One is a male of Arab descent. The other a Caucasian male."

"That's right," said Melanie. "Two bombings, three years apart."

"Remarkable," said the esteemed professor.

"What is?" Jon asked, frustration seeping into his tone.

"When analyzing the nail fragment, I initially thought I had inadvertently re-printed the hair results, but I reviewed it twice. *Both* the hair and nail show the same rare plant derivative, Chrysanthemum Exotic, which means—"

"Both assailants were taking the same drug!" Jon blurted

out.

Stunned, Melanie said, "The likelihood of that is…"

"Infinitesimal," the professor offered.

"Unless they knew each other," said Melanie.

"Or had the same dealer," added Jon.

"Correct," said Professor Breitler. "Given the time and geographical distance between the two assailants, it would be statistically sound to conclude they knew someone in common. One has to ask why anyone would keep the existence of Chrysanthemum Exotic under wraps when they could sell it to Big Pharma for a sizeable fortune."

Jon theorized. "Maybe they intend to use it for their own purposes or wanted to test without FDA guidelines."

"My thoughts precisely. If someone had nefarious intentions, it would be in their best interest to keep their discovery quiet." He paused. "It may be time to speak with the authorities."

Melanie and Jon looked at each other.

Jon said, "We've already attempted to speak with a high-ranking FBI agent, and he didn't want to follow up on it."

"But you didn't have this information then. Holding back now could be construed as obstruction of justice."

"True."

When no more was forthcoming, the professor said, "I'll leave that up to you. For now, I have uploaded these early results on a flash drive. Would you like me to secure them for you?"

"No, please overnight them to my grandmother's house in Boston."

"I can do that. Or should I say, I'll have my assistant do that. I'm likely to forget." The professor called out, "Martin, can you come in here please?"

"Yes, professor?" a voice off-screen asked.

"Please take this flash drive and send it overnight delivery to the address my friends here will provide."

"Okay."

Jon recited the address and both he and Melanie thanked the professor profusely.

"It was a welcome challenge given the tedium of grading papers all day. Not to mention the excitement of playing with the new equipment. If I learn any more about the origins of the drug, I'll let you know forthwith."

They repeated their thanks and signed off. Melanie shut the computer and faced Jon. "That was exciting and scary at the same time. What do we do now with all this information? Go back to the FBI?"

"No way," Jon said with determination. "Now, we call an old friend."

* * *

Professor Breitler was nearing the end of the exam pile, pleased to find that most of his students were grasping the material. Also, he was gratified to be nearly done. The large pile of papers on his messy desk was now significantly smaller.

He had been impressed with Melanie and her friend. They were using their knowledge of science to make a difference in the world, and he hoped he had been a help to them. The TR-X discovery was disturbing. Though he found it a leap to think there were people out there planning to use an unknown drug for harmful purposes, he also knew there were those who would do anything for money, prestige or deep-seated beliefs. He decided to further research Chrysanthemum Exotic.

Setting aside the exams, he spent the next several hours hidden in his office, learning everything he could on the subject. What he found was unimaginable. Deciding he was done for the day, he typed up the main points and transferred them to a flash drive. As an afterthought, he decided to create a passcode that he would email Melanie tomorrow. *Can't be too careful.*

With Martin gone for the holiday, the professor put the flash drive in a padded envelope, addressed it and stuck on the postage. He locked his office and set out.

The campus was quiet on this day before Thanksgiving, but he'd always enjoyed the solitude. He walked to the corner mailbox and dropped in the envelope. *One less thing on my to-do list.* He would pick up the grading where he left off in the morning. His sister was expecting him for the turkey dinner at 4:30.

He walked to his car, finding his keys, after a search, in his pants pocket. With no traffic, he'd be home in fifteen minutes. He'd feed his cat, microwave a frozen dinner and get back to his book. Hawking was his hero.

The roads were slippery from an earlier rain, but his Subaru was made for these conditions. Always a cautious driver, he kept just under the speed limit. Approaching a red light at the corner of the main thoroughfare, he noticed traffic was heavier than usual. People were heading out to visit family for the holiday weekend.

Professor Breitler tapped the brakes.

Nothing happened.

Panicked, he tried again. And again. The slick hill caused his car to accelerate. Unable to stop, he knew he'd pass through the busy intersection. Fear struck him as he jammed the car in neutral and leaned desperately on the horn. It was too late. The last thing he saw were the bright lights of a semi only moments before impact.

CHAPTER 19

South Boston

Thanksgiving Eve

E unice Steadman was a tough old broad. A hair above five feet, she was small in stature but a force to be reckoned with. She had emigrated as a child from her native Scotland to the Lower East Side of Manhattan, eventually moving to South Boston when she married Jon's Grandpa Earl. Eunice and Earl's love affair lasted for thirty-six years until Earl died at fifty-nine, making Eunice a widow at fifty-seven.

She never had a desire to remarry, and in her characteristic manner, relayed to anyone that asked, "I had a great one. I'll never find anyone that good, and less than him I don't want." And that was that.

She kept busy with her friends who were more like sisters to her, and as the last driver standing, she shuttled them around in her five-year-old Honda to their doctor appointments, bridge games, and senior outings.

Despite surviving the tragic deaths of Jon's parents and losing Earl so young, Eunice kept an upbeat attitude. She told racy jokes, wore clothes designed for younger women, and stayed up late on social media enjoying pictures of her friends' grandchildren.

When Jon was eight, he came to live with his grandparents in Boston. They enrolled him in the local public school where he excelled.

After Grandpa Earl died, Jon became the man of the house, fixing latches on doors, grocery shopping, even balancing the checkbook. They lived on a tight budget, getting by on Granny's meager salary from secretarial work, Grandpa's pension and the three small life insurance policies. They shared a close bond built on deep respect and common tragedy. Granny never judged Jon, only offered her undivided attention and the occasional bit of wisdom.

When he was accepted to BTI, she had been as excited as he was, literally jumping for joy when he read the acceptance letter. Though she knew he would be moving on and leaving her behind, she never once showed an ounce of selfishness.

Granny opened the screen door when Jon pulled into the driveway. The familiar creaking was a welcome sound of home, even as the house looked tired and in need of TLC. Jon ran up the steps and wrapped Granny Eunice in a bear hug, Melanie in his wake.

"Granny, it's so good to be home."

"How's my boy? You hungry?"

Jon laughed. Even now his grandmother babied him. He loved every minute of it.

Eunice turned to his lovely companion. "You, my dear, must be the sweet Melanie. I'm so glad you could come. Welcome to my humble home."

Melanie had not yet walked in the door, but already felt a sense of comfortable familiarity. A wonderful aroma wafted from inside.

Jon dramatically sniffed. "Are those my cookies I smell?"

"You always did have the nose of a bloodhound." Granny took their hands and led them inside to the kitchen table, where a plate of warm chocolate chip cookies awaited. She poured them glasses of milk before sitting and facing them from across the table.

The house had not changed since he was a child with green and pink linoleum in the kitchen, cracked plastic-covered chairs, and an ancient cuckoo clock hanging on the living room wall.

A new odor now filled his nostrils—mothballs and medicine, smells of old age. Sadness filled him.

"You all right, honey?" Granny asked.

"Just tired, I guess. We had a long day of travel."

"I want to hear everything about your new school and friends. But if you're too tired, we can catch up after you have a rest."

He moved around the table, bent down to kiss her. "Thanks Granny. You know you're the love of my life, right?"

"I sure better be." She chuckled. "I suppose you two would like to share a room. Jon can show you the way."

Melanie raised her eyebrow at Jon as he grabbed her bag to take up to his old room. There was comfort in things remaining the same, he thought. His BTI league soccer trophies, shiny and dust-free, stood frozen in time on the shelf above his desk. A paper calendar was three years old.

Jon adopted a British accent. With a bow and flourishing hand gestures, he proclaimed, "Here we are, madam. Your accommodations for the next three days. Dinner is called for seven, and breakfast is served from six-thirty until ten AM. Please let me know if you will require turn-down service."

Melanie laughed. "I'm loving it. Your grandmother is so, so...what's the word I'm looking for? Cozy?"

"Perfect description." He kicked off his shoes and let out a loud yawn. "If you don't mind, I think I'll close my eyes for a quick doze."

"My thoughts exactly," Melanie said, collapsing beside him.

* * *

Jon woke up two hours later in a dark room, unsure where he was. The open window let in the cool night breeze billowing the curtains above his head. A bright moon hung high in the sky. Melancholy still hovered above him like a grey cloud. *Snap out of it*, he told himself. He looked over at Melanie sleeping peacefully. He was going to enjoy these few days with Mel and his grandmother. He closed his eyes and fell back to sleep, dreaming of his mother.

CHAPTER 20

South Boston

Thanksgiving Day

J on felt better than he had in a long time. After a quick shower, he changed into a deep blue button down oxford and chinos, then grabbed the bag he'd brought for his granny.

She was in the kitchen preparing the feast, Melanie beside her wearing a worn-out Minnie Mouse apron, sautéing onions filling the room with their aroma. There was stuffed turkey with rice and mushrooms, sweet potato pie, and corn on the cob.

"There you are, sleepyhead," Melanie chided him. "Granny and I have been getting to know each other. I've enjoyed all the stories about you as a little boy. Were you really stuck up that oak in the front yard trying to get your balloon?"

Jon groaned. "Granny! Tell me you didn't show her any bathtub pics."

"Don't be silly. I'm saving those for after dinner."

Melanie laughed. "I'd better go change. I smell like onions." She took off the apron. "I'll be back in a jiffy."

Eunice looked at Jon. "You look so happy, which makes *me* so happy. Mel's a keeper."

"I couldn't agree more. We're lucky to have found each other." Looking at the spread, Jon asked "Did you invite all the neighbors without telling me?"

"Very funny...Oh, I almost forgot to mention it. I was shopping at the market earlier this week, and guess who I bumped into?"

"Your parole officer?"

"Ha! Guess again."

"Oh, that guy who gives out cheese samples. The chubby one who has a crush on you."

Granny let out a hearty laugh. "Freddie? Don't be ridiculous!"

"I saw the way he looks at you. And he always seems to have the premium samples when you're walking by."

"Jonny, you're a hoot. Actually, I saw Officer Kearns. She was just ending a shift and was picking some things up before heading home."

"How's she doing?"

"I thought you had stayed in touch with her since...BTI."

"We did for a while. We still email sometimes but I don't know much about her personal life. I got the impression she's lonely."

"Precisely what I thought. And why I invited her for Thanksgiving."

"Oh, okay. That was nice."

"A few months ago she confided in me about a tumultuous marriage in her early twenties. Claimed it turned her off from pursuing another meaningful relationship. She has no family around, and since she took a liking to you, I thought she'd enjoy the camaraderie."

"After what happened, she checked on me regularly, like she was taking me under her wing. Showed a real interest in my studies, even sent me cards on my birthday."

"Not too many like her that truly care."

"It will be nice to see her again but-"

"I know what you're going to say. Not to discuss what happened. I've always respected that."

"Yes, you have. Just add it to the list of reasons I love you so much."

"Done." Suspiciously eyeing the bag he held, she asked, "What have you got there?"

Jon handed her the bookstore bag.

Granny took out the Mean Green t-shirt with a big grin on her face. "I love it! I'll wear it Senior Poker Night. Oh, before I forget, here's the mail that came for you." She handed him a small envelope from the table.

The early drug results. He pocketed them. "Thanks."

She eyed her grandson. "Everything okay?"

"Sure."

"Just be careful, honey."

"Always."

Jon saw Granny look past him. He turned around and found Melanie standing there, dressed in a red sheath, open-toe pumps, diamond studs adorning her ears, her wavy hair falling naturally. She was holding a bottle of red wine.

Jon crossed the room to her, kissed her tenderly on the lips. "You look breathtaking."

Granny beamed at the couple, took her iPhone from her apron pocket, and took a photo. Mel placed the wine on the dining room table and followed Eunice into the kitchen to help.

At 5:00 p.m. on the dot, the doorbell rang. Donna Kearns stood in the doorway holding an arrangement of yellow mums. Her auburn hair showed some gray but her freckles were still in place, giving her a youthful appearance.

"Jon! So great to see you," she said cheerfully, as she stepped inside, setting down the flowers.

"Happy Thanksgiving, Lieutenant."

"Donna."

"Donna," he conceded, taking her coat.

Melanie emerged from the kitchen, holding a platter of hors d'oeuvres.

"Donna, this is my girlfriend, Melanie Ridgefield. Mel, this is Donna Kearns."

Donna smiled. "Pleasure to meet you. I heard about you from Eunice."

"Nice to meet you as well. Are you a friend of the family?"

"Yes, we've been friends for several years."

Before Donna could explain how they had met, Granny Eunice emerged from the kitchen, her apron off, wearing her favorite dress. "Hello, Donna. So glad you could make it."

"Thanks for including me. I hope you like mums."

"I love them. I think I'll plant these. Maybe Melanie will give me a hand with that tomorrow."

"It would be my pleasure," Melanie said.

Granny Eunice sat at the head of the table and everyone took their seats. Melanie poured out four glasses.

Eunice raised hers. "It's a Steadman tradition to clink glasses as a sign of our thanks."

They all did so, each guest enjoying the joyful holiday spirit.

✽ ✽ ✽

When dessert was finished and the coffee cups drained, Donna took her leave, thanking Eunice with a warm hug, then embracing Melanie and Jon as well.

The next hour was spent cleaning up and answering Granny's countless questions about how Jon and Melanie met, their school, their friends, and life in Texas. She hung on every word, chiming in when she needed follow-up info.

When the dishes were done and the food put away, they relaxed on the living room sofa, sipping hot apple cider.

"Jonny, it sounds like you've acclimated real well. I'm proud of you, honey."

"I hope you'll come down for a weekend. Don't forget the cake and cookies." He grinned.

"My long-distance travel may be coming to an end, sweetheart," Granny Eunice said.

Jon put his fork down. "What do you mean? Are you feeling okay?"

"Sure sure. It's nothing specific. Just plain old age. Happens to the best of us and there's no avoiding it, only need to make accommodations."

Jon looked despondent.

She continued, "It's merely another stage of life. I'm not going anywhere for a long time. We'll simply see each other on my turf."

Jon forced a smile. "Whatever you say, Granny. I'll do my best to come more often."

She stood up, leaned over and kissed the top of his head, then began clearing the cider mugs.

Jon stood quickly. "Let me do that for you."

"Don't be silly. I'm not an invalid. "

"Fine. I know when I can't win. I thought I'd take Mel downtown tonight and check out O'Grady's. Wanna come?"

"Not a chance. Run along and have a good time. I'm in the middle of a real page-turner. Gonna get in bed and fall asleep with the book on my chest."

"Sounds divine," Mel said.

Jon stood up, leaned over to give her a peck on the cheek. "See you in the morning, Granny."

❊ ❊ ❊

Jon gave Melanie a driving tour of downtown. They cruised by Prudential Tower, Quincy Market, Fenway Park and the Boston Common. He pulled up along the waterfront.

"And for our tour finale, before you is Boston Harbor, site of the Boston Tea Party."

Melanie looked out the windshield window. Twinkling lights cast by seafaring boats reflected on the habor like a sea of stars.

It was warm inside the heated car, and Jon's hand felt damp

in hers. She said, "Boston is a big city that feels like a quaint town." She turned to Jon. He was staring at her. "What is it? Is everything all right?"

"You're so beautiful."

Melanie blushed, lowering her gaze. "Thank you."

Gently, he tilted her chin up and looked into her eyes, where he saw a yearning. He leaned in, her whole body coming to greet his kiss. Her lips were soft as silk, igniting the passion building below the surface, Jon's hunger overpowering his senses. Their kisses became longer and deeper, more intense.

"I love you, Jon," Melanie whispered, her lips so close to his.

"I love you too."

❈ ❈ ❈

Their next stop was O'Grady's, an old-time pub frequented by the locals, serving the best brews on tap. A bell above the door jingled as they entered. Recaps of the Dallas Cowboys game were playing on large screens above the bar.

"Is that Jonny?" the barrel-chested barkeep called out as they entered.

"'Tis I, along with Lady Melanie."

"Ha! How're you doing old man?" Connor put down the beer stein he was drying and came around the bar. He gave his friend a bear hug.

Jon introduced him to Melanie. "Connor and I went to school together." Facing his old friend, he asked, "How's it been here?"

"Nothing's changed since you left. Same old, just how we like it." Jon enjoyed hearing the familiar Boston Irish brogue.

"How's Pauly?" Jon asked.

"Real good. Prepping for the big day."

"Big day?"

"Haven't you heard? He's getting married on New Year's Eve."

It was the first Jon heard of his pal's upcoming marriage. Theirs was the longest friendship Jon had, lasting from childhood through college where they'd shared an apartment at BTI. The news was welcome. Pauly deserved to be happy. Despite wealth and privilege, things had never been easy for him. As far back as Jon could remember, Pauly and his father had shared a troubled relationship. And like Jon, he'd lost his mother at a young age.

After the bombing, their lives went in different directions, and they'd drifted apart.

"Who's the lucky gal?" he asked.

"Angela Callahan."

"Angela from PS 87? You're kidding. The girl with eternal braces?"

"Her overbite's gone and she's one hot chick now. Teaches spinning. Has her own sports club."

"That's great. I'm real happy for him. Please tell him I said so."

"Why don't you tell him yourself?"

"We sort of lost touch."

"Then get back *in* touch. No time like the present. Gotta put the past behind us, man."

Melanie wasn't sure what that meant.

"So, Melanie, right? Why are you hanging out with this doofus?"

"Mostly because of the friends he keeps."

"Ha, she's a quick wit, this one. I gotta get back to work before the boss fires me. Oh, wait, never mind, he's my dad. First round's on me. Welcome home, buddy."

"Thanks, man."

Mel and Jon took a table in the back, and a waitress stopped by to take their drink order.

"Connor seems like a fun guy," she said.

"Sure is. Didn't realize how much I missed it all."

"Who says you can't go home again?"

"Not sure who said it, but there's something to it. It's great to be back but things seem different."

"How so?"

"My grandmother is getting older faster. The house seems neglected, and most of my friends have moved on, without me knowing much about it."

"What did Connor mean about leaving the past behind?"

"Pauly hasn't had the easiest of childhoods. He and I have been through some rough times."

"Want to talk about it?"

"Nah, not now. Tonight's special."

She smiled. "It sure is—the day we professed our love for each other."

"Is that an anniversary I'll have to remember?" he teased.

"I'll make sure to remind you."

Their drinks arrived, an Appletini for Mel and a local lager for him.

"Here's to coming home again." Jon raised his glass. Scooting closer to her, he leaned in for a kiss. They sat like that until it was time to go home.

CHAPTER 21

South Boston

It was the morning after Thanksgiving, the heaviness of the previous day's feast lingering. Melanie and Granny Eunice had gone to the market, leaving Jon behind on the enclosed patio with a cappuccino and his laptop.

Checking his phone, Jon saw that Pauly and Angela's wedding invitation had arrived by email. The informality of the delivery method was consistent with the type of affair they were planning, an intimate but casual beachside wedding in Miami. Jon wasn't surprised. Pauly had never been comfortable in the uber-wealthy circles of his childhood. Smiling photos of the couple were attached, the most recent one taken in front of O'Grady's. If he hadn't been told whom Pauly was marrying, Jon would never have recognized her. Angela had grown into a lovely young woman, teeth in their rightful place. They looked very much in love, and for that Jon was grateful. He hoped this would be the beginning of a happier, more settled chapter in Pauly's life.

Jon and a guest were invited to attend. Given that they'd lost touch, he was surprised to be included.

Studying the invitation, he noted that Pauly's stepmother was now *U.S. Senator* Jasmine Hendrix. As far back as he could remember, Mrs. Hendrix was a reputed powerhouse, serving on the boards of well-known charities, and involved in various community projects. Last he heard, she was entertaining aspirations of political office, and Jon wasn't shocked to see she had succeeded.

Mrs. Hendrix had come to the U.S. as an Iraqi refugee when she was nineteen, seeking asylum. She enrolled in university, learned fluent English, and graduated valedictorian of her class. By the time she married Pauly's dad, she was practicing as an immigration attorney in downtown Boston.

Looking at the photos, Jon couldn't help but reminisce. Despite their wealth and privilege, the strain had always been palpable in the illustrious Hendrix household, with frequent clashes between Pauly and his father. As a child, Jon thought Pauly's dad unapproachable—always too busy to play or talk with his son.

Back when they were in the fourth grade, Pauly told Jon his father was going to marry a lady from overseas who had no kids of her own. She spoke English but with a strange accent. Pauly didn't seem particularly upset about it. Just sad. Always sad. After they got married, Pauly began seeing a therapist. Jon confided he did as well. They agreed it didn't help. They missed their moms, and nothing would ever change that.

No one ever mentioned the drastic difference in the boys' economic status, and they never noticed it. Pauly told him he went to public school because his father had, and felt strongly that his son would get a better "real life education" than that from an expensive parochial school. "The school of hard knocks got me where I am today," he used to say. A self-made man, Mr. Hendrix had built his business from the bottom up. He now ran a corporation with hundreds of holdings and subsidiary companies.

On one after-school visit, curiosity got the better of Jon, and he meandered into the part of the house off limits to children. Huge oil paintings hung above ornate mantels lined with shiny trinkets, and colorful rugs draped the floorboards. Jon was startled to hear Mrs. Hendrix on the phone only feet away from where he stood. She was sobbing, speaking rapidly in a foreign language. He nearly knocked over a crystal vase in the hallway as he ran to Pauly's room. "Your stepmom is crying."

"Yeah, she does that sometimes."

"Why?"

"Dad told me she grew up very rich and then when the government changed, they took away all their money. Her family was kicked out of their house and forced to move into a tiny one when she was thirteen. She had to work in a field, and her parents were beaten if they didn't do what they were told by the government. Her dad left to work one day and never came back."

One rainy afternoon the boys looked up Pauly's stepmother's native country, finding pictures that stayed with them for a long time. Dirty skinny kids without shoes, never smiling at the camera. The place looked hot and scary.

Now, as Jon thought of Pauly's upcoming marriage, he rejoiced for his friend's new lease on life. He could start his own family, build strong connections with his own kids, and put his past behind him. If anyone knew the value of moving on, it was Jon.

Rather than RSVP by email, he ventured a call. The phone rang several times and was hastily answered just as Jon was about to hang up.

"Yell-o." Pauly's voice was unmistakable. Jon couldn't help but smile. *Some good things stay the same.*

"Pauly, your email was a wonderful surprise. Congratulations, man."

"Jonny? Hey, pal. Thanks. I just saw Connor at the bar, and he told me you came by. I regretted not keeping in touch."

"Me too. It was kind of you to include me."

"Wouldn't be the same without you. Do you think you can make it to the wedding?"

"We're going to try our best to be there."

"We?"

"Yup, I'll be bringing my girlfriend as the plus one."

"Good for you, buddy. Anything serious?"

"Yeah, I think so."

"We'd love to meet her. It's going to be a small affair—mostly family and close friends."

"Sounds awesome. How are your dad and stepmom?"

"I'm still butting heads with Dad. Jasmine plays interference."

"Sorry."

"S'okay. They're paying for the wedding, so I really can't complain. Dad's way of showing he cares is by writing a check."

"Things okay with Jasmine?"

"Yeah, she's cool. Working to fund her projects around the world."

"I'm sure my girlfriend Melanie would love to speak with her. She volunteers for various causes."

"Sounds like you found yourself a bleeding heart."

Jon laughed. "You bet."

"I'm happy for you. Now tell me, what have you been up to?"

"Way more than I bargained for."

"Oh yeah?"

"I'll tell you more about it when we see each other, but in a nutshell, Gabe and I are working on a thesis for assessing motives for crime sprees."

"No kidding. You think that's a good idea?" Pauly asked, tentatively. When that was met with silence, Pauly continued. "You ever find someone to talk you through it? I did, and I have to admit once I found the right therapist, it helped a lot."

"Seems like everyone's suggesting that lately."

"Seriously, Jonny, trauma doesn't just go away on its own."

"I've got way too much on my plate right now to start counseling."

"Okay, pal, I'll stop mothering you, but think it over. And thanks for the call. We'll see you in a couple weeks."

"Hope so, Pauly. Congrats."

No sooner had he hung up than his phone pinged with a news update. Another attack, this time in Los Angeles. No motive, shooting followed by a bomb explosion.

Not again.

CHAPTER 22

Los Angeles

The once glamorous Hollywood sign appeared neglected and sad, much like the city itself. Jon didn't like LA. Too spread out, terrible traffic, and the awful smog, an asthmatic's nightmare.

Why do people live here? Jon wondered, staring out the window of Sheryl's Coffee Shop. His foul mood was likely a result of a long flight without sleep. Or maybe it was his visit with Granny Eunice. He'd been living in denial: but it was time to accept his grandmother was getting older and less self-sufficient. The thought of losing her one day was unbearable.

He had arrived before sunrise and found an open café on Ventura Boulevard, glad to have come upon an old-fashioned Mom and Pop shop. Overpriced chains could never make a cup of coffee like the one he now sipped.

Sheryl's was nearly empty, morning rush a good hour away. Square Formica tables, black and white parquet flooring, and a stainless-trimmed counter with attached barstools, gave the place a '50s vibe. He couldn't tell if it was designed that way or authentic. Jon watched as cops on the early shift came and went, armed with mega-cups of java. A blinding orange glow filled the shop as sunrise broke. He pulled down the window shade beside him and perused the *LA Times*.

The headline screamed, *YMCA Under Attack!* It was the

reason Jon had flown to Los Angeles, cutting short his time with Granny. Fortunately, this time only the bomber was dead, but not before leaving three others wounded.

The article was written by Edward D. Hernandez, the man Jon was hoping to meet this morning.

His phone rang. Gabe's familiar voice greeted him. "Hey bro, how're you doing?"

"Gabe, what's up, man? How's the Holy Land treating you? Did you meet Dr. Lavi? Was he helpful?"

"Whoa, slow down." Gabe laughed. "Yes, we met. I've got a lot to share with you. But you probably should change your pronoun."

Jon didn't miss a beat. "Terry is a woman, then?"

"Sure is. I kind of made a fool of myself on that one but turns out she's the perfect person for the job. A brilliant, beautiful geneticist, specializing in DNA splicing."

Jon noted how energized his friend sounded. Of course, it was late afternoon where he was. "Beautiful? Sounds like you're taken with the good doctor."

"Maybe I am, but she's all business. She wanted time to think over our request, but I still haven't heard back from her. Looks like I may need to extend my stay by a day or two. Not that I mind. This city is incredible. And the food, out of this world." Gabe heard glasses clinking in the background. "So tell me, what's happening on your end? Sounds like you're on the move. I'll bet you're glad to be back in Boston. How's your granny?"

"She's fine. Thanksgiving was a feast like no other. But seriously, bro, haven't you been checking the news? There's been another bombing. Same M.O. as the others. I arrived in LAX a few hours ago, and plan to do some digging. I tried to reach Dr. B. to get his okay to come out here and meet with a reputable resource, but he never got back to me. I used grant money to get here. Let's hope he won't have a problem with my game time decision."

"That's a lot to take in. I guess I'm living in a bubble here.

Haven't heard anything about it. These attacks are coming closer together."

"They are, and if my hunch is correct," said Jon, "the FBI is getting more involved, putting things into high gear trying to find similarities between them. Remember the crazy meeting Mel and I had with an FBI agent earlier this month?"

"Yeah, why? You guys haven't been getting into trouble, have you?"

"Nah, I'm just glad we covered our backs with the specimens by offering for them to check them out."

"That was a good move," Gabe agreed. "Where are you going to start in LA?"

"Mel's dad is well connected here. He knows the lead crime reporter at the *Times*. Mr. Ridgefield emailed him on my behalf, asking if he would give me a few minutes of his time. The piece he published today included interesting facts of the attack. My guess is he has more info than he wrote about. While he may need to have corroboration to print something, hunches are good enough for me. I'm waiting till 8:00 a.m. to call him and hope he'll be willing to talk to me."

"Ok, good luck," said Gabe. "Keep me posted."

"One more thing. You'll never guess what the compounds yielded before I gave them to you. We got initial results back."

"Okay, I'll bite. What?"

"Both specimens revealed drug usage by the killers."

"Not exactly shocking. Makes it easier for them to do the deed."

"True, but what *is* shocking is that the drug was a rare psychotropic found in plants grown only in the Amazon. You can't find Chrysanthemum Exotic on the market—legal or black. It's not out there. TR-X only found a match because of its extensive comparative database that some genius decided should include plants rarely seen by the human eye."

"Incredible! But there's no evidence they knew each other."

"True again, but now we can assume the killings are linked. It's less likely we're dealing with a copycat. We may be looking at something bigger than we thought."

"Jon, are you thinking organized terrorism?"

"Yes."

"Did you call the FBI again?"

"After the last fiasco, not a chance. We need more proof before I talk to them again."

Gabe sounded unsure. "This is crazy. You think we're doing the right thing, going ahead with this on our own?"

"We need to see this through," Jon replied with conviction. "All our work depends on it. Your parents deserve real answers. "And," he added more lightly, "we'll not only be published in the *Journal of Applied Sciences* but in the *LA Times* as well. We'll be the next Woodward and Bernstein."

Gabe laughed. "Great, as long as I'm Robert Redford and you're Dustin Hoffman."

"Deal! Stay safe, buddy."

"Will do. Talk to you soon."

The aroma of fresh baked bread emanated from the café kitchen making Jon hungry. He left the phone on the table and picked up a coffee-stained, laminated menu. He glanced over the breakfast specials and checked the time on his phone. 7:28. Earlier than he planned, but he was getting anxious. He scrolled through his contacts, found the number and dialed.

"Hello?" The man sounded wide awake. *Phew*. Jon had not wanted to start off on the wrong foot by waking up the reporter.

"Mr. Hernandez, this is Jon Steadman. I got your number from Peter Ridgefield. He sent you an email, said you might be able to help me out." *Not exactly what he said but it can't hurt to push things along.*

"Never saw it. What's this about?" The guy sounded annoyed.

"I'm working on a project relating to the mass killings that happened around the country in recent years. My partner and I have been studying the forensics and profiles of the terrorists."

"Terrorists. That's a presumptive description." He paused. "You say you got my number from Peter?"

"Yeah, that's right."

The reporter warmed up. "So how can I help your project?"

"I've been reading your reports, including today's piece. My sense is you have a good bead on these individuals and could speculate as to their motives and frame of mind."

"I have many thoughts on the subject, most of which I can't put in print."

"I'm not looking to quote you, just get your expert opinion. How does an all-you-can-eat breakfast sound? On me, of course."

"It would sound pretty damn good if I could hear it over my grumbling stomach."

"I'm in Sheryl's Coffee Shop on Ventura."

"I know the place. Be there in fifteen." Hernandez hung up.

Jon put down his phone and waved to the waitress for a refill. He couldn't believe his luck, getting the guy to meet him with almost no resistance. He had fifteen minutes to organize the thoughts inside his sleep-deprived brain.

CHAPTER 23

Jerusalem

G abe was zipping up his suitcase when the hotel room phone rang. He wanted to check the latest news on the LA attack, but first needed to reach out to Terry. He hadn't heard from her since their dinner two nights before, and couldn't afford to wait any longer. He was on a tight budget and his funds were nearly depleted. Check-out was at 11:00 a.m. He would need a clear yes or no to his request, and soon.

He yanked up the phone mid-ring. "Hello?"

"Mr. Lewis? This is the front desk. A package was just left here for you."

"I wasn't expecting—" But the deskman had already hung up.

Gabe took out his phone, dialed Terry and got her voicemail. He hung up without leaving a message. He turned on the television, tuning into CNN. The typical pundit debates were raging about gun control laws and radical Islam. He shut it off, deciding instead to check later from his phone. He grabbed his bag, shut the lights and left the room.

A young man stood at the front desk, dressed in suit and tie and sporting a nameplate that read *Oded*. "Checking out, sir?"

"Yes, and I understand I have a package here."

"One moment, please"

Oded went into the office and retrieved a small box. Gabe's name and room number were written on the package. Gabe lifted the box. It felt empty.

"Do you have a pair of scissors I can use?"

"Certainly."

Gabe pulled a twenty shekel note out of his pocket and tipped the man. Using the proffered scissors, he cut through the packaging and found a paper envelope inside. As he lifted it up, a pink bracelet fell out. *There must be some mistake.*

He noticed the writing on the side, realizing he was looking at a hospital wristband with Hebrew letters.

"Oded, can you read this for me, please?"

"Hadassah Medical Center, dated two days ago."

"That's all?"

"And the patient's name, of course. Theresa Lavi."

CHAPTER 24

Hadassah Medical Center

Jerusalem

"**A**re you a family member?" The nurse sat at her station, wearing a look of pure exhaustion.

"I'm Theresa's brother from the States." Oddly, the lie came easily to Gabe, but the anxiety in his voice was genuine.

"She's in Room 217. Down the hall to your left. Please make your stay a short one. Visiting hours are nearly over."

Gabe all but ran down the hall. He found the room's door ajar and gently tapped on it. A soft spoken response in Hebrew was all he needed. Gabe stepped inside and had a shock.

Terry lay in bed, her head wrapped in gauze, the right side of her face scraped up.

"Gabe? She spoke his name softly as he came into view. He guessed she was taking something for the pain.

"Are you okay? How are you feeling?" he asked, taking a small step forward. She looked so fragile.

"Better today. I had a concussion after my fall. Some bruising but no real damage. I guess I'm lucky it wasn't worse."

"Why didn't you call to tell me?"

"They had me sedated and I just woke up a few hours ago. I must have lost my phone in the melee. All my contact information was in there."

Gabe glanced at her wrist, noting a pale pink band. Identical to the one now in his possession.

He sat in the chair beside her. "I'm so relieved I found you. Do you remember what happened?"

"It's fuzzy, but the doctor says I may get more of my memory back in the next few days. Time will tell. The nurse told me a couple of teenagers found me about fifteen minutes after I left you. I was unconscious on the ground a block from the hotel, bleeding from my head."

Anger boiled up inside him. "Damnit! I knew I should have escorted you back. What a fool I am!"

"Don't be ridiculous. I trained in krav maga and was armed with pepper spray. Clearly, my attacker knew what he was doing. Based on my injuries, he came up from behind. The mugger took my wallet and phone. Had you been there too, it's more than likely there would have been two victims."

"So you didn't see who did this?"

She shook her head. "All I know is I smelled cigarette smoke. I have no idea if that was from the attacker or my mind playing tricks on me."

Gabe approached the bed. Carefully, he took her hand. "I'm so grateful that you're all right."

Terry squeezed his hand. "Thank you. It was just one of those bad luck things. He must have been after my purse. I'll be more careful in the future." She continued, "You never did mention how you found me."

"We can discuss that later when you're feeling up to it." He paused. "But you need to know that this was no random attack."

Her eyes grew large with worry. "How do you know that? Who would want to target me?"

Gabe took out the envelope and showed her its contents. "This arrived in a package at my hotel, addressed to me."

Terry gasped. "Dear God. The nurse came in shortly after I woke up, dismayed my bracelet had been misplaced. She said that sort of thing never happens. The attacker must have followed me to the hospital." She held her wrist. "He touched me while I slept!"

Gabe saw her fear and anger blossoming.

Terry sat upright, eliciting a moan. "I need to get out of here."

Gabe gently leaned her back again. "You still need medical care. I can stay here with you in your room until they discharge you."

"Whoever is behind this isn't going to stop until they get what they want." The full weight of what had happened to her seemed to sink in. "This was just a warning...but who would do such a thing?"

Gabe had thought of little else on his way to the hospital. "The only connection between you and me is our meeting about the DNA samples. Maybe this person is involved in one of the recent attacks and thinks we can identify him."

"We need to call the police."

"And tell them what? We have no useful information or even a clue who did it. And if we do report this, we'll need to tell them of our research. They may confiscate the DNA samples as evidence. There's too much at risk."

"I can't just go back out there unprotected. I have a job to get back to. Looking over my shoulder for the rest of my life is not an option."

She was right. Gabe looked at her. "Terry, I have an idea."

CHAPTER 25

Hadassah Medical Center

Jerusalem

G abe stepped into the hospital hallway, making sure there were no other people around. Visiting hours were nearly over and they would soon ask him to leave. He knew cellphone use was frowned upon in hospitals, but wasn't willing to leave Terry alone, even for a minute.

The hotel desk clerk picked up on the first ring.

"Oded, It's Gabriel Lewis, the man who picked up the package a few hours ago."

"Yes, sir, how may I be of assistance?"

"When you called my room, you mentioned that the package had just been dropped off. Were you manning the desk at the time?"

"I was."

"Who delivered it?"

"Eli, the bike messenger. He comes by twice a day, dropping off and picking up parcels in the downtown area. It's easier and quicker than mail service."

"Can you describe him?"

"Maybe twenty-five at most. Light hair, sabra through and through."

"Sabra?"

"You know, born and bred Israeli. Probably finished his

army service recently."

"I see. How can I find out who gave the package to him?"

"Usually by the return address, of course. The one you received would have been quite the mystery, no, Mr. Lewis? No return address and no name."

"Will Eli be back again today?"

"Today is Friday, Mr. Lewis. Everything shuts down by early afternoon for the Sabbath. I will not see him again until Sunday."

Just my luck. He was about to hang up, thinking he hit a dead end.

"Wait, you said it *would have been* a mystery."

"That's correct. In order to deliver a package, one must sign their name. Security, you understand."

"So who sent it to me?"

"When Eli dropped it off, I noticed the name was illegible. Like someone was in a rush and didn't have time to write their name completely. Normally, I wouldn't think much of it, but the signature had one distinguishing feature. A very large accent above the name. I have only one regular guest who signs his name that way."

"Who?"

"Mr. Lewis, please understand. I have no idea if this man is the sender of your package. I'm simply guessing."

"Yes, yes. I understand, and there will be no consequences if you're wrong." *For you, anyway.*

"Very well. Monsieur René Leduc has stayed with us on several occasions. I imagine he does so when he wants to keep a low profile. He is clearly a man of means and can afford more luxurious accommodations than what we can offer here."

"How can I find Mr. Leduc?"

"I am not at liberty to divulge guest information sir."

"Oh," he said with disappointment. "Then, would you please describe him to me? I'm thinking we've met, and can't seem to place him."

"He is tall, about six feet, slim with dark hair. Early thirties, but I could be off a few years. He is of Mediterranean descent. Oh, and he has an impressive moustache."

An alarm went off in the back of his head. *The airplane.*

"Do you know his country of origin?"

"I cannot give you this information."

"Would you happen to know if this man smokes?"

"Like a chimney. He always requests a smoking room for his stays with us."

Gabe said, "I greatly appreciate your assistance. I will be happy to put in a good word for you with your supervisor."

"That won't be necessary sir. I am happy to help. I never really liked Monsieur Leduc."

* * *

When Gabe returned to Terry's hospital room, he was surprised to find her fully dressed, flitting around the room with nervous energy.

"What's happening? Shouldn't you be lying down?"

Terry stopped pacing to face Gabe. "I'm getting out of here. Now."

"Is that wise? You're still weak and probably drugged from all those painkillers." He gestured to the pills the nurse left on the nightstand.

"True, but I would much rather be in this condition than dead."

Gabe was impressed she wasn't descending into victim mode, becoming paralyzed, or falling apart. He could see she was in pain, her face pale and drawn. But she was resolute. *This is one strong lady.*

She said, "I'm leaving as soon as I figure out how to get out of here without the nurses noticing. You are welcome to join me if you like, but I refuse to be a sitting goose."

"Duck"

"Excuse me?"

"The expression is 'a sitting *duck*.'"

"Thanks for the language lesson. Maybe we can find a better time for it than now?"

"Just trying to add a little levity. We don't know what we're dealing with at this point, so let's hope for the best and plan for the worst. And for the record, you may find it helpful to know that one of my most attractive traits is my ability to remain calm under pressure. When others panic, I keep a cool head,"

Looking relieved, Terry said, "Does that mean you're coming with me?"

Gabe motioned for her hand and took it once again. Gently he said, "I'm not making the same mistake twice. This time, I'm staying right by your side."

With a smile, she said, "Okay, then tell me, Mr. Lewis, how do we get out of here?"

He smiled back. "Funny you should ask."

* * *

Distraction was the best plan. Having interned in a hospital, Terry knew they wouldn't discharge a patient in her condition, and she had no intention of waging a battle with the staff.

Gabe surveilled the corridor. The coast was clear. Finding the supply closet he had spotted when making the call to Oded, he ran inside. Heart racing, he grabbed a set of scrubs and stealthily ran down the hall, turning a corner to find an unoccupied patient room. There, he began pushing buttons on the machinery until an alarm sounded. He briskly retreated back to Terry's room and heard rapid-paced footsteps pass by.

In seconds, Terry donned the scrubs, grabbed her pill bottle, and left the room alone at a fast clip, passing the empty nurses' station. Not wanting to wait for the elevator, she headed unsteadily to the stairwell.

Gabe followed closely behind. As he stepped outside, the

mid-morning sky was laden with heavy grey clouds, threatening an impending storm. Gabe hoped it was not a harbinger of the day ahead.

They met in the parking lot where Terry shed the scrubs, tossing them into an industrial dumpster.

Gabe caught his breath. "That went better than expected. I feel like the lead in a spy film, running a caper with my beautiful sidekick."

Breathing heavily, Terry leaned against a parked Citroen, looking pale in the dim lighting. "I'm glad you're enjoying this, but I'm terrified and already exhausted. I feel like I just ran a marathon. Might I remind you that our lives may be at risk, and a crazy guy has my smartphone and wallet? He knows where I live, where I work. While you may not agree, it's time to call the police. Our lives are more important than your specimens."

Feeling chastised, he knew he couldn't argue. "All right, let's do it."

Terry asked for his cellphone and dialed emergency. She spoke in rapid Hebrew and was put on hold for a few seconds, then had to repeat the same thing to another party. After a few minutes, she raised her voice, growing increasingly agitated until she abruptly ended the call.

"What was that about?" asked Gabe.

Terry took a deep breath trying to control her temper. "The officer on duty said there's nothing they can do, now that two days have gone by since the incident. After I told him I couldn't identify my attacker, he told me to be realistic! Can you believe the nerve? None of this is realistic. I am being stalked by an unknown attacker looking for DNA samples that I don't even have, and who could strike again any time. The officer suggested that I stop by the closest precinct to file a report and loss of property claim form, but also very bluntly told me not to expect any results. If I'm feeling threatened, I should hire a bodyguard. The police would only intervene in the event that something should happen again."

"How frustrating. I guess you're looking at your new body-guard."

Calming down, Terry offered a small smile. "By the way, where *are* those samples?"

Gabe patted his front jeans pocket. "I probably should find a better hiding place."

CHAPTER 26

Los Angeles

Late middle-aged and bespectacled, reporter Edward Hernandez sported an unconvincing comb-over and a burrito-stained, button down shirt fighting a losing battle with his paunch.

Jon waved him over, barely recognizing him from his newspaper photo. He waited as the journalist slid into the booth facing him, the red vinyl making an embarrassingly sticky suction sound as he settled in.

"Thanks for meeting me, Mr. Hernandez."

"You said breakfast is on you, and that's all I needed to hear." He sounded more like a resident of the Jersey shore than a highly respected journalist. Jon supposed the written word required a different set of skills than spoken language.

"I'm sure you don't take the time to meet every caller on the promise of an omelet and coffee."

"Fair enough. Pete's been a buddy of mine since grade school. After your call, I found his email. He said a friend of his daughter needed a favor. I owe him one or ten. So, how is little Melanie doing anyway?"

"She's great, and all grown up. One more semester till graduating from UNT in biochemistry."

"Unbelievable. Where did the time go? It was just yesterday I held her on my shoulders so she could reach her birthday piñata," he laughed. "Such is life. Good stuff is fleeting, and the crap never ends," he said to himself then adding, "Hmm, I should print up posters with that quote."

"I bet you see a lot of crap in your line of work."

Hernandez took a roll from the basket, buttered it. "There's lot of depravity out there. The world is a cesspool of criminals. All I can do is let the world know to beware." He studied the menu, then called the waitress over and ordered the breakfast special. "Two eggs sunny-side up, flapjacks and hushpuppies. And a large black coffee." The waitress took the order without writing it down and left.

Jon tapped his newspaper. "I read your article on the Y killing. I'm working on a thesis project and have some questions."

"Shoot."

"Did they identify the perpetrator from yesterday's shooting?"

"Not officially, but my sources tell me it was a woman."

"Wow, that's a new wrinkle."

"Not really. While it's true the vast majority of mass killings—successful and attempted—are perpetrated by males, there have been women as well."

"I didn't know that."

"Generally, female shooters don't get the same press coverage for any number of reasons. Women tend to garner more sympathy from society since people will often assume they were victims of abuse who cracked. And since nearly all those cases happened outside the U.S., there has been significantly less coverage here."

His order arrived and Hernandez dug in. "Watching your figure?" he asked Jon.

"I ate already. Got in on the red eye. I've been sitting here for hours."

"Hmm." He chewed noisily and with gusto.

"Did they find motives for those female killings overseas?"

"I assume you're asking that because not one of the recent killing sprees yielded a motive."

"Correct."

"You're paying attention. I alluded to that in my article but had to be careful as there's always the possibility that the cops have some info they're not sharing with the public or media, even off the record."

"What do *you* think?"

Hernandez gobbled a heaping forkful of syrupy pancake, talking around it. "Based on everything I've heard through various channels, the cops and FBI are at a complete loss for motive. They haven't been able to pin a single killer with a revenge or emotional disability motive. No 'disgruntled student' leg to stand on."

"What do you make of it?"

"I thought maybe it's a religious extremist thing but haven't found anything to back that up."

Jon leaned forward lowering his voice. "Mr. Hernandez, I think we can help each other out. I have a proposition for you."

"What sort of proposition? You got something on one of the cases?"

"No, on two of them—BTI and Georgia Tech. I'm hoping together we can find a pattern that matches them with this latest one."

"Okay, what have you got for me?"

"First, I need to know two things. One, that you'll keep it confidential. It can't leave this room until I let you know it's okay to go public. I can assure you it will be worth the wait for the best exposé you've ever written, attracting worldwide attention. Pulitzer material."

Hernandez raised his brows. "That big, huh? What if someone beats me to it while I'm waiting for your go-ahead?"

"Not going to happen. There are only five people with this information and all are holding on to it tightly."

Hernandez looked tentative. "Okay, let's assume I'm buying into this, what's second?"

"Second, I want to trade. Info for assistance."

"I'm helping you now."

"I need more."

"What do you want from me, other than what I've already told you?"

"I need your connections to obtain a piece of DNA evidence from the LA killer. It can be anything—hair, nails, skin."

"Are you nuts? The gal blew herself up. There's nothing left of her."

"You bring up an important point. Don't you find that odd?"

"What?"

"Why has that become standard operating procedure? Are there no other ways to get the job done? Even the shooter in BTI ended it with a bombing."

Hernandez looked up from his plate, interested in where the conversation was going.

Jon continued. "My sources tell me extreme heat has the potential to wipe DNA from a crime scene." He had Hernandez's full attention now. "But what I'm learning is there's always *some* DNA left behind. It may be nearly impossible to find it, but it's there."

"That has crossed my mind," said Hernandez. "It seems like Abadi was trying to cover something up. The others that followed may have been copycats."

"Possibly," said Jon. "My theory is that they're all part of the same system, following a protocol they agreed to use."

Hernandez kept his voice down to match Jon's. "Why would you come to that conclusion? You talking conspiracy?"

"That's what I would share with you. But I need to know that you will do your best to deliver on my request." He paused. "Do you accept the terms?"

"Hold your horses. You understand I may not have that sort of access."

"Don't be so humble. Your reputation precedes you, Mr. Hernandez."

"If we're going to be working together, you should call me

Ed."

"Does that mean you're in?"

Ed took a long swallow of his now tepid coffee. "Okay, I agree to try but I can't make any promises." He put down his cup. "Since we can't exactly write this down, let's make a journalist's contract."

"What's that?"

"A verbal agreement signed with a handshake."

"Fine. If Mel's dad trusts you, I trust you." The men shook hands.

Hernandez asked, "So, what have you got?"

"My co-researcher and I have recently learned that two of the bombers had a very rare opioid in their systems when they blew themselves up."

"When you say rare, how rare?"

"It's not available by prescription or even on the street. Chrysanthemum Exotic can only be found in the Amazon and requires specialized knowledge to elicit its drug potential. My partner on this project, Gabe, is in Israel meeting a genetic expert to learn more."

"Interesting. If that's the case then they either knew each other or someone in common."

"Correct. But there's no evidence linking the perpetrators. Which leaves the second option. They knew someone in common."

Hernandez was riveted. "How did you learn all this?"

"Suffice it to say we gained access to DNA specimens from two of the attacks."

"Incredible. Looks like we may have a bigger story than I could have imagined."

Jon smiled broadly. "You're welcome."

Hernandez looked up. "Obviously I'll need your proof."

"You'll have it."

Itching to get the ball rolling, Ed asked, "What do you need from me that I can go forward?"

"To build the case even further and eliminate any statistical possibility of strange coincidence, we'll need DNA from the LA killer. If she also took this drug, we can be certain there is a terrorist network out there finding students to do their dirty work. It would explain why there is no motive for any individual bomber. The perpetrators may not even know the true motive."

"You think people would perpetrate such atrocities without a good reason?"

"Wasn't it you who said, people are depraved? Maybe they did it for money for their family, or posthumous fame."

"Touché, but the kids from those two cases didn't sound like that at all."

"I can't say I figured all of this out yet. There are pieces still missing, but I know we're on to something big."

"Did you take this to the FBI?"

That annoying question again, Jon thought. "I went to them early on before I knew about the drug. The agent in charge blew me off. I don't feel a need to return without ironclad proof."

"Works for me."

"Do you think you can get me the DNA?"

"I agree with you that the bombers had another thing in common. All seemingly wanted to burn any evidence beyond identification. Finding DNA will be like finding a needle in a haystack."

"Even for one of California's top investigative reporters?"

"No need to kiss up to me. I'm motivated enough. Let me see what I can do. Twenty-six years at the paper has built up good creds. I've established the trust of some LAPD higher-ups. I also have connections at local hospitals. I'll get back to you as soon as I get something."

"Try to make it quick."

"Don't worry. You've managed to light a fire under me with your Pulitzer talk." Having wiped his plate clean, Hernandez stood up, hoisted up his drooping pants and departed, a man on a mission.

CHAPTER 27

Jerusalem

"I need to go home and get some things." Terry said, gazing out over the Jerusalem Forest. After leaving the hospital, drained and in need of rest, they had slowly walked to an adjacent park, sitting beside each other on a wrought iron bench. From this angle, they had an incredible view. The threatening clouds had blown away and a clear blue sky stretched before them. Perched on a cliff, Yad Vashem, the Holocaust memorial, was visible to the south, its imposing structure framed by towering pine trees spanning both sides of the valley.

While Terry regained her strength, they decided that the safest course of action was to travel to the States together, meet up with Jon, and get help from the authorities. Perhaps with Professor Breitler's help, she could also learn more about the value of the specimens.

Leduc had followed Gabe from Dallas, and logic dictated they would need to go back to the U.S. to bring this matter to a close. Terry was disturbed about leaving her work behind, but the situation was dire enough for her to temporarily disappear off the grid. She agreed to find a colleague to temporarily cover for her.

Gabe turned to Terry. "I know you never asked for any of this. I brought you into something you can't easily extricate yourself from." He took her hand in his. "I'm sorry."

"I know you are, Gabe, but none of this is your fault."

"If I hadn't come here, you would now be back at work no worse for the wear."

"But this *has* happened, so we need to face it head on. You'll just have to make it up to me."

This woman amazes me. Gently, he replied, "There's nothing I'd like more."

❋ ❋ ❋

Dallas

Gabe invited Terry to stay with him at his apartment off-campus from UNT. It was the quintessential bachelor pad, but more upscale than the average college student could afford, decorated in masculine shades of blue and beige, chrome fixtures and warm lighting. Modern, but with exposed wooden beams in the living space. There was a small chef's kitchen with Cuisinart pans hanging above the stainless steel stove-top and a well-stocked wet bar just outside the master bedroom. A good size full bath made up the space.

Terry dropped her purse on the floor and collapsed on the leather sofa. "I'm looking forward to seeing Professor Breitler. The last time I saw him was at a conference in Prague. He's a brilliant man."

Gabe took her suitcase and set it in his bedroom. He would let her have his bed. Upon his return, he said, "Your meeting should shed light on what's so important about the specimens. And no doubt Professor Breitler will be thrilled to pick your brain since you're so familiar with the TR-X. I'll give him a call so you can arrange a time."

Gabe pulled up the number. He'd met the professor only briefly to discuss the thesis, but read all his correspondence, and had a good sense of the man—a congenial genius.

"Chemistry department, Martin speaking."

"Hello, Martin, this is Gabriel Lewis. I would like to set up an appointment with Professor Breitler on behalf of Dr. Terry Lavi."

His request was greeted with silence.

"Martin, are you still there?"

A somber voice replied. "Haven't you heard? Dr. B. was in a horrible accident. His car was hit by a tractor trailer the night before Thanksgiving."

"Oh no! How awful. Is he okay?"

"I'm sorry to be the one to tell you..." Martin choked back a sob. "He didn't make it."

* * *

The news hit Jon hard, but Melanie was devastated, her mascara streaking her cheeks. He had only just returned from Los Angeles to learn of Dr. Breitler's demise. Reunited in Gabe's apartment, they sat together across from Gabe and Dr. Lavi.

Jon was impressed with the Israeli geneticist. Though petite, she gave off a formidable air. By all accounts, she had been through a harrowing experience, but chose to accompany Gabe back to the States in hopes of finding answers.

"Dr. B.'s death is suspicious at best," Jon said.

"What are you saying?" Melanie dabbed her eyes with an already moist tissue.

"Maybe it wasn't an accident," he replied.

Terry sat forward. "Do you think the same person who attacked me killed Professor Breitler?"

Jon nodded. "It's too much of a coincidence."

Gabe turned to Jon. "What did we get ourselves into?"

"Whatever it is, we must see it through now," Jon replied. "I'm not willing to sit idly by, waiting for another attempt on one our lives."

"But what can we do about it?" asked Melanie.

"We need to devise a plan," Jon said.

"You want us to take on a killer on our own?" Gabe asked, alarmed. "Are you crazy?"

Jon thought a moment. "I have a seed of an idea. If all of you think it makes sense, I'll get us real help."

"From whom?" Gabe asked.

"Lieutenant Donna Kearns."

CHAPTER 28

Cincinnati, Ohio

J on crossed the Roebling Bridge, leaving Kentucky behind. A mild autumn had kept the Bluegrass State a verdant expanse of pastures speckled with grazing thoroughbreds. It was a snapshot of Americana.

With the Ohio River flowing below and the South in his rearview mirror, Jon caught sight of the Cincinnati skyline with Great American Ball Park and Paul Brown Stadium overlooking the waterfront. It seemed like forever since he had sat at a game with a hot dog in one hand and a beer in the other. God, how he missed it. If they ever finish writing their article and Abadi's motive was established, he'd take Mel to a ballgame, this time MLB.

She was asleep beside him, breathing softly. He'd tried to discourage her from making this trip, worried that they were getting involved in something dangerous, but she would hear nothing of it. She said she wanted to be by his side and see this thing through to the end. Since his parents' deaths, there weren't many people that expressed such devotion to him. Just Granny Eunice and Gabe. Now Melanie. He wanted to open up to her about his past but didn't know if he could. Maybe after all this was behind them, he'd give therapy another try.

His thoughts turned to Gabe and Terry, who were taking the overnight Greyhound, thinking it best for everyone to show up using different methods. The plan was to meet at the Cincinnati Hilton and put their plan into motion.

Melanie fluttered her eyes open, yawned and sat up.

Jon turned to her. "Welcome to Cincinnati."

* * *

Boston

Detective Kearns was at her desk, looking at a cold case file when her personal cellphone rang. The caller ID came up on her screen as *Unknown Number*.

She hit *accept*. "Kearns."

"Hi, it's me," Jon said. "Please don't say my name aloud."

It took her a moment to recognize Jon's voice. "Um, okay. Are you all right?"

"We are for now."

"We?"

"Yes, I'll explain later, but I need to talk to you. Face to face. There's more about the circumstances of when we first met than you realize." He spoke the last sentence slowly.

Dumbfounded, Donna asked, "Where are you?"

"In Cincinnati."

"Cincinnati?" she repeated, incredulous.

"Yeah, I know it's not convenient, but this can't be done over the phone or email."

"Wait. You want me to go there? Why can't you come here?"

"No time for that. By then, it will be too late."

"Too late for what?" she asked, exasperated with his cryptic answers.

"I promise I'll explain everything when we meet. You know I've never been an alarmist, and we need your help.

You're one of the few people on Earth I trust. Can you come?"

"That depends. First, you'll need to answer my next question truthfully and without exaggeration... Is this a matter of life and death?"

Jon answered without a moment's hesitation. "*Many* lives and deaths."

"Okay, I'll come but you do understand that I have no jurisdiction in Ohio, right?"

"Yeah, but I trust you. You're the only one we can share this with. Please hurry."

"I'm looking up airlines now. Hold on."

Jon heard her tapping on a keyboard.

"Okay...There's an American non-stop departing in an hour. Meet me at the arrivals terminal at the Cincinnati airport at 7:00 p.m."

"Thank you, Lieutenant."

"This better be good, kid," she said. "Usually, I don't need to leave Boston to find trouble."

CHAPTER 29

Cincinnati

Donna was surprised when the hotel room door was opened by an attractive, petite woman with green eyes, her golden hair tied in a loose knot. The stylish woman wore a long sweater over leggings, sporting a bruised cheek and a chewed pencil lodged behind an ear. Gabe Lewis stood beside her, his hand at her back.

"Hello, Lieutenant," he said. "Thank you for coming all this way."

Donna had met Ashleigh's brother Gabe at the dedication of the BTI memorial. Now he was older, broader in the shoulders. Serious. She supposed living through the tragic loss of a sister had matured him.

She instantly knew that Gabe and this woman were an item, even if they didn't. The looks they gave each other were not of lust, but admiration.

An adjoining door opened, and Melanie walked in. "Donna, thank you so much for coming. There's no way we can do any of this without you. Can I offer you some coffee?"

"No, thank you. If it's all right with everyone, let's get started."

The five of them sat in the suite's living space, Gabe beside Terry on the sofa, the others pulling up chairs. Still in uniform, Donna placed her academy-issue duffle on the floor beside her.

She always kept a change of clothes at the precinct for emergencies. Like this one.

Gabe introduced her to Terry, the one person in the room she had never met.

Then Jon took over, bringing Donna up to speed. He told her about their research project, Terry's assault and Professor Breitler's death. "When Gabe and I decided on our thesis, our initial objective was to learn if some people are wired to kill. That endeavor has taken a major detour."

Jon described the drug Chrysanthemum Exotic and how they could prove at least two of the killings had the same M.O. He said, "I can't believe what happened to Terry and Dr. B. is a coincidence. There's something bigger going on. Leduc and whoever he's working for, are intent on getting their hands on the specimens." Jon paused, then said, "I believe it could be an organized terror network."

Donna was incredulous. She sat riveted, her jaw dropped open, hanging on every word.

Jon continued. "We're here to set a trap for Leduc and determine who his employers are. Over the last few days, we've left breadcrumbs we expect him to follow. We created a dialogue between me and Gabe on Facebook, making seemingly disguised plans to meet here in Cincinnati to transfer the samples and flashdrive back to me after Gabe's trip. Before you ask, we picked Cincinnati, because Gabe's uncle once lived here for many years and Gabe knows the city like the back of his hand. It would save us time on reconnaissance. While it isn't the most convenient location from Dallas, luring Leduc here would definitively confirm suspicions we're being targeted."

As Jon finished speaking, Donna was speechless. The conversation was fantastical. She sat pensively for a long minute, everyone's attention on her, hoping she would offer much needed input.

"This is a lot to process and I have many questions. I'm amazed at all that's happened to you in a matter of days." She paused, organizing her thoughts. "I have connections with the

FBI that I can reach out to. They're the ones to call in a situation like this. From here forward, you'll need to keep this low profile, contain the information you have. Do not discuss this with anyone without my okay. Doing so may put those people in jeopardy."

"I agree," said Jon. "We don't know who's involved and at what level. There's real money behind this guy. Acquiring a rare drug and travelling the world to stalk Gabe takes serious backing. And for the record, we attempted to alert the FBI. The agent we approached was a conceited fool and let us leave with the specimens, telling us there was no way to use them in the investigation."

"What makes you think he's wrong?"

"The TR-X analysis already yielded significant results, and with Terry's expertise we expect to learn even more."

"Okay. For the time being, I strongly suggest all of you stay here in the hotel. If you need to go out, be extra cautious and don't go out alone."

Donna asked several follow-up questions, then stood up and walked to Terry's bedroom, pulling out her phone. "Let me make some calls," she said, and closed the door behind her.

* * *

Nassau, Bahamas

Leduc was enjoying his third cigarette in the last twenty minutes. A piña colada sat chilled on the table beside him, a cool breeze blowing the pages of his Esquire magazine. Then his work cell rang.

"Can you talk?"

He was not expecting a call from his employer. Leduc looked around the pool area. Two bikini-clad beauties were flirting with a bow-tied waiter in navy shorts as he balanced their order of champagne and health salads on a silver-plated tray. Two buff, hairy Italians were playing pool volleyball. The Bahamas were just the place for the rich and distracted. No one paid him any attention.

"Yeah, what's up?"

"Change in plans. Our next trial will take place in a different city and sooner than previously discussed."

Figures. Now that I finally got a break. "Why the last-minute change?"

"The package you're after will be in Cincinnati on Friday, so Phoenix is postponed. You can kill two birds with one stone. First, get the specimens. I'll send details."

"They're becoming a real liability."

"Keep that itchy trigger finger in your pocket. We've brought enough attention to ourselves. Secure the package. Only eliminate the men if the situation demands it."

"I don't like loose ends."

"You will do as instructed. We require a successful trial, which you will need to assist with the following day. The last thing we want is unwarranted police attention."

Leduc remained silent, which the caller took as acquiescence. "Once the specimens are in your possession, go to ground. The equipment needed for the trial on Saturday is already in Cincinnati. Keep it near you and available for the student operative to complete the mission during the Cincinnati Marathon."

"Understood." He hung up, breathing in the beach air and closing his eyes, milking these last few minutes in paradise, knowing his next stop was hell.

* * *

The mole hung up the phone, turning to the employer, a leader of the worldwide syndicate. "Cincinnati's a go. I'll send the information."

"It's fate," said the employer. "Saturday is a big day in Cincinnati. The Annual Flying Pig marathon is scheduled. Runners will be crossing the Roebling Bridge at midday. We will have a surprise waiting for them."

Hesitantly, the underling asked, "Do you think this could be a trap?"

Unperturbed, the Boss answered, "I have made accommodations for that possibility."

"Leduc didn't like leaving Steadman behind. Said he doesn't want loose ends."

The employer looked at the underling malevolently. "Neither do I."

CHAPTER 30

Cincinnati

The meeting with Donna proved to be everything Jon hoped for. She called in favors, explaining only what was necessary, claiming confidentiality to some and national security to others. She was waiting to hear back from Agent Jim Fields, an old work colleague from the Boston PD who now worked for the Midwest FBI office in Ohio. Jon felt uncomfortable with Donna contacting the Feds, even if it was someone she trusted. The FBI had proven more than once to be less than competent. But to implement their trap there was no choice but to involve them.

They all agreed to stay the night at the hotel. Jon booked a room for himself and Mel. Donna would take the extra bed in Terry's room, and Gabe would bunk on the pullout sofa. In the morning, they would set up a game plan.

It was getting late and Jon wanted to check in on Granny Eunice. He had not spoken with her since leaving for LA. While he had no intention of telling her all that transpired in recent days, he needed to know she was okay. Jon left the room to make the call from the quieter hallway. As always, Granny Eunice picked up on the first ring. She was in good spirits and, after sharing the local goings on, asked what he had been up to.

"Lots of work, and time with Melanie."

"Did you accomplish what you needed in LA?"

"Yeah, it was a successful trip. Sorry again for taking off prematurely."

"No need to apologize. Of course, I would have loved for you to stay the whole time, but Melanie is a darling, and thanks to her and Donna I finally have mums in my garden."

"Speaking of Donna, can I ask you something?"

"Sure."

"Did she ever mention a guy named Jim Fields?"

"Yes, from time to time. They were partners on the police force for a year. She saved his life."

"I never heard about this."

"You know Donna. She's a private person. She rarely speaks of that incident. But it was in all the papers at the time. She was decorated for bravery."

"What happened?"

"A drug addict became belligerent when a pharmacist refused to fill a fake oxycodone prescription. Donna and Jim took the call. When they arrived at the pharmacy the man went crazy, attacked Jim, got hold of his gun and aimed it at his head. Donna shot the guy before he could pull the trigger."

"Wow. That's some story."

"It certainly was. Seems Jim left town after that. Took a job elsewhere. It's too bad."

"Why?" Jon asked.

"Because Donna once referred to him as the man who got away. Why are you asking about this now?"

Time to go. "No reason. His name came up and got me curious. I need to get going but I'll call again soon. Love you."

"Love you too. No matter what you're up to."

As he wished his grandmother a good night, Donna stepped into the hallway, pulling the door shut behind her, and leaned against the opposite wall.

"How's she doing?" Donna asked.

"Just like when you saw her. She's still her spunky self but getting older faster. I haven't fully accepted that yet."

Donna cleared her throat. "Listen, Jon, we need to talk."

Jon raised his eyebrows. "What's up?"

"I'm seriously pissed off. You should've come to me as soon as you suspected something dangerous was going on, especially after Terry was attacked. I get why you didn't want to approach the FBI again, but I could have helped you."

"Sorry about that, but everything happened so fast. I didn't want to involve you until we knew more."

"It's sheer luck none of you has been seriously hurt." She paused, switching gears, looking him square in the eye. "How've you been?"

"Good. School's going well. Mel is terrific."

"She sure is…and I couldn't ask for a better segue. This may not be my place, but your grandmother is a dear friend, and frankly since BTI, I've considered you something of a godson. So hear me out."

Touched by what she said, Jon wasn't sure what to expect.

Donna continued. "Have you told Melanie?"

Jon quickly averted his eyes. "I don't know what you're talking about."

"I think you do. It was pretty clear on Thanksgiving she doesn't know a thing about your past. It's time to trust someone else with what you've been through. Melanie will never completely know you until you share your history."

"The bombing?"

"All of it."

Jon kept his eyes down. "I don't think I can."

"God knows you've been through more adversity than most, it's a big part of who you are. But you've figured out a way to rise above it, succeeding despite it all, demonstrating fortitude well beyond your years.

"I had no choice."

"Sure, you did. Other people in your situation would have jumped on the 'woe is me wagon' as an excuse for living a mediocre life."

Jon shrugged.

Donna continued. "I've seen a lot of tragedy in my line of

work, and while I'm no psychologist, I do know that PTSD is real. Repressing tragic experiences never ends well. It's like a pressure cooker. Something's gotta give. I don't want it to be your relationship. Mel deserves better. Talk to her, maybe with the help of a professional. Vent some of that pressure in a healthy way."

"Weird. You're the second person to tell me this, this week."

"Maybe there's something to it."

"Maybe."

Donna walked away without another word.

＊ ＊ ＊

At 5:00 a.m. Donna's phone rang. It didn't wake her, as she hadn't fallen asleep. There was too much on her mind.

"Kearns"

"It's Jim."

Donna had known Jim since starting out together in law enforcement in Boston. They'd been partners on the force for nearly a year. And while there had been an attraction, they never took it further. When Jim was offered a position with the FBI, he jumped on it, relocating to Columbus.

Though they remained in loose touch, Donna thought it serendipitous that he had emailed her only yesterday, asking how she was doing. As such, his was the first name that came to mind when Jon called, her asking for help. She emailed Jim back over a secure department server, explaining there was more to share than just how her life was going. She emphasized the urgency of the matter and that Special Agent Doug Matthews from the Dallas office had been contacted previously with preliminary information, if he wanted to speak with him.

Donna was surprised that Jim was awake so early. It got her thinking that maybe the FBI knew all along this was a bigger deal than they were letting on.

"Got anything?" she asked.

"I've been in touch with the several field offices on both coasts, as well as with Special Agent Matthews in Dallas, ergo the early hour. He told me about the specimens and wants more info on the drug findings."

"All right, I'll pass that along to Jon and Dr. Lavi. What else?"

Jim took a deep breath. "We haven't pinned down the real name of Dr. Lavi's attacker, so for now let's stick with Leduc."

"Go on."

"There's been chatter picked up on the web about a planned attack in downtown Cincinnati. Looks like Leduc is taking Steadman's bait after all. That kid may have a future in law enforcement."

"What sort of chatter?"

"There's a bridge there, the Roebling Bridge. It was a prototype for the Brooklyn Bridge and may be a target. There was a spike in activity on sites known by intelligence agencies to be used by terrorist elements. The bridge was mentioned twice as a soft target. With limited security, it would be way easier to hit the Cincinnati version than the New York one. While it may not cause the same collateral damage, they could claim it's a sign of bigger things to come—a highly effective scare tactic."

"I'm not following. Why do you think there's a connection between Leduc and this threat?"

"We can't know for certain whether Leduc will risk making another attempt at getting the specimens, but it's too much of a coincidence that Jon chose Cincinnati as his drop site, and within a matter of hours a terrorist group is looking at the same city as a soft target. We need to prepare for both an attack on Steadman *and* the bridge."

Better to be cautious than sorry. "How confident are you in the intel?" asked Donna.

"That's why I've stayed up all night. Looks legit."

"When is it supposed to go down?"

"This weekend. But unfortunately, the chatter we mined didn't yield a specific day or time. They're being careful."

Donna was beside herself. "It's too soon."

"We have no choice. We're lucky we got wind of it when we did."

She knew he was right. "Okay, so what's the plan?"

"Since you're with the Boston PD, we'll need to get the Cincinnati police involved, with you as liaison. If Steadman and his friends are up for it, we'll use them to lure this guy from the shadows, then get whatever info we can out of him."

Donna was appalled. "You want to use these kids as bait? No way!"

"You got a better idea?"

"Not at the moment, but that one doesn't work."

"How about you run it by them? They're adults. I can't think of any other way to get the perp to show himself. Keep in mind, there's no reason for him to suspect Steadman's team is even involved with us."

"I just got through telling Jon to be more careful. I can't in good conscience now put him in harm's way."

"If you can come up with a better suggestion, I'm all ears, but do it fast. If Steadman and the others give the go-ahead, we'll have enough time to prep them."

She felt the conflicting pressure of her job and her personal feelings. "I don't know what to do."

"If I know you, you'll think of something."

CHAPTER 31

Cincinnati

J on opened his eyes, finding Melanie beside him on the bed, already dressed, the computer in her lap. She leaned in for a kiss. "Good morning, sleepyhead."

"Up early," Jon said, lazily.

"Only if you count eight o'clock as early."

He sat up quickly. "Eight o'clock? I can't believe I slept that long."

"You earned it, with all your running around. I'm worried about you."

Jon rubbed a hand over his eyes and asked, "What are you talking about?"

"I didn't sleep well last night and didn't want to disturb you, so I went to the lobby and had a tea from the reception area. When I came back upstairs, I couldn't help but overhear Donna on the phone. The walls are paper thin and she was pretty worked up. I admit I lingered in the hallway longer than I should have, but at 5:00 a.m. I thought it might be important."

"Who was she talking to?"

"My best guess is another cop. Seems she didn't want to ask you and Gabe to take risks. Something about being bait."

"Does that mean Leduc followed our breadcrumbs?"

"Probably. But bait doesn't sound too safe."

"I'm sure the cops would do everything to keep us as secure

as possible. Let's see what Donna has to say."

"Okay, but right now it's not sitting too well with me."

"And why's that?"

"Because... I love you," she replied, shyly.

As he leaned in to kiss her, a text came in on Melanie's phone.

"Lousy timing," Jon said, passing her the cell.

"It's from Terry." She read it aloud. "Meet us downstairs for breakfast." She scooted to the edge of the bed. "Okay, let's go."

Jon pulled her back to him, taking her phone and putting it aside. She leaned into his embrace. He stroked her hair gently and felt his heart swell. The chaos could wait just a little longer.

* * *

"Good morning," said Jon, cheerfully.

When he and Mel entered the breakfast area, the working group was reunited.

Donna said, "Glad to see someone's in a good mood. Have a seat. I was about to tell Gabe and Terry about an early call I received."

Mel and Jon made eye contact but said nothing. Mel said, "Give us a minute to catch up with y'all in the breakfast department and we'll be right back."

Carrying the teetering plates back to the table, Jon fended off their friends' exaggerated looks of surprise and disgust. "Free buffet is all I gotta say."

Donna interjected. "Look everyone, we better get to work. Early this morning, I took a call from Jim Fields with the FBI's Midwest office."

Jon interrupted. "Did you tell him I had contact with Matthews?"

"I had to. He would have found out anyway, and I'd rather be upfront than come across as holding back valuable national security information without at least attempting to notify them. He seemed to understand, and contacted Agent Matthews to get him on board this time."

Jon was skeptical. He didn't trust Matthews or his instincts.

Donna went on. "Within the last twenty-four hours, there's been intel on a possible attack here this weekend. It looks like your trap is working. Both Fields and Matthews suspect the same man who attacked Terry is likely to show up. They want to flush him out and get whatever information possible from him to shut down the operation."

"How do they plan to do that?"

"Matthews asked Jim to contact local law enforcement for help with a sting operation. I won't beat around the bush." Donna paused. "It would require your help—mostly from Gabe and Jon. I told him I didn't want you to do it, it's too dangerous. That's what this meeting is about, to find another way. If we brainstorm, we can come up with something equally effective without putting the two of you in harm's way."

Gesturing to herself and Melanie, Terry asked, "Why use the men and not us?"

"This guy knows Gabe and Jon from the online breadcrumbs they left. He's only expecting them. Anyhow, he presumably wouldn't recognize Melanie and we'd like to keep it that way. Terry, you've already been targeted by this man, and we agreed not to put you in that position again."

Pursing her lips, Terry replied, "I appreciate the concern but I'd love an opportunity to get my hands on that guy."

"That's part of the problem. We need to keep our heads straight for this trap to work. If he feels threatened, he'll run, and we may lose our chance at catching him."

"So what was their idea?" Melanie asked.

"To wiretap the guys, make it look like they're swapping back the specimens from Gabe to Jon along with a flash drive. Leduc will think it holds the analysis report and will want to relieve you of it. Nevertheless, I want us to come up with a better plan."

Melanie suggested, "What if we found a way to contact him and bait him with the data, grab him when he shows up?"

Gabe said, "Smells too much like a trap. This guy is a pro."

Donna agreed. "It has to appear to him like he's in the driver's seat tracking you. Not the other way around."

Gabe shrugged. "If we need more personal contact, their plan seems the best option. Will there be back up?"

"We would have plainclothes agents all over the area. You would never be alone."

Jon had been eating silently, listening to the whole exchange. He took his last bite of pancake. "I'm in."

"That's it? I'm in?" Donna sounded annoyed.

"It's a no-brainer. The only way to get this guy out in the open is for Gabe and me to be in his face, give him a chance to get what he wants and finish the job he took on from whoever he's working for. You're saying we'll have backup and recording devices. There's no point in coming up with a second-rate plan."

Donna was conflicted. "There's still danger. You can't predict how it will go down or how desperate this guy is. There's a limit to what backup can do in an unstable situation."

Jon said, "You up for it, Gabe?"

"I'm not letting you do this alone, so yeah."

Donna searched the women's faces for help, finding none. The decision had already been made.

* * *

Agent Jim Fields arrived at the hotel with a quick peck on the cheek for Donna, which raised a few eyebrows around the room. He was carrying a large bag of Chinese take-out, making him the most popular man in the room. Once the decision had been made to go ahead with the plan, Jim had driven down from Columbus to meet them.

Other than the occasional Facebook photo, Donna hadn't seen him in years. He looked much as she remembered, if not fitter than before. She had heard the FBI had stringent rules on personal fitness and he had obviously taken that to heart. He was tall and poised. His large nose and thin lips somehow combined well within the angles of his face. Though his hair was thinning and graying at the temples, it only seemed to contribute to the image of distinguished competence.

As they ate, Jon made the introductions. First Gabe, then Melanie and Terry.

When it was Jim's turn, he gave them updated information, including Leduc's true identity.

"His name is Hugo Carrera, age thirty-five, a native of Spain. Studied in Britain, which explains his excellent English. He has several aliases, one of which is Leduc. He's been a wanted man for fifteen years. Does mostly thug work but suspected of being a hired gun."

Gabe asked, "What do we have to do?"

"I'll leave that to Matthews. Seems he's en route. He'll be here in a couple hours. He wants to be the one to lay out the plan.."

"And size us up," Jon said, contempt in his voice.

Jim shrugged. "Yeah, I suppose so."

CHAPTER 32

Cincinnati

Gabe drove the rental up Interstate 75. He had an errand to run that was long overdue and today was the day. He took the Glendale exit, pulled into the parking lot of the Swap Shop, and cut the engine.

A bell rang as he stepped on the seedy establishment's welcome mat. A heavily tattooed Hispanic man sporting a well-groomed goatee stood behind a glass display case, rearranging a set of his and her Movado watches. His black bowling shirt read "Jose."

"Hello, how can I help you?"

"I'm looking for a new or used firearm. Preferably a 9mm with a night scope."

"Sure thing. You've come to the right place." Jose walked over to another case, unlocked it and slid the glass open, taking out a small handgun.

"This here's the Sig Sauer 9mm with night scope, rosewood grip. It comes with two magazines holding seven cartridges each, clip holster, and carrying case. Minimal kickback, minimal jamming. Top of the line semi-automatic, which is why I own three of 'em."

"How much?"

The man told him. "It's steep but you get what you pay for, friend. If you want something lower end, I can show you those as well."

"My uncle Carl used to live around these parts. He told me you're fair and give the best prices in town."

Jose took a good look at Gabe. "Carl Lewis? He your uncle?"

"That's right."

"Why didn't you say so from the get-go? Any kin of Carl's is a friend of mine. How's about a 20 percent discount on the Sig? I'll throw in a box of ammo on the house."

"Sounds like you got yourself a deal."

The man asked for ID, checked Gabe's concealed carry license, ran a quick background check and rang up the purchase.

He handed the items over. "You take good care now and send regards to Carl for me."

As he headed to his car, Gabe thought, *Thank heavens for the Second Amendment.*

CHAPTER 33

University of North Texas

Sam Delgado felt a mixture of pride and disappointment. He had accomplished a great deal with the ADHD trials. His recent grades at UNT were hard proof. He liked Dr. Siddiqui and was going to miss coming every week for their sessions. From what he was told, the project was only funded for eight weeks and would be closing down any day.

In the office, Ming, the professor's assistant, was packing up boxes. Files were neatly piled on the desk. "Hi, Sam. Last session today?" Ming asked with a smile.

"Yep. Too bad it's over already. I hope I can keep my good grades going."

"I'm sure you will. Sounds like you got a lot out of the treatment."

"Definitely. And the money wasn't bad either."

"You can use it to buy more textbooks," Ming joked.

Sam laughed. "That far gone I'm not."

"Have a seat. Dr. Siddiqui will be right with you. He's just finishing up with another student."

Sam watched as a blue-haired, multi-pierced woman exited the professor's office. She looked disappointed. "Doc, why can't I have a watch?" she said.

"I'm sorry, Jennifer. I only have so many and must select those who responded optimally to the treatments. But we

143

thank you for your participation and I wish you much success. Ming will give you your final payment. Best of luck."

Frowning, the young woman went to the assistant, took the proffered envelope and left.

Professor Siddiqui spotted Sam sitting quietly. "Hello, Sam, please come in."

Sam followed the professor into the treatment room, taking a seat in the comfortable leather recliner, the same chair where he'd learned to relax and improve his concentration. "Last class, huh, Doc?"

"Yes, but it seems you have benefitted tremendously from the study. Would you agree?"

"Definitely. I can sit in the library for hours now with only a few short breaks and understand the material. I expect my GPA to skyrocket. Can I call you if I need a tune-up?" he asked, only partly joking.

"That won't be possible," he said firmly, bringing Sam's mood down a few notches. "I'm relocating. After the semester ends, I'll be leaving Dallas to work on studies elsewhere around the world. When you feel the need to improve your concentration, use the relaxation techniques we've practiced. I'm sure that will help you going forward."

Sam started to panic. What if he needed a refresher course? He wasn't sure why he was reacting so strongly to the news, but it was like he was addicted to the treatments.

The professor patted him on the shoulder. "You'll do just fine. But before you leave, I want to give you something special."

The professor opened a drawer and took out a velvet jewelry case. "The work we've done here together will help many other people living with ADHD. We're giving these only to the students who've benefitted the most from the project. And you are one of those exceptional few." He handed over the box. "This is for you, Sam. Congratulations. If you wear it every day, it will help your time management." He handed the box to Sam.

Opening it, Sam found a watch, its wide silver band engraved with the words, *Carpe Diem*.

Sam was honored. "Wow. This is really nice. What does it mean?"

"It's Latin, meaning 'Seize the day.' You earned it. I hope you will look at it every day as a reminder of your success."

Sam put the watch on. "Thanks, Doc. That means a lot. I won't ever take it off."

"That's just what I wanted to hear." He stood up, shook Sam's hand and led him to the front office where Sam received his final check, said goodbye to Ming, and left, feeling the best he had in years.

CHAPTER 34

Cincinnati

After twenty-four hours straight of no sleep, Special Agent in Charge Doug Matthews arrived in Cincinnati. His trip to D.C. had been fraught with tension. An unknown opioid was out there being used for terror, with what was likely a nefarious organization bent on protecting it. The intel inevitably triggered a hurricane of activity at the Bureau.

The Director ordered Colonel Gomez to get all hands on deck to prevent an attack, demanding regular status reports. In turn, the Colonel expected a smooth operation. The fate of many careers, including Matthews, were depending on it.

They wanted Carrera alive, to lead them to the bigger fish and take down the syndicate. The burden of responsibility was crashing down, landing in Matthew's lap. The Colonel had summoned him to D.C. to represent him while he was out of town dealing with even more urgent matters of national security. While others in Matthew's shoes would view it as an enviable vote of confidence, he knew it to be more about his superior passing the buck and covering his ass. If anyone would take the fall in the event of a terrorist attack that was later proven preventable, it would be Matthews, the Colonel walking away unsullied.

At least, the Colonel had given credit to Matthews' team for finding a solid lead. Matthews never told him he had let those kids walk out of his office and had no intention of sharing that information. He considered it good luck that Jim Fields contacted him when Kearns brought up his name. Sharing intel on the Cincinnati chatter with Jim was a prudent move on his part. After meeting with higher-ups, Matthews wanted to sit face-to-face with the lieutenant, Steadman and his gang. Too much was on the line for Matthews. If they failed, he failed.

He deplaned, entering the terminal, taking his phone off airplane mode and dialing Detective Kearns.

"Lieutenant Kearns, are you here?"

"Pulling up now, sir. I'll be at baggage claim."

Matthews took an underground shuttle to the baggage area and spotted a middle-aged woman with reddish hair and a face best described as pleasant, standing alongside the carousel assigned to his flight. Her demeanor was not that of the long-serving officer she was purported to be, but he knew she was there to meet him by her regulation shoes and alert, scanning gaze.

Donna gave him a warm smile. "I appreciate you taking time out of your busy schedule to meet."

"It's not a favor, Lieutenant," Matthews said brusquely. "The situation is dire. If we don't handle this carefully, we'll have a real disaster on our hands."

Donna didn't necessarily expect a thank you for chauffeuring him, but she certainly didn't need a lecture. She made a move to wedge herself between the others waiting on their bags.

"I have no checked luggage," he informed her. "D.C. was a quick trip. Where to?"

Annoyed by his abrupt manner, Donna nonetheless kept her tone cordial. "We're meeting the others at the hotel. They're eager to help and get Carrera off their backs."

"Good. From what I heard you're not fully on board with this operation."

"I wouldn't quite put it that way. Actually..."

Matthews cut her off. "They agreed to it so that's all that

matters. If there was another way, I would have considered it. I'm here to make sure everything's under control. The objective is always to do these things quietly. Let's see if you all can manage that."

The drive to the hotel was made in silence.

* * *

Everyone rose from their chairs when Agent Matthews walked into the hotel room escorted by Donna.

Consistent with his meticulous personality, Jim was fully prepared when his boss showed up. It was one of his qualities that Donna admired. He stood to greet Matthews, who nonetheless extended his hand to Jon first.

"We meet again, Mr. Steadman." They shook.

"So it would seem, sir."

"Perhaps I should have afforded your visit more weight. For that, I apologize." Matthews planned to eat as much humble pie as necessary to get his hands on the specimens.

"No need, sir. You're onboard now. No one could have predicted any of this."

"Quite gracious of you." He turned to Melanie. "Ms. Ridgefield, I'm glad to see you're well."

"Thank you, sir."

Matthews was ready to get down to business. "Dr. Lavi, I understand that you've had a trying few days. But the upside is that you and Mr. Lewis are in the invaluable position of being able to identify your attacker as the same man we'll be monitoring on Friday."

Terry responded, "I never actually saw his face. Only Gabe has, as far as we know."

Everyone sat.

"Be that as it may, now that we know his identity, we're hoping to get him alive and learn more about his employers through interrogation. However, if that isn't meant to be, we need to take him out."

The situation was beginning to settle in, with talk of someone potentially dying.

Matthews paused, facing Jon. "Mr. Steadman, under the current circumstances I must reconsider and ask you for the specimens you offered when we met last."

"I'm sorry, sir. I no longer have them."

Everyone in the room was stunned into momentary silence.

Matthews broke it. "Excuse me?"

"After what happened to Terry and Gabe, I got rid of them."

"Define *got rid of*." Agent Matthews felt an ulcer coming on.

"Flushed them down the toilet. If I don't have them, we can't have any more trouble. There are surely more hitmen like Carrera on the payroll. They won't hurt us if we don't have what they want."

Matthews was shocked and bordering on irate. The others appeared astonished they had no knowledge of this. Trying hard to keep his voice calm and professional, the FBI agent said, "That was foolish. What makes you think they won't still come after you, mistakenly believing you have them? We could have used them for analysis or as a lure if needed in the future."

Knitting his brow, Jon replied, "Sir, I'm confused. You were very clear that they could not be accurately analyzed and that fully reliable mapping technology for the quality of those specimens was not yet available."

Rubbing a hand over his face, Matthews was beyond frustrated. "The way you came into my office that day...oh forget it."

"There's no point in crying over spilled milk," said Donna. "You must admit, Agent Matthews, these young people are going above and beyond any citizen's call of duty."

Matthews ignored her. "And the flashdrive?"

"Destroyed."

"I see." Matthews was barely holding it together.

"We can use decoys for the trap," said Donna. "It's what we would have done anyway. This is a good time to discuss the plan."

Agent Matthews asked Jon, "You didn't perhaps learn anything from the professor's work *before* getting rid of them? Or is that also too much to hope for?"

"Of course, we did. That's how this began. Didn't Agent Fields get around to updating you on Professor Breitler's findings? I would think you'd be the first to know."

It was a direct blow to the agent's pride. Matthews was Fields' superior, not the other way around. It took every ounce of self-control to let the comment pass unanswered. Of course, he knew everything Fields did! He was only asking for more details. To keep his mouth occupied, Matthews poured himself a glass of water from the pitcher on the table and took a long drink.

Resigning himself, he leaned his forearms in his lap and clasped his hands together. He studied the motley crew before him. They instinctively drew in closer. "Okay," he said, "here's the plan."

When they were through, Matthews stood up to leave, saying he needed to contact his office urgently to deal with the latest developments. With any luck, he'd be in his own hotel room and asleep within the hour.

* * *

Agent Jim Fields had come prepared with wiring devices, and he explained how they worked. A map of the area around Roebling Bridge was spread out on the coffee table. Movements and timing were reviewed. After their umpteenth rehearsal, Jim asked them to huddle in close. To lighten the mood, he put a hand in the middle. The others followed suit. In a coach-like fashion, Jim shouted, "Ready?"

They replied in pumped-up unison, "Ready!

CHAPTER 35

Cincinnati

Repairs to the Purple People Bridge were taking longer than expected. The pedestrian walkway stood parallel to the Roebling Bridge, its brick bases fenced in by construction metal framing. Spanning the Ohio River, it connected Cincinnati, Ohio's southernmost metropolis to Newport in Kentucky. The bridge, a popular attraction for tourists and locals, had earned the quirky moniker from its distinctive hue, a cheerful lavender. Senior centers made it their business to beautify the bridge with an array of colorful seasonal flowers.

The man pushed his cap low over his brow, shuffling along from one flower planter to the next, taking close-up photos of the blooms. Dressed in a light jacket, tan chinos and rubber-soled shoes, he seamlessly blended in, just another flower lover out for a late-autumn stroll. Every few minutes, he raised the high-powered camera, refocusing the lens in search of his true subjects.

Hugo Carrera aka René Leduc had followed these two from New York to Jerusalem, and now to Nowheresville, USA. Itching to go home, he was glad to put an end to this assignment. Things had quickly escalated, and the Boss wanted the problem to go away.

His disguise allowed him camouflage, and besides, neither

subject had ever seen him clearly. Not on the plane, in the restaurant or when he hit the woman from behind. Amateurish mistake, he admitted, not verifying she was in possession of the items before approaching her. The mistake tipped his hand, but he did what he could to use it to his advantage, delivering the hospital wristband to Lewis, sending a clear message of warning.

The Boss's hackers must have tracked them down in minutes. *Stupid kids!* They had no sense of privacy, posting every little thing for the world to see, from what they ate for breakfast to their pets' antics.

While Carrera didn't overly concern himself with being spotted, he wasn't taking unnecessary chances. He zoomed in on the bench. Luck shone down on him when he spotted Gabe Lewis pull out the familiar pouch. He was waiting for someone. Sure enough, a young man wearing sunglasses and a ballcap walked over and sat next to him.

Carrera focused his lens for a better view. It was Steadman. The last time Carrera had seen him was at the school cafeteria giving Lewis the specimens. He walked with a limp Carrera hadn't noticed before. *This is too easy.* About time he caught a break.

They didn't stay long. Lewis handed the pouch and flashdrive over to Steadman, stood up and walked away from the river. Steadman got up, heading in the opposite direction towards the bridge.

Another stroke of luck. All Carrera had to do was wait.

✳ ✳ ✳

Jon walked as casually as possible, hoping Carrera was out there. The bridge's purple color reminded Jon of Ashleigh, calming him. *She's watching over me.*

He had followed the FBI's instructions to the letter and was now making himself a lone target. In his pocket was a fake lab pouch and blank flashdrive. Despite what he'd told Matthews and the others, Jon had not destroyed the authentic ones. They were in a safe location that only he and Gabe knew about.

Jon felt beads of sweat dripping beneath his shirt, causing the wire to slightly slip on his bare chest as he reached the purple bridge. Several people were strolling along the span, admiring the skyline and flowers. A young mother pushing a baby carriage, an older woman resting on a bench, and a middle age man taking pictures of flowers in their planters.

As he passed the photographer, Jon was quickly jerked back, and felt a sharp jab in his side.

"Stay calm," the man whispered in his ear. His breath reeked of cigarettes. "You scream or bring attention to yourself in any way, and I won't think twice about shooting you."

Jon was stunned by how quickly he had been assaulted. "What do you want?" he asked with genuine fear. "My wallet's in my back pocket."

"I don't want your money asshole, I want what's in your other pocket."

"I don't know what you're talking about."

He felt the gun jab deeper in his kidney, causing him to stumble sideways, his bad leg seizing up. The man held on tighter. "I have a silencer on this piece. I can shoot you, take what I came for, and walk away before anyone gets a whiff of what happened."

"Okay. Let me get it out."

"Do it slowly. If I sense you're playing around with me, I'll kill you."

Jon shuddered. The fear was near paralyzing as he reached into his pocket and took out the pouch, awkwardly handing them to the man behind him. "What do you want these for anyway? I'm just using them for a research project."

"That's none of your concern. Now the flashdrive. I know you have it, so save the innocent act."

Jon took out the flashdrive. The man grabbed it from him,

placing it in the pouch with the tubes. "Okay, now we walk."

"You said you'd leave me alone if you got what you want."

"I never said that, so shut up and move."

"I'm just a student—"

Before Jon could finish his sentence, the young mother pulled out an assault rifle from her baby carriage and yelled, "Drop it!"

In a split second, Jon dropped to his knees, as he had been instructed to do if those words were spoken, as a message both to the perpetrator and himself, should he be held at gunpoint.

The man tried to keep a hold on him, lost his grip, and quickly racked back the slide of his pistol.

With her Colt M4 carbine held steadily in hand, the mother barked, "One more move and it's between the eyes! Drop it, Carrera!"

Hearing his name, Carrera sized up the situation. A SWAT team surrounded him, guns drawn and pointing in his direction. He lowered his gun.

"Drop it," she repeated.

He did so.

"Kick it over here."

He did so.

Jon scurried to the opposite side of the bridge as several agents ran in his direction. Positioned all over the area, they had been ready for Carrera's move. The elderly person on the bench was now holding a semi-automatic. Without Jon's knowledge, everyone around him had been undercover. The Feds had picked Carrera out within minutes of Jon's meeting with Gabe and had been listening to the whole exchange. Any civilians in the area were shielded from the action by well-positioned agents. Feeling dizzy and weak in the knees, Jon held onto the railing to stay vertical. The sight of the gun brought back the night at the BTI. It was as if Abadi was standing right there.

Donna came up beside him, "You okay, Jon?"

"I need a minute."

"You did great, just as we practiced. We got him."

They watched as the mother/agent held Carrera at bay, gun pointed at his chest. Two local police officers carefully approached him, cuffs at the ready. Without warning, Carrera bent over, swiftly pulled an army-issue knife from an ankle holster and held it out menacingly. The policemen halted, pulling out their guns.

Donna yelled out to Carrera. "Don't be stupid. You can walk away from here. Put the knife down."

Cornered, he darted his eyes between the two approaching cops, waving his knife back and forth. Carrera sneered, and as if to himself, muttered, "I'm never walking away from here. They'll get me wherever I am."

"Who will?" Donna asked in an even-toned voice.

"Haven't you figured it out? The syndicate! You fools don't have a clue what's coming. It's not even on your radar." In his other hand, he held up the flashdrive and pouch. "This is only the tip of the iceberg—test runs proving the system works. They're building an army right under your noses."

He was surrounded, the Ohio River churning behind him. A dazed look of resignation flooded his features as he turned to look at the view, as if he was a tourist admiring the scenery.

"What syndicate?" Donna asked, more urgently than before. She was losing him.

Carrera looked out at the riverbank, registering surprise. He turned back to face his adversaries, laughing perversely. Now delirious, he shouted, "New beginnings!"

Those words sealed his fate.

❋ ❋ ❋

Snipers are trained to be patient. The scope was perfectly aligned, breath even, attention focused. Carrera could be clearly seen from this vantage point. He had Steadman in front of him, held tight against his body, preventing a clear shot.

Even at a distance, Carrera looked like a trapped animal ready to strike.

The Boss had hoped this hit wouldn't be necessary, but circumstances had taken a quick turn in the wrong direction. Now it was the only way to get back on course. Their timeline depended on it. Too much was at stake.

The sniper listened remotely to the verbal exchange on the long-range device.

It was time. The sniper allowed a few seconds to re-check the alignments and, with a steady trigger finger, took the shot, watching as Carrera, knife in mid-air, fell backward over the bridge railing and down into the Ohio River.

Disassembling the rifle, the assassin took out a fishing rod from its case, replacing it with the weapon, and kicked dirt around the area with the tip of a black sneaker. Moving at a fast clip, the assassin stepped onto the landing above, serpentine steps leading up to the waterfront park. Donning a beat-up fishing hat and dark sunglasses, the killer slowed pace, weaving through the growing number of pedestrians gawking at the bridge. Five minutes later, the sniper was on the highway heading south...on to her next assignment.

CHAPTER 36

Cincinnati

S everal hours were spent dredging up Carrera's body and searching for his shooter. Police boats and divers were summoned to recover the remains, and despite a moderate current that made the job tedious, they were successful. Donna watched it all unfold from atop the purple bridge.

The sniper search, however, was as short and fruitless as anticipated. No one expected to find any trace of the assassin. The kill was quick, achieved with pinpoint accuracy, and the perpetrator believed to be long gone. Nevertheless, standard procedure warranted a full-on search of the area. A BOLO order was sent to all law enforcement in the tri-state area and the FBI cyber system was updated to include an unnamed and unseen assailant who may be in the Midwest with a cache of lethal weapons. The description was ludicrous and given the easy and legal access to high-powered weapons by residents of Ohio, Indiana and Kentucky, the likelihood of any unusual sightings was slim. As such, Jim, Donna, and Captain Lawrence Johnson of the Cincinnati Police Department were not holding their breath, deciding instead to focus on viable leads.

Upon Jim's request, the local police captain ordered his men to study the trajectory of the sniper's bullet. They worked side by side with Jim's crew, gathering potential evidence.

When Carrera went over the side, Jon had appeared fine, but Donna knew better. She'd seen it a thousand times. Trauma leaves its mark.

She'd pulled Melanie aside, explaining that Jon was going to crash and would need time to process what he'd just been through. His adrenaline would drop like a brick, causing extreme exhaustion. Knowing she would be working through the night, Donna asked Melanie to go back to the hotel and keep an eye on him. She handed over the keys to her rental. "The Feds will pick up the tab. We can debrief tomorrow."

Melanie nodded solemnly and asked Gabe to drive so she could sit in the back with Jon. Without hesitation, he ushered them into the car and drove away.

CHAPTER 37

Cincinnati

"Get down! Run, run!"

Gabe and the others heard the screaming from Jon's hotel room and bolted, Gabe getting there first, crashing the door open. Jon was lying in the bed, eyes closed, covered in sweat, writhing from side to side. "Ashleigh, get out!" he shouted.

Gabe stepped aside, miserable, allowing Melanie past him, the others looking on. She went to the bed and put a hand on his sweaty forehead, whispering. "Jon, wake up, sweetie. You're having a bad dream."

"Help!"

"Everything's okay," she cooed. "Open your eyes."

Jon slowed his rocking, and his eyes shot open. He looked at Melanie, slowly becoming aware of the others in the doorway.

"What? What's going on, guys?"

"You had a bad dream. You were yelling."

"Oh God, not again."

"Again?" Gabe asked. "How long has this been going on?"

"I used to wake up in a sweat, but that stopped long ago."

"Maybe today's events triggered something."

"You were very upset," said Melanie. "Who's Ashleigh?"

Terry looked perplexed. "Gabe, isn't that your sister's name? The one who was killed in the bombing?"

Gabe turned to Jon, saw the terror in his eyes.

"What bombing?" asked Melanie, sounding confused as well.

Gabe said, "Buddy, it's time. Now or never. Do or die."

"What are you two talking about?" asked Melanie.

A protracted silence settled in the room, ending abruptly when the phone rang.

CHAPTER 38

"**W**hat happened in Cincinnati?"

"It was a trap, just as you suspected. The Feds were waiting for Carrera. Turns out he couldn't keep his mouth shut."

"Then abort the detonation. There will be too many cops crawling around. Not what we want for a trial."

"Already done."

"And what of the specimens and flashdrive?"

"They've been disposed of. No evidence remains. They were using decoys to reel Carrera in. I learned it too late to warn him."

How can you be sure it was destroyed?"

"We have them under audio surveillance."

"And what of my student?"

"Collateral damage. Taken care of."

"Pity. I had high hopes for Cincinnati, but it's a sign. We need to step up our mission and prepare for the Event. If those interlopers should get involved again, take them out."

* * *

Cincinnati

Jon leaped at the phone. "Yeah?"

"*Yeah?* That's how you answer a call?" The voice of Ed Hernandez came over the line. "Is this Jon?"

Jon sat up, trying to calm himself down and get his bearings.

"Hello? You still there?" Ed asked, louder.

"Sorry. Ed?"

"You okay, kid?"

"Uh, I guess." Jon gestured to the others that he needed to take the call, and they shuffled out of his room.

"What's going on? You don't sound so good."

"The adventure continues," Jon replied with a note of sarcasm. "You saw what happened in Cincinnati today?"

"Yeah, it's all over the news. I'm writing a piece as we speak."

"I was there. Front line and center. Guy had me at gunpoint."

"No way! Are you okay?"

"I will be."

Ed didn't spare a moment. "Can I get a quote from you?"

"Seriously?"

"Yeah, it would help with my article. Exclusive from someone at the scene."

"Sure, but—"

"I want every detail. Of course, that's not why I'm calling."

"You find something?"

"Yes. A reliable source who will have to remain anonymous, told me the police found DNA evidence at the Y."

"Great! What did they find?"

"Cartilage from the bomber's right ear. That's all that was left of her. Shari Kordivan. A senior at UCLA. She frequented the YWCA, played women's basketball. No motive, just like the others. The explosives were well beyond what was needed to take the place down."

"Sounds like the same M.O. How and when can I get a sample?"

"Slow down, friend. Things don't work that way. I can't get it that easily."

"So how does this help?"

"The FBI needs to analyze it. The good news is they're looking for a specialist who can get the job done quickly. Most of these tests take weeks, days if expedited. I recalled you mentioned the geneticist who your friend was meeting in Israel. My thought is we could have him…"

"Her."

"Okay, have *her* assigned to the analysis team. Then you could quickly view the results."

"Why on earth would the FBI agree to hire someone I recommend?"

"Because it wouldn't be you doing the recommending. I would whisper the name in my source's ear. He passes it along, assuming your doctor is qualified and willing to do the job fast. He'll look good to his superiors having found someone so quickly, and you gain access."

"Very impressive."

"It's what I do. The writing is just the flourishing finishing touch to a lot of digging, negotiating and favors."

"Sounds down and dirty."

"It is, but you have to play by the rules of the game if you want any chance at a win."

"And the Pulitzer is the prize."

"You're learning. I'll be in touch as soon as everything is arranged. Once you have data from the ear, I'll expect a quick turnaround on the story. But for now, let's get your quote on today's events."

Jon answered Ed's questions with the stipulation that he leave his name out of the article. When they were winding down, Jon let out a loud yawn, the earlier adrenaline taking another nosedive.

Hernandez said, "That's enough for now. Get some rest. Sounds like you still have a wild ride ahead."

CHAPTER 39

Cincinnati

Donna polished off her third black coffee of the night. The Cincinnati PD's brew tasted like mud, but she needed caffeine to keep her going. Atop a nearby file cabinet, an open package of mint Oreos teased her, threatening her latest attempt at dieting.

After the crime scene was cleared and the body taken away by the medical examiner, the team met back at the local police station, a more convenient location than the nearest FBI field office.

She sat in an uncomfortable metal chair in the station's dreary assembly room facing Jim, Captain Johnson, and Officer Sarah Barkin, a bright-eyed recruit sporting no makeup and an easy-care bob. Low maintenance kind of gal.

Most of the team members involved in the takedown had left for the night, shortly after the incident review. Everyone was in agreement that procedure had been followed and no further inquiry was needed. What remained was deciphering what Carrera said before his death. They had reviewed the recording repeatedly but found no workable leads. His last words—"New beginnings!"—were perplexing as well.

Given the late hour, Donna was impressed with the captain's presence. He was a large dark-skinned man, broad in the shoulders and gut. She supposed he'd used his intimidating appearance to his advantage when working rougher parts of town.

Donna pulled the box of cookies closer, deciding which to take. "Find anything on Carrera?" she asked Jim while the others listened in. Despite the late hour, she thought he looked refreshed. Maybe even handsomer, with his unshaven face.

"He had a driver's license with the name René Leduc, an American Express Black Card, and four hundred bucks in cash."

"Personal effects?"

"A pair of reading glasses, remarkably found intact in his jacket pocket, and the pouch he took off Jon. We'll need to formally confirm his identity as Hugo Carrera. I have my guys running his prints through the FBI system to see if anything else turns up."

Donna said, "Good. Any increase in online chatter in the last few hours?"

"It's been crickets since the shooting. These people know what they're doing. In the meantime, we need to figure out who Carrera's employers were."

Barkin chimed in, "We've gained access to Carrera's bank accounts, but so far the money trail's run dry. No unusual deposits. Too bad he wasn't carrying his phone."

Donna said, "He must have had one. Any luck finding his vehicle or hotel?"

"Still working on it," Jim replied. "We have five agents canvassing the area."

Officer Patel knocked on the open door. "Excuse me sir, one of the agents just called in. Said he found a boutique hotel on Race Street in Over-the-Rhine. A man matching Carrera's description booked one night, checking in earlier today. The times match up. They said if we need to look at the room, they'll allow it without a warrant. They were just hoping it might get done before the early bird guests get moving, so there's no police activity when breakfast service begins at 6:00 a.m."

They all instinctively looked at the clock on the wall. 3:55.

"Wouldn't want to upset anyone over breakfast," said Captain Johnson.

Jim stood up with newfound energy. "Okay, let's go."

CHAPTER 40

Over-the-Rhine, Cincinnati

U nique furnishings and artwork adorned the hotel's small lobby, giving it an upscale feel. Clearly, Carrera had good taste, not to mention deep pockets.

His room was freezing. Donna zipped up her coat. Flanked by two modern side tables, the king size bed had been slept in and made up haphazardly. Jim began searching the dresser drawers. Donna opened the bathroom door, feeling the residual heat from a shower hours before. Condensation remained on the glass-tiled mirror. A jar of actor's glue—a staple for use with stage wigs and fake facial hair—was left open by the sink. A white terry robe lay sprawled on the wet floor. Donna used evidence tweezers to pluck several hairs from a comb found in the leather vanity kit, hoping there was at least one viable strand. Nothing to lose by comparing it to the specimens acquired by Jon and Gabe.

Finishing in the bathroom, she opened the sliding door to the room's only closet. She found a compact umbrella, a newly pressed, button-down and a navy blazer with cough drops in its side pocket. A nearly empty pack of Marlboros and a silver lighter were in the inside breast pocket. She didn't expect to find a wallet and there was none. A standard issue safe was perched at knee height. Locked. She texted Patel to ask the clerk for the password override. Two minutes later, she unlocked the safe. Inside were an iPhone and an envelope with one thousand dollars cash. She called Jim over, who carefully placed the phone into an evidence bag.

"Let's get this back to the lab ASAP. We won't be able to access deleted text streams but maybe we can find something of value."

Donna took a slow second look around the room. She had a strong feeling she was missing something, and had learned long ago to trust her instincts. She took mental inventory. Bed made, but not by a housekeeper, wet robe, actor's glue, typical male toiletries. The contents of the closet—unlocked safe, shirt, blazer, umbrella. On the top shelf were extra blankets and down pillows.

"Jim, come over here. Take a look at this."

"What've you got?"

"It's pretty chilly in this room, and he only has a light blanket on the bed."

"So? Lots of people like to sleep in a cold room."

"Yeah, but not this cold." She walked to the thermostat mounted on the wall. "Something's wrong with this. It's set to seventy-one degrees but it must be sixty in here. Why wouldn't he use the extra blankets?"

"Where are you going with this?"

"Can you reach them?" She said pointing to the top of the closet. Jim was only an inch or two taller than Donna, but that made all the difference. He reached up and attempted to pull down the blankets. They stayed securely intact.

"Huh? There's something anchoring them down. Get me a chair."

Donna pulled the desk chair over and Jim climbed up. "I can't seem to dislodge them." He took out his iPhone and engaged the flashlight. "Okay, here we go. There's a black hard case underneath. Looks like it was intentionally hidden. Help me get this down."

Together they managed to dislodge the comforters enveloping the case. With a great deal of effort, the two laid it on the floor. It was equipped with a recessed combination lock.

"I've seen a similar suitcase once before," Jim said to Donna, his face ashen. "With its weight, we either have a substantial cache of firearms or a ticking time bomb. Let's move out of here. Time to call the bomb squad."

CHAPTER 41

Over-the-Rhine, Cincinnati

T he hotel needed to be evacuated, making the manager very unhappy, but Agent Jim Fields gave him no alternative.

As they escorted guests outside, a police bomb squad entered the hotel lobby dressed in lime green bomb suits, stomping awkwardly like astronauts on the moon's surface. One carried a sophisticated robot, known to the team as Bo.

Outside, Jim joined Donna and Patel ushering hotel guests and staff past the police barriers. Some were in their pajamas, others with sopping wet hair, pulled from their morning shower. No one wore a coat. To keep them from freezing, they were guided to a coffee shop a half-block away.

Twenty minutes after everyone was out, Jim got a call from the Ohio PD bomb squad team leader. "Sir, all clear."

"What did you find?"

"Bo took hi-res x-ray photos of the device. The case was filled with explosives. Properly armed, it could bring down a four-story building, no problem. Top of the line material, but inactive. No detonator was in place for a charge to occur. This guy was careful. Knew what he was doing."

"Thank you, Officer. Clean it up and move out. When you're done, we'll send everyone back inside. Please keep this intel on the QT. No need for the public to get worked up."

"Yes, sir."

Jim ended the call and faced Donna, who was staring at a large poster stapled to a wooden lamppost near the entrance of the hotel.

She said, "It appears we put a wrench in their plans. A few more hours, and we could have easily been dealing with a very different situation."

Jim followed her gaze and read the advertisement. "The Flying Pig marathon takes place tomorrow by the river," he said. "The route crosses the Roebling Bridge. You think that was their intended target?"

Donna thought a moment. "Were there enough explosives in Carrera's room to bring down a bridge?"

"If placed strategically, it's possible."

Jim's phone rang. "Fields." He paused to listen. "I'll be right there." Hanging up, Jim said, "That was the captain. A body was found, washed up on the Kentucky shore, not a mile from where they dredged up Carrera. Too much of a coincidence."

"I'd like to tag along, if you're okay with it."

Jim nodded, and jogged to his car, Donna close behind.

CHAPTER 42

Newport, Kentucky

The barefoot corpse was badly mangled, its bloated arms at an odd angle, legs twisted in a disturbing way. His clothes were drenched and torn, embedded with debris. He was maybe twenty years old, dark-skinned, dressed like most kids his age in skinny jeans and an A & F fitted t-shirt. His eyes were open, staring at nothing.

The M.E. van was parked adjacent to the riverboat dock, a gurney at its backdoor, awaiting its next passenger. Thick shrubbery lined the riverbank. Barren shrubs and broken branches lay on the frozen ground, making it rough-going to reach the victim. A dog walker had found him. Her mutt wouldn't stop growling until he pulled her close enough for a bare white foot to be seen.

Donna spotted Captain Johnson, his posture weighed down by fatigue. Surrounding him was a skeleton crew of the police force, those not at the hotel corralling guests. They stood clear of the corpse, giving space to the medical examiner kneeling beside it. An officer was hanging yellow crime scene tape around the perimeter.

Eschewing any greetings to Jim and Donna, Captain Johnson got right to it. "Another unexplainable shooting within a twenty-four-hour period. Same execution style as Carrera. Not good for city business. The mayor wants answers fast. Let me hear your feedback."

Jim answered, "I'll need to get the M.E.'s report but short of that, Donna and I think Carrera on the bridge was not just a place to scout out Steadman, but also reconnaissance for an attack on the Roebling Bridge. The bomb left behind in his room corroborates that theory and is consistent with online chatter. The way we figure it, Carrera was going to use the opportunity that brought him to town for the specimens to also supply the vic with explosives for tomorrow's marathon. The plan was aborted, and Carrera and this kid needed to be taken out of commission."

Donna noticed that Jim gave her equal credit.

The captain nodded. "Sounds right. Keeps them from talking to us if captured. This was a clean job, professional. I'll ask the M.E. to put a rush on it."

"You get an ID on him?" asked Donna.

"Not yet. But a good place to start would be local colleges."

"Any missing persons reports come in?"

"Too early for that. It's possible no one is missing him yet."

The M.E. stepped over to join them. The captain asked, "Doctor, what can you share with us?"

"For now, looks like a single shot to the back of his head. Instant death."

"Can you estimate the TOD?"

"Not at this point, but I'm confident he hasn't been in the river more than thirty-six hours. I'll have a better idea once I open him up."

"So we can safely say his death could have happened around the same time as Carrera's?"

"It's possible, but I wouldn't jump to that conclusion at this time. It's still premature."

"I would wager the same gun was used to shoot both men," said Captain Johnson. "It will help if you find the two shells to see if they came from the same gun. Fred, can you put our John Doe at the head of the line, just after Carrera?"

The M.E. sighed. "Everyone asks me that...but given the

high profile nature of this case and its implications to the wellbeing of our citizens, I'll do it."

"Thank you."

Jim asked, "Can we have a minute to look at him?"

"Go ahead. Just don't mess up the integrity of the scene."

Jim and Donna put on shoe covers and gloves offered by the doctor's assistant, and approached the kid's body. Even with the river wash, the stench was overpowering. Instinctively, they covered their noses.

"Such a shame. He looks so young," said Donna. "I'll never get used to seeing this. A young life wasted."

Visible at the base of his skull was a single, perfectly round hole. The bleeding had stopped hours before in the water, though reddish-black stains were left behind on his clothes.

Jim said, "Looks like a high-powered rifle round. Consistent with Carrera's wound. But why would both be taken out on a dry run? It takes a lot of money and effort to arrange an attack like they had planned. Why stop at the last minute?"

Donna bent down to get a better look. Without touching the corpse, she pointed to the wristwatch on his left hand. "Take a look at this. Still running. Too bad. Maybe we could have a better TOD if it had stopped when he hit the water."

"Hard to tell. He could've been shot hours before being dumped. Let's see what the M.E. comes back with."

Jim and Donna left the somber scene. She offered a theory. "To answer your question, 'the syndicate,' as Carrera referred to them, needed to shut the attack down fast. Maybe they worried Carrera would talk. If someone was watching the bridge, they would have seen us closing in on him and knew an interrogation was coming. A shot to the head would keep Carrera quiet."

"And this kid?"

"Once Carrera was taken out and the operation was off, the kid was a loose thread, hanging in the wind."

"Sounds like a solid theory." Jim yawned loudly. "Sweetheart, it's time to put myself to bed. I'll get a ride from one of the officers and catch up with you later."

He gave her a quick peck and walked away.

❊ ❊ ❊

Cincinnati

After leaving the crime scene, Donna also went back to the hotel to get some shuteye. She slept four hours and woke disoriented when the alarm went off. She showered, changed clothes and was back at her adopted precinct desk by noon. There was no sign of Jim. No doubt he was crashing somewhere. As she walked into the situation room, Donna overheard Sarah asking the captain, "Can I see that watch again?"

The captain gestured to Patel standing nearby. "Please go down to the evidence room and bring us the wristwatch."

"Yes, sir," he said.

"What watch?" Donna asked trying to keep up.

"We've identified the victim as Farad Jackson, a student at UC," said Sarah. "His mother called the precinct saying she hadn't heard from him for three days."

"Is that so unusual, or have things changed since I went to college?"

"She had celebrated her fiftieth birthday and Farad was meant to go home for the festivities but never showed up. When she finally got hold of his roommate and heard his bed hadn't been slept in, she called us."

"What's the deal with the watch?"

Sarah said, "My dad's a watch enthusiast. He owns something like three hundred watches. He tinkers with them, taking them apart and putting them back together. His father was a collector of old timepieces and left them to my dad when he died. Anyway, when I saw Farad's watch in the evidence bag, I'd never seen one quite like it. Given my exposure, that's pretty unlikely. Just thought I'd take another look."

"That's fine," the captain said. "Sign of a good investigator when she notices the small things."

Sarah beamed at the compliment. "Thank you, sir."

Patel returned to the room, placed the evidence bag on the table and stepped back.

Sarah donned plastic gloves, and extracted the wristwatch from the evidence bag, carefully turning it over in her hands. "Odd."

Donna was looking over her shoulder. "What is?"

"I've never seen this name, Quantos."

"Maybe it's very rare."

"Perhaps, but I'd at least recognize the manufacturer. It may not be of any significance, but it sure has piqued my curiosity."

Captain Johnson asked, "Do you think your father would be willing to come in and take a look?"

"I'm sure he would. I'll give him a call."

Donna asked if she could take photos of the watch and ask around. The captain agreed, but reluctantly. "Be cautious. I don't want to see anything about this in tomorrow's paper."

Donna agreed, took out her phone and snapped a few photos of the watch from different angles. As she left the office, she had a funny feeling they were onto something important.

* * *

Donna wasn't surprised that Jon didn't recognize the watch, but she figured it was worth a shot when she emailed him the pictures. While she planned to stay on in Cincinnati to work the case, the others were returning to Dallas.

Donna was walking to her car in the PD lot when her cell rang. She dug the phone out of her pocket. It was Officer Barkin. "Hi Sarah, what's up?"

"The captain asked me to update you. Carrera's phone was

fully encrypted and Apple's not willing to hack into his account. No word back yet on the hair."

"Damn. We need to catch a break. If Carrera was to be believed, more deadly attacks are coming. Soon."

CHAPTER 43

Cincinnati

Melanie knocked softly on Jon's hotel bedroom door. Without waiting for a response, she entered the room, finding him sitting up in bed. "Hey there. How are you feeling?"

"Getting back to normal, I guess, whatever normal is."

She smiled, sat on the edge of the bed. "Glad to hear it. How did the call go with Ed?"

"Pretty good. He's going to pull strings to get Terry named as specimen analyst for cartilage the LAPD found at the YWCA site, believed to have been part of the killer's ear."

"Incredible. Have you spoken to Terry about this?"

"Not yet."

There was an awkward silence as both avoided each other's eyes. Until they didn't, when Melanie said, "Can you tell me who Ashleigh is from your dream? You were screaming for her to run. Wasn't that Gabe's sister?"

Jon broke eye contact. "There's a lot I need to share with you about that, but I'm not sure I'm ready."

"Okay." Disappointment seeped into her voice. "I hope you know you can tell me anything."

"I do, but that has never been my way, with the exception of Granny Eunice, of course."

"I hope at some point you'll feel comfortable enough to

talk to me freely."

"I will."

Though not convinced, she let it go and changed the subject. "I've been thinking...about the upcoming wedding you mentioned."

"Pauly and Angela."

"Yes. Maybe we should go."

"You can't be serious. Someone just tried to kill me! Whoever he worked for is still out there."

"Please just listen. I know it sounds reckless, but it would only be for the weekend. We'll be careful. Only Terry and Gabe will know where we're going."

"Mel, I can't just drop everything and fly off to Miami."

Melanie took Jon's hand. "I know you want to see your old friend get married. And you need to relax and recuperate. These last few days have been trying and dangerous." Sensing his skepticism, she added, "You—no, *we*—deserve a break."

Melanie's expression was solemn, sincere. Pleading. He ceased arguing.

Jon asked, "Are you sure about this?"

"Absolutely. I have airline points we can use."

"That's generous."

"Well, you know...I love you and all that."

Jon pulled her close. "What did I do to deserve you?"

"You donated a dollar to Haitian orphans."

"Best dollar I ever spent."

＊ ＊ ＊

Officer Sarah Barkin escorted her father into the precinct. They stood in Captain Johnson's open doorway.

"Excuse me, sir. My father is here," Sarah said, knocking politely on the door.

"Please come in."

Sarah was followed by a short, thin gray-haired man wearing a sweater vest and bifocals.

The captain stood, extending his hand. They shook and everyone took seats.

"Thank you for coming, Mr. Barkin. We hope your expertise might help with our investigation."

"Glad I could be of use. These days, I don't have a whole helluva lot going on."

"From what I hear, you're very knowledgeable in timepieces."

"Been around them my whole life. My pop was a big collector. Taught me everything I know."

The captain passed the evidence pouch to him, and Sarah gave him gloves.

"What can you tell us about this watch?" asked Captain Johnson.

Mr. Barkin took a magnifying glass, tiny tools and a table lamp out of his workbag. He cleared a place on the captain's desk, put down a clean cloth and put on the gloves. He picked up the watch, looked at it front and back. "May I open it?"

"Certainly."

With the agility of a seasoned craftsman, Mr. Barkin used the tools to open the back of the watch. Sarah couldn't help look over his shoulder. "Dad, what on earth is that?"

"That my dear, is a Wi-Fi receptor." It was wedged inside a tiny compartment. The captain and Sarah took turns with the magnifying glass.

The captain asked, "Is the backing material typical of old-time watches? It appears almost membrane-like."

"I've never seen anything like it."

Sarah asked, "Is this a smart watch?"

"Not one that I've ever seen before. With this receptor, it can't do any of the functions a smart watch could do. The Quantos name is not known to me and I've seen just about every make of watch out there." He looked up at his daughter and her boss. "Did you Google it?"

Sarah nodded. "Nothing came up."

Captain Johnson was befuddled. "In your opinion, what do you make of a Wi-Fi receptor inside a watch?"

"The only thing I can fathom, is that a signal could be sent to the watch from another location, remotely activating it to do something. Why would someone need another party controlling their watch?"

"That's the question of the day. Thank you, Mr. Barkin. You've been a tremendous help."

"Really? It seems I'm leaving you with more questions than you started with."

"Maybe so, but with more questions often come better answers. Sarah, why don't you take your dad out for lunch on the precinct?"

"Thank you, sir."

Officer Barkin left the office, her arm around her father's shoulders.

CHAPTER 44

University of Cincinnati

Niles Petrolli flung open his dorm room door, looking ready to bark at whomever was pounding on it. Donna put down her fist, sizing up the pimply, skinny teenager staring back at her. He was wearing noise-cancelling headphones around his neck and a pissed look on his face that quickly changed to confusion. His doorway was jammed with police officers two deep.

"What the—?"

Jim took the lead. "Is this Farad Jackson's room?"

The kid flipped greasy hair out of his eyes. "What's this about?"

"Kid, we asked you a question," Jim said in an authoritative tone.

"Can I see some ID?" He was scared but trying not to show it.

"What, all our gear isn't good enough?"

Donna didn't want to waste time on a testosterone showdown. It had been Jim's idea to come out in full force and scare the kid into coughing up everything he knew. "Jim, just show him." He pulled out his ID.

"Now, let's try again," said Jim. "Is this Farad's room?"

"Yeah. Can you at least give me a clue what happened? Is he okay?"

The kid was pushy, impressive given that five armed officers had eyes on him.

"We're asking the questions," said Jim. "We suggest you cooperate."

Donna moved past the kid into his dorm room, glancing at his computer. "Candygrams, huh? I'm not too bad at it myself."

"Really? You play?"

"Sure. But beware, it's addictive."

"I know, I've been playing for an hour nonstop."

Donna knew Jim didn't like the chitchat, but she laughed lightly. "What's your name?"

"Niles Petrolli. Farad's my roommate."

"Okay, Niles. I'm Donna. I'm sure you want to help us. Maybe you can fill us in on your roommate's activities."

"I don't know what he does."

If she was the good cop, Jim was the bad. He growled, "Withholding information could land you in serious trouble."

Donna thought he was laying it on a bit thick. If Jim didn't back off, the kid would shut down and ask for an attorney, which would slow down the process considerably.

"Seriously, Farad and I are not really friends."

"But you live with him," said Donna. "Tell us what you do know about him. Did he play sports? Spend a lot of time online?"

"He has a few friends that come by now and then. I think they're in the drama club."

Jim interjected. "Did he ever express sympathy for any terrorist organization?"

Niles eyes grew wide. "What? Should I be getting a lawyer?"

"Why? Are you involved in anything illegal?"

"No!"

Donna would need to have a conversation with Jim about his bedside manner. How he ever got anyone to willingly provide information was beyond her. She took over again. "Let's calm down."

She faced the assisting officers. "Guys, I think Jim and I have this. Why don't you take a break?" They didn't need to be asked twice. "We'll meet up with you at headquarters."

"With or without the kid?" one of Jim's men asked obnoxiously before leaving.

Niles' face paled. "I don't know how to help you." He paused, thinking intently. "Hey, you know, Farad keeps a calendar. Said writing stuff on it helps him remember what he has to do every day. Would that help?"

"Possibly," said Donna. "Where is it?"

"Behind his bed on the wall, next to the photos."

Pictures of Farad's family were taped to the wall above the bed. He looked like a normal teen, goofing around with what Donna assumed was an older brother. An old-fashioned calendar hung on a loose nail above the bed. Each month displayed a pro-shot of a different NFL team. December was Green Bay Packers. The grid was filled with Farad's schedule. Each Friday of the month had the same reminder penned in.

One entry was scribbled in for Saturday, the day of the would-be bombing. "Extra C.T. 8 a.m."

Donna took pictures of the calendar.

Niles spoke up. "He made lists of everything. His shopping lists, study notes, schedules, you name it. He told me he was trying to get more organized. I think he was getting help with that."

C. T. coincided with the marathon.

She turned to Niles. "Farad has C.T every Friday, and also this Saturday. Know what that is?"

"That's the program I was talking about. They're actually paying him. I would've done it too to make a few bucks, but didn't qualify."

"Why not?"

"'Cuz you have to have ABCD."

Jim asked, "ABCD. What's that?"

"Ya know, when you can't concentrate on stuff."

Donna got it. "He means ADHD."

"Yeah, that," said Niles. "Farad goes for treatments at the Psych office."

Donna looked at Jim, who said, "I'm on it." He got on his phone and called the guys who just left for lunch, telling them to find the Psych Department, and look into a therapy program for ADHD students.

"What does C.T. stand for?" Donna asked.

"Cure Theory," Niles answered with annoyance. "I'm still pissed they wouldn't accept me." He paused. "You guys done? I have a lot of studying to do."

Jim said, "More Candygrams?'

Niles shrugged.

CHAPTER 45

Dallas

J on had mixed feelings about being back home in Dallas. In a way, it felt comforting to get back to his routine, and catch up on missed schoolwork. But he also knew there was unfinished business out there. Carrera was the tip of the iceberg. With just over two weeks until Pauly's wedding, he still wasn't sure he made the right decision to attend it. But he had already committed and saw the positive change in Melanie's demeanor.

After a good night's sleep, he made a cup of coffee, went to his desk and checked his email. He had 2,178 unread messages. Most were junk but without the downtime to sift through and trash them, the number would just keep rising.

He found an email from Hernandez with the subject line, "For Your Eyes Only" and clicked it open. It read, "Good news. The FBI rep from LA is desperate to get the work done quickly on the ear sample. If you can confirm Dr. Lavi's immediate availability along with her credentials, we'll pull this off. Keep me posted. My Pulitzer awaits. -Ed."

A link was attached. There, Jon found a formal boilerplate request from the FBI Los Angeles Field Office for "Expedited Analysis." The name on the form for lead analyst was filled in —Dr. Theresa Lavi. Results were to be sent classified to an address in LA. All expenses would be reimbursed, and a hefty fee for service would be paid upon completion. A signature was required as an affidavit of agreement to the terms and laws of confidentiality. Once they reviewed her credentials and the form was signed and returned, the specimen would be shipped to Terry for examination.

Jon printed out the form and grabbed his car keys. He peeked out his window, establishing all was clear. It was a lot of work constantly looking to make sure no one was tailing him. The simple task of getting to his car had become stressful. Though he wasn't a fan of firearms, he was thankful when Gabe told him he'd bought a gun for protection.

After checking the brakes, Jon drove to Melanie's apartment. He dialed his phone while letting himself in with the key she'd copied for him. Melanie sat at her desk, working online. Seeing him on the phone, she blew him a silent kiss.

When the call was answered on the first ring, Jon said in sing-song, "Happy Birthday, Granny! How old are you now? Thirty-five?"

"Thank you, sweetheart. And yes, thirty-five...in dog years.""Seems someone sent me an all-expense paid trip to Foxwoods Resort and Casino for me and a friend of my choosing."

"Incredible. Who would send such an amazing gift?"

"Hmm. There's a postmark from Dallas with your zip code."

"Ha! Maybe you should be a private investigator."

"Sweetheart, it is generous of you but too expensive. I can't accept this."

"You have to. I can't return it. You're having a special birthday and I feel bad that I can't be there to celebrate with you. So have a good time with a friend, on me."

She relented. "Okay, I will. Thank you."

"You're welcome. So who will you take?"

"Shirley Donato. She's been so kind to me over the years. This time, I'll treat her. Oh, by the way, another small package came for you. Sorry I forgot to mention it last time we spoke. My memory's not what it used to be."

"Sure it is, Granny. Who's it from?"

"Looks like from the same address as the last one. The chemistry department in UNT."

Jon was stunned. Professor Breitler must have mailed it before his death.

"Granny, this is very important. Please put the package somewhere safe and don't mention it to anyone. You haven't already, have you?"

"No, why would I?"

"Good. Can you go tomorrow and overnight it to my post office box? But be careful."

"What's going on, Jonny?"

"Everything's fine."

"Doesn't sound like it, but I'll do as you ask. You should have it by the day after next."

"Thanks. I'll call you soon."

"I look forward to it. Love to Melanie."

They signed off and Jon let out a long sigh. "Oh God."

"What was that all about?" Melanie asked.

"You're not going to believe this."

❃ ❃ ❃

Jon unlocked his post office box and set aside the FedEx envelope, separating it from the junk mail. It was strange and sad to receive a package from a dead man. He tore it open along the familiar emblem, retrieving the enclosed flashdrive and attached post-it note. In cat-scratch penmanship, it read, "Fascinating!" "Be careful with this data!" "Only my toy can do it!" "Keep me posted!" "Good luck!" Clearly, the professor had been a fan of pithy sayings and exclamation points. Jon pocketed the flashdrive and note and called Gabe.

"Ready for this one?" he announced as soon as Gabe answered his call. Before Gabe could reply, he continued. "I got another flashdrive from the professor."

"Creepy. Must be he found more info."

"That's what I was thinking. Let's meet where we used to go after lab on Thursday nights and we can look at it together"

"Sounds like a plan. I can be there in thirty minutes."

"See you then."

* * *

It felt cloak-and-dagger meeting Gabe on a chilly December afternoon on a park bench looking out on the basketball courts. For nearly a year they had come here to catch a pick-up game and play off their excess energy after studying all week.

Jon thought it fitting that he was wearing his dad's old trenchcoat, one of the few articles of clothing he had from him. It was out of fashion, but Jon loved wearing his dad's clothes and would never get rid of this coat. For the full effect, he pulled up the collar when approaching Gabe.

When Gabe spotted Jon, he immediately picked up on the espionage vibe. Casually, he lifted a discarded newspaper left behind on the bench and shielded his face with it.

"Think we'll ever grow up?" Jon asked as he sat beside his friend, getting out his laptop.

"Hope not." Despite the gravity of their situation, they laughed.

"Okay, let's see what the good professor found out," Jon said, shifting closer to Gabe to see the screen.

"You ready for this? Another step deeper in the muck?"

"No turning back now."

Jon powered up the computer and inserted the flashdrive. A request for a password popped up. Dismayed, he said, "No way. Why would he install password protection without telling us what it is?"

"Maybe he intended to but never got the chance."

"Know anyone who's good at hacking?"

"Hold up. Maybe he picked a password he knew we'd guess."

"The spy thing is really getting a hold of you."

"It's worth a shot. How about "Melanie?"

"Sounds too easy, but let's try." Jon typed in her name and was denied entry. "We could be here all day, trying things. For a guy who used so many colloquialisms, you think he would've sent the password as well."

"What are you talking about?"

Jon pulled out the crumpled post-it note from his pocket. "This was attached to the flashdrive."

"Wow, the good professor wasn't the most eloquent man ever...but hey, wait a minute. What does he mean by, *only my toy can do it?* Seems a strange thing to put on a sticky note."

"He was extremely proud of the TR-X machine. Called it his toy. When we had the Skype call with him before Thanksgiving, I had to keep redirecting him to talk about data results, and not the new equipment. That machine was his baby."

"Then let's work with that. What does TR-X stand for?"

"No idea."

"Google it."

Jon typed *TR-X lab equipment* in the search bar, then read the first result. "The Titanium Radioactive X edition is a state-of-the-art analyzer used by geneticists to map chromosomal attributes of all living matter by employing precise radioactive wave technology."

Gabe interrupted him. "Okay, let's try TR-X."

"It's too short to be a password."

"Then titanium."

"Okey-dokey." He tried it. No luck.

They made several more unsuccessful attempts.

Gabe said, "We need to look at this from another angle." They sat quietly thinking. Gabe asked, "Does TR-X sound to you like T-Rex?"

"I suppose it does, now that you mention it. Professor Breitler kept a toy dinosaur on his desk. It was visible throughout our webcam conversation."

Gabe lit up. "That's it...dinosaur!"

"Bit of a stretch."

"If it was easy to figure out, it wouldn't be a good password. Only you and Mel saw that toy. Try it."

Jon typed *dinosaur*. The file opened.

Gabe jumped up, cheering as if his team won the World Series.

"That was awesome!" said Jon.

Gabe took one more victorious leap, fist bumped his friend, then settled back down. "Okay, we're in. Let's see what the professor went to such pains to protect."

✻ ✻ ✻

Breaking the password code proved the easier part of the job. The flashdrive held three files. The first was a series of formulas and chromosomal maps. Both men were familiar with chemical formulae and advanced math, but these calculations were new to them.

"We're going to need help with this," Gabe said.

"Terry comes to mind."

"True, but might I remind you that we lied about destroying the first flashdrive. Not sure how well she'll take the news we've been holding out on her."

"We did it to keep her and the others safe. No culpability if the Feds—or anyone else—questions them."

"I'm not certain she'll see it that way. Terry does not like feeling manipulated. Take it from someone who knows."

"I guess you'll just have to find the best way to tell her and ask for her help deciphering this mess."

"Great. And just when I was starting to grow on her."

"Want to attempt the second document?"

"Sure, what's another hour sitting outside in freezing temperatures?"

"Your Southerner is showing."

"Your Northerner is too."

The men huddled closer and Jon clicked open the second file.

* * *

"Where have you guys been? Terry and I were getting worried." Melanie asked as the two men entered Gabe's apartment.

Two hours had gone by since Gabe met Jon at the park. They were astonished at what the professor had unearthed and were no longer second-guessing the circumstances of his death. Someone wanted him dead to keep the information from getting out.

Gabe subconsciously felt for his gun holster. He'd been wearing it wherever he went. With Donna back in Boston, he was the group's full-time protector and took the job seriously. When the women went out, he'd be with them.

The men wanted to ease into the conversation as smoothly as possible. Gabe agreed to let Jon do most of the talking.

Melanie and Terry appeared dubious when asked to sit. "What's happened?" said Melanie.

Jon said, "I'll start with the email I just received. A third sample, one from the LA attack, will be available if you, Terry, are willing to analyze it for the FBI in an expedited manner. If you locate traces of Chrysanthemum Exotic, there can be no doubt of a conspiracy."

"How'd you pull that off?" asked Melanie.

"Long story, but your dad's connections made it possible. We'll just need to send them Terry's credentials *asap*."

Terry said, "I'm on leave from my job so I have nothing but time. Tell your contact I will do it. If the UNT lab is available, I can work there."

Melanie said, "I'll arrange that for you."

Jon handed Terry the forms. She glanced over them and signed.

"There's more," Jon said. "Mel, remember I told you the professor sent a second package to Granny's house?"

"Yes."

Gabe took over. "It was another flashdrive."

"Incredible," said Terry. "After all we went through to get rid of the first one, there's another."

"That's part of what we need to discuss with both of you." Gabe continued as Jon evasively looked away. "This flashdrive had three documents on it. The first will need to be deciphered by you, Terry. It's a series of complicated algorithms and chromosomal maps."

"Let me have a look."

"Before we get to that, you should both know there were two other files. The second file contains detailed medical profiles of the two bombers, Abadi and Capaletto, which we should go over carefully for commonalities. Mel, will you be able to take that on?"

"Sure."

"Great," said Gabe. "The third and final document is a history of Chrysanthemum Exotic, including its potential effects. We should start there. You'll both find it informative. The last thing we need to tell you before reviewing the file ..." He looked at Jon who gave a small nod. Gabe continued "We weren't fully honest with you."

Melanie and Terry leaned in closer, brows knit.

"Oh?" Terry asked in a clipped tone.

"In a sincere effort at keeping you both safe and believably unaware should you be questioned, we told you that we destroyed the samples and first flashdrive with the initial Chrysanthemum Exotic results. In fact, we did not. We kept them hidden."

Melanie looked annoyed while Terry shook her head in disappointment. Her demeanor changed from conciliatory to wary.

"I hope you're not mad," said Gabe. "Understand, Terry, that besides doing my best to keep you safe after what happened in Israel, we couldn't allow anyone to believe we were still in possession of the data and specimens, as they would've been confiscated. And telling Donna would've been problematic. She'd be torn between her job and her friendship with us."

Melanie stayed quiet, mulling it over.

"I'm not angry," said Terry, even as her tone sounded contrary. "But once again, I am disappointed in your choices, especially those involving me. I am a respected scientist, more than accustomed to taking care of myself. After all we've been through, you had no right to keep us in the dark."

"We realize that now and apologize," Jon tossed in.

Melanie said, "At least their motivations were pure. Chivalrous even."

"I don't need a knight in shining armor to rescue me," said Terry. "But since I want to bring these murderers to justice, I will help with the analysis. After that, I will immediately be returning home."

Gabe was stunned. "What if they come after you again?"

"I'm not one to live in fear."

"That seems to be a bigger risk than you should be taking," said Jon.

"It's my risk, for which I will take precautions. I don't want to discuss this any further. Melanie, would you be so kind as to help me find other accommodations for the remaining time I need to be here in the States?"

"What do you mean?" said Gabe. "You can stay here. I'll give you all the privacy you want."

"No, thank you. Melanie?"

"Um, sure. You can stay at my apartment. One of the beds is available. It's not as luxurious as here, but it's a place to sleep and get work done."

"Thank you. It's all I will need." She eyed the men. "I lived on a military base for two years so I'm certain it will exceed those accommodations."

Gabe was speechless.

Jon tried to smooth things over. "All right then, since we don't want you walking around with the data in hand, you'll need to review them here. No copies should be made or emailed. Agreed?"

Melanie said "Yes, agreed." They turned to look at Terry. She was still hot under the collar, but after a moment offered a reluctant, "Agreed."

* * *

Melanie read Professor Breitler's research aloud. "Chrysanthemum Exotic grows only in a few areas deep within the Amazon rainforest. The plant was used by indigenous Indians in rituals as a meditation-inducing ointment. When applied, an Amazonian was given directions to carry out certain religious rites. The tribes were vegetarians and meat was considered holy, similar to Eastern Indian culture. To slaughter an animal was antithetical to their conventional belief system. However, after applying Chrysanthemum Exotic, the users repeatedly did so, without question or hesitation, forgetting these deeds when the drug wore off.

"In the 1950s, twenty Canadian members of a religious cult, followers of a man many believed delusional, went on retreat to northeastern Peru. Ten days after they were expected back, they were found by a search party in a remote part of the rainforest, all dead, apparently by their own hand. Each follower had an oily substance on his arm—a residue of Chrysanthemum Exotic." Melanie finished reading and looked up at the others.

"What do you make of it?" asked Gabe.

"Remarkable," said Terry. "I've never heard of anything like this. A drug with the ability to compel its users to engage in actions completely out of character, even contrary to their moral code."

Melanie added, "It sounds like a morose fairytale."

Jon said animatedly, "Think about it. The user can be forced to do another's bidding. What if a criminal mastermind is somehow manipulating unsuspecting people into carrying out terrorist activities on his behalf?"

Melanie and Terry looked shocked.

Terry asked Gabe, "Do you think Carrera was one of the manipulated?"

"Good question. I don't know."

"But Donna might," she said. "They probably did an autopsy on him."

"We need to bring her in on this and let her decide what to do with this new information."

Terry nodded. "Definitely. This needs to be brought to the attention of the authorities. At this point, mistrust of them is nothing short of dangerous."

No one missed the jibe at Gabe. He said, "Okay, let's call her."

Jon dialed Donna's personal line and got her voicemail.

"It's me. Please call as soon as you get this message." He hung up, hoping they were doing the right thing.

* * *

Boston

Donna was on the phone with Jim when Jon called. They'd been speaking nearly every day for the past week. It began as work-related conversations—when he first called to say Carrera's hair came back negative for drug use. But more personal anecdotes slowly seeped into their late-night talks. Both seemed to enjoy the development. Donna didn't recall Jim as a sensitive man, but he clearly had evolved over the years and she found herself increasingly attracted to him.

"Any regrets moving out of Boston?" Donna asked lying on her sofa, the television muted on the HSN channel.

"Some," he answered, his voice husky. "Mostly about my lost friendships."

Donna felt her heart skip a beat. *Was he referring to her?* "Columbus can't be so bad."

"It's all right, but you can't compare it to Boston. For one, there's no ocean."

"I suppose there's not much you can do about that."

"I've meant to get back east more often, but work's been crazy...for the last three years."

She laughed. "I know how you feel."

"I have lots of vacation days coming to me but never seem to find the right time to use them."

"New Year's is around the corner. Why not use your vacation days then? The fireworks show in Boston will be something special this year."

"They still doing that over the harbor?"

"You bet. A few of us on the force are getting together to ring in the New Year. We rented a cruiser to take out on the water. We'll have a sideline view of the show."

"Sounds incredible. I love boating."

It was one of her favorite pastimes as well. Donna decided to take a risk. "Why don't you come? You'll be my guest."

"That's some invitation but—"

Donna felt the rejection coming. "If you have other plans, it's fine."

"Not at all. I was going to say, I'll only come if I can get you alone for a few hours."

Donna wasn't sure she heard him correctly. She sat up straight. "Wh-what?"

"I'm not sure if it's wise to say this now but I've always regretted leaving town before we could see if we had something real together. It was going so well. I've often wondered if you were the one that got away."

It was the last thing she expected him to say. She blurted out, "I feel exactly the same way."

"What a relief. I can't believe I put myself out there like that…and that you did too. Let's do it… Skip the boat. It'll be just the two of us, ringing in the New Year together."

Overjoyed, she said, "I'll bring the champagne."

* * *

Donna was still on cloud nine when she picked up Jon's message. Before returning his call, she closed her eyes, and laying her head against the sofa's chenille pillow, basked in the excitement that comes with a blossoming relationship. It had been a long time since she'd been on a proper date. She'd buy a new dress and heels. Jim was a terrific guy, someone she could imagine a possible future with. But now she had to get back to reality. She called Jon back.

"Hey Jon, how are you doing?"

"You sound cheerful."

"I'm in a good mood. What's the vital information you wanted to share?"

"You better get comfortable because there's a lot to tell

you. And I may as well apologize now because I can assure you what I have to say will ruin your good mood."

It was fun while it lasted, Donna thought. "Bring it on."

As he filled her in on Professor Breitler's package, countless dark thoughts crossed her mind. Using Chrysanthemum Exotic, the potential for great tragedy was mind-blowing.

Jon fell silent.

"Listen Jon, this has become much bigger than you originally thought. It's no longer just a thesis paper."

"What do you suggest we do? I don't want to turn to the wrong people for help."

Donna wasn't sure how to guide him. "You've told me that you trust me. Is that still the case?"

"Yes, of course."

"Good. I'll talk to you later." And with that she hung up, and made another call. To Special Agent Doug Matthews.

* * *

FBI Regional Office
Dallas

Matthews was livid. Steadman was a never-ending thorn in his side. If it weren't for Donna's negotiating skills, he would have sent someone over to arrest the sonofabitch for obstruction of justice. *Not to mention playing Russian roulette with my career.*

Once he calmed down, he agreed to Donna's terms— not to prosecute Jon, and to keep the information he'd be given close to the vest. Matthews would confide it only to his superiors and the team of men and women who worked directly with him at the Dallas office. He could vouch for them. In return, he got full access to whatever Steadman found out. If he wanted to get ahead, this was the only way. The agreement would stand, provided Steadman didn't pull any dirty tricks again. If he tried, all bets were off. Matthews would go after him with everything he had.

CHAPTER 46

University of North Texas

J on, Gabe and Terry waited in the hallway outside the chemistry department office. With the help of Dr. Lewitis, the interim professor who stepped in for the late Professor B., Melanie had arranged for uninterrupted use of the laboratory through winter break. She was inside getting the keys from Martin.

It was two long weeks since Terry had signed the paperwork. A delay in obtaining a release from the killer's family had pushed everything back. While the others used the time to focus on their schoolwork, Terry anxiously awaited her return to Israel.

Melanie joined them in the hallway, a key ring dangling from her finger, which she entrusted to Terry. "Martin is devastated. He said Dr. B. often shared his research ideas with him, but over the last few days before his death he became more secretive. Martin never found out what he was working on."

Jon said, "Lucky thing for him Professor B. kept his mouth shut. It probably saved Martin's life."

* * *

In Gabe's opinion, the machine looked like something out of a sci-fi film. It consisted of three panels, each the size of a shower door, its surface was made of the same element as a smartphone screen. The only other embellishments were two small engraved metal panels that read "TR-X," and below it, "Genesis Corp."

Gabe, Jon and Melanie watched as Terry donned a white lab coat, goggles and gloves. Locating the switch, she turned on the machine. A low hum filled the room, along with a quickening vibration.

From the freezer, Terry retrieved a box labeled "Human Remains. Biohazard. Handle with Care." Her name was on the sealed package with the UNT address. It had been sent from the Los Angeles Medical Examiner's office.

She laid the package on the stainless table. Breaking the seal, she took out a small plastic container surrounded by dry ice. Inside was a tiny piece of cartilage, a section of an earlobe, with a woman's faux diamond stud attached. Using miniature tweezers, Terry took out the lobe, positioned it in a petri dish, and placed it on the shelf fixed inside the TR-X's triad of panels. She swiped the screen in front of her—causing the machine to close around the specimen—and continued tapping and swiping, creating the desired settings for testing. Several laser beams were directed at the dish, which began turning as if in a microwave.

"Radioactive and magnetic waves are penetrating the sample," said Terry. "Within several hours, it will produce a detailed chromosomal map of the earlobe, providing extensive information about the Y bomber's medical history, predispositions, sexual tendencies, as well as other data points. Once I have that, I can isolate the gene associated with the Chrysanthemum Exotic found in the other two samples and see if it's present here as well."

"Fascinating," said Melanie. "The advances made in the field of genetics over the last decade are truly remarkable."

"None of you need to stay here," said Terry. "I have at least another half hour of paperwork before I can leave and you must all be tired."

"We're not leaving you here alone," said Gabe.

Terry looked annoyed. "I'll be fine."

"He's right," Jon said. "There's no point in taking unnecessary risks."

"Okay," Terry conceded. "I'll try to finish as quickly as possible." She went to the adjacent room, sat at the desk and began typing on the computer. Thirty minutes later she emerged with her workbag over her shoulder. "I'm done for now. The machine will continue working overnight. I'll come back tomorrow to finish up."

The foursome left, Terry bringing up the rear, and locking the lab door behind her.

* * *

"They have more information." The Boss was seated on a silk-lined chaise overlooking the snow-covered city, a martini in hand, a rolled-up newspaper nearby. "The Event is quickly approaching, and warnings have gotten us nowhere. They need to be stopped once and for all."

The subordinate was one of the elite permitted direct dealings with the Boss, both an honor and a responsibility. "I don't have another professional ready at this point to take care of them."

"Find another Carrera or do it yourself."

"I can't afford to get my hands dirty now. But come to think of it, I have just the person in mind. One of our successful trial students."

The Boss raised the chilled cocktail both as an acknowledgement and a dismissal. "Spare me the details. Just get it done."

CHAPTER 47

Dallas

"You do realize Gabe has feelings for you?" Melanie asked Terry as she pushed closed her carry-on bag, sitting on it. The men would be picking them up shortly, allowing Terry a few hours at the lab before Mel and Jon headed to the airport and sunny Florida.

"Maybe so, but they are not mutual," Terry replied without conviction.

Melanie jumped off the luggage and eyed Terry. "If I may be so bold, that's not the vibe you've been giving off."

"Any feelings I may have had for him have faded. He is a nice man but too provincial for my tastes."

Melanie wasn't buying it for a second, but there was no point in forcing the issue. She had offered for Terry to remain at her place while she went to Miami with Jon, and Terry graciously accepted.

On the way to the lab, Melanie watched the freeze-out. Gabe made several attempts at conversation with Terry but was met with one-word answers. When they arrived, Terry unlocked the lab door and immediately got to work.

Jon felt bad for Gabe. Terry was giving him the cold shoulder. Icy cold. He took a seat between Gabe and Melanie, watching as Terry approached the TR-X machine, tapped the screen, and then waited. Within minutes, a printer in the corner of the room spat out a lengthy printout. "I should have a readable report ready for the FBI by the end of the weekend," she said.

"How soon until you can share results with us?" Jon asked.

Terry sat down abruptly and sighed. "I've given this serious thought. Disclosing the data to you would be a direct violation of the contract I signed with the LAPD. In order to do the testing, I bound myself to their terms of confidentiality."

Jon couldn't believe what he was hearing. "Isn't that why we're all here and why you agreed to do the testing?"

"I agreed because they were in a bind and needed an expert who could do the job quickly to move along an important investigation."

The others exchanged glances, confused.

Gabe said, "We would never want you to jeopardize your professional ethics. But we need to know at the very least if there's a match with the other two samples regarding Chrysanthemum Exotic and if any other unexpected commonalities are discovered."

Jon was distressed at Terry's change of heart. All the legwork to get the sample and arrange to have Terry analyze it would be wasted if she didn't share her findings.

Terry shook her head. "I'm sorry."

"What about the ethics involved in bringing these killers to justice?" Jon retorted. "And in keeping us safe?"

"That's a job for the FBI, not for us."

"The FBI doesn't even know what Chrysanthemum Exotic is capable of," said Jon.

"It may be time to tell them," she persisted.

Exasperated, he said, "We've discussed this. Once we share this information, we lose control of it. If it gets into the wrong hands, we'll have made the situation exponentially worse, putting our lives in even greater danger. That's why we contacted Donna, as a way of containing the situation while still working to solve it. It worked for catching Carrera, and hopefully will work again to bring down his bosses."

"I'm sorry," Terry repeated. "I'm not comfortable with all

this."

Melanie said, "Look, we don't have to decide anything right now. Terry, maybe you can think things over. Jon and I will be back Sunday. We can reconvene then and figure out the best course of action. In the meantime, Terry, you need to complete the analysis anyway."

Jon looked like he had more of an argument to make, but trusted Melanie to size up Terry's disposition. She had amazing intuition, and he didn't want to risk alienating Terry even more. "I'm cool with that. How about you, Gabe?"

"Sure, let's do that. Terry, where will you be staying while Melanie and Jon are out of town? You're still welcome to stay with me."

"I'll be fine at Melanie's until I leave."

"When do you expect that to be?"

"After I submit my report."

Jon could tell that Gabe was distraught, but Gabe kept his voice even as he said to Terry, "All right. Let's make the best of the time you have left."

CHAPTER 48

Miami Beach, Florida
New Year's Eve

T he Alexander Hotel had been an architectural main-
stay of Miami Beach for the last six decades. The
gilded edifice colored the fifty-sixth block of Collins
Avenue with its pink façade, overlooking the yacht pier on the
Intracoastal Waterway. Mercedes convertibles, Lamborghinis
and Bentleys took turns parading slowly down the palm-lined
stretch. The hotel had been renovated within the last two
years, but the sweeping spiral staircase, the centerpiece of
the wood-lined lobby remained, staying true to its origins by
maintaining the fine balance between art deco and old world
elegance.

Jon and Melanie had checked in the night before. Festivities
would begin in late afternoon with a poolside cocktail hour,
followed by a sunset ceremony and reception.

They woke up early, eager to make the most of their time.
They rode rented bikes around South Beach, stopping for
drinks on Ocean Drive, and ice cream in a cute shop in Lin-
coln Mall. Returning to the hotel, they walked hand-in-hand
through the airy lobby and out the back exit to the boardwalk. Tropical flowers in dense foliage framed the walkway.

Jon observed the beach filled with sun worshippers, sand-
castle builders, and seashell collectors. His mind went to Ash-

leigh and the Caribbean honeymoon that never came to pass. "These people have no clue of the evil lurking in this world."

Melanie stopped walking, frowning at the comment. "I'm also deeply concerned about the terrorist threat. We'll see what Terry's research yields. The timing may be lousy, but I appreciate you agreeing to this trip. We both needed it." She looked out on the ocean, leaning on the wood railing. A stream of joggers angled by them in both directions. "I love it here. The tropical feel, everyone happy and healthy looking."

Jon remained somber, pensive.

Softly she asked, "Did you go to the beach as a child? Take family trips?"

Jon was caught off guard. He wasn't ready to speak of his childhood. He'd hoped this would be a vacation from the insanity. All of it. But somehow his problems followed him wherever he went.

"No, we didn't go away much," he said curtly.

"So how did you spend your summers? Camp?"

"There was no money for that. I stayed home and played with other kids that did the same."

"You must have good memories of that."

"I guess."

Melanie seemed to catch the vibe and changed tacks. "How long have you known Pauly?"

Jon breathed an internal sigh of relief. *Easier territory.* "We met in grade school, and then later went to the same college."

"You mean BTI?"

"Yes, that's right."

"He must be very bright, too."

"Pauly has the brains *and* the bucks. His father owns a large corporation in Boston and is priming him to take the reins one day."

"What sort of business?"

"I'm not really sure. He bought it after Pauly and I parted ways. From what little I know, it was a declining company. He renamed it, brought in new leadership, turning it around."

"Sounds like an impressive man."

"Don't know about that, but he sure is business savvy. Haven't seen him in years."

"What about Pauly? Did he have any girlfriends before Angela?"

"Many. He even had his eye on Ash-." Jon caught himself. *Please stop.*

"Were you going to say Ashleigh? Isn't that who you were calling for in your dream? You were yelling for her to run."

Feeling lightheaded, Jon knew he needed to quickly end the conversation. "Look, Mel, I'm sorry but I'm not comfortable with this topic."

As if she didn't hear him, Melanie asked, "Is that why you and Pauly had a falling out? Over a girl?"

Jon let go of Melanie's hand. "I can't do this. I'm going back to the hotel to get ready for the wedding. I'll see you there." And with that he walked away, Melanie staring dumbfounded at his quickly retreating back.

* * *

When Melanie returned to their hotel room to dress for the wedding, Jon wasn't there. She was distraught at his reaction to her questions, things she had wanted to ask him for so long but sensed he was avoiding. She reminded herself they had enjoyed a wonderful day, and that couples sometimes argue. That was normal. But it poked the back of her mind. *This is not normal. Something is wrong. Is he still in love with Ashleigh? Why won't he talk about her?*

Melanie would apologize for upsetting Jon, though she wasn't clear what she'd done wrong. It was important not to let the situation fester. Once they were back in Dallas and things settled down, they would have a serious conversation. No relationship could progress if one person had to walk on eggshells. Jon was as closed off as a No Trespassing sign, and that was no way to build something together. But right now, Melanie would forget all that.

She brushed out her hair, carefully applied her makeup and put on a flowy bright blue beach dress matching her eyes and beaded sandals. She sprayed her favorite perfume into the air and glided through it. A glance at the clock told her she needed to get downstairs. The festivities were about to begin. She grabbed her clutch and left the room.

* * *

The pool area was closed off to the public. Stringed lights provided an elegant touch. Milling the area were about fifty people, dressed in casual but expensive attire, champagne glasses in hand. Hors d'oeuvres were offered by black-tied waiters while soft music played from hidden speakers. It was the perfect day for a wedding—puffy white clouds painted onto a deep azure canvas of sky, and a soft breeze floating off the ocean. Melanie took an offered glass of Asti, wondering where Jon was.

An attractive dark-haired woman laden with diamonds and dressed to the nines approached her. "Welcome. I'm Jasmine Hendrix, Paul's stepmother. And who might you be?"

"Melanie Ridgefield. It's a pleasure to meet you, Senator Hendrix."

"Please call me Jasmine." She smiled, extending a bejeweled hand. "How do you know the happy couple?"

"I'm here with Jon Steadman, a friend of Pauly's."

"Of course. We're so glad some of Paul's friends came down to be here on this special day."

"Jon was delighted to be invited." She looked around. "What a beautiful setting for a wedding."

"Yes, I agree. We wanted to give Paul and Angela the wedding they dreamed of." She scanned the area. "Where's Jon? I haven't seen him in years."

"*That* is a good question. I was wondering that myself."

"Let's hope you find him before the ceremony," said Senator Hendrix.

"I'm sure I will." Melanie changed the subject. "I understand that you're involved in various charities."

"I try to help where I can."

"I would love to discuss your work. I'm interested in becoming more involved in non-profits and philanthropy."

"It would be my pleasure, Melanie. Perhaps we could find a few minutes while you're in town to sit and chat."

"That sounds wonderful."

Senator Hendrix caught the eye of a distinguished man in his late fifties. "Excuse me, dear. I should continue my rounds. We'll talk soon." The senator walked on.

Within seconds, a young man—with whitened teeth, dressed in a flashy Armani light beige suit, open-collar button-down, and pretentious leather mules—took Senator Hendrix's place beside Melanie.

"I couldn't help but notice the most beautiful woman at the party," he cooed.

Melanie blushed, uncomfortable with the opening line. "Thank you."

"You are most welcome. Are you on the bride or groom's side?"

"The groom's. And you?"

"It so happens that the bride is my younger sister. Allow me to introduce myself, Sean Mulraney."

"Pleasure to meet you."

He extended his hand. "And you are…?"

"She's Melanie, my girlfriend." Melanie wasn't sure where Jon materialized from but was grateful he had showed up just in time.

"Jon? How long's it been?" asked Sean, annoyed at the interruption.

"Not long enough, Sean. I see you're still in rare form."

Ogling Melanie from head to toe with stops on the way

down, Sean said, "Looks like you hit the winning numbers again. Care to share your secret?"

"And why would I do that?"

"To help an old friend."

"We were never friends."

"Jon!" Melanie said in a loud whisper, incredulous at his rude behavior, particularly at a wedding *and* to the bride's brother, no less. It was then that she realized he smelled of alcohol. "Why don't we find our seats for the ceremony? It was a pleasure meeting you, Sean."

"The pleasure was all mine. If you should ever tire of Jon, please look me up."

Jon looked livid. Before he could respond or pull a punch, Melanie steered him to the organza-covered folding chairs. They were arranged in rows on a wooden beach platform overlooking the ocean.

The sun would soon begin its descent. Melanie and Jon were the first to find their seats, the other guests still socializing near the pool.

"Sorry about that," Jon said with slightly slurred speech. "I never liked that guy."

"Are you okay?"

"Yeah, fine, just fine."

"I'm sorry about what happened earlier," Melanie said. "Let's try to have a good time."

"I'm sorry too. I shouldn't have walked away like that."

"Apology accepted." She took his hand and they sat quietly as other guests began to fill the chairs.

An officiant took his place at the front. Senator Hendrix and a fit, severe-looking man in his sixties—Melanie assumed he was Pauly's father—took their seats in the front row. A harp began to play, quieting the crowd. Pauly appeared at the back, and walked slowly down the aisle, a determined look on his face. He stopped beside the officiant.

Next was Sean, Pauly's best man. As he walked past, he made full eye contact with Melanie. She felt Jon's body go rigid with anger beside her. Once Sean reached the front, he turned left, found his chair and sat.

The harp was silenced and a string quartet began playing "Here Comes the Bride." The bride was lovely, escorted down the aisle by her parents. She resembled Sean. Her face shone with emotion and joy, emanating true happiness. Pauly broke out into a wide grin, his eyes drawing her closer to him. Melanie teared up as she always did when witnessing unbridled love.

Jon looked over at her and squeezed her hand. "I'm sorry, Mel. I don't deserve you."

The non-denominational ceremony was touching, the vows short but meaningful. When the service was over, Pauly twirled Angela around and backwards, kissing her deeply. Everyone laughed and applauded. Hand in hand, they ran down the aisle and disappeared from view.

The guests were invited to the reception hall, a room adorned with elegant crystal chandeliers and colorful tropical flowers. The dance floor was surrounded by round tables bedecked in white satin tablecloths and fine bone china. The bride and groom table sat directly across from the stage, a smaller table displaying the wedding cake alongside it.

Melanie and Jon were seated with Connor and his girl-friend, Candace. A salad of mixed greens was served while they made small talk.

When the band picked up, Melanie turned to see the newly-weds enter the hall, taking their place in the center of the dance floor. One of the singers announced, "Ladies and gentlemen, for the very first time, Mr. and Mrs. Paul Hendrix." Everyone clapped enthusiastically. "The happy couple would like to perform a dance for their guests. Please enjoy."

The band began to play the theme song from *Dirty Dancing*. Pauly and Angela nailed the routine. Melanie was enthralled. When they were done, the guests were invited to join the couple on the dance floor.

Jon stood, putting his hand out for Melanie. She accepted,

and he proceeded to lead her in a slow dance. She finally felt right again. The last few hours had been upsetting, not to mention the last few weeks. So much had happened in such a short time.

Since Melanie had met Jon, they'd grown close, spent the holidays together, witnessed a murder, discovered possible terrorist activity, and now were here in Miami Beach dancing the night away. Like a rollercoaster. Who could blame Jon or anyone else for strange behavior? Melanie spent the next two dances in the moment, enjoying the feel of Jon's breath on her cheek, his sweet nothings, and the glide of their smooth, coordinated movements.

The guests were asked to take their seats for dinner service, which consisted of prime beef, scalloped potatoes and wild rice. Before dessert was served, the lead singer announced that the couple wished to address their guests. Pauly rose from his seat, accepting the mic handed to him.

"First of all, thank you to our parents for giving us the wedding of our dreams. Angela and I are humbled that all of you chose to spend your New Year's holiday with us here in Miami Beach. Many of you have come long distances to witness our marriage. It means the world to us." He paused taking a deep breath. "I would like to single out one old friend in particular. We've lost touch over recent years, which is why I am so happy to see him here tonight. He and I went through the tragedy of the BTI bombing side by side, barely escaping the flames with our lives. This friend demonstrated the meaning of selfless heroism that day. He was badly injured but ran back to the burning building to try and save the woman he loved. When he lost her, we all grieved. Because of him, I have learned how to love deeply and wholly," Pauly said, tears glistening in his eyes as he gazed at his bride.

The guests were clearly touched, several women dabbing at their eyes. Regrouping, Pauly continued. "But today, my heart is full knowing he has found true love again. Thank you, Jon." He raised his glass.

Melanie's jaw dropped. She was stunned. Pauly was looking directly at *her* Jon, who was white as a sheet and glassy-eyed.

Pauly cleared his throat. "As a thank you to all our guests, we've arranged a spectacular fireworks show preceded by the countdown to the New Year. Please make sure you have your significant other nearby at midnight. I certainly will." Pauly looked adoringly at his bride.

Melanie looked back at Jon. He was gone. Again.

CHAPTER 49

Miami Beach

Melanie decided not to look for Jon. He obviously didn't want to be around anyone. Including her. Besides, she needed to process what Pauly had just disclosed.

Candace, Connor's girlfriend, noticed Jon's absence and intuited that something was up, engaging Melanie in idle conversation about her job. Melanie appreciated the distraction. She ate dessert, a generous slice of chocolate mousse cake. Empty glass in hand, she stood for a refill, when Sean stopped by.

"May I walk you to the bar?"

Not wanting to deal with his not-so-subtle overtures, she replied, "Come to think of it, I probably shouldn't have anymore."

Sean smirked, his thoughts written on his face. "Then at least allow me a dance."

"Well—"

"Not even for the lonely brother of the bride? Please."

Melanie couldn't think of a good enough reason to decline. "Why not?"

Sean guided her to the dance floor, placing his hand firmly on her back. He was a good dancer but tried to draw her closer than she was comfortable with. She stepped back a bit, waiting for the music to end.

Sean didn't seem to notice her discomfort. "Nice what Pauly said about Jon. I always thought it was weird that the two people closest to Ashleigh—besides Gabe of course—lost touch."

"Ashleigh was Gabe's sister?"

"Yes, that's right. From your question, I surmise Jon has maintained his ever-close-lipped stance on all things personal. He's always been like that, even in high school. Feel free to ask me anything. I'm at your service."

She wasn't sure she liked the sound of that. "I'm not sure if Jon would want me to know."

"It's common knowledge, at least in Boston. I wouldn't be divulging anything that you couldn't find online in seconds."

Melanie considered he had a valid point. She knew exactly where to begin. "What happened with the three of them at BTI?"

Sean told her about the BTI killing spree.

"Yes, I know all about it. I saw the memorial when I visited the campus."

"Did you also know that Jon was the last one out the door before the place exploded. He got knocked unconscious. He tried to go back inside for Ashleigh. Took all of Pauly's two hundred pounds to restrain him, even with Jon's broken bones."

Melanie was mortified.

"Didn't you wonder where he got his limp?" asked Sean.

"I did but was hesitant to ask. I figured he'd get around to telling me eventually."

"Not Jon. He wouldn't have ever said a word. Seems the explosion threw him a good distance, lifted him straight off the ground and he landed wrong. Took months of rehab to arrive at how you know him today."

Melanie didn't know what to make of it.

"The guy always rubbed me the wrong way and it's mutual for sure. But I always felt a little bad for him. Growing up without parents and then losing his fiancée."

His fiancée?

"Word is he experiences occasional PTSD, post traumatic stress disorder—like what veterans experience after coming home from war. You know, they go psycho? He gets anxious and can't tolerate loud noises or crowds."

Melanie felt like Sean was speaking about a stranger, not the man she loved. She saw more distaste than empathy in Sean's expression, but had to ask. "What happened to his parents?"

"They were killed in a car crash when he was a kid. His grandparents brought him up."

"Oh my god." Now she understood Jon's unusually close relationship with his grandmother.

The song finished playing and Melanie, reeling from the new information, declined a second dance, needing to get some air. All this time she hadn't really known Jon. Now she understood more clearly what Terry must be feeling. Someone you care for withholding vital information. At least, in Terry's case, it was to protect her. In this case, Jon was emotionally scarred, mistrustful.

Melanie stepped onto the terrace overlooking the ocean. The sky was filled with twinkling diamond stars. Under other circumstances, this would have been a wonderfully romantic evening, but instead she stood alone, alienated and confused.

Guests began spilling out of the reception hall wearing New Year's hats and holding noisemakers, a spirit of anticipation in the air. Looking at her watch, Melanie saw it was 11:52. Couples waited expectantly for midnight, holding each other close. Pauly embraced his bride Angela from behind, while Sean seemed to have found a willing partner to ring in the New Year. It was a perfect evening for a fireworks display.

At one minute to midnight, Pauly said, "Get ready—we'll count down together." And that's what they did. Everyone cheered, "Happy New Year!" Couples and new friends kissed, some a friendly peck, others passionately. The band struck up "Auld Lang Syne" as the fireworks began, explosions of color illuminating the night sky. Everyone around her was oohing and ahhing, but all Melanie could think was, *I'm starting the new year alone.*

* * *

Jon sat in the sand, knees bent, looking out on oblivion. The sound of gentle waves meeting the shore was the only clue to the presence of the vast ocean before him, the utter darkness a reflection of his mood. After the big reveal by Pauly, he'd needed to escape, his anxiety reaching a crescendo. He swiped the first bottle of liquor he found and ran outside, wandering aimlessly until he found a random spot, far from late-night beachcombers. With everyone celebrating the new year at the posh hotels and clubs, the beach was deserted, just as he'd hoped.

The bottle of whiskey lay at his feet, a third of it gone. He was spiraling downward, the worst he'd been in years. Snippets of that night came rushing to his mind. Crouching as he ran from the social hall, waking to the madness on the quad, Pauly tackling him to the ground. Losing Ashleigh.

The old questions crept in with no answers, only a circle in his mind that tortured him. He pulled his phone out of his pocket. It took two tries till his fingers obeyed and dialed Gabe.

"The cat's outta the bag," he slurred into the phone when Gabe answered.

"Jon? What are you talking about? Are you drunk?"

"Pauly made a toast to his old friend Jon, and..."

"Oh no. Are you okay?"

"I blew it. Big time. I had to get out of there. Left Mel sitting there alone." He took a pull from the bottle. "Second time I walked out on her. I can't lose her, Gabe. She's the best thing that's happened to me in a long time," he sobbed.

"You're damn right she is. Melanie has a heart of gold. And

she loves you. Clean yourself up and go find her. Apologize, answer all her questions and tell her you'll get help. It's long overdue."

Jon was about to agree with him when the first burst of fireworks exploded. Instinctively, he threw himself to the ground, covering his head, dropping his phone.

More explosions threw him into a tailspin, his drunken mind allowing repressed memories to rush back in one fell swoop. Jon stayed down on the sand, yelling "Ashleigh, run!" over and over until the fireworks ended and he finally passed out.

CHAPTER 50

Dallas

"Hello, Hello. Jon?" The call abruptly disconnected. The last thing Gabe had heard was an explosion. He prayed it was nothing more than background party noise. He knew his friend was struggling. There were times over the last three years Gabe would see a heavy darkness come over him, a despondency that had never been there before the BTI bombing. A shadow came on suddenly, draping a depression around Jon's shoulders, then passing just as quickly.

Gabe tried to call back but got Jon's voicemail. He left a message, asking him to call back. New Year's Eve, and both of them were alone, having messed up with the women they cared for. He tried Melanie's number and got her voicemail too, leaving an intentionally vague message asking her to call him.

He hung up and looked at the muted television. The ball had dropped in Times Square. Thousands of elated people stood jammed together in the bitter New York winter just to say they did. *This would be a terrorist's dream come true,* he thought. They needed to redouble their efforts to find the syndicate and cut it off at the head, but his friends were splintered, making a team effort even more challenging.

He shut off the TV and set his alarm for 5:00 a.m. Given

Terry's work ethic and the time crunch, she would continue her research on the holiday. He wanted to position himself well, so he could keep a close eye on her. His priority was keeping Terry safe. Five hours of sleep was better than nothing.

❊ ❊ ❊

Miami Beach

When the fireworks ended Melanie went back inside with the other guests. Exhausted physically and emotionally, she returned to her seat to retrieve her clutch, hugged Candace and Connor and wished them good night.

Candace squeezed her hand. "Hope to see you again soon in Boston."

"Me too."

Connor took her aside. "Don't give up on Jon. He's a good guy."

Melanie held back tears. "I'll try," she said noncommittally. She walked warily to the elevator and pressed the button for her floor.

"Going to bed already?" asked a familiar voice. Last thing Melanie needed was another round with Sean.

"It was a beautiful wedding but I'm tired. It's time for me to call it a night."

"Oh, come on. The night's just getting started, not to mention a new year. Don't you want to make it a memorable one?" He raised a brow. "Or if you prefer, I'd be happy to escort you to your room."

"Back off, Sean. She isn't interested." Senator Hendrix strode over. Sean looked mildly embarrassed, clearly intimidated by the imposing, powerful woman.

He cleared his throat. "Right, then. Good night. Regards to Jonny. When you find him, of course." He sauntered away, trying to maintain his dignity.

The senator shook her head. "He still behaves like they're in high school."

"Thanks for coming to the rescue."

"Don't mention it. I was hoping we could set a time to meet in the morning. Talk about our favorite charities."

"That would be great. My flight back to Dallas is at eleven."

"How about breakfast on the veranda? Just you and me. Eight o'clock? Then I'll have my driver take you to the airport."

"Perfect. I'll look forward to it."

She gave Melanie a proper kiss on both cheeks. "Sleep well, dear."

CHAPTER 51

Boston

Early New Year's Day

Donna lay spent in Jim's arms, basking in the afterglow of sweet lovemaking. Her body felt utterly relaxed as his soft, sleep-laden breaths landed like feathers on her cheek.

They had met at an Italian restaurant with views of the harbor, eating an indulgent meal, dancing to Sinatra tunes, and laughing at each other's corny jokes.

After toasting the new year with champagne and a sultry kiss, Jim suggested a nightcap at his waterside condo. Donna was surprised to learn he'd kept his Boston place all these years. He explained that he couldn't part with it and, though he returned only once or twice a year, he still thought of it as home.

He'd been a perfect gentleman throughout the evening, but Donna was hoping that would change. At his place, he offered her a glass of red wine, sat beside her on the soft leather sofa, and without warning, took her face in his hands and kissed her, softly at first and then with building, hot passion. An hour later, she was in his bed, feeling blissful.

As Jim sat up, she thought he looked lean and fit.

"I'm so glad I saved your ass," Donna said.

Jim laughed, pulled her closer. "The drug addict? Me too.

What brings that up?"

"If I hadn't shot that lunatic, we wouldn't be here together."

"True, and thanks, by the way, for saving my ass, as you so delicately put it. Not my best moment."

Donna caught Jim's gaze, her expression sobering. "No one could have foreseen what happened, that he would go for your weapon."

"Still, it was our job to anticipate everything."

"And we handled it."

"*You* handled it," Jim said.

"We were partners, same difference." She paused. "Tell me, is that why you left the force?"

"It was one of the reasons. A call like that leaves its mark. But I also got a job offer with the FBI, one I really wanted."

Donna nodded her understanding.

"Feeling hungry?" he asked, changing the topic.

"Not anymore"

He laughed. "I mean for food."

"Sure. Can I help?"

"No, stay right there, looking beautiful. I'll be back."

She stayed put for a minute but was antsy. The smell of toasting bread drove her out of bed. She put on Jim's button-down and walked to the living room, wandering the space, impressed at his substantial digs despite a federal career. A bronze sculpture of a man on horseback caught her eye. Beside it was a small photo album. She picked it up, flipping through the pages. One photo drew her attention. A ragtag group of men and women grinning as they huddled together in a forest or jungle. She didn't recognize anyone. Putting the album down, she scanned the books on his shelves.

A copy of *Jane Eyre* was on a side table and she picked it up, paging through.

"You like that one?" he asked as he walked toward her, two steaming cups of aromatic coffee in his hands. "You can borrow anything you like."

"I don't have much time to read these days, but I love the classics."

They took seats next to each other on the couch and he handed her the cup. "A performance of *Pride and Prejudice* is coming next month to the playhouse in Columbus," he said. "Maybe you'd consider coming out for a visit and I could take you." He looked at her longingly.

Donna felt breathless, excited, knowing what was coming. The food would have to wait a little longer.

＊ ＊ ＊

As the morning sun shone through the windows, Donna curled up beside Jim. They had spoken on and off as the night progressed, talking of this and that, past histories and funny stories, ice cream preferences and pet peeves. She wasn't surprised to learn that Jim had never fired his weapon in the line of duty —a sign of wisdom and restraint in this age of shoot first and ask questions later. She wanted to enjoy the inner happiness and forget the outside world, but her mind wouldn't allow it for long.

"Jim, I have a dilemma."

Jim stirred drowsily. "What's the matter?"

She kept her voice low, not wanting to change the mood too quickly. "I'm not sure how much to tell you without it getting you in trouble." She turned to face him. Jim kissed her nose. *He's happy too.*

Pulling back, he saw her serious face. "That doesn't sound good."

"It's not."

Jim sat up, back against the headboard. "Can you give me any information that will allow me to help you but not incriminate anyone?"

She positioned herself beside him, taking a minute to collect her thoughts. "I don't see how."

"Then I'm not sure that I can objectively guide you. But you know I'll do anything I can to help."

"Even if it means it could create professional issues for one or both of us?"

"You're one of the most ethical people I know. I have confidence in your choices."

Not one to get emotional, she was surprised to feel her eyes water. "Thank you. That means a lot."

"Does this have anything to do with the Cincinnati bombing and those kids?"

"Yes." She sat quietly for a moment, then took a deep breath. "Ok, I'm going for broke. I trust you and hope you'll forgive me if it leads to any trouble. I need input on this. I've spoken to Doug Matthews but so far he's gotten nowhere and I know you have other resources."

Jim said, "Okay. Matthews is in the loop. Go ahead."

"Jon Steadman called me a few days ago. We had a long conversation about highly sensitive information he provided."

"What about?"

"A terrorist network."

"Oh jeez."

"Jon and others suspect there are people in the U.S. who are involved—possibly at high levels—so they're trying to limit whom to involve."

"Do you think their information is good?"

"I read everything he had. It's very damning. Terrifying, actually. I'm between a rock and hard place. I don't know how to help them without involving more law enforcement. However, that could further endanger them."

"Do they feel that there's an imminent threat?"

"Wouldn't you? Professor Breitler, who was assisting them, died in what the police deemed foul play. And you remember what Carrera said on the bridge. Since then, Jackson's body— the Cincinnati student—was found, and there was another attack in LA."

"Are you saying the LA attack is definitely connected to the others?"

"I don't know but there are too many similarities. The perpetrator was a student with no motive who blew herself up."

"I see."

"The info Jon sent me was shocking. Essentially, they linked several killing sprees over recent years, all·across the country."

"What sort of link?"

"Jim, if I go further with this, you could be implicated in withholding vital national security information."

Now he was fully awake. "You need to tell me all of it." He took her hand and squeezed. "We'll figure this out together."

Donna resigned herself to dragging him into her dilemma.

"All right. Here goes." She told Jim everything she knew. "Jon has concluded the bombings were meant to vaporize any physical evidence. If it weren't for the new level of genetic technology, they would have succeeded."

Jim looked floored. "Incredible."

"Now do you see what has had me all worked up? Jon and the others are fearful of who can be trusted, but I've spoken to Doug Matthews."

"Makes sense. There's no way they can handle a threat of this magnitude alone."

"So you think I did the right thing?"

"Of course. From what you're telling me, Jon's team has hit a wall."

Donna was relieved having a trusted and objective party agree with her assessment.

Jim said, "I have connections throughout law enforcement and, of course, at the Bureau. There are some higher ups I would trust with my life...and have. Doug Matthews may not appreciate having less control but we need to get the full power of the Feds behind this. This is too big for a few laymen and a small team to crack on their own. Let me call Matthews and work it out with him."

"But what if it gets back to the wrong people?"

Jim's face turned grim. "It's just a risk we'll have to take."

CHAPTER 52

Miami Beach

Melanie entered the Garden Terrace, the Alexander's open-air restaurant, and asked the Maître D' to seat her with Senator Hendrix. She was led to a table with a magnificent view of the ocean. Overhead fans enhanced the fresh breeze coming off the water, dispensing with the early morning humidity.

The senator stood and smiled as Melanie approached. She was elegantly dressed in a white sundress that accentuated her tanned complexion. "Please have a seat. What would you like for breakfast?"

"Oh, I'm not very hungry."

"Everything all right?" Mrs. Hendrix asked.

"I hope so. Jon never came back last night. It seems Pauly's toast brought back troubling memories. Honestly, I never knew anything about his involvement in the BTI bombing. It took me by surprise."

"Surely he wouldn't deliberately keep you in the dark about such an important part of his past."

"But that's exactly what he did...I'm sorry. I had no intention of burdening you with any of this."

"It's no trouble at all. Everyone needs an ear sometimes."

A waitress in crisp white uniform brought them a pot of fresh coffee. Mrs. Hendrix ordered fresh-squeezed orange juice and an assortment of fruit and pastries.

The two women spoke for nearly an hour, Melanie learning about the senator's patronage of Doctor's Without Borders and Oxfam. Before Melanie knew it, it was time to leave.

"Thank you for a lovely breakfast," she said, putting down her napkin.

"It was my pleasure."

"I look forward to getting your packet on humanitarian college internships."

"I'll send it out this week. Hopefully we'll recruit capable UNT students. We can use all the help we can get."

Melanie stood, exchanged kisses, bidding the senator farewell. She gathered her bags, stole one last look at the sunny beach and walked out to the waiting car.

* * *

"Hey buddy, wake up. I gotta put the chairs over here."

Jon opened his eyes to a Hispanic young man wearing a lifeguard tank top and carrying a huge, bright yellow sun umbrella, nudging him with his foot. Jon groaned, head spinning. "Sorry. Can you give me a hand?"

The lifeguard dumped the umbrella and helped pull him upright. "Some serious New Year's partying, huh, man?"

"Uh, yeah," he croaked, throat parched.

The guy laughed heartily. "I hear ya, bro. You should see the pool area. Beer cans and champagne bottles floating in the pool, confetti all over the place, and I won't tell you about the vomit stench."

Jon looked at his watch. 9:45. "Oh no." He was going to miss his flight. He checked his pockets for his phone. Not there. Searching the area, he found it in the sand. But when he tried to turn it on, nothing happened. It was either out of juice or broken from sitting in the sand for hours.

"Happy New Year." The lifeguard was way too cheerful.

"Yeah, same to you."

Jon looked around, trying to get his bearings. He vaguely remembered walking the beach at night, upset by Pauly's announcement. Then he recalled the explosions. The fireworks. The display had been planned, Pauly had even announced it, but in Jon's compromised state, he was unprepared.

A street number was painted on the boardwalk—Forty-fourth Street. He'd walked half a mile south of the Alexander. His suit was covered in wet sand and he looked like a homeless person. He found a bin and threw out the empty whiskey bottle.

How on earth would he explain this to Mel? He'd need to think of something. And fast.

CHAPTER 53

Dallas

T erry looked out the window, scouring her surroundings. No unusual activity. Dressed in her favorite jeans and a Technion sweatshirt, she rushed from the apartment to the waiting Uber. She checked the car make and model, and the driver's face. Few people were milling about this New Year's Day, following a late night for most.

She got in the car's back seat and leaned back, trying to dismiss her conflicted feelings. Her plan was to complete the report for the FBI and send it out by the end of the day. The work would surely help the investigation, but was confidential. She had been both shocked and relieved when she found Chrysanthemum Exotic in the female bomber's results. Knowing there was a verifiable connection among the killings could be a significant step in tracking down the conspiracy's ringleaders. Whether Terry would tell the others was something she had yet to decide.

The Uber ride took ten minutes. She tipped the driver via the app and rated him five stars. He had let her sit with her thoughts. She exited the car and crossed the street to the campus entrance.

The stone archway was still decked out with New Year's regalia, evidence of a rowdy night. She passed through the gates and walked at a good clip to the Science building. For a fleeting moment, Terry felt there were eyes on her, but she dismissed the thought. Gabe had stoked her paranoia, but she wasn't about to cower in fear.

The Science building's long hallway was devoid of people. Terry took the stairs to the second floor two at a time. Outside the lab door she opened her bag, searching for the key, and was unexpectedly yanked backward into the stairwell.

A firm whisper hissed in her ear. "You're going to take me quietly into the lab, hand me your report and erase all other copies. If you resist, I will make use of this knife." The man was pushed up against her, the cold point of a knife's edge piercing her jacket.

He was huge, at least six-three, and husky, wearing a ski mask. Her own reaction surprised her. More than scared, she was pissed off...at this asshole, and even more so at herself. How could this happen twice without her having a chance to react? What happened to her krav maga training?

What she needed now was a chance to grab her mace, spray him and kick him where the sun didn't shine. She worked on slowing her heart rate, allowing years of training in the military to kick in. *Pay attention. Find his weakness.* His voice sounded young.

Feigning more fear than she actually felt would make him believe she wouldn't fight back. Of course, he had another thing coming.

"I've already given copies of my initial results to the Feds," said Terry. "You're too late."

"Nice try, Doc. I know that's a lie. The syndicate has eyes everywhere." He pushed her toward the lab, keeping a tight grip on her arm. Stumbling, a knife at her back, Terry could only hope someone happened by.

"Just what's this syndicate's agenda? What's so important that so many people had to die?"

The question didn't rattle him. "We're bringing justice to those who can't achieve it themselves. A few innocents are collateral damage, casualties of war. The new order is around the corner. And it begins with getting the world's attention."

His speech sounded off, like he was reading from a script. *Was he drugged?*

"How do you get the world's attention?"

He spoke in a monotone. "With killing exercises. Soon everyone will know about us." He pushed against the lab door. Locked.

"Unlock the door. And no funny business or you won't leave this building alive."

The lab key was in the pocket next to her canister of mace. Terry reached into her bag. *There it was!* She only had to remove the cap and position it for firing. She managed that while her hand was still in the bag.

"Hurry up!"

"Here it is." She pulled out the mace, turning it toward him, poised and ready to spray. She aimed for his eyes, the rest of his face hidden behind a mask. Like a striking asp, he grabbed her hand and twisted it with force. A searing pain ran up her arm.

"You bitch!" He raised his knife, aimed at her chest, then unexpectedly stopped in mid-air, eyes blinking as if waging an internal battle.

It was all she needed. With her back to him, she broke away. Behind her she heard the familiar sound of pulling back a slide, forcing a cartridge into a chamber. *He had a gun!*

As she bolted down the hall, a shot rang out, echoing off the empty corridor walls. *He missed!* She didn't stop to investigate.

"Terry!"

Confused, she turned and saw her attacker on the floor, a blood stain spreading on his pant leg, his knife fallen, out of reach. Mumbled curses and groans told her he was still alive.

And then Gabe was running towards her. Seeing his concerned face, she was overcome and dropped to her knees, realizing how close she'd just come to dying.

Gabe leaned down to help her up, embracing her tightly. "Terry, please tell me he didn't hurt you."

She swallowed a strained sob, massaging her wrist. "I'm all right."

"Your hand looks swollen. What did that sonofabitch do?"

"I tried to mace him and he saw it coming, twisted my wrist. I'll be okay." She looked up at him, tears in her eyes. "Where did you come from?"

"Don't you remember? I'm Gabe, your guardian angel. Not that you need protection."

"I was angry."

"I noticed. And I know how angry you can get." He laughed and put both hands on her shoulders, "Give me a second." He walked over to the attacker, gun at the ready.

"I should finish you off right now, jackass. Tell me who you are and why you attacked her."

The big man remained silent.

"Is he badly hurt?" Terry asked.

"My bullet got him in the knee." Then to the attacker, Gabe said, "Cat got your tongue?"

Still no response.

"Time to make your acquaintance." Gabe bent down, hovering over the man and pulled off the mask. He nearly fell off his feet in shock as he looked into the glazed eyes of Sam Delgado.

CHAPTER 54

Miami Beach

By the time Jon got back to the Alexander, it was close to eleven o'clock and he knew he would miss his flight. He ran through the lobby and up to the room, plugged in his phone, hoping it was just a dead battery. He used the room phone to call the airline. The next flight wasn't for several hours and he booked himself a seat. A call to Melanie went straight to voicemail.

"Hey Mel. I don't know how to say this again and come across as sincere. I'm so sorry. I hope you'll be willing to hear me out. I'm on the next flight back. Please call Gabe and have him pick you up. Don't take any chances."

He hung up knowing his plea was weak. He showered, changed into fresh clothes, and packed. He was famished. Leaving his suitcase with the concierge, he went to the terrace restaurant. As he was being led to a table, Pauly's stepmother walked up to him.

Prior to this trip, it had been several years since Jon had seen Senator Jasmine Hendrix. He knew Pauly's relationship with his stepmother was best described as polite—not family-like. Pauly had confided that they had never really bonded. There was something unapproachable about her.

"If it isn't the elusive Jonathan Steadman."

"Hello, Senator Hendrix."

"You're old enough now to call me Jasmine. Your girlfriend was worried about you. She's a lovely young lady, by the way."

"I'm really sorry to have worried her."

"You know what Paul said was from the heart. You should call him when they get back from their honeymoon and catch up. I know he would want that."

"I'll do that."

"And how has school been? I heard you moved to a smaller university in Texas. It must be quite a change from New England."

"I'm at UNT. Great school, and an even better criminology program. I like it there."

"Have you been working on anything interesting?"

"Actually, I've been writing my thesis on the correlation between chromosomal makeup and criminal activity."

"Fascinating, but way over my head."

He smiled weakly. "How are you and Mr. Hendrix?"

"Diligently working on our respective projects. As you know, Paul's father never takes a break. Honestly, I can't wait until Paul graduates and we can pass the torch. Maybe I can entice his dad to take me on a world cruise, something I've been wanting to do forever."

"Please send my best to your husband."

"I will." She glanced at her watch. "I'm running late for a work call. Good to see you again."

Jon smiled a goodbye to the senator, and followed the patient waitress to his seat. At a table set for one.

❊ ❊ ❊

Melanie sat next to an empty aisle seat. The one Jon should have been in. About to turn off her phone for takeoff, it pinged with two new messages. Anxious to see if they were from Jon, she surreptitiously listened to them, knowing a flight attendant would make her put the device away if she was seen. The first message was from Gabe asking her to call. The second was from Jon. She heard the contriteness in his voice but was still hurt that it took all this for him to suggest talking things out. She'd call Gabe when she landed. Jon was right to avoid taking any chances. Exhaustion set in. She shut off her phone, closed her eyes and fell asleep.

CHAPTER 55

University of North Texas

The police showed up within minutes, followed by a campus security guard. Gabe wondered where he'd been the whole time. While an officer was putting handcuffs on a semi-conscious Sam, a medic readied him for transport to the local ER. Before the police arrived, Gabe had the foresight to pull a few hairs from Sam's head.

Pocketing them, he returned to Terry. He was willing to bet that Sam was under the influence. It was the only explanation. Gabe knew Sam wouldn't hurt a fly. His behavior was completely out of character.

The cops kept them at the precinct for over an hour, taking their statements. Gabe held Terry close the entire time, while informing them of his acquaintance with Sam. Terry gave an account of what had happened, allowing the cops to assume it was a mugging attempt rather than Sam's true objective—namely, to hijack the lab report.

Though Gabe's gun license was deemed in order, his firearm was confiscated. He felt naked without it, certain their pursuers would not stop.

He and Terry were told to be available for further questioning if necessary, and then given permission to leave.

"Let's get out of here," Terry said.

"It can wait a few more seconds."

"What for?"

Gabe took her face in his hands and kissed her deeply. She didn't resist.

* * *

Gabe guided Terry outside. "I still need to finish my report... and test Sam's hair for Chrysanthemum Exotic," Terry said.

Gabe stopped in front of his car. "The lab's going to be off limits while the police do their job." He opened the passenger door for her. "So, Dr. Lavi, would you agree that maybe there are times when depending on someone other than yourself is not so bad?"

Terry smiled. "I'm beginning to learn that."

"May I drive you home- my home?"

"Yes, and thank you for saving my life." She kissed him full on the lips.

Gabe wrapped her in his arms. "Mmm. You're welcome."

His phone vibrated with an incoming text message. "It's from Melanie. She just landed and needs a ride."

"No mention of Jon? What do you think that means?"

"I have a lot to catch you up on."

"Let's go pick her up. Tell me on the way."

* * *

Dallas

Melanie exited the terminal weighed down with a garment bag, handbag and pulling a wheelie. She looked glum.

"There she is." Gabe jumped from the car to help. He took her bags. "How are you doing?"

"Hanging in there."

"Have you heard from Jon?"

"He left an apology message, but I have some thinking to do."

"I'm sorry I couldn't tell you about his past. It wasn't my place," he said.

"I don't blame you. This is about Jon and our relationship. If he can't trust me, we won't get anywhere...but I'm so sorry about your sister."

"Thank you. If it's any help, try to keep in mind that despite all his challenges, Jon came out on top. It just takes him more time than the average guy to trust. He's lost so many people close to him that he keeps a distance, especially in a new relationship."

"That makes sense, I suppose. I just need to see if I can handle it."

"Gotcha. Hop in. By the way, Terry and I have made up."

"I knew she'd come around," Melanie said nudging his shoulder.

"It took a lot for that to happen. I'll let her explain."

Melanie got in the back seat and Terry turned to face her from the front. "Welcome home. Boy, have we got a tale to tell," she said with a shaky laugh.

After the two women exchanged stories of the recent days' incredible events, complete with laughter and tears, Melanie looked out the window at the passing traffic. "Where are we headed? My apartment's the other way."

At the wheel, Gabe shook his head. "You can't go back there, Mel. Powerful people after us. If they got to Sam, anything's possible. We need to stick together. Terry's coming to my place and we'll make room for you. After that, you can decide if you want to stay on or bunk with Jon."

"I don't think that would be wise right now."

"Whatever you decide. I can sleep on an air mattress in the living room, you can have the couch and Terry my bed."

"I appreciate it," said Melanie, "but at some point, I'll need to go home and get some things."

"Then we'll all go together. We're stuck with each other

until this terrorist syndicate is brought down. For now, how does pizza sound?"

Melanie was starving. "Like music to my ears."

* * *

The moment Jon stepped into his dorm room he understood that his roommate Ken must have hit his tolerance limit. The space was spotless, clothes folded and in their rightful place, laundry in the hamper. He owed his roommate a beer.

Jon was unpacking his bag when Gabe called. "Hey Jon Jon, so glad you picked up the phone."

"Just got back. Sorry about my drunk call. Hope it didn't freak you out."

"I'm just glad you're home. Listen, buddy, I have a lot to catch you up on. But first, tell me where your head is at."

"Don't wanna think about it. All I can say is, I'll do whatever it takes to get back into Melanie's good graces."

"Now you're talking. Give her some time to come around. You need to start including her in your world. Scars and all."

"Is she okay?"

"Yeah. She's staying with me and Terry. Sleeping soundly in the other room."

"Thanks, man. So what happened on your end?"

Now Gabe had to share the shocking story of Terry's attack by Sam Delgado, complete with ski mask and knife.

"Sam? *My* Sam?" Jon was dumbfounded. "It makes no sense."

"Maybe it does. He might have been under the influence of Chrysanthemum Exotic, like the others."

Jon was shaken. "I don't know. It doesn't add up."

"It was a wake-up call for Terry. She decided to share the results from the LA bomber's ear cartilage."

"And?"

"She asked that we all be together when she tells us. Can

you come over?"

"I'm not sure Mel wants to see me."

"She's cool with it. You guys don't need to talk about any-thing right now." As an extra push, he added, "We ordered pizza from Luigi's. I'll heat some up for you."

Jon allowed himself a laugh. "Okay, I'm on my way."

"Before you go, I have a favor to ask, if you can get around to it in the next few days."

"What do you need?"

"For you to pay Sam a visit, get some answers."

"In jail?"

"Yeah. He's still being treated for the gunshot wound but because of the recent campus attacks, they're going to transfer him to a state prison instead of the local jail, while he waits to see a judge."

"That's awful."

"You up for it?"

"I guess. Can't say I've ever been to a state penitentiary. But I suppose there's a first time for everything."

CHAPTER 56

Dallas

T erry was on her second glass of red wine, snuggled up to Gabe on his sofa. Melanie sat across from them, Jon at a safe distance near the breakfast table. She had barely glanced at him. Two empty pizza boxes lay open on the kitchen counter.

Terry put her glass down. "Before Sam attacked me, I was conflicted about sharing the TR-X results. Medical ethics are paramount in my field." She paused. "I am fully aware that if it should come out that I violated the confidentiality agreement, I would lose all credibility, possibly my license." Gabe tried to interject, but she held up a hand. "Nevertheless, recent happenings lead me to believe that some things are more important. In this case, world security. Therefore, before I go forward, I beseech each of you, to do everything within your power to protect this information and if I may be so bold to ask...my involvement in divulging it."

Gabe's response was solemn. "Terry, none of us wants you to risk your job."

"I appreciate you saying so, but the results are vital in the investigation." She took in a deep breath, then exhaled. "The LA bomber was also exposed to Chrysanthemum Exotic. It's my belief that transference was made by a concentrated cream or liquid applied directly to the skin."

Gabe was perplexed. "So the attackers were unaware the

drug was being applied to their skin?"

She shrugged. "I have no idea. There's something else I want to mention. Just before Sam was going to take his final strike, I swear he hesitated. It gave me the moment I needed to get away. I'm wondering if this drug has limitations."

"Are you suggesting that his true self was holding him back?" Melanie asked.

"I suppose I am. It's amazing that he could inhibit the drug's effects, especially with his ADHD."

"Eyewitnesses of the LA attack reported the same thing," said Jon. "Shari Kordivan hesitated before detonating the bomb. Several survivors said it saved their lives."

Melanie froze. "Maybe you're on to something, Terry... What did you just say?"

"Which part?"

"Oh my God! How did I not see this sooner?" She ran to her bag, rifling through papers. The others watched as Melanie scurried around the room.

"What are you looking for?" Jon asked.

"It's been staring us in the face the whole time," she said, as if speaking to herself.

"What has?" Terry asked.

Melanie sat, looking for something in the printouts. "Remember when we got the results back from the fingernail? Professor Breitler said there are medical history profiles we could get now that were never available before. We looked at mental illness, depression and aggressive tendencies and found nothing. But the regular panel showed blood type and medical data."

Gabe nodded, though unsure where she was going. "Yeah?"

"I didn't give it any thought then because it's so common. We were so excited to have the more detailed genetic mapping that we overlooked the obvious. Abadi had ADHD."

Terry said, "Okay, so? There are no known links between ADHD and homicidal tendencies."

"Here it is...oh my God...take a look," Melanie said, pointing a finger to Andrew Capaletto's diagnosis line. "If my hunch is right, we'll see the same with the other one from LA. Where are Terry's reports?"

Terry got out her iPad, entered the password and opened the classified files with the female bomber's results. "Bingo. Shari Kordivan had ADHD too!"

Jon interjected. "I just remembered something. Niles Pertrolli, Farad Jackson's roommate, told Donna that Farad was taking classes to improve his organizational skills. Something called Cure Theory. The cops checked it out but it looked legit. They thought it was a dead end."

Mel asked Terry for her device, typed frantically and opened five screens side by side, each one showing one of the five college sites. BTI, Georgia Tech, University of Cincinnati, UCLA, and UNT. Randomly, she selected the Georgia Tech website, and clicked on the page for the Psychology Department. From the drop menu, she selected *Student Clinical Trials*.

Melanie read aloud, "Cure Theory is a worldwide study initiative whose mission is to treat adults and adolescents diagnosed with ADHD by using innovative behavior modification therapy designed to help participants achieve greater performance, deeper concentration, optimal grades, and better relationships. Twenty dollars per hour will be paid for accepted subjects."

She checked out the other schools. Each one offered the program. Next, she typed *Cure Theory* into Google, and cross-referenced it with locations, and pressed *Search*.

Her jaw dropped. There were four hundred locations around the world.

* * *

The shock wearing off, Jon looked at Melanie. "I heard about this study from Sam."

"Have you seen any changes in his personality?" asked Melanie.

"Maybe some subtle things. He does seem more focused. He told me he liked the program. It was helping his grades. If he *is* involved, he definitely didn't realize the study is actually a front for terrorist recruitment. And if Sam was exposed to Chrysanthemum Exotic, he isn't accountable for his actions."

Gabe said, "We need to find the connection between the study and the attacks. Mel, is there any way to check the timeline of the school trials and see if they correspond with the dates of the attacks?"

"Great idea. I'm on it." She took Terry's iPad to the breakfast table and sat beside Jon. Gabe grabbed his own laptop and got to work.

It took about twenty minutes to track down the trial information. They studied the dates together.

Melanie said, "It looks like there was a five-month gap between the onset of Cure Theory interviews and the attack on BTI. Four and a half for Georgia Tech and UCLA."

"Now, we need to go back five months from today, and figure out which other school has already begun trials." Gabe typed furiously.

Jon said, "I see where you're going. We'll be able to figure out which school is next."

Eighteen colleges were conducting interviews over the summer months. Terry said, "There's no way to figure out which location is next. It could be any of them."

"Or *all* of them," Jon said.

Terry asked, "Are we ready to take this to Agent Matthews? We're racing against the clock."

Melanie said, "We still don't know who's involved in this and how high up. These studies required an enormous budget with government and private funding."

Jon was conflicted. "I see your point, but running down all the schools alone would take too long. And anyway, I agreed to keep Matthews in the loop. If he finds out we didn't share this breakthrough with him, he'll come after us with the big guns

—prosecutors."

"All right," said Gabe. "Let's contact him, but first things first."

"What do you have in mind?" Terry asked.

"Jon's been good friends with Sam for years. It's time for him to pay him a visit."

CHAPTER 57

Hutchins State Prison

Dallas

"**Y**ou gotta believe me, Jon. I don't remember a thing."

Jon was having a hard time grasping that he was in Dallas' Federal Correctional Institute, sitting on the opposite side of a plexiglass divider, speaking through an old-fashioned handset to his buddy. Sam wore an orange jumpsuit, looking shell-shocked, his leg in a soft cast.

Jon couldn't make eye contact. This was his friend, lovable Sam. But he needed to remain stoic or he would lose his objectivity. "That's hard to believe, Sam."

"I swear. Last I remember I was in my room, setting my alarm. I was planning to wake up early to review my spring registration. See if I wanted to drop any classes before the semester started. Next thing I know, I'm lying in the ER, my hands cuffed to the bed!" Sam must have noticed the skepticism on Jon's face. "Jon. Bro. I've known you for how long?"

"Years."

"Have you ever known me to do anything like this?"

"No, but I don't know what kind of people you're involved with." He didn't hold back. No point, with so much on the line. He changed gears. "Tell me about your ADHD trials."

"What? Why? We only have a few minutes left before the

guard comes back."

"It's important. Could be connected."

Sam shook his head. "You're barking up the wrong tree, man."

"Humor me. Unless you have any better ideas of how this happened."

Sam looked down at his cuffed hands. "Fine. They call it Cure Theory. Professor Siddiqui is in charge. He's a really smart guy. Has two PhDs. He helped me a lot."

"What's the treatment—a pill?"

"No. Just one on one time. They use meditation techniques. The professor took notes and stuff."

"Did they videotape your sessions?"

"I think there was some equipment. Never paid it much attention."

"So no pills, creams, nothing?"

"No. Why?"

"I had a theory but forget it."

Sam looked dejected. "Thanks for coming by. Tell Dr. Lavi I'm sorry."

"Will do."

"Can you do me a favor?" Sam asked.

"Sure, what?"

"Ask the warden if I can get my watch back. I was one of the few to get one because I did so well in the Cure Theory trials. It means a lot to me, and I don't want it to get stolen in this hellhole."

The guard came in. Sam hung up the phone receiver, then looked directly at Jon. Sam's sad gaze tore through him. This time, he couldn't look away. Even as the guard helped Sam to his feet and escorted him from the room.

❋ ❋ ❋

Jon believed Sam. He knew his friend, and trusted his own gut.

He approached the guard posted at the visitor's desk.

"Excuse me."

The guard looked away from the surveillance monitors showing live feed of the exterior of the prison. Yes?"

"I just visited an inmate. He asked if it was possible for him to get his watch back."

"I'm sorry, no." The guard turned back to the monitors.

Jon was irritated. "Are you the man in charge of that?"

"Actually, no. But I know procedure."

"I'd like to speak with the person who *is* in charge of that, if I may." Jon noted the guard looked annoyed but was unsure how to handle this atypical request.

"Hold on a minute." The man picked up his phone and dialed a number.

"Sir, there's a visitor here that wants to get a watch back for an inmate." He paused, listening. "I told him that, sir. He wants to talk to you." Another pause. "Yes sir." He hung up, looked back at his monitors. "Warden Smith said to go to his office. I'll call someone to escort you."

❊ ❊ ❊

"What's your name, son?"

"Jonathan Steadman."

A big man, Warden Smith sported a military-style haircut, and a prison-issued firearm on his hip. He looked at his computer screen. "You came to see Samuel Delgado?"

"That's right."

"He's being held without bail for attempted murder."

"That's a mistake."

The warden laughed. "If I had a quarter for every time I heard that line."

"I'm not here to try his case, just ask for a favor."

The warden raised his brows and took a closer look at the young man standing before him in his office. He was dressed like a cowboy but spoke like a lawyer. "What sort of favor?"

"Sam asked if I could help get his watch back." Jon left out the part where he was concerned it would get stolen.

"That's not procedure, Jonathan."

"Somehow, I knew you were going to say that...and maybe it's not, but let's face it—he can't exactly break out of here with his watch."

"True, but when the warden does favors for one inmate, it can cause problems with others. We don't want the natives to become restless." He laughed.

Jon smiled conspiratorially. "Who would know? I'll tell him to keep it out of sight."

"Have an answer for everything, do you? I like you, Jonathan. Ever consider a job in law enforcement?"

"It's funny, Special Agent Matthews asked me the same thing a few weeks ago." *Drop the hook.*

"Hmm, Matthews...isn't he one of the top FBI honchos working the killing sprees?"

"Yeah, that's him."

The warden leaned back in his chair. "You have connections at the Bureau? And you know Matthews?"

"I helped him recently on an operation." *Catch the fish.*

"As a civilian?"

"Extenuating circumstances. But let's get back to the watch."

The warden was quiet a moment. "Jon...may I call you Jon?" Seeing Jon's nod, he continued. "Please have a seat."

Jon sat. Dropping Agent Matthews' name was working. *Reel him in.*

The warden put his hands behind his head and gently bounced in his faux-leather office chair. "You may find it helpful to know that in this field, the squeaky wheel often gets the grease."

"Does that mean you'll get Sam his watch?"

"What it means Jon, is grease flows both ways."

Jon was wary but curious to see where the conversation

would go. "What do you want?" he asked, doing his best to swallow his disgust.

"Put in a good word with Matthews for me. He's well-connected, knows people in Corrections. I've been wanting to move onto bigger and better things and in this field, it's all about who you know."

Jon decided to go with it. "If you show me the watch and send it down to Sam, I'll call Matthews as soon as I leave here."

The warden picked up his phone. "Officer James, bring me the personal effects of Samuel Delgado."

Five minutes later, a bag was placed on the warden's desk. He opened it and took out the watch. "Strange-looking watch."

Jon peered over. He blanched. "May I have a look at that?"

The warden handed him the timepiece. It was an exact replica of the one from the would-be bridge bomber.

"On second thought, may *I* have the watch?"

"What? It doesn't belong to you. I can't just give you an inmate's personal effects."

"I'm certain Sam would want me to have it. It may help in his case."

"That definitely does not follow pro-." He stopped himself. "If you think it's evidence, it needs to go through his attorneys or the police."

"And I will contact them forthwith....after I phone Agent Matthews and sing your praises." Jon made an exaggerated show of looking around the dreary office. "Which field office were you considering?"

The warden sighed, then nodded. "South Florida would work out fine." And he handed Jon the watch.

CHAPTER 58

University of North Texas

P rofessor Siddiqui's office was a mess of discarded papers, Styrofoam packing nuts and unused moving boxes. Dust bunnies had accumulated in the corners of the room, and furniture had been moved out, leaving discolorations on the threadbare carpet. The school-issued metal desk where the professor's assistant sat looked different without all the paperwork piled up on it. Melanie led the way into the back room, Jon and Matthews following close behind.

Things were not the same since Jon got back from Florida. After meeting at Gabe's apartment, Jon initiated a conference call with Donna and Agent Matthews. He told them how they'd posited that Cure Theory trials were a cover for terrorist recruitment. Following his visit to Sam in prison, Jon phoned them again, arranging secure delivery of the watch to Matthews. He was determined to get Sam's charges dropped, and that watch was the clincher. *Quantos.* The same unusual timepiece found on Farad Jackson, the would-be bridge bomber.

With Matthews' consent Jon had informed Sam's lawyer, who notified the D.A. of the new developments in the case. A hearing was scheduled for next week.

In the interim, Agent Matthews obtained a warrant for UNT's Cure Theory office. As a show of good faith, he informed

Jon that testing had revealed the hair taken from Sam after the Science building attack showed traces of an unknown opioid.

After seeing Melanie at Gabe's apartment, Jon had spoken to her just once on the phone. She'd been cordial, but not ready to see him in person.

When Agent Matthews called Jon, however, requesting they meet at the UNT Psych office, Jon used it as an excuse to contact Melanie. After clearing it with Matthews, Jon sent her a text, inviting her to come along. She reluctantly accepted.

Jon assumed Matthews was including him in the search since he'd proven his worth. And, if Jon should learn anything helpful to the investigation, Agent Matthews would be right there.

Melanie stood in the back room office. "This must be where they held the treatment sessions," she said.

Matthews looked around, touching nothing. "I looked up Professor Siddiqui's background. Not much to report. No criminal record. The school didn't want to disclose any info on faculty members without a court order, but I called an old friend at the Bureau who's an alumnus of the school."

"And?" Jon asked.

"Siddiqui has an impressive background in groundbreaking psychological research. He's authored several articles published in top journals. He came to UNT for the express purpose of conducting ADHD trials."

"What else do we know about him? Personal stuff," Jon asked.

"Unmarried, no kids, no listed religion. He's travelled extensively and while teaching here, lived just off campus in a faculty rental. But he's gone now, left no forwarding address. I have a guy tasked with tracking him down for questioning."

The three of them donned gloves and took their time rummaging through what was left behind, unsure what they were looking for. Melanie steered clear of Jon, searching areas of the room farthest from him.

A few minutes went by before Jon called out, "Over here!"

Matthews looked up. "What have you got?"

Jon was peering into a large brown U-Haul box.. "Looks like a DVD. No markings."

"It's probably blank, or they would have taken it."

"Maybe in the hurry to leave, they missed this one."

Matthews appeared skeptical. "All right. I'll take it to the office and have a look." He ripped a paper towel off a nearly depleted roll sitting in the corner of the room and used it to pick up the DVD without getting his fingerprints on it. "We've done all we can here. Let's go."

"Can we tag along and see if there's anything on the disc?"

"Okay. Just don't get in my way."

* * *

FBI Regional Office
Dallas

Agent Matthews unlocked his office and ushered Jon and Melanie inside. It had been several months since the two had seen him here, and much had changed since. Matthews took a seat behind his desk and powered up his computer.

Melanie and Jon stood behind him, looking over his shoulder. He took the DVD out of the paper towel and inserted it. Much to their surprise a frozen image came up of the Cure Theory therapy room they had just left. Matthews clicked Play, and increased the volume.

Within seconds, they knew they had found something important. The first person to appear onscreen was none other than Sam Delgado.

* * *

They watched transfixed as Sam entered the therapy room.

Dressed in formal attire, Professor Siddiqui, a middle-aged man of Indian descent, was there, waiting for him.

"Sam, you know the drill. Have a seat. Get comfortable. I'm going to dim the lights. All you have to do is listen to my voice."

Sam sat in the cushioned chair and closed his eyes. He remained that way several minutes before the professor spoke again.

"You're doing very well. You are safe and secure. You are visualizing yourself succeeding. What you study stays with you, and you are able to access your knowledge during exams."

"Yes, I can."

"Are you sleepy, Sam?"

"Yes."

"That's good. Are you comfortable?"

"Very."

"Okay, relax. All you need to do is listen to my voice. I will be giving you directives to follow that will help you achieve your goals." He spoke in soothing tones, pausing after each sentence, giving it time to sink in. "We're going to practice again what we did last time. When I place this vibration on your arm, it will put you into a deep sleep. Understand?"

"Yes."

"What do you understand?"

"When I feel the vibration, I can sleep."

"That's right. Same as last time."

Siddiqui took a small electric vibrator out of his pocket and turned it on. Gently, he extended Sam's arm and placed the vibrator an inch above his wrist.

Within seconds, Sam was snoring loudly.

"Sam, can you hear me?"

No response.

Siddiqui took out a vial from his pocket. Using a tiny dropper, he placed a droplet of clear liquid on Sam's wrist, just where he had introduced the vibration.

"Sam, open your eyes."

With effort, Sam opened his lids and looked at the professor, his eyes glassy.

"Stand up and go to the drawer closest to your chair. There you will find a pistol and silencer. Take them out and screw the silencer on the pistol. Do you understand?"

"Yes." Sam got up and, with dazed movements, walked to the cabinet, took out the pistol and silencer and screwed them together.

"Now shoot me."

"Hmmm?"

"Raise the pistol, aim and pull the trigger."

Sam didn't move.

"Sam, do you need me to repeat the directive?"

"Okay."

"Raise the pistol, aim at me, and pull the trigger."

Sam hesitated, but this time, he lifted the piece, aimed at the professor and pulled the trigger. Three times.

Click. Click. Click. No bullets.

"Well done, Sam. You're ready. Now put the pistol back where you found it and sit back down."

He did so.

"When I tell you to come out of your sleep state, you will do so, and forget everything we did today. You will have the desire to study for several hours and focus on schoolwork. Do you understand?"

"Yes."

"Okay, I will count. On five, you will awaken, feel refreshed, no memory of the gun... One. Start coming awake."

Sam stirred, his breath coming softer.

"Two. Forget all about the gun. Three. You feel rested and refreshed. Four. You are ready to study with concentration for your next exam. Five. You are fully awake."

Sam sat up, his eyes open and clear. "Hey, Doc. Great session."

"How do you feel?"

"Awesome. Actually, if it's okay with you, I think I'll get out of here early. I really need to study for my test on Tuesday."

"Certainly. See you next week."

* * *

In Agent Matthew's office, Jon was shocked. Watching his friend so utterly manipulated had been eerie and unnerving. Stunned by what he just witnessed, Jon asked Matthews to make a copy and send it to Sam's attorney and the DA's office.

"Doing that as we speak. This drug is something else. In the wrong hands, it could cause a world war."

"The way things look, that ship may have sailed," Jon said.

"Let's hope it's not too late," Melanie said.

Jon agreed, but more than anything, he was thankful, as there was no question now. This DVD would get Sam off.

CHAPTER 59

Dallas

A t his apartment, Jon logged into his email account and found a note from Granny Eunice. She'd apparently found a joke website and selected several to send him. He would read them later when in a better mood.

Another recent email was from an address he didn't recognize. The paperclip icon told him it contained a photo attachment, but he knew better than to click on it. He was about to delete it when he read the subject line. Jon...this should help you find what you're looking for. While the words were ambiguous, spam mail never referred to him as Jon. It was always Jonathan. This was a personalized email. He clicked it open.

Above a link was written, You may find this interesting. Pack layers. The hairs on the back of his neck stood up. Still hesitant to open an unknown link, he looked more closely at the sender's Yahoo email address. He had no way to trace it.

"Here goes nothing," he said aloud. He clicked on the link, Slowly, a photo began to upload, its pixilation making it difficult to see properly. He resized the photo. A group of men and women stood huddled together, grinning for the camera. They were surrounded by dense foliage, dressed in tank tops and hiking boots, all wearing sunglasses. While they all appeared rugged and tanned, one guy stood out. He was built like a bodybuilder, muscles bulging, skin parched, hair in Rastafarian braids. The picture was captioned with red marker reading "Happy Holidays from New Beginnings." Signatures of the assembled crew were scribbled beside their images. All but one were blurred out. Only HeMan's was legible. *Chase Larson.*

Jon looked closely at the image. *What the hell was going on?*

And then it came to him as a sudden flashback. "New beginnings" were Carrera's last words before being shot.

Who is Chase Larson and what could he have to do with a paid assassin from Spain shot off a bridge in Cincinnati?

He printed the photo, and picked up his phone.

❊ ❊ ❊

Chase Larson sounded like a self-absorbed jerk. "I don't have time for this now."

"This is urgent. Peoples' lives are at stake. What's so important that you won't help us?" Jon demanded.

"I didn't say I wouldn't help you. Just not now. In all fairness, you call me out of the blue and expect me to drop everything to help you—a stranger—figure out a national security issue."

"What do you mean out of the blue? You sent me the photo!"

"Look man, I didn't send you anything. And if I were you I'd stay clear of whatever *was* sent to you. You don't know what you're getting yourself into."

"So you do know what this is about?"

"I have a hunch. And if I'm right it could be dangerous territory."

"Then tell me! What do you know?"

"This isn't something I'm comfortable discussing over the phone," Chase said firmly.

Was it fear Jon heard in the man's voice?

"Then let's meet in person." Jon said, forcing down his exasperation.

"I can't come out east right now. I'm in the middle of an important project and working on a deadline. The university is holding a symposium in two weeks on fossils found here, deep in the canyons. I need to get out to the dig site and finish my work so it's ready in time. I simply can't allow anything to derail me. If I'm late, I'll lose my job. And I won't find another one. So, excuse me, but my livelihood comes first."

Jon saw Chase Larson wasn't going to budge. He obviously knew what this was about, at least to some extent. Jon needed to wrestle some answers from this guy, learn the truth about New Beginnings and its connection to Carrera. "What if I come to you?"

"Fine," Chase said, reluctantly. "I think I can shed some light on the issue."

"Where can we meet?"

"Where I currently make my home. In God's country. Springdale, Utah."

CHAPTER 60

Springdale, Utah

The rented cabin was tucked into the woods of southwestern Utah, a good ten minutes from the closest paved road. A new ATV was parked off the side of the pebbled driveway.

Melanie and Jon got out of the rental car. "It's adorable," she said.

"Come on, let's go in," Jon said.

Melanie agreed to put aside their differences for the sake of learning more about New Beginnings. After online searches had yielded hundreds of businesses with that name, they had called Donna. She was also going to do some investigating on the group from her end.

The log cabin was new and well-built, potted poinsettias lined the entranceway. Jon entered the code he was given into the door keypad. A waist-high carved wooden bear welcomed them. There was a small, updated kitchen to the left, with forest-themed dishes set neatly on a round pine table. Steps led up to a great room, a carpeted space filled with deep sofas covered in chenille pillows and throws. A floor to ceiling fireplace was the room's focal point, with sliders on either side leading out to a spacious veranda overlooking the mountains. Another set of stairs opened onto a charming master bedroom with en-suite bathroom. The king-size bed was decked in a patchwork quilt and more pillows.

"I think I've found my forever home," Melanie said.

Jon was glad to see her relaxed and smiling. Renting the cabin rather than separate hotel rooms was more economical. And potentially more romantic. "I'll bring in the bags."

"I'll make hot cocoa and meet you out on the porch."

"Sounds wonderful."

❊ ❊ ❊

By the time they unpacked and changed into sweats, the sun had set. Melanie stared in awe at the breathtaking starlit sky. The temperature had plummeted to near-freezing. Bundled up in a thick pile of throws, they leaned back in the Adirondack chairs, gazing skyward. Jon pointed. "There's the Milky Way. That's Saturn over there."

He looked over at Melanie. "I know we're not here on vacation, but I'm glad we're together."

"Me too. What's the plan for tomorrow?"

"We're meeting Chase at 8:00 a.m. at a local gas station before he sets out to his dig site. It was the only way to get time with him."

"He sounds like quite the character."

"Sure does, but at least we'll get a chance to look around. From what we've seen so far, it's going to be magnificent."

❊ ❊ ❊

Chase met them at the Texaco station. He looked to be in his late fifties, lean build but still muscular. He wore a bandana, saber-tooth necklace and well-worn hiking boots. The dreadlocks were gone. It was shortly after sunrise, yet his sunburnt face sported a five o'clock shadow.

He put out a calloused hand. "Chase Larson, good to meet

you."

The air was cold, around forty degrees, but all Chase wore were jeans and a long-sleeve t-shirt. He eyed the two young people with amusement, clad in thick jackets, hats and gloves.

"You'll be shedding those layers within ten minutes." He sized them up. "We've been lucky, had no snow in a week. Makes it easier." He paused, nodding at them. "Glad you two could make it out here."

Irritated, Jon replied, "Way it sounded, we didn't have much of a choice. We need answers about New Beginnings. Now. Someone sent me that photo and you're in it. Which means you're our only solid lead."

Melanie gave him a stern look, so Jon added, "But we appreciate you meeting with us."

Chase did a three-sixty spin, hands outstretched. "Where better to meet? I've travelled the world and there's nowhere I'd rather put down whatever roots I have than here, tucked away between Zion and Bryce."

Done with the small talk, Jon said, "We have a lot to ask you and time is of the essence." Jon took out his phone, pulling up the photo emailed to him. "Can you take a look at this?"

Chase took the mobile device. "Wow, someone emailed this to you?"

"Yeah. Thought it was you."

"Definitely not me." He studied the photo. "Looks like someone blurred all the faces except for mine. I remember posing for this picture. There's me in my dreads. Nasty things, impossible to keep clean. Chopped 'em off the day I got back to the States."

Melanie said, "You all look happy, like good friends on a fun work trip."

"I suppose we were. This photo was taken at the start of our project. We hadn't found the chrysanthemum yet. No reason for discord."

Jon was stunned at the admission. "You're the ones who found Chrysanthemum Exotic?"

Chase hesitated, "Yes. That's what the expedition was about. But I had nothing to do with it beyond that point." He saw the skepticism in Jon's face.

"We were hoping you could identify the others," Melanie said.

He pointed. "That's Shannon Pierce, geologist. I heard he got a good job with NASA. Moved to Florida. Next to him is Portia, the Brazilian conservationist. She acted as our overseer, making sure we followed the local laws. Right next to me is Lorne, an ecologist. Retired to some warm weather place. Heard he had a heart attack. Beside him is Juan, our guide, and finally, Kel, our team leader and New Beginnings rep." Chase looked at his watch. "We need to get moving, take advantage of the daylight. I'm heading out to Coral Peak to check on a dig site. There's something down there I think you should see."

Jon shook his head vehemently. "There's no time for that! We need you to tell us what you guys were doing on that expedition."

"Then you'll need to join me." Chase said calmly.

"What do you want to show us?" Melanie asked.

"I kept samples of extremely rare botanical specimens I brought back from the expedition undetected," Chase admitted. "I put them in a box and buried it. Out here. If you join me, we can dig it up together. You'll get your answers and not have to just take me at my word."

Amazed, Melanie said, "I don't understand why you risked bringing contraband back to the States."

"As the expedition proceeded I began to sense something was amiss and I might need them as an insurance policy."

Melanie looked at the rocky landscape. "Wouldn't a safe deposit box be more convenient?"

"We're dealing with powerful people. I needed a place I knew was secure. The dig is my turf. No one would find it there unless I told them where to look."

Jon said, "Can't you just dig it up yourself? We'll meet you back here when you're done."

"Mr. Steadman, you've come all this way. If you want answers I suggest you assist with digging, both for the box and my fossils. I could use the help. And from what I gather, you need mine. Besides, joining me in the canyons will give you a better understanding of what I do and an appreciation of this beautiful unspoiled country. Coral Peak was once the ocean floor. You can still find fossilized seashells and fish on the mountain."

Jon was ready with his retort, when Melanie, enthralled, said, "No kidding? Sounds fascinating."

Content that at least one of his visitors was interested, he said, "Sure is. Grab your packs. We'll take my pickup. Your car won't make it up those roads. We can talk on the way."

❊ ❊ ❊

Melanie sat up front, Jon behind her, watching as three colorful hot air balloons drifted above, the red mountain peaks soaring in the background. She asked, "Chase, how did you get caught up in this mess?"

"If you mean the New Beginnings project, I'll tell you. Nearly five years ago, I got a call from an old colleague who I had previously worked with. He was asked by a non-profit to join a six-month expedition to Brazil. His wife was expecting, and he couldn't take the assignment. He asked me if I was available and I jumped on it. I was thrilled to get the job. It's every naturalist's dream. Journalists and photographers—from top periodicals such as *National Geographic*—vie for those jobs. I knew it was a once in a lifetime opportunity. The point being, I didn't ask too many questions. The budget was there, I would be getting well paid and doing what I love."

"What was the job?" Melanie asked.

"To join an elite team of scientists, commissioned to explore areas of the deep Amazon and study its natural resources, then write up our findings."

Melanie was intrigued. "What sort of resources?"

"Soil characteristics, plant and wildlife, air quality, and such."

Melanie said, "If I may ask, what were you trained in?"

"I studied anthropology in college with an emphasis on primitive tribes."

Melanie turned in her seat and gave Jon a knowing look. "Was the expedition a success?" she asked.

"Very much so. We spent several months, day and night learning about the territory, meeting with local tribesmen and conducting the best tests we could under the conditions. We photographed species of insects we never knew existed, learned about the behaviors of indigenous primates and reptiles."

"Sounds like you accomplished a great deal in those few months."

"Indeed," Chase said, jerking the vehicle to the right to avoid a muddy pothole. "We assembled an extraordinary team of experts in several fields of study. Each member was expected to focus solely on their area and not be distracted by anyone else's work."

"Did it play out that way?" asked Melanie.

"For the most part, yes. But six months is nothing when making new discoveries. Each member was given a grant to continue the analyses stateside, and an NDA to sign. All data was sent to the sponsor."

"An NDA?"

"A non-disclosure agreement. No findings were to be released to the public until the sponsors reviewed them."

"Is that legal?"

"I don't know but that wasn't my problem. The lawyers could deal with that. I only wanted to do my job. But thinking about it in retrospect, there was no government funding involved, so it probably was on the up and up."

"What about plants specimens? Who oversaw that project?"

Chase smiled grimly. "For better or worse, that was my project. And as I suspected, that's why you're here. I knew this day was coming and I'll do my best to answer your questions." Chase hesitated. "Brazilian and international laws are strict regarding specimen acquisition. Permits for the expedition were nearly impossible to get, and taking samples is strictly monitored. A field representative from the Brazilian conservation authority accompanied us to make sure we didn't violate any rules."

He pulled off the road into a makeshift parking spot. "Here we are. Coral Point."

The scenery was unlike anything Jon had seen before. The landscape was rocky, chiseled into red-toned cliffs giving it a timeless and majestic aura. The canyon walls were striated with beige and amber otherworldly waves. The air was cool but invigorating.

"I first came here in '08 when I was hired by the Museum of Natural History in New York," said Chase. "They were looking for paleontologists and anthropologists to work an excavation after hikers came across early petroglyphs in these mountains. From those rock carvings, we learned a great deal about the early indigenous tribes that lived here forty thousand years ago."

He turned off the engine, leaving the keys in the ignition and opened the door.

"I finally bought myself a cabin in the area. Couldn't get enough of the place. Well, then, that's enough about me. Ready for the dig?"

Melanie answered. "Sure, as long as we can talk while we do it."

"Great! I'll grab our gear and we can get going. Take a pack with bottles of water and a hat. I have sunscreen in the back seat for you to put on. You'll need it. Last chance to leave your coats behind."

Melanie and Jon took them off.

Chase ruffled around in the bed of the pickup, filled his

large backpack and effortlessly put it on. He began walking towards the monoliths, Jon and Melanie a few steps behind.

Melanie whispered to Jon, "Is this a good idea?"

Looking at the challenging trail before them, he replied, "I sure hope so. If it's not, we're screwed."

CHAPTER 61

Coral Point, Utah

J on and Melanie had silently followed Chase hiking at a steep incline for twenty minutes, building up a sweat. Chase stopped, giving them a chance to catch their breath and enjoy the view of vermillion bluffs blending seamlessly into crystalline skies. He dropped his pack alongside a foot-high cairn, and extracted two collapsible shovels, handing one to Jon. "This is our first stop, where we dig for the plant specimens. It's approximately two feet down. Shouldn't take long."

Jon and Chase dug into the red earth, softened by winter rains. Within minutes they heard the clunk of metal on metal. Chase knelt down to retrieve a small steel box secured with a padlock. He dusted it off and handed it to Jon.

Jon wiped a bead of sweat from his forehead. "Let's see what's inside."

"Later. When we're done at the archeological site. Excavating and photographing the artifacts will take a few hours and I can't waste a minute of sunlight."

Jon put the box in his pack. Together they scooped dirt back into the hole, patting it down with the backs of their shovels.

Melanie handed out water and granola bars, which they quickly finished off. Chase pulled three harnesses from his pack, supervising as Jon and Melanie donned their gear. After checking that they did it correctly, Chase gave them each a helmet.

"What do we need all this gear for?" Melanie asked, gesturing to her harness.

"See that cliff?" Chase pointed. We're going over the side."

Melanie looked ahead, where the rocky ground abruptly ended. She dared a peek over the edge and what she saw made her stomach flip. A sheer drop of two hundred feet ended in a narrow ravine. "Wait...what? No one said anything about mountain climbing!"

"We're not climbing, we're rappelling to the bottom." Chase said, as he prepped the ropes, looping them through metal caribiners.

"Why can't we hike down?"

"It would take three times as long and we're short on daylight this time of year. I need to get to the dig site."

Melanie blanched. "I can't do this."

"Sure, you can. The first time is the hardest. After that you'll be fine."

Jon interjected. "We'll go down together."

"That's right," said Chase. "I'll hook you up and come down after you. If you need help, I'll be right behind you."

Melanie thought she would be sick. *How did I get myself into this?*

"Mel, I know you can do this," said Jon. "Watch me. I'll go first and wait for you below. You'll see how easy it is. Just don't look down."

Melanie watched as Chase inspected two trees several feet back from the cliff's edge. He wrapped a rope around one trunk, then threaded it through a belay device. Chase walked over to Jon, attached the rope to his harness's caribiner pulling down on it firmly. He neatly coiled the rope before tossing it over the edge. "See? Secure. Ten men could attach to this and be safe." He then did the same on the second tree.

Jon had done this once before on an all-guys weekend in

Maine. Though nervous, he knew once he took his first steps back over the cliff's edge, it would be an exhilarating experience.

Melanie gasped as Jon positioned himself backwards at the edge of the abyss. Slowly, he let out rope, walking back a step at a time, over the side of the cliff. Before she knew it, only the top of his helmet was visible.

"Jon?"

"All good. See, there's nothing to it."

Turning to Melanie, Chase said, "Now your turn."

Terrified, all she could do was nod. She allowed Chase to rig her up and position her to where she would begin her descent. He showed her again how to let the cord out.

"You're going to do great, Mel," Jon called out.

Instinctively, Melanie turned to Jon's voice and immediately regretted it. They were so high off the ground. She became dizzy, closed her eyes and moaned audibly.

Chase said, "Melanie, look up at me. That's it. Now slowly, lean back and let out some cord, while you take a step."

She couldn't move. *Breathe*, she told herself. *Breathe, like you do in yoga class.* Slowly, she moved her left leg back, tapped into her reserve courage to lean back, and let out a bit of cord. Standing at a forty-five-degree angle, the tautness of the cable provided a sense of security.

"Well done. Take another step." And she did.

"I'm so proud of you," said Jon. "Now try to enjoy it."

"That would be a big leap. Um, bad choice of words."

Jon laughed, looking relieved when Melanie was beside him.

Chase called out. "I'll watch you two get to the bottom and bring up the rear."

Gradually, they started down the sheer mountainside, taking each step with more confidence.

* * *

Chase was monitoring the couple's progress, and hooking up his own harness, when he heard a noise behind him. Expecting a deer, he was shocked and took a stumbling step backwards when he saw a woman emerge from the bushes. She was dressed in military camouflage, a tactical backpack slung over a shoulder.

He did a doubletake. "Kelly? What are you doing here?"

"I could ask you the same thing."

Startled and confused, he replied, "I live near here. I'm showing my friends a dig site."

"Your friends? Chase, don't insult my intelligence."

A sense of foreboding came over him. "Why are you here?" he repeated.

"The Boss sent me here to talk to you. You've betrayed us."

"I did no such thing. You sent me on a job and I did it. And well, I might add."

"True. Without you, we never would have secured the drug. But it seems you've gone rogue."

"Had I known what the expedition was really about, I never would have taken the job. But I kept my word. Never told a soul about it."

"How kind of you, given that your own involvement would have put you behind bars for a long time."

Chase couldn't deny it. He hadn't taken what he knew to the authorities, fearful he wouldn't be granted immunity.

Kelly went on, "And yet here you are, spending quality time with two people determined to expose what we've accomplished. Your work, however, is finished. Hand over the box."

A prickle of fear ran up his spine. "What are you saying?"

"We set you up to see if you would take the bait. An email from us led Steadman to you for information. And what possible reason could you have to invite them here? Why else but to expose us?"

Chase began to respond but Kelly cut him off. "We have a policy at the organization. Traitorous behavior is dealt with swiftly and without mercy. It's the only way to keep moving forward."

She took a gun from a holster at her back, aimed and approached him. "The box."

"I don't have it."

Kelly grabbed Chase's pack, searching it. "You gave it to them?"

Chase remained silent.

"I see you brought a shovel. How convenient. You'll save me the trouble and bury the bodies. I've been busy silencing traitors lately. Had to take one out just a few weeks ago in Cincinnati. Nice clean shot. Put him over the side of a bridge, never to be heard from again. Before that was a pathetic professor—in the wrong place at the wrong time."

She was only feet from where Chase stood. He stepped back, watching her holster the gun, then pull a Swiss Army knife from her pocket. She flicked it open, bent down on one knee and grabbed one of the rappelling ropes.

"What are you doing?" he yelled in fear.

"Solving a problem. One that you created."

"Are you crazy? Someone is attached to that line." He took a step forward.

Pointing the knife's edge at him, she replied, "Not for long. Stand back." Kelly sawed at the rope.

"They're just kids," said Chase. "Don't do this." Chase stepped closer.

"Those *kids* have caused too much trouble." The cord frayed quickly. With each cut, Kelly became more manic, a visage of pure rage on her face. "That's it. One more to go."

* * *

Halfway down, Jon felt a sudden jolt. His rope slackened and he dropped ten feet fast, hitting his head against the side of the mountain. The helmet took the blow, but he was shaken up.

Startled and scared, he yelled up, "Chase! What happened?"

Melanie was below. "You okay, Jon?"

"My rope just gave way."

He felt another pull and slack. "Someone's cutting my line!"

"Find something to hold on to!"

He scrambled desperately, looking for anything to grab hold of. He was still one hundred feet off the ground. The drop would kill him.

Melanie called from below, "There! Next to your right leg. It looks like a ledge."

Jon looked down. Sure enough, there was an outcropping a few feet below. He shimmied his body slowly, placing his right foot on the ledge. Relieved to have stability, he took a deep breath.

"Okay, now try to find a handhold," said Mel. "I'm going to swing my rope next to you."

Jon felt the blood drain from his face.

Melanie shouted, "Jon, look at me. Remember what Chase said? Lots of people can attach to one cord."

She tested a small pendulum movement, making a narrow arc with her body, then a larger one. "When I get to you, grab hold of my harness. You ready?"

He was about to consent when there was another jolt. Jon's rope slackened, causing him to lose his grip, dropping him ten more feet.

"Jon!"

Instinctively, he held tight to the cable, though it was counterproductive. He loosened his grip, careful to move as little as possible, aware the rope was likely down to its last threads. He scanned the surrounding area and found a place for his feet.

"Hold tight. I'm coming." Melanie lowered herself to Jon's new location. She used both arms and legs, alternately pushing off the rockface in a back and forth manner. When Jon couldn't bring himself to lean her way, her first attempt failed.

"Let's try again," she said. "This time I'll try to get closer. You'll need to reach out to me and hold on."

"Okay. I'm ready."

Melanie pushed off again, this time with more pressure. When she was within an arm's length, he reached out and grabbed her around the waist and let his feet go.

At that moment, Jon's rope snapped, the length of it falling inches from their dangling bodies and into the abyss.

"Oh God!" he cried. He was completely untethered.

"Hold on. Don't let go." Melanie held onto him tightly.

They swung for a few moments, dangling in a life-or-death embrace. Melanie steadied the rope, allowing Jon to find a foothold. While he held her, she located Jon's caribiner and looped an extension of her rope through his harness hooks. "We're attached!"

Jon shoulders slumped, though he kept the hold on her. "Thank you, Mel," he whispered.

She let out a sob. "I got you now. We're going to be okay. Let's get to the bottom before he gets started on my rope."

Together, they worked their way down until they reached terra firma.

* * *

Chase felt sick as he saw the rope snap, rip apart and fly over the cliff, like a snake shot by a rifleman. There was nothing left holding Jon up, and no way for him to survive that fall.

He also knew Kelly had no intention of allowing him to walk away from this. He had just witnessed her commit murder. He had only one chance.

As Kelly grinned at her handiwork, Chase bent over, grabbed a rock, took quick aim and threw it. It hit her on the side of the head. He didn't wait. He clipped his cable to the anchor and went over the side. Bullets came flying, soaring over his head.

But she had no vantage point without risking her life lean-ing over the edge. Unable to gauge his position, she was firing blindly. He quickly leaped from one spot to the next. Know-ing it would take her too long to dislodge his cable, he was fairly confident that—if he didn't get hit by a stray bullet—he'd make it to the bottom alive.

CHAPTER 62

Coral Point, Utah

Jon and Melanie lay on the ground, spent, their adrenaline tapering off.

They sat up and undid their harnesses. Melanie wrapped her arms around her legs and took a deep breath. Jon put an arm around her shoulders.

"Anything broken?" he asked.

"I don't think so. How about you?"

"I hit my head a few times, but the helmet took the brunt of it. We're lucky to be alive. Thank you for saving my life."

In response, Melanie squeezed his hand. "I can't believe Chase tried to kill us. He had me fooled." She stood. "We need to keep moving." She took her phone out of her back pocket. "There's no signal. And no navigation. You have any idea how to get out of here?"

"No. Just that we need to head east. Chase is an outdoorsman. He can track us. We need a plan."

"Oh my God! Look at that!"

Jon looked up the side of the mountain to see Chase racing downward. Suddenly the distinct sound of bullets ricocheted off the canyon walls.

"Oh God. Someone's shooting at him. What's happening?"

Jon grabbed Melanie's hand. "I don't know, but we need to get out of here, and take cover until we figure it out."

Jon and Melanie left the heavy gear behind and ran, side by side between the canyon walls.

"Wait!" Chase yelled from above.

"Don't stop," said Jon. "He's probably armed."

The two of them ran as quickly and quietly as they could, even as the sound of their footfalls echoed through the gorge. Every few steps they encountered another boulder to maneuver around or over, scraping elbows and knees in a mad rush.

Chase called out again, his voice echoing in the cavernous space. "Jon, Melanie, please, wait up. Kelly is out there! She has a gun! You won't find your way out without me!"

Catching his breath, Jon whispered to Melanie. "Who's Kelly?"

"I don't know. Wait. Kelly...the name rings a bell."

"Keep moving. We need to get away from him. He could be trying to trick us."

Exhausted and out of breath, Melanie said, "Listen to his voice. He sounds desperate too. At this pace we'll never outrun him, and we haven't a clue how to get out of these mountains. We need to find something to defend ourselves with."

Quickly, they stockpiled fist-size rocks, then hid behind a large boulder and waited.

Melanie called out. "Stop where you are and tell us what happened."

Chase called out. "When you were halfway down your rappel, Kelly Flanagan showed up."

"Who's that?"

"She hired me for the Amazon expedition I told you about. She's one of the higher ups at the syndicate."

"Describe her."

"About five foot eight, usually in a business suit, though not today, red hair worn in a bun. Very fit."

"That sounds like Kelly—the woman who works in Matthews' office," Melanie said.

"That makes no sense." Jon called out to Chase, "What does Kelly want?"

"To kill you. Said you're causing too many problems for the syndicate. Her boss put a contract out on you as the ringleader. If I hadn't stalled her with a well-thrown rock, I'd be dead now. She has no gear, but plenty of firepower. You need my help or she'll catch up to you before you find your way out."

Jon said to Melanie angrily, "I never trusted Matthews. All this time he's been one step ahead of us."

"If what Chase is saying is true," said Melanie. "Do you believe him?"

"I don't think we have a choice." Jon looked at Melanie, "I'll go first. If he shoots, run for it. Got it?"

She nodded. Jon stepped out.

Chase stood in the clearing, looking ragged and terrified, relief flooding his features. No gun, no knife. "Thanks for believing me. Where's Melanie?"

Jon didn't move. "Show me you're unarmed."

Chase pulled up his shirt, emptied his pockets and lifted his pant legs. He opened his backpack for Jon to check.

"Mel, he's clean. You can come out."

Melanie stepped from the hiding place, a large rock in her hand. "Okay, now what?"

Chase took a compass out of his bag. "Now we get out of here." He turned in the opposite direction from where Jon and Melanie were headed. "Follow me."

* * *

As he guided Jon and Melanie through a slot canyon, Chase took in Jon's appearance. No blood. Same limp as before. "How did you survive the fall? I don't see any broken bones."

"Melanie swung over to me, and I grabbed hold of her just in the nick of time."

Turning to Melanie, Chase said, "For a fearful rappeller, you did good. Real good."

Jon asked, "Why does Kelly want to kill you?"

Chase deftly maneuvered around a boulder in their path, followed by Melanie. Jon struggled to keep up, his leg throbbing.

"By inviting you here, her superiors believed I was going to blow the whistle on them."

"About what?"

"Chrysanthemum exotic. When I found it I had no idea what it was. Its appearance was similar to opioid poppies in Afghanistan but was clearly a different genus. I knew it was something to be studied. I was permitted one small sample. I documented our precise location and let Kelly know where I had found it. Later, when I returned to the base, I did all I could to classify it, with little success, so I decided to speak with the locals."

Melanie said, "They told you when it was ground down and stored properly it had powerful characteristics."

Chase looked stunned. "How'd you know that?"

"We obtained DNA from three individuals who attempted or succeeded in carrying out killing sprees."

"Oh God. Then they're carrying out their plan after all." Chase sounded defeated. "While on the expedition, I couldn't sleep one night, so I left my tent and went out for a short walk. As it happens, I overheard Kelly on the satellite phone. I could only follow her side of the conversation, but it was clear she was talking to her boss. She spoke of testing Chrysanthemum Exotic on unsuspecting subjects. I was horrified. The drug derivation is psychotropic. Users would not be in control of their actions."

"You still brought the plant home, knowing their plan and despite the strict laws?"

"When I understood what could be done with our research, I spoke up. I was reminded of my NDA and threatened with legal action. I never thought they would go through with it." Chase looked down to the ground. "They were bringing the opioid back no matter what I did. I have no clue how they circumvented the rules. In retrospect, maybe well-placed bribes, but we left with a sizeable amount of Chrysanthemum Exotic."

Jon said, "We need to know who runs New Beginnings and put a stop to the terror. We have reason to believe they're planning something big."

"But I don't know who's running it. The only one I had contact with was Kelly."

"What about the other members of the expedition team?"

"All subcontractors. With one or two exceptions, I brought them in."

"And the boss Kelly was calling from Brazil?"

"I don't recall a name being said. I'll have to think about it. In the meantime, we need to speed up. Night falls quickly here, and we don't want to be stuck in the canyons after dark with a madwoman on the loose and no overnight gear. We still have a good hike to the Suburban."

Jon felt his leg swelling up. "Let's hope she doesn't get there before us and disable the truck. That's what I would do if I were her."

* * *

Kelly opened her small pack and took out a first aid kit. Her eagerness to finish off the interlopers had caused her to let down her guard for a moment. Which Chase exploited. The Boss wanted him taken alive for questioning to assess how much he'd already divulged. But now Kelly would not stop until she killed him along with the other two. She did her best to clean and bandage the cut on her head without the benefit of a mirror. The way it felt, she would need a few stitches. *Bastard.*

She turned on her satellite phone and used the tracking app to locate Chase. It was her good fortune that he still had the same phone since the last time they saw each other a few days after returning from Brazil, when the group reconvened to submit their findings. Given his inside knowledge of their research and his righteous indignation, she had come to the meeting prepared, and slipped a tracker into his phone. In the early weeks following their return, she periodically checked Chase's whereabouts. During that time, he never went near a police station or FBI office.

Kelly's phone screen tracked him moving at a slow but steady pace, making a beeline for their vehicle. With the rope cutting, one was surely dead, and now their slow progress told her at least one of those remaining was injured. She would intercept them and take them down. Painfully.

* * *

"Hold up," Jon told the others. "I can't keep the pace. My leg is killing me."

"I have an idea," Chase said, "The two of you go ahead, follow the direction we're heading in, and you should be back at my truck in twenty minutes or so. The keys are in the ignition."

"Where are you going?" Jon asked skeptically.

"I'll backtrack and try to slow Kelly down. She is a trained mercenary. Even though she has more ground to cover, she's alone and can move faster than we can. I'll be close behind you. If I'm not back within a few minutes of your getting to the truck, leave without me."

Melanie and Jon glanced at each other. Jon said what they were both thinking. "You up to something, Chase?"

"What do you mean?"

"How do we know you aren't sending us in the wrong direction and that your keys are actually in the truck?"

"You checked everything in my pockets and pack. You see any keys?"

He had a point, but something still seemed off.

"How about this?" said Chase. "You can have my phone. It has a virtual compass that works without a signal. I'll need to hold on to my real one just in case."

Jon felt better accepting the phone as collateral. It couldn't be easy for Chase to forfeit it.

"Okay, we'll do our best to wait for you. Good luck."

"Do what you need to do. If nothing else, it will be penance if you have to leave me behind. I can handle myself out here."

Jon put the phone in his pocket and grabbed Melanie's hand. "Okay, let's go."

＊ ＊ ＊

Kelly checked her tracking device. Chase was slowing. At this pace, she would catch up quickly. She raised her binoculars and peered out on the canyons before her. There, she saw movement. She spotted a split second of long brown hair. *The girl!* She was moving carefully, squeezing between the rocks, 250 yards due north. Kelly had the advantage, knowing where her prey was, and now she saw the most direct way to them.

＊ ＊ ＊

Chase stayed still, sneaking a glance beyond the rock wall getting a quick view of the clearing. A flat limestone surface lay directly below an outcropping fifty feet above. He had done the best he could, devising a crude trap, no different than the kind he learned back in Boy Scouts.

He waited, refusing to allow himself to think of what would happen if the trap failed. He would draw Kelly out, make himself a target. Chase owed the kids that much, having put them in harm's way. He was bait without an escape plan.

CHAPTER 63

Coral Point, Utah

K elly was making excellent time. Ahead was a fifty-foot drop, one she could hike down in a few minutes. She looked over the side and was surprised to see Chase. That made no sense. According to the tracker, he should have been several minutes ahead of her. But he was crouched behind a boulder, his moans reverberating off the stone walls. He's injured and the girl left him behind. Easy prey.

He gave his phone to his surviving companion. No matter. Kelly would pick him off now and get the other one later. She walked determinedly to the edge, preparing for the descent when suddenly she was yanked off her feet, dangling upside down from a tree, swaying over the cliff's edge.

"Ahh!"

Chase watched his handiwork with a mix of pride and revulsion. He emerged into the open.

Kelly struggled, squirming like a worm on a hook. "Get me down from here!" she screamed.

Chase called up to her. "Maybe after you tell me what the hell is going on."

She wriggled furiously. "I'm going to get out of this and then I'm going to kill you."

Chase was impressed with her defiance. He watched from

below as Kelly, with incredible core strength, bent her body upwards and held on to her ankles, unsheathing her knife. She was going to try to cut herself free.

"You're in no position to threaten me," he said.

Kelly lost hold of her ankles and fell back. The knife dropped from her grasp, ricocheting off the rocks below. She reached for her gun.

"If you shoot me, you'll be left here with no one to cut you down. And you don't have a shot. I could walk away slowly before you could even aim that thing."

"Do I have your word that you'll cut me down if I tell you what you want to know?"

"Yes. You have my word. Now tell me who's in charge of New Beginnings."

"I don't know."

Chase crossed his arms, staring at his quarry. "I don't believe you. You were in touch with someone while on the expedition."

"There are new people involved now. I don't know who, but I can give you the name of someone who does know."

Annoyed with her evasiveness, Chase asked, "Who?"

She told him.

"From the expedition?"

"Yes. He has a higher position than me. Closer to the top."

"What has New Beginnings morphed into?"

"We've built an army of underground followers. A syndicate," Kelly offered with a note of arrogance even as her voice weakened. "Now get me down."

Chase strained to hear her from where he stood. Her eyelids fluttered, blood rushing to her head. He would need to get answers fast. "What are they trying to accomplish?"

Weakly, Kelly said, "The Event."

"What's that?"

"We'll demonstrate the full power of Chrysanthemum Exotic on an global scale. Then sell it to the highest bidder—one who will kill in the name of the greater good."

Appalled by what he heard, Chase asked, "Where? When?"

Kelly closed her eyes. She was losing consciousness. She didn't deserve to be cut down, but he'd keep his word.

"Drop your weapons and I'll cut you down."

Kelly pulled the firearm from her holster and held it out.

"Throw it over the edge."

She let the piece go. It produced a loud clanging echo as it hit the ground.

He ran to retrieve the gun and knife and then nimbly scrambled up the rocks to the top. He approached her from behind, scaling the tree that held her, then reached out, pulled her twisting form toward him, and grabbed onto the binding that held her. Using Kelly's knife, he began to cut her loose. Just then a black raven flew towards them, its wingspan a good three feet across. It squawked and landed on the branch beside her bound legs, showing no concern for them. The sudden noise roused Kelly.

Despite her weakened state, her fear was evident. "Get it out of here! I hate birds."

Chase made a motion to shoo the bird away, but it didn't budge.

Kelly jerked sharply to distance herself from the creature, her body now spinning perilously over the edge, her face blood red.

"Don't move!"

The raven spread its wings wide and flitted towards Kelly's hanging frame.

She jerked once more, causing the rope to give way, screaming in terror as she fell fifty feet to the red rocks below.

CHAPTER 64

Coral Point, Utah

The hike back to the truck was harrowing. Chase had given them a phone without service and vague directions. Still, after taking one short break to catch their breath, Jon and Melanie reached the SUV, relieved to find its keys in the ignition, just as Chase promised.

Jon's leg was numb, his limp more pronounced as he did a quick scan of the area and the truck, checking the tires. No slashes. Melanie got into the driver's seat.

"What do we do now?" she asked.

"We follow Chase's instructions and wait five minutes. If we see Kelly, we take off, calling the police as soon as we get a signal."

The minutes crawled by in silence.

Melanie looked at the digital clock on the dash. "I don't want to leave him behind. What if he's in trouble?"

"He told us he could manage. He knows these mountains like the back of his hand."

"But there's a killer out here."

"Exactly. I'm not risking our lives any longer. Let's go."

Melanie turned the key and the engine came to life. She stepped on the gas, kicking up a dust cloud as they took off.

"Mel, stop!"

She peered in the rearview mirror, There was Chase, coming their way in a full-on run. She slammed the brakes. Jon had already rolled down his window. "Come on!"

Chase pulled open the back door and jumped in. "Go!"

Melanie hit the accelerator. They swerved a moment, then sped as fast as the truck would take them out of the canyons and back to civilization.

❊ ❊ ❊

Southern Utah Medical Center

An unmistakable smell of antiseptic filled Melanie's nostrils as she watched orderlies and nurses wearing rubber-soled clogs, come and go. Despite constant movement, the ER was eerily quiet.

Chase sat beside her in the waiting room. Jon had been taken up to Radiology for x-rays. She glanced at the clock. 6:35. They'd been waiting nearly two hours. She fidgeted, going over recent events in her mind.

"While you were seeing the doctor, I called the cops from the hospital payphone," Chase said. "Gave them my name. I kept you both out of it. The cop on call knows me—he'd taken one of my classes. Anyway, he took down my story about Kelly's accident. Said he'll go out to Coral Point at first light, or there won't be much left of her to clean up."

Melanie winced.

"I'll go downtown to give a statement in the morning. Not sure how I'm going to explain everything. It might look like foul play, with the trap and all. But it was self-defense, no way around it."

"Thanks for what you did."

Chase patted her hand. "I know I'm a self-absorbed asshole, but I wasn't going to let her come after us without a fight."

A nurse in light blue scrubs and a warm smile walked towards them, addressing Melanie. "Ms. Ridgefield? Mr. Steadman asked for you. Please follow me."

"I'll be out here," Chase said.

The nurse led Melanie to a small space, cordoned off by a cloth curtain. A bleary-eyed doctor was leaning over Jon listening to his chest with a stethoscope. "Heart sounds strong. Good blood pressure too. Now let's take a look at your leg."

Jon was lying on the hospital bed, dressed in a shin-length fabric gown.

Melanie asked, "You sure you want me here? I can wait right outside."

"Please stay."

The doctor palpitated Jon's leg gingerly. "Does this hurt?"

"Not too bad."

"Good. Looks like nothing's broken but you're going to have some scary discolorations for a while. Give it a chance to heal....now what's this? You've had a previous injury?"

Jon took a deep breath and answered the doctor's question, looking instead at Melanie as he did so. "Yes, a few years ago, I broke my hip, leg, and a few ribs."

"I'm so sorry. Any complications since then?"

"A limp." Still looking at Melanie, he added, "And what I'm learning is called PTSD."

Melanie's eyes watered.

"Are you seeing someone for that?" asked the doctor.

"No... but I will," he said to Melanie with determination and promise. "Can I go now?"

"Soon enough. I'll have the nurse bandage up your scrapes and give you discharge forms to sign. The films confirm no breakage in your leg, but you suffered a mild concussion. You'll need to stay awake for the next several hours. Call if you have any discomfort, headache or double vision."

When the doctor left, Jon opened his arms for Melanie. She went to him, careful to hug gently. Though no words were said, she understood that she was being welcomed into his inner circle and that was all she needed to know for now.

* * *

"Kelly was dangling from the tree, fighting like a trapped bear cub," Chase said quietly, on their drive back to the rental cabin. He'd relayed everything that had happened after their separation.

A minute passed in horrified silence as they absorbed all that had transpired.

"Chase, did Kelly tell you how the syndicate is funded?" Melanie asked.

"We didn't get that far. She was losing consciousness, and I needed to get her down." Chase shut his eyes as if trying to erase the image.

"If what Kelly said is true, countless lives are at stake. We have to find someone who has information about the so-called Event." Jon said.

Chase pulled up to the cabin. "Before she died, Kelly gave up the name of a top guy at New Beginnings. He was with us on the expedition. Worked security. Maybe you can track him down."

"Who is he?"

Chase killed the engine and looked at Jon and Melanie. "His name is Jim Fields."

CHAPTER 65

Springdale, Utah

B ack in the cabin, Jon tried but couldn't make sense of it. He and Melanie sat across from a bedraggled Chase who was cracking open his second beer.

Jon allowed his mind to go back to that night at BTI. If Chase had it right, Jim was there from the very beginning. Then it dawned on him. *How had I not see it earlier?* Jon said to Melanie, "He was in Boston at the time of the BTI attack."

Melanie asked, "How can you be sure?"

"Donna had a partner. I remember he was on the car radio. It had to be him."

"Why wouldn't she have mentioned it?"

"She did. I just didn't pay attention. Remember the first time Jim came to meet us in Cincinnati?"

"Yeah, he kissed her on the cheek. I thought that was weird for a colleague."

"Right. She mentioned they had worked together a short time before he moved to the FBI. Now I know it overlapped with the BTI attack."

"Do you think he was part of it?" Melanie asked, aghast.

"I know it," said Jon, fury in his eyes. "Three people died that day, including Ashleigh. I'll never give up till he pays for what he's done."

Melanie noticed it was the first time Jon mentioned Ashleigh's name to her while fully conscious. She said, "Agent Matthews is Jim Fields' and Kelly Flanagan's boss. What have we gotten ourselves into?"

"We need to warn Donna."

"You think she'll believe us?"

"I don't know, but we have to try."

It was the middle of the night on the East Coast. He would wait till morning to call Donna, which also gave him time to figure out the best way to break the rotten news.

Jon stood, brought his pack over to the sofa and handed the metal box to Chase. "Time to open this."

Chase placed the box on the coffee table, grasping the padlock. He aligned the numbers in their proper sequence, unlocking it. "This box could get me into a whole lot of trouble."

Inside were several labeled plastic bags with dried plant specimens.

"These are extremely rare botanical specimens I brought back from the expedition undetected."

"I don't understand why you risked bringing contraband back to the States." Melanie asked.

"After I learned about the plant's potential, I knew I might need a sample as an insurance policy."

He handed one bag to Melanie. A red label identified it as Chrysanthemum Exotic. Melanie passed it to Jon.

Chase said, "A truly spectacular find. In this preserved form the plant is harmless, but given the right conditions, its power is extraordinary."

Jon scrutinized the bag's contents. "Can we borrow this? Maybe it can be used to formulate a viable antidote."

"My thoughts exactly. If it can help stop the syndicate, then yes, take it, with one condition. If anyone asks where you got it, leave me out of it."

"Fair enough. I'll bring it to our friend, Gabe. He's a skilled chemist," Jon said, putting the bag in his pack.

Melanie asked Chase, "What will you do with the other specimens?"

"I'll hold on to them for now. Never know when they'll come in handy." He stood to leave, tossing two empty bottles in the trash bin.

Jon said, "One minute. There's something I meant to ask you." He clicked on the photo of the New Beginnings group. "If Jim's been with the syndicate from the start, why isn't he in the picture?"

"Simple." Chase shrugged. "He's the one that took it."

CHAPTER 66

Boston

J im lay in his king-size bed, exhausted. He hadn't slept well
the last few nights. Waiting till daybreak to rise, he
trudged into his galley kitchen and turned on the shiny
espresso machine. He'd miss the waterfront bachelor pad. But
what awaited him was worth it.

Jim impressed himself. He walked a tightrope with great
finesse, learning from Donna what Dr. Lavi and the others un-
raveled while also keeping the Feds one step behind.

Donna trusted him entirely. He thought of the night they
spent together here in his apartment. It was sexy as all hell.

Truth be told, she was growing on him. If things had been
different, he would have recruited her for New Beginnings,
even involve her in plans for the Event. She'd been keeping
him on his toes over the past few weeks. But as bright as she
was, she had yet to discover his link to the syndicate. As the
Boss said, "Love is blind...so let's exploit it."

With only one day left until the Event, he was glad to
finally end the charade. He'd been with the syndicate since its
infancy. The expedition with Chase to Brazil was his third trip
in search of a new drug. The original plan was to sell what they
found to raise funds for their cause, but when the chrysanthemum was discovered, the plan took on a wider scope.

Jim poured himself a double espresso, added three lumps

of sugar. He needed the energy boost for what would be the culmination of years of hard work. He had always known he was destined for greater things, certainly well beyond a mid-level job at the Boston PD, a position that had served only a short-term purpose—he'd been instrumental in executing the first successful drug trial at BTI. After that, he moved onto the Bureau.

As he rose in the ranks at the FBI, he also assumed a more prominent role with the syndicate, first as one of their sleeper agents, and working his way up from there.

Cure Theory was the Boss's brainchild, a lofty endeavor that really took shape after Chrysanthemum Exotic was dis-covered. With successful trials now behind them, only the Event remained, a choreographed exhibition of the drug's true power.

Jim's motives were less pure than others inside the net-work who were tirelessly working for the disenfranchised. He was in it for the power and money, and not in the least bit ashamed of it. He considered himself akin to a VP of corpor-ation. He worked hard, dedicated himself to the organization and earned fair, if not, substantial compensation.

Jim sat at the breakfast bar, took out his phone and con-nected to the device planted inside Donna's phone—the same technology used by the syndicate to track trial participants. Though he was fairly certain Donna would confide any im-portant updates, the bug kept him current on intel passed along to her. Sometimes he even saw it before her.

The log said Jon Steadman had placed several calls to Donna's phone over the past few hours without leaving a mes-sage. He was surprised. By now, he would have thought Kelly had eliminated him. It had been the Boss's ingenious idea to lead Jon and Melanie into the middle of nowhere, and for Kelly to follow.

He opened Donna's inbox. She wouldn't be alerted to his hacking; her emails would appear as unread. There was one from Jon. Jim clicked it open.

* * *

Donna let out a loud yawn, shook off the morning sluggishness, and pushed the comforter away. Despite the craziness, she couldn't help admitting she was truly happy having Jim in her life.

Doug Matthews had been a surprising help, speaking with her superiors, explaining how useful she'd been to the investigation. Her commander agreed to her continued FBI involvement, as long as she kept up with her paperwork.

She reached for her phone on the nightstand. Its battery had died overnight, and she plugged it in. Moments later, it dinged repeatedly, emails and messages coming in one after the other. *Something must have happened.* She had missed calls from Jon and Jim, and had seven emails. She checked those first. All were spam but the one from Jon. It had a photo attachment.

The email read, *D- Here's the expedition that found the chrysanthemum. Jim took the pic. So sorry about this. Please call me a.s.a.p.*

A sense of foreboding came over her. The doorbell rang. She took her phone with her as she walked to the door. *Stop being an alarmist.* Donna clicked open the image. She was looking at the same photo she saw at Jim's condo on New Year's Eve, their first night together. She couldn't make sense of it. The doorbell rang again.

"Who's there?"

"Honey, it's Jim. Open up."

CHAPTER 67

Dallas

G abe stood in the Old City of Jerusalem at the base of the Tower of David. Terry looked down at him from atop the citadel, her hair long and golden like Rapunzel. A distant bell tolled four times, and he was dragged back to consciousness. Another ring. Gabe opened his eyes and looked at his phone screen. Jon.

"What's going on?" Gabe asked. "You okay?"

"We are now, waiting for a plane."

"What happened? You still in Utah?" He whispered, not wanting to wake up Terry in the next room.

When Jon filled him in, Gabe was shocked. "You guys all right?"

"Bumps and bruises but we'll be okay. Got spared the police interrogation. Get this…before Kelly fell to her death, she implicated none other than Jim Fields as a major player in the syndicate."

"No way!" Then, "Does Donna know?"

"Not yet. But think of the info she's been passing along to Agent Fields all this time. I've been trying to reach her for hours. If you hear from her, tell her to stay away from Jim."

"I'm not sure she'll listen to me. I think she's in love with him."

"Yeah, I think so too. But first and foremost, she's a cop. If nothing else, we'll give her pause to think."

"Let's hope so," said Gabe. If he gets wind that we're on to him, she could be in jeopardy. We have to alert Matthews. If he's in on it, he can't do any more damage. If he's not, he'll help us track Jim down."

From the other end of the phone line, Gabe heard an airport announcement, a flight's last call.

"Gotta go, buddy. Say hi to Terry. See you back home."

As soon as they hung up, Gabe woke Matthews.

CHAPTER 68

Boston

L ooking in the rearview mirror, Donna slowed her black Camaro. If she stayed at this speed, she would get pulled over.

She was at a loss for how to deal with Jim. When he rang her bell, she had feigned a loud cough. Through the door, Donna said she felt ill and didn't want him to catch what she had.

Once she heard his retreating steps, she didn't wait. She hightailed it out of the back door. Her phone had been beeping for the last ten minutes. Texts and voicemails, most likely from Jim. She needed a place to think.

There was one place she knew she could stay a few days and be off the radar. She dialed the number. "Eunice. Hi, it's Donna. How would you like some company this weekend?"

* * *

Salt Lake City International Airport

Jon was not a worrier, but after trying to reach Donna since the previous evening, he was concerned. He checked his phone for missed calls. With everything going on, he couldn't imagine why she wouldn't be answering. As an afterthought, he sent a quick email. "Donna, watch your back...talk to you when I land."

The flight attendant hovered, waiting impatiently for him to turn off his phone. Jon felt his frustration rise, but there was nothing more he could do until his layover in LaGuardia. Nearly five hours away.

CHAPTER 69

South Boston

T
he brisk morning walk with Eunice past "Southie's" old-school diners, gastropubs and waterfront trails, did Donna good. Now she had a game plan on how to move forward with Jim. She tried calling Jon, but it went straight to voicemail.

The two women entered the house, Eunice locking the door behind them. Donna walked into the living room and let out a shriek. Sitting in an armchair was Jim.

"Oh God! You scared the life outa me! What on earth are you doing here?"

Eunice was livid. "Who is this guy? I'm calling the police. How dare you break into my home!"

Donna said, "Eunice, I *am* the police. And unless I'm mistaken, Jim is with the FBI. I'm sure he has a perfectly good explanation for why he's sitting uninvited in your living room."

Jim scrutinized her with a piercing gaze, his voice restrained. "You said you were sick and here you are, looking hale and hearty."

A chill went up Donna' spine. "I *was* sick. Must've been something I ate. I felt better so I decided to get some much-needed R & R. Eunice offered to host me." The lie fell flat.

"Let's call it, Donna, shall we? We both know *some* of the other's cards. Time to fold."

Eunice started walking towards the front door.

"Sit down, Mrs. Steadman." When she didn't respond, he added, "Here, now."

Donna looked at Jim's face, shrouded in malice, his features distorted. How had she been so blind? "What's gotten into you? If you need to speak with me, let's go get coffee. There's no reason for Eunice to be involved in our issues."

He shook his head. "Still holding onto the ignorance façade? Impressive, but I don't have time." He pulled out a Glock.

"Oh, dear Lord!" Eunice cried. "Get that thing out of my house."

Donna was stunned. "What do you want?" she asked, matching his cold demeanor.

"Tell me what you know about the syndicate."

"I've shared everything with you. Why would you believe otherwise?"

"You received a photo from Jon shortly before I arrived at your door this morning."

"How do you know that?"

"That's not relevant."

Anger burned inside her. "How long have you been spying on me?"

Jim placed the gun in his lap. "Since the beginning. And let's not get weepy about it. I care for you Donna, but you've become a nuisance. And Jon has created enough havoc as it is."

Eunice stood up, balled her fist. "You keep away from Jonny. You hear me? You lay a hand on him and—"

"Save the histrionics, lady. Though I see where his perseverance comes from. Last time...sit down!"

Donna's phone rang.

"Don't answer it."

She let it go to voicemail. Moments later, it rang again.

Jim stuck out his hand. "Hand it over."

She gave Jim the phone. Though he was no longer holding the gun on them, she knew he could draw quickly and effectively. Unfortunately, she was unarmed.

Jim looked at the incoming call ID. "Jon is eager to speak with you."

"He's left several messages. I never had a chance to get back to him."

"If he calls again, tell him you aren't feeling well and taking a few days off. Tell him you'll speak to him when you're better." He turned to Eunice. "If you so much as whimper while she's speaking with him, I won't hesitate to silence you in a permanent fashion."

The look Eunice gave him in return was deadly.

Donna's phone rang, and she answered.

"Donna! Thank God. Where have you been?"

"Sorry I didn't call you back. I've been under the weather. Let's talk in a few days," she said curtly.

"Hold on. I have so much to tell you. You need to be careful. Jim is in on this."

Donna coughed. The cuckoo clock chimed.

"Sorry, Jon, I'm exhausted. You woke me up. Gonna run. Talk to you soon." She hung up.

"Nicely done. Another place and time and you would have made an excellent recruit."

"Not a chance."

"Your phone," he said, putting his hand out.

Very reluctantly, she relinquished it.

* * *

LaGuardia Airport
New York City

Jon hung up, bewildered. There were no missed calls, no messages. He tried reaching Donna again without success. Even if she wasn't feeling well, it was as if she didn't want to hear what he had to say.

Melanie was in the ladies room. She was worried too. He began pacing at the gate. The connection to Dallas was not for another hour and a half. He felt a headache coming on, sat down, and began massaging his temples. Something was off. He leaned his head back, closing his eyes. As he began to drift off, in the space between consciousness and sleep, it came to him.

His eyes popped open wide.

The cuckoo clock.

Donna was in trouble. And she was in Granny Eunice's house.

CHAPTER 70

Outside Boston

"The best-laid plans of mice and men often go awry." The old adage came to Jim's mind as he attempted to suppress his frustration at the unexpected detour from his agenda. He'd learned from his time on the force to devise contingency plans. For situations such as this. He felt his heart rate quicken as he contemplated the magnitude of what was soon to come. *Then I'll be sitting pretty.*

They had been driving south on the interstate for nearly an hour, en route to his summer cottage, where he would sequester his now ex-lover until the Event was completed. The frigid temperatures meant no traffic. Headlights from the opposite direction offered the only illumination. Seated in the back of the silver Lexus SUV, he instructed Donna to take the next exit. Eunice sat in the passenger seat breathing heavily, face pale. Once both women were dealt with, he would contact the Boss as planned.

Donna said, "Stay calm, Eunice. I don't want you to hyperventilate. We'll be fine."

Jim saw Donna look at him in the rearview mirror.

"I have to hand it to you," she said. "You had me fooled. How could you share my bed while undermining me? Have you no feelings at all?"

"I'm not the cold bastard you'd have me be. It wasn't all an act. It's too bad it came to this, being on opposite sides of an issue greater than the two of us. But it's taken too many years of hard work to get to this point."

"You've been involved with this for *years*? Since BTI?" she asked, incredulously.

When Jim didn't reply, Donna shook her head in disbelief. "You were with me that day. That was no coincidence, was it?"

Still no response.

"*Was it?!*" she shouted.

"No," he replied, simply.

"I saved your life for heaven's sake!"

Jim said, "It's the only reason you're still alive. Consider it a debt repaid. That, however, does not apply to your friend here."

Eunice moaned. Her eyes were closed.

Alarmed, Donna said, "She's sick. We need to get her to a hospital."

"Not a chance."

"We don't have to stick around, just drop her off at the ER entrance and drive away. She will only be a burden on you. What happens if she gets sicker...or dies?"

Jim peered out his window at the deserted roadside. "Pull over. She's getting out."

"We're in the middle of nowhere. There's no hospital here. There's nothing here at all."

"You're right, I can't deal with a sick hostage."

Donna exclaimed, "It's bitter cold! She'll freeze to death."

"I can't risk her calling someone when we're still nearby. Pull over."

Eunice was conscious but breathing heavily. With fear in her voice, Donna asked, "Eunice, can you manage in the cold? We'll call for help for you as soon as we can."

Eunice opened her eyes. "Um, I don't know. Where are we?" They were idling along a dark, isolated road.

"About a mile off the interstate."

"I can't walk that far," she answered weakly.

"Jim, find a better place to let her out. This could kill her."

He replied with the wave of his pistol.

Donna choked back her horror. "Take my coat and put it over yours. And my hat." She helped her put them on. "See that tree? Go sit there. It's close enough to the road for drivers to see you. We'll call an ambulance. If someone drives by, wave them down."

Donna was impressed to see Eunice bundle herself up, and seemingly find an inner strength.

"Okay, I'm going. And you, jackass, if you hurt Donna, I won't stop till I'm certain you're put away for the rest of your miserable life."

"Get out," he said.

Eunice left, hunched over, walked to the tree next to the road and sat down. Donna saw her frozen breath coming in short spurts.

"Drive," Jim commanded.

As Donna pulled back on the road, she said "I can't believe we just left a frail woman on a deserted roadside in the freezing cold."

* * *

After Donna's pleas and assurances of obedience, Jim allowed her to call 911 from a roadside gas station. Jim hovered over her as she gave them Eunice's location, declining to provide her name but emphatic that her friend wouldn't last long without medical care. Donna prayed they would get to her in time.

Thirty minutes later they passed a sign announcing their arrival in Sagamore Beach, Massachusetts. The quaint seaside village was deserted, vacation homes and shops boarded up for the harsh winter months. They pulled up to a red-shingled bungalow at the end of a long driveway. As Donna got out of the car, the wind slapped her in the face.

Jim took the car keys from her and ushered her in the

house. Dust particles floated in the dappling sunrays streaming through back windows. The house was cold.

"The place isn't winterized so we'll have to use blankets."

Reading her expression, Jim said, "Don't look at me that way. I have no intention of continuing where we left off."

"Why did you bring me here?"

"It was either dispose of you or keep you quiet until the Event is completed. Be thankful I chose the latter."

"Event?"

Jim looked Donna in the eye, holding her gaze. "New Beginnings' ultimate display of power."

"You are repugnant." Donna said, turning away from him. "What are you planning?"

Jim tossed a log in the fireplace, kindled it. "All in good time."

Donna hugged herself, looked out the window to a stretch of white sand beach and the ocean beyond.

"How do you afford a place like this on your salary? The syndicate paying you a bundle, huh?" Silence. "I guess it's not only about the righteous mission."

She had annoyed him. "I won't deny it. They're very generous. Doesn't take away from the vital impact we'll be making on the world. I'm going to set up the rooms. You'll be staying here until our work is complete. There's no phone or Internet access and no one within miles. I trust you won't be foolish enough to go out, dressed such as you are. You won't get far."

Irate, Donna sat down on the nautical blue sofa, not knowing what her next move would be. Yet.

CHAPTER 71

LaGuardia Airport

J on called Captain Hutter in Boston to immediately get over to his grandmother's house. As Donna's precinct commander, he knew both her and Jim. Jon told him he had good reason to believe Jim Fields was a mole for a terrorist syndicate and to be careful what correspondence went out because he likely could access it. Hutter sounded skeptical about Jon's assumptions based on a grainy photo and a cuckoo clock. The captain said he'd call Matthews about it. In the meantime, he'd send someone over to Granny Eunice's house.

Jon had to assume Agent Matthews was involved, given his ties to both Kelly and Jim. However, there was no choice but to involve him.

Fifteen minutes went by before Captain Hutter called back. Melanie went to check flights to Boston.

"The officers found your grandmother's door unlocked. Her car's in the driveway, but no one's home. Donna's car was found nearby."

"So where are they?"

"They could be anywhere—maybe the grocery store, using a friend's car."

"They're not at the grocery store! Granny Eunice never leaves her door unlocked."

"I understand your concern, but there's no sign of foul

play."

"Have you looked for Jim's car?"

"We put out an APB but haven't found anything. Until I hear back from Matthews, my hands are tied." A pause. "I'm getting another call. Could be him."

"I'll hold." Jon turned on the speaker and ran through the terminal, Melanie now beside him, trying to locate their new gate.

✽ ✽ ✽

Captain Hutter came back on the line. "Seems Jim's off the radar. Matthews is buying into your theory that Jim could be working for this so-called syndicate."

Thank God. "Listen, Captain, my grandmother has been having some age-related issues. Please call me when you find her. I'm on my way up there."

"Will do. If you're right, Donna is in serious danger."

CHAPTER 72

Quincy, Massachusetts

The ambulance sirens wailed while at the wheel Patrick Shaw turned off I-93. The dash registered an outside temperature of twenty-eight degrees. The caller had said the old lady was at the Route 3 intersection. No one could last long in these temps, especially with the wind factor.

A steady snow had begun to fall.

"What's that?" asked his partner Marley, pointing at two o'clock.

Patrick slowed the ambulance to a crawl. "Where?" He squinted.

"That bundle by the tree," said Marley

A pile of clothing shimmered under a sheath of crystalized snowflakes, an oblong mound a few feet from the side of the road. The bundle wasn't moving.

Patrick grabbed his emergency kit. Marley was prepping the gurney. He pulled open his door. "Let's go!"

* * *

Sagamore Beach, Massachusetts

With urgent details to review with the Boss before the Event, Jim needed to find reliable Internet service, unavailable in Sagamore Beach during the off-season. Using his unsecured phone wasn't a risk he was willing to take. The question was whether or not to take Donna along. Even if she managed to get away, there was no one within miles. Making his decision, he said, "I need to go out for a while."

"You're leaving me here?"

"You'll be fine for a few hours. In town, I can't exactly trust that you'll behave yourself."

He led her to a guest room, took two neckties from the closet and bound her hands and feet. Without a word from either, he turned and locked the door behind him.

* * *

Donna waited exactly ten minutes from when she heard the car ignition. The pounding surf made it hard to hear if his car had driven away. Using her teeth she gnawed persistently at the knots with little success. At least Jim hadn't tied her hands behind her. She took a breath, stood and studied the room, settling her gaze on a small wooden desk. Note pad, pencil holder. Donna shuffled over and with a bound hand took a yellow pencil, placing it in her mouth. Sitting back down, she carefully stuck the pencil into one of the knots, moving it back and forth until the fabric loosened. It took twenty minutes till her hands were free, another five to unbind her legs.

She tried the doorknob. There was a slight give.

Beside several signed baseballs in glass display cubes, a Louisville slugger signed by the entire Red Sox team of '86 was mounted on the wall.

She pulled down the bat and took some practice swings. Last thing she wanted was to break the bat and not the door. She got into a classic hitting stance and took a swing. It hit the doorknob head-on, knocking it right off on her first try, leaving a gaping hole.

She assessed her handiwork with satisfaction. "Home run!"

CHAPTER 73

Sagamore Beach, Massachusetts

Donna searched every closet for something warm to wear. She had to get out of there and make sure that Eunice was okay. She prayed her friend wasn't still on the side of the road.

She found a fleece jacket, garden gloves and a baseball cap. She walked out the front door, into the numbing cold, her gaze drawn downward. There, stuck between the concrete cracks, was a small slip of paper, crumpled up like an old receipt. The cop in her made her bend down and pocket it.

She studied her surroundings. Not a human in sight. No cars on the street. Every nearby cottage was buttoned up tight. She estimated the closest thoroughfare was a forty-minute walk, not possible in her current attire.

She ran to the house across the street, and peered through the windows. Sofas and chairs were covered with sheets. Hoping to find a working phone, she tried the door. Locked. She picked up a rock from the front garden and broke the window beside the door, reached her arm in and unlocked it.

Inside it was only slightly warmer than Jim's place, her breath still visible. She searched the kitchen and bedrooms for a landline. No luck. A modem sat under the work desk near the kitchen island, but it wasn't working. All utilities had been cut off. She wondered how they kept the pipes from freezing. She ran to where the garage should be and found a golf cart, open on all sides, keys in the ignition. She knew that residents of beach communities used them for local transportation. She'd check a few more houses and, if necessary, come back for the cart. She had no idea how far it could take her, but it was the best option so far.

After the next two houses offered nothing helpful, she came to a quirky cottage painted a coastal blue, with concrete seashells bolted to the siding and a wind chime on the front porch, tossing furiously, noisily, in the wind. She needed to break in again. Walking through the house, Donna was struck by the number of framed family photos. With crocheted quilts and ceramic figurines, the home had an old person's feel to it. No working phone or computer.

In the garage, she hit the motherlode. A seafoam green 1949 Oldsmobile 88—in pristine condition—was in the narrow space, facing out.

Donna said a silent prayer and looked on the garage walls. There they were. Keys on a hook. She grabbed them, raised the garage door by hand, and jumped into the driver's seat. *Please make it run.* She put her foot on the brake and turned the ignition. The fuel needle jumped to *F*, the car purring like a well-fed kitten. She shifted into drive and hit the gas.

* * *

Auntie Em's Internet Café was nearly empty at this hour. It would be dark soon and locals were home eating dinner and keeping out of the frigid cold. Jim Fields logged into New Beginnings' secure chatroom and initiated a one-on-one with the Boss. Each day at this time, the top-tier personnel made themselves available for internal communication. If no one came online within ten minutes, the chatroom was closed. With the Event imminent, Jim expected that many others would be logged in, but he required personal time with the

Boss.

His superior got right to the point.

Everything on schedule?

Yes. Will arrive in NY hours before the vote.

Good. The others will be in position. Word from K?

No contact since she left for Utah. Emails from Steadman to Lt. Kearn's phone suggest K failed. He is alive and well.

Jim had never cared for Kelly Flanagan. She scared him, a wolf in sheep's clothing ready to strike at anyone she deemed competition. If she were somehow out of commission, he wouldn't miss her.

We will proceed without her.

Jim was not surprised by the Boss's lack of sentimentality. It was all about the project, all the time. The Boss's reaction had been similar when Carrera was killed. Of course, it might have been the Boss who ordered that hit. No single individual was vital enough to impact the success of the project. The Boss wrote,

The most important elements are timing and coordination. Any miscalculation and the Event will be compromised.

Jim took offense to the lecture, but let it go. Ready to log off, he saw one last message come through. This one thrilled him.

The new world order awaits.

CHAPTER 74

Marshfield, Massachusetts

I t was ten minutes before Donna saw another car on the road. She had the heat cranked up full blast, her knuckles white on the steering wheel.

Spotting a 7-11, she parked and ran inside. "You sell phones?" she practically yelled at the clerk.

"Right there behind you."

She took the first one she saw off the wall display. Thankful to not have been relieved of her wallet, she paid for the phone along with one thousand minutes, and asked the clerk to help activate it.

Donna's first call was to Captain Hutter. She was redirected from one desk sergeant to the next until they tracked him down. In the background. she heard the sounds of an active police station.

"Donna, is that you?"

His voice nearly brought her to tears. "Yes, sir."

"Thank God. Where have you been?"

"Agent Jim Fields of the Midwest FBI office was holding me hostage in his summer cottage by the shore. East of Brockton." She was breathless. "We need to locate him. And Eunice Steadman. An elderly woman we left on Route 3 off the interstate. Can you find out if she was picked up and what hospital she was taken to?"

"Done. We'll make calls to area hospitals. Where are you now?"

"I'm at a 7-11 in…" She turned to the clerk. "Where am I?"

He looked confused by the question. "Marshfield."

She told the captain, then recited her new phone number.

"I've pinged where you are. I'm sending someone to get you."

"I have a car. Had to commandeer one to get away."

"Leave it there. Wait for our pick-up."

"Got it. Thanks, Captain. But what about Jim? He said he would be back in a few hours."

"Jon Steadman told me of his suspicions. We'll have a local team at Fields' place in fifteen minutes. If he shows up, they'll be waiting. Do you know where he might have gone?"

"No, but I can tell you that whatever he and his organization are planning is going to be devastating. He calls it the Event."

"The Feds are taking this over. They're digging through Fields' profile, looking for terrorist connections."

"I don't think that's the way to go. Jon Steadman will have the best leads. He's been onto this syndicate for months."

"I'll have someone contact him." A pause. "Donna?"

"Yes, sir."

"I'm so relieved you're okay."

"Thank you, sir, but I'll only be okay once I know that Eunice Steadman is safe."

Donna hung up, 993 minutes remaining on her phone plan.

* * *

Jim took back roads to the beach house. About two miles out, he noticed increased activity when there should have been no one around. Something felt off. The last three cars he saw were Crown Vics, a classic old Fed car.

They were onto him. He slowed down, took the next turnabout and drove back the direction he came. After Jon had sent the expedition photo to Donna, Jim had no intention of going back to the Bureau. He'd known it was just a matter of time until someone connected him to Kelly Flanagan and New Beginnings. He was unfazed. After all, he would soon be on his way to New York, leaving his old life behind.

CHAPTER 75

South Shore Hospital
Massachusetts

Donna rushed from the police cruiser into the hospital. At the information desk, she asked for Eunice Steadman's room.

"Let me see." The white-haired woman smiled and checked the computer. "Looks like she was transferred from the OR to ICU about an hour ago. Room 406."

Donna didn't know if she should be relieved or worried. She was alive but in critical condition.

"Donna?"

She turned around. And was facing Jon, Melanie beside him, their faces riddled with worry.

She went to Jon, hugging him tightly.

As they waited for the elevator, Jon asked, "So, what the hell happened?"

Donna quickly filled them in.

"Oh jeez. Granny could have died!"

Distraught, Donna said, "I'm so sorry."

The ride up to the fourth floor felt like an eternity. The moment the doors parted, Jon darted past the nurses' station, beelining to room 406.

* * *

Eunice lay covered in heavy blankets, her head slightly elevated. Attached to a heart monitor and IV, her eyes were closed, sunken into her pale face. Jon teared up, sat beside his grandmother and took her clammy hand.

"Granny, it's Jonny."

There was no response.

"I'm so sorry that I wasn't there to protect you. Please wake up and come back home. I need you." Melanie put a hand on his shoulder.

"I'm going to find him, Granny. I swear." A single tear escaped, falling down Jon's cheek.

A middle-aged woman in a white coat, a stethoscope draped around her neck, tapped on the door. "I'm Dr. Petersen. I understand you're Mrs. Steadman's grandson."

Jon stood, nodded. "Please tell me she'll be okay."

"The medics found her unconscious by the side of the road. She's suffered acute hypothermia. Two fingers on her left hand were frostbitten. We tried to save them but were unsuccessful."

Jon noticed the bandage for the first time. "Oh God."

"I'm sure this is very upsetting and scary, but your grandmother was incredibly lucky. Had she been found even a few minutes later, she would have succumbed to the cold."

Jon let out a sob.

"She's stronger than she looks, Mr. Steadman."

"She's the strongest person I've ever known."

"Let's hope she'll come through this, only slightly worse for the wear. Stay here with her if you like, but the others must leave by 8:00 p.m."

After Dr. Petersen left, Jon returned to his post beside Granny Eunice's bed, the two women quietly beside him, all silently praying for a full recovery.

* * *

At 8:00 p.m., Donna broke the silence. "My apartment isn't far from here. You're both welcome to stay with me. Jim won't take a chance going there. As far as he knows I'm still locked up in his house."

Jon handed the bag of Chrysanthemum to Melanie. "Please get this to Gabe. You two go get some rest," Jon said, his voice subdued. "I'm not leaving her."

Donna didn't argue. Melanie kissed the top of Jon's head and walked to the door.

With controlled rage, Jon said to Donna, "We need to find that bastard Fields. First Ashleigh, now Granny."

❃ ❃ ❃

Boston

Melanie sat at Donna's kitchen table, staring out at a snow-laden parking lot, a lone streetlamp offering the only illumination. She sipped her hot tea, thinking of Granny Eunice and all she'd been put through.

"Donna, did Jim say what he was planning?"

"Only that New Beginnings will display their power at an Event, something big. But truthfully, I was more focused on getting myself out of there." A pause. "Oh, wait a second. As I was leaving the cottage, I found something. I picked it up and..." She put her hand in Jim's jacket pocket.

Melanie peeked over. "What's that?"

"I found it near his doorstep. I'm guessing it was Jim's."

Melanie took it from her, studying the sticky note. No more than one square inch, it had been unfurled, leaving behind a web of wrinkles. Scribbled on it were the numbers "3-3," followed by "A/RES/71/293."

"Any idea what this means?" Melanie asked.

"Not a clue."

"What could 'res' stand for?"

"Maybe reservation. Like with an airline or online purchase?"

"Yeah, that could be it. And the three-three when he plans to travel or a delivery date."

Donna said, "That's possible, but the number is no use to us without an airline."

"Let's see what we get on Google." Melanie took out her laptop and typed A/RES/71/293 in the search bar. The first result was, *UN resolution #71/293 to be voted on March 3.*

"That's next week," Melanie said as she clicked on the link. Reading beside her, Donna pointed to the screen, halfway down. "Take a look at this." She read aloud. "One of the biggest proponents of the resolution has been the CEO of Genesis Corporation. A highly regarded philanthropist, Carlton Hendrix has rallied along with his wife, Senator Jasmine Hendrix, to provide aid to the underprivileged, primarily in Third World countries."

Melanie couldn't believe it. "I just met Senator Hendrix." She paused, absorbing what she'd read. "Why would Jim be interested in a UN resolution on World Bank funding of Third World countries?"

Donna was perplexed. "No idea, but the UN must be where Jim's going for the Event. We need to stop him. I'll get Matthews on this." Donna pulled up his email address, copied and pasted the section about the UN resolution, and added a note that he should expect her call. She would explain what she and Melanie had concluded. A catastrophic event was planned for the United Nations.

Melanie was still pondering the implications. "Do you think Pauly's father is linked to whatever this Event is?"

"Good question. There's one surefire way to find out."

CHAPTER 76

Genesis Corporate Offices
Boston

O fficer Donna Kearns shoved past Carlton Hendrix's executive assistant and bolted into the man's office. She caught the Genesis CEO, seated behind a sleek glass console, in the middle of a videoconference.

"What is this?" he demanded.

His assistant rushed in behind Donna. "I'm sorry, sir. I tried to stop her."

He faced a large screen, split in quarters, each square with a different man's face. "Gentlemen, I have unexpected company. Allow me to call you back in ten minutes so we can resume our discussion." He pressed a key on the computer on his desk and the faces were replaced with the Genesis logo screensaver.

An austere man with a distinguished demeanor, Hendrix was irate. He swiveled his chair to face Donna, who carried a thick folder. "Who are you?"

"Lieutenant Donna Kearns, Boston PD, special consultant to the Federal Bureau of Investigations."

He registered surprise. "What does the FBI want with me?"

"Answering that might take longer than ten minutes, Mr. Hendrix."

A mixture of confusion and annoyance cloaked his features. "That's more time than I can spare. Now what's this all about?"

Donna was unintimidated. Something dire was about to happen, and this pompous man was involved. "You can either spare the valuable time now or be escorted to the FBI headquarters for debriefing."

Hendrix cursed under his breath. "Lois, email the partners and reschedule for the same time tomorrow."

"Yes, sir. Sorry again, sir."

"It's not your fault. Now, run along."

Lois left, looking fearful for her job.

Donna took off her coat and pulled out two photos from a folder in her bag. She showed Hendrix the one of Jim. "Do you know this man?"

"No."

"Look closer. He may have changed his appearance. Ignore the hair and eye color. Those can be altered. Look at the jawline, nose structure and such."

To Hendrix's credit, he studied the photo more closely. "I still don't recognize this man. Who is he?"

"Jim Fields. We believe he will soon perpetuate a grand scale terrorist attack against this country."

Hendrix paled. "Why would you believe I have any association with such a person?"

"New Beginnings is one of your companies." It was not a question. "A photo Fields took several years ago was found in his home. It was signed by a team of New Beginnings employees on an expedition to Brazil. At least one of them is a known member of the terrorist syndicate."

Mr. Hendrix said, "Lieutenant, I have thousands of holdings and employees around the world. There's no way I can know each one of them."

"Maybe so."

"If that's all—"

"How about this woman?" Donna showed Hendrix a photo of Kelly Flanagan.

Hendrix said, "Never seen her before. Who is *she*? An accomplice?"

"An assassin. Killed while trying to stop our investigation." That silenced him. "Tell me about Genesis."

The sudden change in topic didn't throw him. "We trade on the NYSE."

"Impressive. What exactly do they do?"

"We're a pharmaceutical company. We manufacture drugs."

"That all?"

"Several years ago, we added an arm to the company—lab equipment. Hired hundreds of engineers to work on building more efficient, less costly methods of bio-genetic assessment."

"Bio-genetic assessment?"

"Testing DNA."

"For criminal cases?"

"In part, but mostly for scientists and researchers to do their jobs more productively."

"Such as the TR-X."

Surprise shone in his eyes. "You've done your research. Yes, the TR-X is one of ours—our latest advance, as a matter of fact. Only a few of them out there on the market and mostly in the academic realm. We're waiting to get feedback from the first users before deciding if we should expand production."

"Getting back to the main part of your business, are all the drugs under FDA approval?"

"No."

"How's that possible?"

"For one, not all drugs are made for use in the United States, and thus don't require meeting those standards."

"Wouldn't you want to meet the highest standards possible?"

"Of course, but the reality is some countries are in dire need of drugs, antibiotics and such. If they went through the rigors of FDA approval procedures, it would slow down the process considerably and be too late for potentially thousands of people. That's not to say we don't carefully test all our products. Even foreign countries have learned the efficacy of litigation. It's in our best interest to make sure our products are effective and safe, regardless of FDA guidelines."

Time to knock him off balance. "Then how do you explain that one of your drugs is killing people?"

"What are you talking about?" Not a twitch, no aversion of eye contact. Hendrix looked truly perplexed.

"A drug, developed by a subsidiary of your company, is being used to control users to carry out deadly attacks."

"Don't be absurd. Perhaps one of our competitors is responsible for this."

"An assassin cited New Beginnings moments before he was murdered by his handlers. You may have seen it on the news. Took a back dive into the Ohio River."

"I remember that story. But this is the first I'm hearing of a connection to one of my companies. I'll inquire with my staff and let you know anything I find out."

"Do no such thing. You likely have at least one mole in your company and we don't want to tip them off."

"So what is it you want from me?"

"Given that you don't know either of these people," she said accusatorily while pointing at the photos splayed out on his desk, "the only thing I will need is an antidote."

"How is that possible when I don't even know what the drug is made of."

"But I know someone who does, and you, Mr. Hendrix, are going to help her."

CHAPTER 77

Boston

Donna made two calls as soon as she left Carlton Hendrix's office. The first was to update Agent Matthews, the second to Terry. The confrontation with Hendrix convinced Donna and Matthews the Genesis top dog was in the dark about New Beginnings' terrorist activities. He was being cooperative, probably more out of fear of a lawsuit than compliance. Under pressure, Hendrix had given Dr. Terry Lavi authority over a team of lab technicians, making his state-of-the-art facility available for any necessary testing.

Early the next afternoon, Terry and Gabe arrived in the lobby of Genesis R & D Laboratories, a facility housed in a modern building with glass façade just south of downtown Boston. Gabe insisted on accompanying Terry, hopeful his chemistry background would be of help, while keeping her close. Upon hearing from Donna they came prepared with a printout of Dr. B.'s Chrysanthemum Exotic profile.

Donna greeted the pair warmly, then handed over the Chrysanthemum sample Melanie and Jon had entrusted her with. The challenge was monumental. Develop a life-saving antidote from the plant Terry now held in her hands.

Donna's phone vibrated with a new message. It was from Matthews. *Meet in NYC asap.*

Hurrying to the exit, Donna watched as Terry and Gabe

disappeared inside the bowels of the Genesis labyrinth and silently wished them Godspeed.

CHAPTER 78

South Shore Hospital

Massachusetts

J on woke to the sound of hail pounding on the window-
pane. Momentarily disoriented by his surroundings, the
beeping heart monitor reminded him where he was soon
enough. Granny Eunice was restless, mumbling something he
couldn't decipher. He patted her hand and she settled down.
The doctors were biding their time on making a prognosis till
she regained consciousness.

An industrial clock over the door ticked loudly. Five a.m.
Fidgety and uncomfortable from hours in the caregiver tor-
ture chair, Jon stood, stretched his back, and paced the room.

The fire in his belly had diminished to a low simmer. He
was now in action mode. Despite the hour, he texted Matthews, informing him of where he was and asking him if there
were any leads. He would demand to be kept in the loop
regardless of his own previous transgressions or vowed to become a thorn in the agent's side until he relented. He was surprised when he received a text back. *On way to NY. Working a
new angle. Will let u know. Hope your grandmother gets better soon.*

He pocketed his phone and looked at his grandmother.
Whatever Jon would one day accomplish would be a direct
credit to Granny Eunice. She had encouraged him to flourish
despite life's challenges, sacrificing her needs for his.

He opened the top drawer of the bedside table and looked at the Bible. He had never been religious, yet felt there was a greater power, and believed in heaven. That's where his parents and Grandpa were now. Sitting back down, he closed his eyes. *What the hell? Dear God...*

He finished his silent prayer. Had let it all go. His anger, fear, resentment. Face wet with tears, he dozed off.

"Jonny, is that you?"

The soft words were like an answer from above.

PART III

The Event

CHAPTER 79

United Nations Plaza
New York City

It had been a long time since Jon walked the streets of Manhattan. Standing on the salted pavement he regarded the crowded sidewalks, honking taxicabs, and nonstop activity with disdain. Forty-sixth Street and First Avenue was a hub of frenetic energy. He looked up at the austere Secretariat building. Its simplistic design was easily identifiable along the New York skyline by its flat façade looming over the East River.

It had been difficult leaving Granny's side, but she was recuperating well at a rehab center with the security of Fort Knox, thanks to Donna's intervention. Her feisty spirit had reappeared, and she insisted Jon stop moping and get back to his life.

When Donna emailed with the news of Jim's intended destination, Matthews summoned Jon to New York, claiming since he had seen Jim in person he could help identify his mannerisms and gait. But Jon suspected it was Matthews' way of keeping tabs on him and preventing him from playing rogue investigator again.

Melanie called from a Starbucks on Third Avenue. She and Donna had driven down to Manhattan in Donna's late-model Subaru. While Donna met the others at the United Nations,

Melanie planned to use the café's Wi-Fi. There was big money behind New Beginnings activities and she sounded eager to find its source.

A caravan of coach buses rolled down First Avenue, spewing exhaust fumes onto slush left from a recent snowfall. Jon observed a steady stream of people clearing security and entering the building through steel revolving doors.

On this unseasonably warm day, students and tourists had descended upon the United Nations building to witness history in the making. Today, the General Assembly was preparing to vote on resolution 71/293 for humanitarian aid to countries under tyrannical rule. If passed, it would provide billions to impoverished nations, the largest handout in modern times, sparking international debates. Dissenters believed that unscrupulous governments would seize any allocated funds, no different than what happened in Nigeria or the Gaza Strip, when corrupt regimes used well-intentioned charity to enrich their personal coffers, while citizens remained destitute. Proponents of the resolution were convinced that with improved UN monitoring, the funds would find their way to the neediest enclaves, bypassing crooked tyrants. The controversy had been steaming for years, stranding the proposed measure in policy purgatory.

It was the resolution that led the FBI to the UN. Despite the uncertain nature of the Event, after speaking with Donna, Matthews determined the sticky note found at Jim's beach house and his talk of imminent terrorist activity, were sufficient cause for mobilizing a SWAT team. He contacted the Under-Secretary-General for Safety and Security to the UN, who readily agreed to collaborate in the pursuit and apprehension of Jim and members of the syndicate, should they appear on UN grounds. In turn, the Office of Homeland Security issued a threat advisory—level orange. The result was extra-tight security with the NYPD and FBI stationed in and around the complex. Armed guards checked bags, and ushered visitors through metal detectors.

Jon thought of Jim Fields, a liar, opportunist, and traitor to his country. He scanned the crowd. *Where are you, son of a bitch?*

With thousands in and around the building, the potential was real for a death toll greater than on 9-11.

Sweating profusely, Jon entered the lobby, his shoes clacking on the checkerboard floors. A middle-aged brunette dressed in a black pantsuit approached him, introducing herself as a member of Matthews' team and handed him a temporary clearance badge, and an ear mic, explaining how to use it. She pointed to Jon's designated post and quickly moved on without another word.

Looking up into the mezzanine he spotted Doug Matthews. The FBI agent had a bird's eye view of the antechamber. They made eye contact. Jon still didn't trust him completely, given his connection to Kelly, but he no longer believed Matthews was with the syndicate. Maybe he simply was a stuck-up asshole.

He heard Matthews in his earpiece. "You wanted to see the FBI from the inside...Here's your chance, Steadman. Show me what you've got."

Feeling his heart rate accelerate, Jon took several deep breaths, and wiped his sweaty forehead with his sleeve, careful not to dislodge his ear mic. He wasn't going to blow it with a full-on panic attack. *Get a grip!*

On mounted screens airing live feed from inside the General Assembly, he watched the Secretary-General approach the podium. Jon's leg still ached, the last pill wearing off. His mind was on too many things at once. *Focus on the here and now.*

Plan A was to thwart any attempts at violence. Each member of the Feds' team was positioned in a strategic spot. Jon was manning the antechamber, while Donna covered the back exit. Her demeanor since learning of Jim's betrayal was professional, yet he could sense the darkness and melancholy. If she was anything like himself, putting Jim Fields behind bars was the only thing that would get her back on track.

Expecting his quarry would be disguised, Jon kept a close eye out for men wearing hats and glasses. There were hundreds of them in and around the building's vicinity.

Spotting Jim Fields would come down to plain old-fashioned luck.

CHAPTER 80

United Nations Plaza
New York City

J im sat on a park bench directly across First Avenue from the UN complex. A soft breeze played a flapping mantra along the flag-lined entrance. From his vantage point, he was afforded direct sightlines to the building's entrance. There, the crowd stood five deep, corralled by metal barriers. Many toted placards asserting America First!, while protestors chanted, "Stop the greed." Cops were everywhere, ensuring the situation didn't get out of hand.

He wore plain slacks, a dark fleece jacket, tortoiseshell glasses, and a fake goatee. On his feet were rubber-soled shoes, in case he needed to make a quick retreat. A wool visor cap obscured the top of his head and the small bud in his ear canal, tuned in to the live feed playing on his smartphone.

Jim watched the Secretary-General preparing to welcome the 193 member states. The man was in his fourth year of a five-year term and expected to extend his tenure. To his left sat the elected President of the Assembly and the Executive Assistant to the Secretary-General. The iconic UN emblem, depicting Earth encircled by a wreath of crossed olive branches, was illuminated behind them.

Leaning into his mic, the Secretary-General began, "Ladies and gentlemen. Honorary members of the assembly..."

* * *

Jim had the trigger ready, its range easily spanning several city blocks. The Cure Theory trials had prepared the syndicate for this day. With the watches activated, all hell would break loose. His phone displayed where each of the subjects was stationed. Despite the heavy police presence, there was nothing for them to look for. The subjects were not even aware of what they themselves were about to do.

Jim stayed focused on the task at hand. By this time tomorrow he would be a very wealthy man.

* * *

Terry and Gabe passed through the security checkpoint and exited into the plaza fronting the Secretariat building. Two armored trucks loaded with emergency equipment were parked near the entrance. There were men donning bulletproof vests and ballistic helmets, carrying assault rifles.

Gabe was stunned. "What the hell?"

"This reminds me of my Israeli military service," Terry said.

Gabe approached an officer holding an MP5/10 submachine gun. His name patch read "Corbin." "Why all the firepower?"

"Precautionary measures, sir. Nothing to be concerned about."

Gabe wasn't going to argue the obvious lie. "We need to speak with Agent Doug Matthews."

The officer eyed them more closely. "Who are you?"

Gabe gestured to Terry. "This is Doctor Theresa Lavi. She's helping the FBI with a related investigation. Please call him."

The man turned away, spoke into his shoulder mic, then

addressed them, "He'll be down momentarily."

Minutes later Matthews materialized. He introduced the SWAT leader to Terry, giving her temporary clearance and issued her and Gabe badges.

"Did you accomplish what you needed in Boston?" Matthews asked.

"I hope so." She patted her briefcase then placed the lanyard around her neck. "Can we look around inside?"

"Alright, but stay out of the way of security personnel. If you'll excuse me I need to get back to work." And with that Matthews disappeared.

* * *

The Secretary-General was completing his opening remarks when the jumbo screen suspended above the chamber suddenly switched from his face to that of a digitally shaded figure.

"It's a true honor to be here," the figure declared in a booming voice eerily altered by a synthesizer. "To all those present and watching around the globe, I have exciting, world-changing news to share with you."

The Secretary-General looked up at the screen behind him, appalled. Aides were scrambling to take back the feed. Ambassadors were confused as they listened to the unscheduled prerecorded speech transmitted through their Taiden headsets in their native tongues. The mysterious figure's words were being aired on several TV stations, broadcasting everywhere cable news aired.

"The country in which you are sitting, as you prepare to cast your ballot, is the one I now call home. This land has allowed me to succeed beyond my wildest dreams, accrue great wealth and garner respect. As a one-time destitute refugee, this is the ultimate twist of fate."

From outside, roars of approval and applause could be

heard emanating from the crowd, some cheering "U.S.A.!"

The usurper continued. "I have never forgotten where I came from. The poverty, abuse, and corruption of those in power. Who is to blame? Who bears the responsibility for countless children being left to live in huts with dirt floors while their corrupt leaders bathe in champagne? Why have the so-called developed countries not shared their wealth to do something about it?"

The figure pointed at the assembly. "You were entrusted with improving living standards and human rights for the less fortunate but have chosen instead to cower behind the guise of humanitarianism. Your countries engorge themselves on possessions, food, money, power while allowing the down-trodden who share the planet to die of curable diseases. And still, today's proposed resolution is doomed to flounder. You, *distinguished* ambassadors have failed to guide your country-men. But know this, you *will* share the wealth.

"Several years ago, our organization acquired a remarkable tool that will finally allow a more even playing field." Each word was said with angry conviction.

The uncanny voice intensified. "A syndicate has been quietly growing, comprised of an army of soldiers hidden amongst you, trained to use this tool to its full potential. Today will be a spectacular demonstration of its power, an-nouncing our mission to the world."

In utter frustration, the Secretary-General sat down. No one was cutting off the feed, or even muting this deranged individual. He looked around at the ambassadors' perplexed faces. They appeared intrigued with what the interloper had to say. Perhaps they were being swayed by the ravings.

"Tonight, the effects will be fast and far-reaching, fierce in their intensity and scope. The greediest of nations will suffer most from rapidly declining economies allowing monies to be diverted to their rightful and just recipients. The time has come for a new world, a new beginning."

* * *

Outside, the tide turned quickly. Protestors began shoving, trying to break through the barricade, alert to a primitive danger. One man called out, "What's happening in there?" Another, "Let me out of here!"

Trained in crowd control, the NYPD opened both ends of the barricade, allowing the gathered throngs to exit the area in front of the UN in a controlled manner. A voice on a bullhorn instructed the crowd to walk, not run.

Jim rose from the bench, trying to steer clear of the bustling crowd. By pressing the trigger on his phone, a Wi-Fi signal would be sent to six subjects. A low-frequency vibration would elicit a hypnotic, almost catatonic state, a Pavlovian response honed over weeks in the Cure Theory program attended by each of the UN Assembly guards.

Seconds later, the serum would be released through the membrane at the back of their watches. Chrysanthemum Exotic would be absorbed instantly into the bloodstream, and the trained behavior would take over.

An alarmed protestor shoved past Jim on the sidewalk, sending him off balance. Head down, he moved aside, shielding himself from the masses. He closed his eyes and listened intently. The speech was over, and the screen went blank. This was his sign.

Jim pressed the trigger.

CHAPTER 81

United Nations

New York City

T he first thing Jon noticed was a moment of stillness. It was fleeting but given the degree of activity surrounding him, the silence that fell after the speech was deafening.

Something inside him set off an internal alarm. *This is it.*

Several security guards had rushed into the chamber when the mysterious activist hijacked the session. Despite all attempts, the feed could not be disconnected. Everyone seemed confused, some fearful enough to leave the security line and exit the building, sensing something serious underway.

Jon walked briskly to the chamber doors and peeked inside. Ambassadors had kept their seats, many talking to their aides, as if consulting on what had just happened while waiting for the Secretary-General to restore order and offer an explanation.

Jon entered the assembly hall, letting the door close quietly behind him. Keeping a low profile, he stood in the back of the mezzanine shielded by a decorative column. Guards were positioned at each chamber exit, six doors in total, one stationed several feet in front of him, his profile visible through the column's gaps, unaware of Jon's presence. He appeared pale, his expression glazing over. It was the same look

Abadi had worn when killing the BTI students.

Only now did Jon notice what he had missed before. Each guard in the chamber wore a Quantos. Each was hypnotized, unaware of his own impending behavior.

Several things happened at once. Jon leapt from his hiding place, landing awkwardly on the guard's back while grabbing his pistol from its holster. At the same time, the remaining security guards drew their weapons, leveling them on the closest ambassador, each a respected member of the Security Council.

Screams rang out. The guards were frozen in position. The one under Jon jolted violently trying to force him off, like a bucking bronco. Jon raised the butt of the gun and brought it down on the drugged man's head, who fell to the ground beneath him with a muffled thump.

Someone yelled, "What's happening? Oh, dear God!" No one moved. UN members were yelling in their languages, fear and confusion creating a modern-day Tower of Babel.

Once a military leader, the Secretary-General called out, "Put your weapons down this instant! Stand down!"

The security guard nearest the Secretary-General shifted his position, cocked his raised weapon, and shot him between the eyes. The round echoed loudly, ringing off the walls. The Secretary-General collapsed to the floor, a plume of smoke rising from his head.

As if on cue, the remaining guards opened fire. Pandemonium broke out.

"Get down!" someone yelled. Everyone dropped.

That's when the lights went out.

* * *

Matthews and Donna stood in the security epicenter, a high-tech space with large screen monitors along the walls. They had left their respective posts to address the video takeover.

Donna noticed a change in Agent Matthews' demeanor. He was treating her more as an equal.

Mike Donnely, the UN chief safety officer and retired NYPD sergeant, held his current position for the past decade. Most of his crew's attention was on trying to regain control of the hijacked feed. Matthews and Donna studied the monitors, searching for Jim's face, when the shot rang out. They turned to the assembly screen and watched in horror as the Secretary-General, a black hole burning between his brows, fell to the ground.

"Oh God. What are my men doing?" Donnely cried in disbelief.

Matthews and Donna didn't hesitate. Unholstering their weapons, they ran from the office.

CHAPTER 82

Third Avenue
New York City

L eft to her own devices at Starbucks, Melanie did extensive digging online. In the end, she could think of only one other person who had a connection to Jim, Genesis and the UN. With the others occupied at the UN, it was a lead worth pursuing, despite the apparent long shot.

She exited the coffeehouse and hailed a yellow cab.

"Where to, lady?" the driver asked.

"Fifth Avenue and 79th Street, please."

❋ ❋ ❋

Fifth Avenue
New York City

The Hendrix duplex was atop a post-war building, its architecture consistent with the statuesque edifices lining

Museum Mile. Gothic stone gargoyles were carved along the façade. The location was prime real estate in one of the country's ritziest zip codes. As Melanie approached the building, the doorman, dressed in a double-breasted suit with gold buttons and a donning a braided cap, opened the door. He smiled, ushering her inside. "Good afternoon, Miss."

"Hello. "I'm here to meet Mr. Hendrix. Has he arrived?"

"Yes, Miss Ridgefield. He's waiting for you in the sitting area at the left of the corridor."

Melanie entered the elegant space. Waxed marble floors reflected light from an extravagant chandelier overhead. She turned left and found Pauly Hendrix on a royal blue velvet settee. He stood to greet her.

"Nice to see you again, Melanie."

"Thanks for meeting me on such short notice."

"Angie and I bought an apartment on the Upper West Side, so getting here was no problem." He had a look of concern on his face. "You said it was urgent."

"Yes, it is." *I need to ease into this.* "How are you and Angela doing? Acclimating to married life?"

"Definitely."

"Nice." An awkward silence ensued.

"You wanted to meet me here, but didn't explain why. You've piqued my curiosity."

"There's a great deal to tell you and not much time to bring you up to date on all that's been going on, but I'll do my best."

She sat beside Pauly and told him everything.

CHAPTER 83

United Nations
New York City

J on was blind. In the dark of the General Assembly, no one was using their phones for fear the light would render them targets. In their hypnotic state, the armed guards did not appear concerned by the darkness. They were programmed to kill. The shooting continued for several seconds after the lights went out but had stopped. Sobs and labored breathing could be heard in the cavernous space.

Jon knew the door was directly behind him. He had to get out. Get help. He expected that as with the other attacks, the place would soon explode. He needed to summon the bomb squad. He stuck the guard's gun in his back pocket and ran for the door.

* * *

Terry heard the God-awful sounds of ricocheting bullets, followed by muffled screams. She felt helpless and terrified for Jon. As she and Gabe watched the lobby's overhead screen they quickly realized their worst fear. The guards firing on the crowd appeared robotic. Drugged.
She spotted a SWAT team officer running past her in the melee.

And had an idea. Quickly she enlisted Gabe's help. He nodded, and caught up with the officer, asking him to radio Matthews and tell him what was needed.

Terry watched the two men run outside to the SWAT truck. Now all she could do was pray her plan would work.

* * *

The UN lobby was empty of tourists. Jon did a one-eighty. Only law enforcement personnel remained, calling for back up, their radios squawking. *Where the hell is Matthews?*

Jon shouted into the mic but got no reply. Then he realized it had been dislodged, probably in the scuffle with the guard. As he attempted to reattach it, he was stunned to see Terry running toward him.

"What are you doing here?" he yelled. "You need to get out! The guards are shooting inside the assembly hall!"

"I know! Gabe and I came to help. We shut off the lights. It stopped the shooting for a while. Listen. You need to start a fire inside the chamber."

Jon stared in disbelief. "Have you lost your mind? Where's the hostage team? We need the bomb squad! An explosion follows the shootings. Why isn't anyone doing anything?"

Terry took Jon's face in her hands, forcing him to look in her eyes. "Jon, calm down. Two more SWAT teams are on the way. In the meantime, Matthews okayed my idea hoping to minimize casualties. Take this." She handed him a large silver and black canister with a red button at the back.

"What the hell is this?" Jon yelled.

"A blowtorch. When you ignite it, direct the flame to the ceiling. Get as close as you can to the ceiling. Do you understand?"

"No, I don't!" But as he said those words, he began to calm down. *This isn't BTI. This is a different situation. I have a chance to do things differently now.* He took a deep breath.

"You know the space. Several others are doing the same thing. Now go!"

Jon pushed his fears aside. *I have to go back in there. Do this for Ashleigh.*

Acting on pure instinct and unfettered adrenaline, Jon grabbed the blowtorch, and went back into the killing field.

*   *   *

Jim Fields watched in fascination as the crowd panicked. He pressed himself along the exterior of the building behind him, avoiding people running past, screaming in fear.

He had one more trigger to push, but he would need to be far away from the UN before engaging it. He ventured into the crowd, aiming for the corner subway station. He would take the first train that arrived, ride to the next stop, then complete the job.

Caught up in a wave of shoving pedestrians, he finally spotted the green lamp of a station entrance. Just as he made it to the stairwell, a mass of fleeing people jammed into him, propelling him down the stairs, his phone flying from his grasp.

It hit the pavement, shattered and broken.

CHAPTER 84

Hendrix Duplex
New York City

"To what do I owe this delightful surprise?" Senator Hendrix stepped aside, allowing Melanie and Pauly into her fifteenth-floor apartment. She wore a cream cashmere turtleneck and tailored camel hair slacks. An exquisite blend of modern and traditional furnishings adorned the vast space. Museum-quality artwork was displayed, as if in a world-class gallery. A magnificent view of Central Park lay before them, a panorama of maple and oak trees beginning to bud.

"You have a beautiful home." Melanie said, noticing the packed Louis Vuitton luggage in the foyer. A stainless steel metal carrier, the size of a shoebox and imprinted with the Genesis logo, sat on a small decorative table nearby.

The muffled sound of a television was audible from an adjacent room.

"Thank you, dear. I was just watching the news." She looked from Melanie to Pauly quizzically. "Your father is in Boston. May I assume this is not merely a social call?"

"You may," Melanie said.

"Well, please have a seat. Tell me what's on your mind."

Melanie and a mute Pauly remained standing. The senator sat on a white satin sofa, crossing her tanned legs demurely.

"Senator Hendrix—" Melanie began.

"Jasmine, please."

"Jasmine. It seems there's been a complication with your beloved pet project."

"Which one are you referring to?"

"Cure Theory."

Pauly and Melanie looked at Senator Hendrix for her reaction.

"You've been doing your homework. Yes, the project has shown tremendous results. Students around the world are showing significant improvement with their ADHD symptoms. Improved concentration, better grades and relationships."

"And the side effects?"

"What side effects?" Senator Hendrix asked with a near-convincing ignorance.

Melanie refused to play this game any longer. "Murderous rampages."

"Oh, don't be absurd. Where did you get such an outlandish idea?"

Melanie pulled up the video of Sam's Cure Theory session from her iPhone. She had shown it to Pauly in the lobby. It had convinced him to join Melanie upstairs. He wanted to see how his stepmother would react to the allegations.

Senator Hendrix looked up from the video, seemingly unaffected. "Why on earth would you believe that this professor and his methods are part of our procedure? He's clearly using our system for his own dangerous purposes. Have you found this man?"

Melanie was impressed with Senator Hendrix's cool-headedness. "It took some real digging, but I finally found the connection. Cure Theory is funded by New Beginnings, one of many holdings of Genesis Corporation, your husband's company."

"So why not ask *him* about it?"

Looking the senator straight in the eye, Melanie said, "We

already have. He knew nothing of it."

"And you believed him?"

Melanie was disgusted that this woman would throw her own husband under the bus.

Melanie continued. "We assumed your assassin, Hugo Carrera, was only spewing the raving gibberish of a madman. Turns out, he was telling us who he worked for! Genesis has been funding this venture for years. They located the drug you saw Professor Siddiqui administering to Sam, creating a potential murderer out of a kind, gentle man. How can you live with yourself?"

Senator Hendrix said, "I don't appreciate the tone this conversation is taking."

Ignoring her, Melanie said. "So many people have died in your attempts at testing the drug. Victims and casualties all over the country. Young lives cut down for a malevolent purpose. Your own people—Carrera, Kelly Flanagan, not to mention dear Professor Breitler, and those who killed others unwittingly on your behalf, as well as their innocent victims."

The senator's features turned distorted. "Innocents?" she spat. "The UN resolution failed to pass five times! There has never been anything remotely comparable. How dare those pathetic bloated ambassadors in their ivory towers dictate who receives aid! Greed needs to be stopped."

Pauly looked aghast at his stepmother's admission to orchestrating the killing sprees. Floored, he asked, "Was BTI the first?"

"It didn't go as planned," she said smugly. "Often the case with early trials. I would of course have preferred that you were nowhere near the scene and was greatly relieved when you emerged unharmed."

"Unharmed? I needed plastic surgery! My friends were killed in that bombing!"

"All for the greater good. When we located the chrysanthemum, I knew we had something special. Something to finally help mankind in the manner I had hoped for so long." She paused, deliberating. "Who else knows about this?"

Pauly replied. "The FBI, local police...Dad. You'll be exposed. A case will be made against you, Genesis and the Cure Theory members. Your foundation and all the work you've done to *legitimately* help the needy will be scrutinized and shut down."

Pauly's phone alarm sounded. "That's my emergency alert." He looked at his cell and blanched. "The UN General Assembly is under siege. A security guard murdered the Secretary-General and other guards are firing on the delegates!"

Melanie swerved to Senator Hendrix. "What have you done?"

"The Event is upon us, proof to our buyers that the drug works as we've promised. We're in negotiation with revolutionary organizations. The winning bidder will buy our drug and we'll use the revenue to expand our work and funnel funds to the places it's most needed."

Pauly was appalled. "What if the UN had voted in your favor? You would have killed them for nothing!"

"After all its failures to pass, the vote has become irrelevant. Today is about teaching the world leaders a valuable lesson. The innocent are suffering across the globe—without food, clean water or any form of modern healthcare—while their leaders ride in Mercedes eating foie gras and caviar. My own people—my mother, sister—live like animals." She calmed. "That's about to change."

Melanie glanced around at the opulence, astounded at Jasmine's tunnel vision. *Is she delusional or psychotic?*

"I know what you're thinking, my dear," said the senator. "But this"-she gestured to her surroundings- "is only a pretense I maintain to gain access to the powers that be. This lifestyle allows me to acquire funds, and pay my assistants."

"Do you mean people like Jim Fields?" Melanie asked.

The senator blinked. "Yes, amongst others."

"You turned a good cop."

"There are countless more like him. If the money motivates them, so be it."

Melanie was incredulous. "*Countless* more?"

Pauly said, "The word will now get out, you'll be stopped."

"That is not my concern. I will soon be running the program from a location outside the country. One with no extradition laws."

"What about Dad?"

"Dear, clueless Carlton. A trusting fool, allowing me to control the reins while he assumed all responsibility."

"But he loves you," said Pauly.

She emitted a low disdainful laugh. "Your father loves no one but himself and the almighty dollar. He was merely a means to an end." She turned to Melanie. "You and your friends, on the other hand, have been quite resourceful. Our many attempts at halting your interference failed. However, in the end, you were unable to stop our progress."

Pauly said, "The Feds know what you're planning."

"It's too late. The world is viewing firsthand both the power of the syndicate and the serum. Buyers will vie for it, seeing that even the UN is within reach. Perhaps you've heard my speech?"

Melanie and Pauly looked at each other.

"But, of course, you haven't. You've been busy finding me. Suffice it to say, we must educate the populace to achieve our objectives."

Pauly shook his head. "I thought you were family, but what you've done is...reprehensible. You give me no choice." He took out his phone and punched in a number.

CHAPTER 85

United Nations

New York City

I t was a horrifying sensation being in a vast space filled with people terrorized into silence. All Jon could hear were stifled sobs and low groans.

The assembly hall was pitch dark. He awkwardly groped the wall with one hand, while holding on to the blowtorch with the other. He felt for the balustrade he'd hidden behind earlier, recalling it had a decorative ledge about three feet off the ground. It wouldn't get him near the ceiling, but it was the best he could do. He quietly climbed up. He had never handled a blowtorch before and hoped he would figure it out without setting himself aflame. He raised it to face the ceiling and depressed the igniter switch. A blinding flash of spraying fire emerged from the torch. It acted as a signal and immediately other torches were lit.

The shooting started once again.

* * *

The bomb squad arrived in the UN lobby, leading K-9s wearing FBI vests. The dogs' handlers spread out, some up the stairs to check meeting rooms, others to the lower level where the cafeteria and gift shop were located. All civilians and UN staff were evacuated. The bustle of tourists was replaced with the scurrying of emergency personnel from the NYPD, FBI, Homeland Security and National Guard. The bomb-sniffing dogs had been trained to bark violently when picking up the scent of incendiary material. So far, they weren't making a peep.

Those inside the assembly hall were scrambling for cover or looking for a way out past the killers stationed beside the exit doors. Only one door was now unprotected, and Jon was there, standing high on a platform, firing a torch toward the ceiling. It was only a matter of time before he'd draw fire.

Suddenly, the smoke alarm went off, its siren deafening, adding to the existing cacophony. Within seconds, the sprinkler system was activated, soaking everything and everyone below. In the pandemonium, several more people managed to get out of the arena. Jon kept the fire going until it was extinguished by the downpour. The room fell into near darkness. Only the flickers of distant still-lit blowtorches provided dim illumination.

"What the hell?" a guard manning the nearest exit, called out. He was shaking his head like a wet dog, eyes blinking rapidly. He looked down at himself and the scene around him. "Wha-What's going on? Why is the room dark? How did I get here?"

Similar proclamations came from other guards. Jon understood the antidote had been released through the sprinkler system, causing the guards to awaken from their hypnotic states. He yelled into his headset, "This is Jon Steadman. It's safe now. Turn on the lights!"

Instantly, the room flooded with light. Dead and wounded lay mangled and bloody on the floor. Jon spotted Agent Matthews among them, an extinguished blowtorch gripped in his soaked hand. He was bleeding from his shoulder but managed to stand up. The Secretary-General was face down in a pool of blood. Horrified, the unsteady security guards lowered their weapons. The doors to the hall were opened and survivors ran out en masse. Agents did their best to prevent a stampede, to no avail.

Jon spotted a young woman, dressed in a business suit, lying on her side, files strewn around her. Her hair was matted with blood. Jon ran to her, bent down, finding her unconscious, her breath shallow. *This can't be happening again.* He applied thirty compressions to her chest, then held back her head, squeezed her nostrils and blew twice into her mouth. Jon repeated CPR twice more until her breathing became stronger. Then, he lifted her in his arms and ran for the door.

A winded medic rushed over to him with a gurney.

Gently, Jon lay the woman down. "She's alive but her breathing is strained. I gave her CPR."

As she was being wheeled away, he heard the medic call out to him. "You saved her life, man. Well done."

Soaked to the skin, the blowtorch at his feet, Jon felt a deep sense of gratitude and relief sweep over him.

CHAPTER 86

Hendrix Duplex
New York City

"**P**aul."

Pauly's expression quickly changed from disbelief to sadness as he saw his stepmother standing before him, a pistol in hand, aimed at him. All he could think of was his father. He would be crestfallen.

"Hand me your phone," she said. "You too, Melanie." Waving the pistol, the senator directed them into an ultra-modern kitchen, and tossed the two cellphones into the incinerator chute.

Addressing her stepson, Senator Hendrix said, "It's a shame it has come to this. However, once the sale has gone through and I'm out of the country, you can resume your lives."

A voice-activated intercom beside her chimed in.

"Yes, Jorge? Is my driver here?"

"Yes, ma'am. Shall I come for your bags?"

"I'll manage on my own. Tell him I'll be down shortly." She led Pauly and Melanie back into the sitting room.

Pauly asked, "Where are you going?"

When she didn't answer, Melanie said, "The senator has made it clear she's leaving the country, but I don't think we can allow that."

"You have no way to stop me, Ms. Ridgefield."

Melanie thought otherwise. Mimicking Senator Hendrix's condescending tone, she said, "Pauly, be a darling and fetch me that metal case next to the luggage." He was standing between the senator and the case.

Senator Hendrix sprang in a fury. She brandished the pistol. "Paul, stop."

He sped up, grabbed the box and brought it over to Melanie. The senator didn't shoot, unwilling to risk hitting the case.

"Be careful with that!"

"What could this be, Senator?" asked Melanie. "Chrysanthemum Exotic? It's the only item besides your suitcase that's ready to go." Melanie walked backward, careful to keep the carrier between the two of them. With the care of a skilled surgeon, she laid the case on a table and opened it. The box was lined with black silk and cradled twelve dropper vials, each nestled in its own narrow compartment.

Senator Hendrix poised to shoot, her face flush with anger. "Give that to me."

Her heart beating through her chest, Melanie carefully extracted one of the vials. "Is this what you're planning on selling to the highest terrorist bidder?"

Simmering over, the senator yelled. "They're not terrorists! The sale will bring billions to the needy. Put it down!" She stalked over to Melanie, ready to reclaim the carrier.

Pauly intercepted his stepmother, causing her to stumble forward in Melanie's direction, the pistol still gripped in her hand.

Melanie reacted instinctively, using the only weapon she had. She pulled the dropper from the vial, splattering it contents in Senator Hendrix's direction. Pauly jumped out of the way.

Senator Hendrix landed on the floor, writhing like a rabid animal. "Ahh! It got on me!" She was turning pale, her eyes glazing over.

Pauly was terrified. He turned to Melanie. "Will it hurt her?"

"No," Melanie said. "The drug will stop her inhibitions, get her to do things she wouldn't normally do."

Pauly was conflicted. His stepmother looked dazed and detached.

"Are you sure?" he asked. "She doesn't look right."

"You saw the video of Sam Delgado. This is what happens."

Pauly watched as his stepmother stopped convulsing, a drugged visage on her face. She seemed to shift to a more tranquil state. "So you're saying she'll just be amenable to any suggestion?"

Melanie offered a grim smile. "Pauly, that's exactly what I'm saying."

CHAPTER 87

United Nations
New York City

T he police dogs found a cache of explosives hidden in the Security Council chamber, behind the dark grey curtain at the back of the horseshoe, a U-shaped grouping of fifteen blue chairs assigned to the representative statesmen. Three more bombs were located in the Secretariat building next door—enough firepower to obliterate the peacekeeping entity within a matter of seconds. After the bombs were defused, it took hours for the building to be declared safe for re-entry.

Flashing lights from emergency vehicles lit up the area. *Like that night at BTI*, Jon thought morbidly as he, along with Terry and Gabe, exited the building. Huddling together on the plaza lawn, they stood beside the statue of St. George slaying the dragon, a gift from the former Soviet Union. It was titled "Good Defeats Evil."

The Secretary-General's body had been bagged and whisked off by the coroner before reporters could show up and photograph his remains.

Shell-shocked members of the assembly emerged from the building, shivering in waterlogged clothes. Medics arrived with Mylar blankets as the NYPD escorted the stunned guards to a police van.

Jon draped a blanket over his wet shoulders and looked around the makeshift periphery. "Any word from Melanie?"

Terry said, "Last I heard she was with Donna."

Jon dialed Melanie's cell. When it went directly to voice-mail, he sent a text asking her to call.

Matthews came jogging toward them, his ripped thin black tie flapping along, the right sleeve of his soaked shirt torn away, exposing his bandaged shoulder. "We're at thirteen dead and twenty-five wounded, but I expect those numbers to rise." He put his good hand on Jon's shoulder. "Had you not done what you did today, many more people would be dead."

Jon put his face in his hands. "That's thirteen we couldn't save."

Matthews addressed him sternly. "If you're going to make it in this business, Steadman, focus on the lives you save, not the number of casualties, or you'll never sleep at night."

Matthews began to turn away when Jon said, "I haven't been able to reach Melanie. She was with Donna earlier and now she's off the radar. I'm worried she's in trouble."

Matthews furrowed his brow. "What makes you say that?"

"Call it intuition."

Agent Matthews sized Jon up. "That's good enough for me. I'll get Donna. Let's see if we can track down Melanie Ridge-field."

CHAPTER 88

Hendrix Duplex

New York City

Melanie and Pauly led Senator Hendrix to her home office, sitting her down in one of the silk-upholstered chairs.

"Jasmine, are you comfortable?" Melanie used the sedating tone of voice she had heard from Dr. Siddiqui use on the video with Sam.

The senator leaned back, her limbs loose, her eyes at half-mast. "Yes," she replied just above a whisper.

"Tell us who you're selling the chrysanthemum to."

"I don't know their names."

"How do you contact them, Jasmine?"

"A shared email account. We log in and update the messages and documents."

Melanie had heard of crooked politicians and high-profile philanderers using this procedure, a simple and secure method of communication.

"How many buyers are there?"

"We're nearing the end of the bidding process. Two bidders are left."

"The highest bid wins the drug?"

"Yes. The standing bid is 1.1 billion."

Pauly gasped but managed to stay quiet.

Senator Hendrix continued, "Now I have to tell them we

are one vial short." She said this without animus.

"We need to stop the transaction," said Melanie.

The senator remained silent.

"Senator, do you understand?"

She closed her eyes as if trying to figure something out. Even with the powerful drug, one's strongest ethos tried to push through, fighting its way to the surface. But as with Sam, Senator Hendrix succumbed.

"It's too late to contact the bidders." She stood up shakily, walked around the desk to her computer and—still in a daze—typed her password, logging into her account.

Pauly whispered to Melanie. "Tell her to give you the login information in case we need it later."

Melanie did, then instructed Senator Hendrix to print out the list of syndicate members and their contact information.

She was given everything without hesitation. At a glance, Melanie noticed names of some of the most powerful people in Washington, New York and Los Angeles.

She registered Kelly's name and was relieved not to find Matthews on the list. Her eyes locked onto one name. *Jim Fields, FBI Midwest Regional Office.*

Senator Hendrix showed them the most recent correspondence with the remaining bidders. The auction would end at midnight, Eastern time. Until then all communications had been suspended. After more questions, she slumped into her office chair, eyes closing.

"The drug's wearing off," Pauly said. "Should we give her more?"

Melanie shook her head. "We got as much information as we can hope for. I just have one more question to ask." She turned to Senator Hendrix. "What is Jim Fields role?"

The response was stated with subdued defiance. "Now that Kelly's dead, Jim is my new right-hand man. I will run the syndicate from overseas, and Jim will take over all U.S. operations. He has been entrusted with the other twelve."

Aghast, Pauly asked, "Do you mean vials?"

"There were twenty-four. Now twenty-three."

Melanie and Pauly exchanged eye contact.

"Where is he, Jasmine?"

She shook her head. "I can't..."

Melanie raised her voice for the first time. "Tell me now!"

Senator Hendrix's eyes fluttered open with the command, then closed once again, the eyeballs behind her lids making frantic, nystagmic movements. She hesitated, her inner desire to inhibit her response battling the fading effects of the drug.

But once again she failed.

CHAPTER 89

United Nations Plaza
New York City

J on nearly dropped the phone in his haste to answer it.
"Mel?"

"No, it's Angela."

Jon was surprised to hear from Pauly's new wife. "Oh, sorry,
I thought you were Melanie."

"That's weird. I'm calling to see if by chance you had heard
from Pauly. I know it's a long shot, but he told me you were in
touch a few days ago, and said you were coming to New York."

"Listen Angie, I don't think it's a coincidence. I have a feeling Mel and Pauly could be in some trouble."

"Why would you think that?" She sounded alarmed.

"We've been right in the middle of the UN attack situation,
and knowing Mel, she may have figured something out to help
the investigation along."

"I don't see how Pauly would be involved in any of that."

Donna came rushing over to the group. Jon told Angela he'd
call her back.

Donna said. "I just learned the drugged guards were trained
at a facility at Long Island University. They were all graduates
of the Cure Theory program."

"How'd they end up here?" Terry asked.

"They were recruited by a security company. Guess who

owns it."

Gabe answered for all of them. "Genesis."

"Bingo. Among their holdings is a mid-size security service, based in Brooklyn. Goes by the name Body Armor, a subsidiary of Genesis just like New Beginnings."

"So Hendrix is behind all this?"

"He claims ignorance, of course. Matthews believes him. I'm leaning that way too since he gave us full access to his lab. What did you need to speak to me about?"

Jon answered, "I can't locate Melanie. And it seems Pauly, Carlton's son, is also missing."

"Wasn't he on the scene with you at the BTI attack?"

"Yeah."

Terry asked, "Do you think Pauly is involved in this?"

"If anything, he would want to stop these maniacs," said Jon. "He was on the frontlines of their dirty work at BTI."

Donna said, "Last time I saw Melanie was when I dropped her off at Starbucks on the way over here."

"Did she say anything about going somewhere else?" Jon asked.

"No, not at all. Actually, she was pretty intrigued by the connection between Jim and Hendrix. She wanted to hang out there and look into it some more."

Jon felt the hairs rise on the back of his neck. "What connection? You said it appeared Mr. Hendrix didn't know anything about it."

"Melanie thinks we missed something."

"I'm going to the Starbucks. Maybe there's something wrong with her phone."

"Keep me posted," said Donna. "I need to review the tapes. See if we can find any sign of Jim."

Jon gave her a thumbs up. Along with Gabe and Terry, he headed to Third Avenue.

* * *

"Go back a second," Matthews directed, looking at the video feed in the UN security center.

"You see something?" Donna asked.

"I'm not sure. Mike, rewind the footage by a minute or so."

Mike Donnely was back in the security office, having been summoned as soon as the last hostage was evacuated from the premises. He rewound the footage.

Matthews gave further directions. "Pan the camera to the street corner, near the protestors."

Mike manipulated the directional with his finger, panning the crowd view as he went along. They watched intently as things happened backwards and in slow motion. "Tell me when to stop."

Matthews shouted, "There!" A man wearing a visored winter cap, despite the warm weather, was being shoved by a protestor. He nearly lost his footing, but never looked up from his phone. He appeared completely uninterested in the melee around him, fixated on his device. Moments later, he tapped his screen.

Donna asked, "Zoom in on that guy."

Mike expanded the frozen image. The man's face was obscured by his hat. Facial hair was viewable on his chin.

Donna couldn't latch onto any identifying markers. "Do you think that's Jim?" she asked Matthews.

He replied. "Too hard to tell from this perspective." They moved in closer, squinting, looking for any identifying detail.

Donna said, "If it's him, he's creative with his disguise. This man looks nothing like Jim." She took another look. "Is that an insignia on his jacket? There's something familiar about it."

Matthews said, "It looks like a design. Maybe a company emblem."

"Let me try something." Mike suggested.

At the computer, he hit some keys. "We have new software designed to enhance even a small object from a distance. It uses GPS technology. Let's see if it was worth the thirty grand."

The screen focused on a wrinkle in the man's jacket, obscuring part of the emblem.

Matthews pounded the desk. "Damn, so close! We can only get a partial view."

Mike was deflated. "Sorry I couldn't be of more help."

"Guys?"

The two men looked over at Donna. Her face had turned beet red. "I know that insignia."

Matthews' eyebrows lifted in question.

"It's from the New York Yacht Club," said Donna, "down in Battery Park."

Matthews appeared skeptical. "How do you know that?"

"I've been around boats my whole life. I took a class there a few years ago."

"Lucky break," Mike said.

"Yeah, but that's not all. I know that jacket. Jim had one just like it at the beach house. Unless it's a crazy coincidence, that guy is Jim Fields."

CHAPTER 90

New York Yacht Club
Battery Park

T he Charley Girl sported two decks, a pool, three staterooms and a fully stocked bar. The yacht 's interior was
finished with polished oak and brass. A crew of three
was on call for when the owners wanted to take her out to sea
but at the moment, only Jim was aboard.

The course had been set months ago. He sat in the chartroom, making certain the fickle weather of early spring
wouldn't delay the journey. The Event had gone smoothly
enough, though the Boss would be disappointed their bombs
had been found before decimating the global organization
she hated so passionately. Nevertheless, they'd dramatically
demonstrated the chrysanthemum's incredible power and
usefulness. On a world stage.

Jim tried not to be impatient as he awaited his sole passenger, reminding himself they would be asea shortly after sunset. At a cruising speed of six knots, they'd make it to the Yuca-
tan Channel in ten days. Once the auction closed at midnight,
Jim anticipated assisting the Boss in completing the drug sale,
an exciting endeavor. Following the UN attack, the bids had
skyrocketed.

* * *

Flashing credentials, Donna and Matthews gained access to the downtown Manhattan dock. This was their only active lead on Jim Fields.

Approaching the guardhouse, they saw a uniformed man inside, on the phone. They tapped the window. The guard responded with a finger in the air, mouthing, "One minute."

Matthews put his FBI badge up to the window and banged on the glass. "FBI. Open up!"

The guard jumped up, put down the phone and slid the window open. "Whoa, you scared me. What's this about?"

They described Fields to the guard, who directed them to slip 27.

Unholstering their weapons, the two ran down the pier, Donna stopping suddenly, causing Matthews to nearly lose his balance.

Donna pointed out to the water. "Take a look at that."

If she hadn't known where to look, Donna would never have recognized him. Jim sported a trim goatee, the hair expertly grayed in spots. The tortoiseshell glasses and his attire were out of character. It amazed her how a few simple changes could alter someone's appearance so significantly, particularly someone she'd known so intimately.

The Charley Girl was cruising by, Jim at the helm. From this distance, Donna saw him glaring right at them, shooting bullets with his eyes.

CHAPTER 91

Hendrix Duplex
New York City

Senator Hendrix blinked wildly, mumbling incoherently. "She's coming out of it," said Pauly. "What do we do now?" he asked Melanie.

"Get her phone and call Matthews. I'll look for something to restrain her with."

Melanie deactivated the intercom. The senator's driver was likely wondering about the delay and Melanie didn't want Senator Hendrix yelling for help. On the terrace, she found tree saplings bound to their stakes with twine. She untwisted them and ran back into the home office. The senator was sitting up, glassy-eyed, color returning to her face.

"What happened?" She looked around, her disoriented gaze landing on Melanie.

Melanie moved quickly. "Stay still, Senator, and put your hands behind your back."

"What on earth—?"

Before she could resist, Melanie had bound her hands.

"Take these off!"

"After what you just shared with us, we need to restrain you."

"Are you crazy? I haven't said—" She noticed the droplets on the rug and the wooden box on the table. "Oh, dear God.

What have you done? Did you use the serum on me?"

"It was an accident," said Melanie. "But we found it very informative."

Senator Hendrix tried to stand but the combination of the drug's dwindling effects and her bound hands made it difficult. She flopped back in the chair.

Pauly was holding her phone, unable to call Matthews because it was locked.

"Tell me the passcode," Pauly instructed his stepmother.

The senator remained silent.

"We're wasting time," said Melanie. "I don't suppose it's wise to leave her here alone."

Pauly looked drained. "I'll stay. I can log into Jasmine's computer and send an email to Jon about what's happening."

"Good, he'll pass it along to Agent Matthews at the FBI."

Pauly eyed his stepmother with disdain. "I'll wait till the authorities arrive."

Melanie readied to leave. "Sorry about all of this."

Pauly nodded. "Good luck, Mel. Keep me posted and stay safe."

* * *

Off Manhattan Island

Using the secure server, Jim updated the crew, all devoted members of the syndicate. He tried reaching the Boss, but his chatroom message and email elicited no replies.

Something was wrong. The arrangement was to check every hour on the hour after the Event. If he didn't receive a response soon, he'd have to text. Even with smartphone technology, it was a security risk.

It was 8:50 p.m. and Jim would be docking again in thirty minutes. The original rendezvous time would be missed. *No worries.* Plan B would be implemented.

CHAPTER 92

FBI National Headquarters
J. Edgar Hoover Building
Washington D.C.

C olonel Victor Gomez was at his desk, a lit Cuban rolling between his fingers, when Matthews called in.

They'd identified one of the main perpetrators of the UN attack but he still eluded them. The president was closely watching the situation and wanted hourly updates from the Director, who would then turn to the Colonel, the man overseeing the investigation. The unfortunate incident presented the Colonel with an invaluable opportunity to raise his profile.

"There are only so many places one can dock a yacht of that size," he told Agent Matthews.

"But we don't have the manpower right now to immediately cover all those places. Our agents are on scene at the UN. We need to narrow down the field."

"I'll move agents to where you need them."

"That's helpful, but I don't know where yet."

"When you do, call immediately."

"Thank you, sir."

The Colonel leaned back, took a deep, satisfying puff of his cigar. He had strategized for years moving his soldiers like a five-star general on the battlefield. The general he was meant to be.

CHAPTER 93

Brooklyn Navy Yard

The Brooklyn Navy Yard was quiet this time of night. The only ships at dock were not in use, their crews finding trouble somewhere in the wilds of downtown Brooklyn.

The yard had survived through various reincarnations. Shipping containers, smokestacks, and cranes dotted the expanse. The buildings had been used in recent years as event facilities, including during the Democratic run for the presidency. Now, the yard and its environs were undergoing a multimillion-dollar renovation. As far as Jim was concerned, gentrification could never fully erase the decades of grime and of rust.

The Boss had used valuable connections within the syndicate to arrange a back-up berth in case one was needed. *Good thinking,* Jim told himself as he carefully approached the inlet. The East River was heavily congested and difficult to navigate, but with the winds in his favor, he arrived with time to spare.

Once docked, he descended below deck to check for the Boss's response. There was none. He knew he'd face consequences for initiating a text. Members were instructed to refrain from texting at all costs given the supposed inherent vulnerability. He thought differently. If Al Qaeda had used them unfettered, why not New Beginnings? And anyway, he had no choice. If he didn't make contact, the Boss wouldn't know about the new rendezvous location.

Jim had met the Boss only once, years before she became Senator Hendrix of Massachusetts, when she had interviewed him before the Brazil expedition. Once they had found the chrysanthemum, their involvement intensified, relying exclusively on remote communications. Over time, she bestowed on him greater responsibility and reward.

Spending the next ten days at sea alone together would not have been his choice, but he'd had no say in the matter. Normally, being secluded with an attractive woman aboard a luxury yacht would be tempting, but he had to admit he was afraid of the Boss, having carried out ruthless orders at her behest.

He took out his phone and created a personal hotspot. As an additional precaution, he blocked his number.

He typed, *Follow Plan B.*

❊ ❊ ❊

Fifth Avenue
New York City

Melanie was walking out the building when she saw the text come in on Senator Hendrix's phone.

Follow Plan B

Thanks to the senator, Melanie knew Plan B and the identity of the sender. As was the case with locked smartphones, she could respond to the text without accessing other aspects of the device.

She thought a moment and then typed, *Confirmed,* hoping the one-word reply would not raise suspicion. She put the phone in her back pocket and approached a middle-aged woman who didn't appear to be in any rush, asked politely to use her device, and shot out a quick update to Pauly. There was no point calling Jon. He would only try to stop her.

Melanie returned the phone, thanking the woman, and ran to the nearest subway station.

* * *

Third Avenue

New York City

Jon stood outside Starbucks, fidgeting beside Terry and Gabe when his phone dinged with an email from Pauly. The subject line read, *Jon-Open Immediately.*

He clicked it open, and quickly perused the content, his brain trying to catch up with what he was reading. Terror gripped him. He forwarded the email to Agent Matthews.

As calmly as Jon could muster, he said to his friends, "We need to get to Brooklyn. Now!"

CHAPTER 94

Brooklyn Navy Yard

Melanie's only hope was to get to Jim Fields in time to stop him from leaving the country with the vials. The sun had set over an hour ago, but she didn't let fear talk her out of what she had to do. If Jim figured out that Hendrix wasn't coming, he would leave with the vials, evading apprehension.

The yard's chain link fence had an old-fashioned padlock. She had nothing to break it open with and no way to get over it. Studying the fence, she realized if she tried, she might be able to squeeze through the narrow opening. *Let's hope I don't get stuck halfway.* Carefully, as to not prick herself with the fencing's metal spikes, she pushed herself through, starting with one arm and leg and then shimmying the rest of her body through. No alarms went off.

The only light came from the moon reflecting off the East River and red airplane warning lights mounted atop the cranes and smokestacks. The air was thick with the smell of rotting fish and turbine oil. Clanging ship bows gently slapped against the sides of the dock, as the waves rocked them to and fro.

Melanie rounded the warehouse abutting the pier. Three vessels were docked in their berths—two cargo ships that appeared abandoned, and one glittering yacht. Under the cover of darkness, Melanie moved stealthily towards *The Charley Girl.*

* * *

Fifth Avenue

New York City

Angela hurried out of the taxicab and dashed into the lobby, passing by the doorman. He called out, "Hello, Miss Angela. Mr. Paul is up in his parent's apartment."

"Thanks, Marco!" She took the elevator up to the twelfth floor, ringing the bell repeatedly.

"Who's there?" her husband's anxious voice asked through the door.

"Pauly, it's me Angela. Open up."

Pauly opened the door only wide enough to peer out. "Angie? What are you doing here?"

She choked back a sob. "I was so worried. You haven't answered any of my calls or texts. This was the last place left to check."

He hugged her close. "Listen, babe, you can't come in. I'll meet you back at home later."

Still standing in the hallway, she tried to peek over his shoulder. "Why? What's happening?"

"I'll explain it all tonight."

"Who's there? Who's voice am I hearing?" Senator Hendrix demanded from inside.

Angela said, "Hi Jasmine. It's Angela."

"Help me!" she screamed. "Paul has me tied up back here!"

"What?" She pushed past her husband and into the living room. There she found her mother-in-law on the sofa, looking exhausted. And true to her word, her arms were bound behind her.

Flummoxed, she asked, "Pauly, what's going on?!"

"It's a long story. Suffice it to say she's behind the UN attack and other killings, even the one at BTI."

"That's insane! How can that be? She's your stepmother!"

"I know it's crazy, but Melanie explained it all to me. She has proof. And Jasmine confessed."

Enraged, his stepmother said, "I did not. You had me drugged."

Angela intervened. "Pauly, you need to let her go."

"That's not possible. The FBI's Agent Matthews should be on his way. I need your phone." He stuck out his hand.

Looking directly at the younger woman, Senator Hendrix spoke firmly, "Angela, untie me."

Angela stared at her, frozen in shock. A moment passed. "Angie?" Pauly said, distraught. She looked at her new husband, a lone tear streaming down her cheek. "Oh Pauly, please know I love you."She pulled a small revolver from her purse.And then resignedly, Angela walked over to Senator Hendrix, and cut her loose.

CHAPTER 95

Brooklyn Navy Yard

J on, Gabe and Terry arrived at the Navy Yard like gangbusters, plowing Donna's Subaru through the chain-link fence. It had taken them forever to get here, thanks to congestion on the Williamsburg Bridge and an accident on the BQE. Despite being in the heart of Brooklyn, Jon was astounded at the yard's desolation.

Terry asked, "What are we looking for?"

"Melanie was coming here to track down Jim. Let's look at the pier. Gabe, take this. I don't know what to do with it." Jon handed him the gun taken from the UN guard. Gabe put it in his waistband, the coldness of the metal bringing him a sense of comfort.

Jon said, "Stay quiet and follow me." As they turned the corner of the warehouse, they saw in the near distance a shadowy figure running in the opposite direction, away from the docks. Jon couldn't tell who it was, and didn't want to yell out. He whispered, "I'm going to check if that was Mel. Catch up with you soon." He ran in the direction of the figure.

Gabe nodded and crossed quietly to the pier, Terry following closely behind.

* * *

The warehouse was marked for demolition, with signs along the exterior warning trespassers. Jon pushed open the heavy metal door, its wheels noisily creaking. The space was dark and cavernous, the pungent smell of motor oil lingering in the air. The dim lighting reminded Jon of the UN, but this time his breath remained steady, his mind sharp.

"Melanie?" he called. "It's Jon. It's okay to come out.."

Something sharp struck his back, bringing him to his knees. He looked up behind him. The figure raised his weapon again, bringing it down once more and Jon fell into total darkness.

❊ ❊ ❊

Gabe and Terry walked the pier, doing their best to stay out of sight.

Terry whispered, "There's light on in the back of that boat."

The yacht's engine came to life, startling them.

Gabe swore. "Jim must have decided not to wait any longer." Gabe grabbed hold of the railing and hoisted himself onto the boat's deck, then pulled Terry alongside him.

❊ ❊ ❊

When Jon woke up, it took a moment for him to realize where he was, and to recall that he'd been assaulted. He was alone in the waterfront warehouse, his assailant gone. He had no idea how much time had passed. He rose, his back burning, bum leg throbbing. The sound of a revving motor resonated off the walls. He stumbled out of the warehouse and ran for the boat.

❊ ❊ ❊

Gabe and Terry snuck along the underside of the chartroom, where Jim was steering the ship out of port. Laying low, they hoped to sneak a look through the windows without being spotted. An open window brought sounds of agitated voices, the words indecipherable over the grinding of the boat's gears. Terry ventured a peek and saw Melanie sitting on a leather loveseat inside a beautiful wood-paneled room, her face the picture of defiance. Someone outside Terry's view was speaking to her.

Gabe took out his gun and led the way to the door. Expecting Jim, they were shocked to find Melanie seated across from Senator Hendrix, a gun directed at her.

Gabe said, "Senator Hendrix, put down the gun."

Terry asked, "What have you done to Pauly, you witch?"

She didn't reply and didn't put the gun down.

Gabe reiterated. "Do you think I won't shoot you after what you've done?"

"I don't question your willingness, Mr. Lewis, but I do believe we have a stalemate."

* * *

Jim walked in, yet another pistol in hand. He leveled at Gabe. "Hey, Boss," he said to Senator Hendrix.

She laughed. She had enjoyed the title, perhaps even more than her political one.

Thanks to Angela, she'd made it out of the apartment, having read Jim's messages with the new meeting place. Her security detail escorted her car through traffic with lights and sirens.

"We can't seem to rid ourselves of these pests," said Jim. "What should we do to make them finally back off?"

"You know quite well that I'm a humanitarian. I have no interest in killing without a greater purpose." Ignoring Gabe's useless gun, she said, "Jim, get the outboard lifeboat and put them on it. Dump its motor fuel. By the time they're rescued, we will be far away."

"The Feds will be here any minute," Terry said, defiantly.

"Then time is of the essence," Senator Hendrix said with a smile.

Jim grabbed Gabe by the arm. "Let's go, all three of you."

The senator said, "Actually, Miss Ridgefield will stay with us."

"What?" the others responded in unison.

"Melanie, you've spent much of your young life on philanthropy. I commend you. I was idealistic and naïve at your age too but you'll come around to understand what we're accomplishing."

"That will never happen."

"Be that as it may, I would enjoy your company and appreciate the benefit of added protection. We're less likely to have our journey interrupted if our pursuers understand we will dispose of you if they interfere."

Melanie went pale.

Gabe spoke up. "Take me instead."

"How chivalrous, but you're too much of a handful." Turning to Jim, she said, "Please escort them out."

* * *

Jim walked behind Gabe and Terry, his gun aimed at their backs. He had Gabe unbind the lifeboat, dump the engine's fuel, and detach the reflector lights. The two got into the small vessel and Jim lowered it into the sea, watching as they drifted away.

Jim retook the helm. He steered the boat into the harbor, the earlier traffic long gone. The crew would meet them on open water—his own inspired security measure. Jim maintained the required speed, but looked forward to being at sea and pushing the yacht to the max.

The intercom squawked with Senator Hendrix's voice. "I'm going below decks. Melanie is locked in the small stateroom. Notify me when the crew arrives."

She treated him like an errand boy but he supposed that was a small price to pay for immense wealth.

A faint but familiar odor permeated the bridge. *Gasoline!* He left his post and followed the odor. As he approached the engine room, it became stronger. *A leak?* He opened the access panel. Inside, an inch of fuel lined the floor. Attached to the corner wall was a digital clock, wires running out of it. *A bomb.* The output read 12:13, speedily counting down to zero.

Jim sounded the fire alarm.

* * *

Jasmine Hendrix went to check on their inventory of Chrysanthemum Exotic. The auction would be done by midnight. *How exciting!* She opened the safe.

It was empty.

Then the fire alarm blared.

* * *

When the alarm went off, Jon was hiding in the galley, waiting for an opportunity to find Melanie. This was his chance. He knew Gabe and Terry were safe when he saw them lowered into the lifeboat.

He swallowed panic, ran from the galley towards the staterooms. One was locked. "Melanie, are you in there?"

When she responded, he called, "Stand back!" He put all in his strength into a kick. The door crashed open and she fell into his arms.

"There's a gas leak. Come, we need to go."

* * *

Jim had no clue how to disarm a bomb. Should he risk cutting the wires and blowing himself up? No, he was going to bail. *The vials!* He had to save the vials. He ran across the lower deck to the safe room. Senator Hendrix was there, rage radiating off her.

"Where did you put the vials?" she spat.

"What? The boat is about to blow! Someone leaked fuel and wired a bomb in the engine room! We need to get the vials and get out!"

"Liar! There's no bomb. Do you actually believe you can deal with the buyers alone and cut me out? You stole the vials, you two-timing thief!"

Jim's own anger flared. "They're in the safe."

"They're not. Where have you moved them?"

He looked in the open safe. His face turned ashen.

"The winning bidder will never agree to dealing with my subordinate. Tell me where they are!"

"Maybe *you* took them and are trying to cut *me* out."

She looked as though she would strangle him.

She sniffed the air. "That smell…what's that smell?"

"I told you there's a gas leak. There's less than ten minutes left. We need to get out of here!"

"I'm not leaving without the vials," she said stubbornly.

"Do what you want, but I'm leaving."

"How? We sent the others away. We have no lifeboat."

* * *

Jim was on deck, wearing a life vest and gearing up the courage to jump overboard, when he spotted Melanie and Jon running along the yacht's starboard side. He gave chase, reaching for his gun. It wasn't there. In his panic, he must have left it below decks.

"I'm going to kill you with my bare hands." He came at Jon in full force. "Give me the vials!"

Jon deflected the incoming blow with his forearm and landed a punch on Jim's right shoulder further infuriating him. The two men pummeled each other with their fists wrestling for the upper hand.

Senator Hendrix emerged from below and saw the two men fighting. "Jim, get the vials. Hurry!" As she went for her gun, Melanie jumped at her, grabbing her hair. The older woman screeched, dropping her weapon. Melanie snatched the gun and pointed it.

"Enough!" Melanie commanded.

Everyone froze.

"We need to get off this boat now. Everything else can wait." Melanie yanked two life vests from a clear plastic bin and handed one to Jon who didn't hesitate to put it on. He then took the gun and allowed Melanie to do the same. He grasped her hand and walked to the deck's edge, keeping the gun pointed at Jim and the senator. To Melanie, he said, "You ready?"

"As I'll ever be."

Hand in hand, Jon and Melanie jumped into the cold waters of the Atlantic.

CHAPTER 96

A massive explosion erupted late last night in New York Harbor. Witnesses say the fireball could be seen from as far away as Jersey City. Authorities believe it was a recreational yacht heading out to sea when it began leaking fuel and ignited. At this time, it is unclear how many passengers were aboard and if there were any survivors. The boat is seen here on security video earlier in the evening docked at the Brooklyn Navy Yard. Stay tuned for further details on this developing story.

* * *

New York Harbor

Moments after they jumped ship, the yacht incinerated, the shockwaves casting Melanie and Jon clear of the vessel. Reverberations caused five-foot swells, dragging them along with the falling debris. The water was near freezing, making the heat from the explosion sadly welcome.

Agent Jim Fields and Senator Jasmine Hendrix had not made it off the ship. Like their many victims, their remains would never be found.

* * *

Nothing prepared Jon and Melanie for their euphoria when

seeing the first Coast Guard boat head straight for them, Gabe and Terry aboard, wrapped in blankets. It was finally over.

PART IV

One Week Later

CHAPTER 97

John F. Kennedy International Airport
New York

T erry stood at the end of the security line at JFK International Airport, her passport in hand.

"I'm sorry you have to leave so soon," Gabe said, handing over her carry-on bag.

"So am I, but I've missed a tremendous amount of work. I can't keep asking other professors to take on my load."

"Of course. It's just that... I'll miss you."

She smiled. "And I'll miss you. I look forward to your visit in a few months when you've completed your thesis. You and Jon have enough material now. I'm sorry I'll miss graduation."

"That's all right. We'll celebrate when I come see you." He gave a playful wink.

She nudged him. "I can't wait."

He opened his arms for a hug. She went to him.

"*L'hitraot,*" Terry said. "That means, 'See you soon.'"

"*L'hitraot,* Dr. Lavi."

Gabe watched as Terry made her way through the security line and waited until she was out of sight.

CHAPTER 98

Potomac, Maryland

T he estate was in full bloom. Crimson peonies and purple rhododendrons framed the mansion's entrance, the aroma of English roses welcoming him home. Colonel Gomez let himself in. Their golden retriever barked a hello, her tail wagging happily as the Colonel ruffled her ears.

His wife met him in the foyer. "Hello, darling."

He gave her a perfunctory kiss on the cheek. "How was your day?"

"Marvelous. I met with Janice about the club's annual tea and things are looking good. I'll tell you all about that later. We have company."

"Oh? Were we expecting someone?"

"They came unannounced. Said it was important. Doug Matthews and his associate. You remember Doug? He was at our last gala."

"Yes, of course."

"They're waiting in your office."

"Thank you, dear."

The Colonel took off his overcoat, hung it on the rack and smoothed out his suit.

Matthews stood up as the Colonel entered the room and closed the heavy doors behind him.

The Colonel eyed his guests. Seated in one of the leather

armchairs was a young man with a sling on his arm and a bandage on his forehead. He did not stand. He noticed Agent Matthews also sported a sling.

"This is an unexpected visit. Is everything all right? Last I heard Senator Hendrix's and Agent Fields' remains were still not recovered. Has that changed?"

"No, sir."

"Were you satisfied with the additional assistance at the scene? We mobilized the Coast Guard as quickly as possible."

"It worked out well enough, sir."

"Then what is this about?" Turning to Jon he said, "Pardon my bluntness, but who are you?"

"Name's Jon Steadman. But something tells me you already knew that."

"I have a steel-trap memory, young man, and I can say with certainty that you and I have never met."

"That may be true, but you know my comings and goings."

Irritated, the Colonel said, "I'll ask again, Agent Matthews, what is this impromptu meeting about?"

A knock came at the door. The Colonel's wife poked her head inside, the dog bounding past her. "Can I pour you gentlemen something to drink?"

"No, thank you, dear. I'll do it."

"Very well. Come along, Charley." The dog followed her out.

The Colonel poured himself a brandy from the bar offering none to his guests. "Well?"

Jon began, "When we arrived at the Navy Yard, I saw someone running away from the boat. That person attacked me. Not until later did I give much thought as to who it was. After the explosion, it occurred to me that someone else was involved in all this. I remembered Jim and Jasmine accusing me of stealing the vials of Chrysanthemum. Someone else had taken them, maybe the person who knocked me out. And maybe that same person set the bomb, destroying evidence. Everyone would think the vials were lost in the accident."

Matthews continued. "Once Jon told me that, I searched for the yacht's registration. Thanks to good old-fashioned leg-work, we tracked it to Major Sherman Pickett. Imagine our surprise when we discovered he's your wife's father. Killing Jasmine Hendrix and Jim Fields was a stroke of evil genius. After they had done all the work, taken all the risks, they would be eliminated so that all the proceeds from the billion-dollar sale would go to only one person. You."

"Don't be ridiculous. There's obviously some mistake." The Colonel looked like a trapped animal, eyes dodging about the room, as if searching for a quick escape.

Matthews said, "I recall you had a yacht docked out back when we were here for the party. I don't see it there now."

"We sold it months ago," he said feebly.

Jon didn't mince words. "We know you have the vials. Surrender them and maybe you'll have a shot at seeing daylight again one day. And one more thing. Your dog. How did it get the name?"

At that, the Colonel blanched.

"Seems years ago, when your wife was a child, your father-in-law owned a beloved dog. He named each subsequent dog after her. Charley. Since then, his daughter...your wife, kept up the tradition. Touching, really."

"So what?!"

"The boat that was blown to smithereens, the same one that was docked behind this house, was christened in 2012. She was named *The Charley Girl.*"

* * *

Matthews sent out a text and within minutes armed federal officers filled the Colonel's office. They found twenty-three vials of Chrysanthemum Exotic in the Colonel's home safe. He was read his rights and taken in handcuffs from his mansion, into a waiting unmarked Buick. As the car rolled down the winding driveway, Charley chased behind, doing her best to catch up to her owner.

EPILOGUE

The untimely death of Senator Hendrix rocked Capitol Hill. Like all political happenings however, the next big scandal usurped the headlines, leaving the senator and her associate, FBI agent Jim Fields in the dust pile of megalomaniac history.

A federal warrant led to many late hours of data mining the Colonel's and senator's Internet servers, resulting in one of the vastest federal takedowns in U.S. history.

* * *

Ed Hernandez earned the best scoop of his life. He was feeling good about the Pulitzer.

* * *

Pauly and Angela separated. The senator had won Angela's loyalty years earlier after hearing of the young woman's secret love for her stepson. She'd agreed to encourage their relationship despite Angela's humble means, making it clear she would one day expect a return of the favor.

Pauly went home to Boston to begin rebuilding a relationship with his father. They shared the most meaningful time since his mother's death.

* * *

Agent Doug Matthews' job security was tentative. Having Kelly Flanagan in his employ for so long had critically exposed the Bureau. The bugs had been eliminated from all the devices in the building, and an updated security firewall was put in place. The powers that be allowed Matthews to keep his job while analyzing the Kelly Conspiracy, as it was referred to.

Ultimately, a decision was made, delivered by phone from the Deputy Director. Given Matthews' lengthy tenure at the Bureau, and the successful apprehension of the Colonel, he resolved to keep the SIC at his current pay grade but move him to a new office to get a fresh start.

This unexpectedly pleasant conversation ended with questions about a student from the University of North Texas who was instrumental in cracking the case leading to the seizure of Chrysanthemum Exotic and the Colonel's arrest. Matthews recommended offering the young man a position with the Bureau and proposed taking him under his wing.

* * *

Gabe completed the dissertation with Jon, expecting to make several revisions before it would pass muster with the dean. A draft of their work was being sent to the *Journal of Applied Sciences* for their spring publication. If all went well, by year's end he would be Professor Gabriel Lewis, Doctor of Chemical Engineering.

* * *

Melanie hung up the phone, excited and nervous. She just accepted a position at one of the top bio-medical facilities in the country. It was the opportunity of a lifetime. Terry had given a glowing reference. The company came after her long and hard, making an offer she couldn't refuse. Orientation would begin the week after next, the only downside being the job was in Northern California, the opposite side of the country from Jon. He was starting a new chapter of his own. They agreed to speak every week no matter what was happening in their busy lives and meet in Napa for the Fourth of July weekend.

* * *

Granny Eunice recuperated nicely but was no longer comfortable living alone. Arrangements were made to move her to a senior living community for active retirees down in Pompano Beach.

* * *

Alone again, and in no rush to meet someone new, Donna put everything she had into her job.

Captain Hutter took notice. He would be retiring soon and was keeping an eye out for his successor.

* * *

The New York FBI headquarters was based in Tribeca, surrounded by heavy security. As Jon exited the building, his workday complete, he thought of Ashleigh, gone nearly four years. His heart ached, but the pain was duller, less intense, some of his burden lightening.

The air was chilly, the Canyon of Heroes creating a wind

tunnel down the avenue. Jon looked back at the imposing building, taking a moment to consider everything that
brought him here, to his new job. A powerful sense of redemp-
tion washed over him.

A glance at his watch told him he'd need to hurry to be on
time for his appointment.

Twenty minutes later he reached his destination, hesi-
tating across the cobblestone street from a weather-beaten
storefront, one block west of South Street Seaport. A white-
haired woman with a kind face spotted him through the window and came out to greet him. "Can I help you?" she called
out.

"I'm Jon Steadman. I'm here for the PTSD meeting."

The woman smiled and went inside, leaving the door ajar.

Jon lifted the collar of his coat and limped forward.

The End

ACKNOWLEDGEMENT

Bringing a work of fiction to life requires a great number of people who believe in you, and if you're lucky also have a discerning eye. Deep-felt gratitude to Karen Sheff, whose attention to detail is unparalleled. To Tali Schwartz and Betty Atlas-Rumelt, for getting in the trenches with me from the get-go. To my mother, Jeanette Neeman aka Granny; Leah Germain, Sharon Auerbacher, Alex Sachs, and Charlotte Adler, who took more interest than I deserved. To the numerous and insightful beta readers whose honest feedback was invaluable. To Dana Isaacson, editor extraordinaire, whose professionalism keeps this ever-changing industry flourishing.

To my husband, Glenn, who listened patiently to my pitch, read the manuscript in one sitting, and continues to hike by my side. Without him, I would never have the time to pursue this great love of mine. With him, mountains can be moved.

And always to my son, Yechezkel, who inspires me every day. My love for you is as vast as the great outdoors.

ABOUT THE AUTHOR

Nellie Neeman

Nellie grew up on the Upper West Side of Manhattan, tapping away on her mother's typewriter. She attended the City University of New York where she earned a master's degree in speech pathology. In 2015, she left the Big Apple and her twenty-year career to pursue her writing passion full-time in the greener and wider pastures of the Midwest.

An avid traveler and hiker, Nellie uses her own adventures as inspiration for her stories. She currently resides in Cincinnati and Jerusalem with her husband and Lexi, the wacky Labradoodle.

Made in the USA
Monee, IL
28 December 2020